I0641101

Daniel Bros

Illustrated Guide for amateur Gardeners

Spring 1912

Daniel Bros

Illustrated Guide for amateur Gardeners
Spring 1912

ISBN/EAN: 9783741198458

Manufactured in Europe, USA, Canada, Australia, Japa

Cover: Foto ©Andreas Hilbeck / pixelio.de

Manufactured and distributed by brebook publishing software
(www.brebook.com)

Daniel Bros

Illustrated Guide for amateur Gardeners

PRICE 1/-

SPRING ·1912·

DANIELS·BROS LIMITED

ILLUSTRATED GUIDE·FOR AMATEUR·GARDENERS

SEEDSMEN & NURSERYMEN
BY APPOINTMENT
M. KING GEORGE V.
M QUEEN ALEXANDRA
Entd. Sta. Hall

DANIELS·BROS·LIMITED
SEED·GROWERS·&·NURSERYMEN
NORWICH

THE ROYAL NORFOLK SEED ESTABLISHMENT,

NEW YORK STATE
COLLEGE OF AGRICULTURE,
DEPARTMENT OF HORTICULTURE,
Head Office and Registered Establishment,
ROYAL ARCADE.Y.
Nat. Telephone :—No. 38.

NORWICH, ENGLAND.

Seed Warehouses,
BEDFORD STREET.
Private Telephone.

Seed Grounds,
IPSWICH ROAD AND EATON.
Private Telephone.

Nurseries,
THE TOWN CLOSE NURSERIES,
NEWMARKET ROAD.
Nat. Telephone. No. 39.

GOLD MEDAL AWARDED BY THE
ROYAL AGRICULTURAL SOCIETY, JUNE, 1911

TERMS OF BUSINESS, &c.

☞ All orders from unknown Correspondents must be accompanied by a sufficient Remittance or Bankers' or other satisfactory References. To save cost and trouble of Booking, a Remittance should in all cases be sent with Orders under 10s. in value.

ACCOUNTS—DISCOUNTS.—All accounts are due net in three months; we however allow a discount of 5%, i.e., 1s. in the pound, on all orders of 20s. and upwards, when accompanied by a remittance, or when paid within fourteen days of date of invoice.

ADDRESSES.—Full Name and Address should be sent with every communication, and nearest Railway Station should be stated with every order, as much time is thereby saved, especially in our busiest season, when we often receive from 1000 to 1500 letters daily. In consequence of this large correspondence, we suggest that, at all seasons, Cut Flower Orders and other Urgent Letters should be so marked on the envelope.

CARRIAGE ON GOODS.—We pay carriage on the following Articles to any address in the British Isles:—
All KITCHEN GARDEN and FLOWER SEEDS offered in this Catalogue.
SEED POTATOES, CULINARY ROOTS, and HORTICULTURAL REQUISITES, if included in a general Garden Seed order of the value of 20s. in all.
DWARF and BUSH ROSES of the value of 7s. 6d. and upwards.
STANDARD ROSES " " 10s. 0d. " "
ROSES IN POTS " " 15s. 0d. " "
We also pay carriage to any Station on the G.E.R. or Mid. & G.N. Joint Line on:—
SEED POTATOES, CULINARY ROOTS, &c.; to the value of 10s. and upwards.
Owing to their heavy weight, in proportion to their value, we regret that we cannot pay carriage on the following:—
ROSES of less value than the amounts mentioned above.
TREES AND SHRUBS } But we continue to enclose extra plants, free of charge, to partially meet the cost of carriage.
PLANTS IN POTS }
HORTICULTURAL SUNDRIES, such as Silver Sand, Mats, Tools, &c., when ordered alone, and of less value than 20s.
MUSHROOM SPAWN.

CHANGE OF RESIDENCE.—We shall esteem it a favour if our customers, on changing their residences, will kindly favour us with their new addresses, so that we may be able to send them our Catalogues as usual.

CHEQUES, MONEY ORDERS, AND POSTAL ORDERS.—Should be made payable to DANIELS BROS. LIMITED, and crossed "BARCLAY & Co., LIMITED," Bankers, Norwich. Letters containing coin must be registered according to Post Office regulations.

CO-OPERATION IN SENDING ORDERS.—Allotment holders, Cottagers, and members of Cottagers' Garden Societies, requiring individually but small quantities of Seeds and Seed Potatoes, if they join together in sending their orders, will be allowed a special discount of ten per cent., to be taken in seeds, besides the usual discount of five per cent. for cash, thus:—for every 20s. remitted, 23s. worth of seeds may be ordered. No order can be recognised under these terms unless over the net value of One Pound, and accompanied by prepayment in full. Each order will be packed separately and all can be consigned in one package, but full name and address of each customer ordering under this arrangement should be sent.

CORRESPONDENCE. Most Important.—Our customers having occasion to write to us respecting any order previously sent by them, will much facilitate attention to their letters if they will kindly state the date on which the order was sent, and if remittance was enclosed name the amount; this will enable us more readily to identify their orders on reference to our Registers.

ORDER EARLY.—All orders are executed in the rotation in which they are received, and we would ask our customers to send us their orders as soon as possible after receiving this Catalogue. If every one waits for favourable weather, or until seeds are actually needed for sowing, it involves such a rush that an excessive strain is put upon our large staff of executants, and sometimes delay is as a consequence unavoidable.

PACKAGES.—All packages are charged at the lowest cost price, and are not returnable, unless sent back in good condition, and Carriage Paid, within fourteen days of receipt of goods. Customers are particularly requested to put their name and address on each package, and to advise us by post when returned, or they cannot be credited.

All Fruit Trees, Roses, and Shrubs, will be so packed as to stand a journey of a week or ten days without injury. Should the packages arrive at their destination during a severe frost, it will be advisable not to unpack them, but to keep them cool and moist out of the reach of frost.

PACKETS.—Will our customers kindly note that, in all cases where Seeds are quoted by the "Packet," this is the minimum quantity that we can supply; smaller quantities or half-packets are not sold by us.

RECOMMENDATIONS.—The many kind recommendations to new customers with which we have been favored in the past have been very gratifying. Should any of our customers have friends requiring Seeds, Plants, &c., to whom a copy of our *Illustrated Guide* would be acceptable, we shall feel much obliged by an intimation of the fact.

WARRANTY.—We believe that all Seeds, Bulbs and Roots sold by us are of the description and kind specified by us at the time of sale, but owing to the practical impossibility in many cases of being certain of this, we give no undertaking that such Seeds, Bulbs, or Roots will correspond with the description under which they are sold, and we make all sales subject to this condition. We further give no warranty, express or implied, as to their growth, description, quality or productiveness, and will not be in any way responsible for the crop. If the Purchaser does not accept the goods sold to him, on these terms, they are at once to be returned to us.

TELEGRAPHIC ADDRESS:—DANIELS, NORWICH.

January 1st, 1912.

SEEDSMEN & NURSERYMEN
— BY APPOINTMENT TO —

H.M. KING GEORGE V. &
H.M. QUEEN ALEXANDRA

EXPORT OF SEEDS, PLANTS & TUBERS.

Important to Foreign and Colonial Correspondents.

REMITTANCES :—A remittance, or draft on a London Bank, should accompany all orders from unknown correspondents.

VEGETABLE & FLOWER SEEDS:—Special Collections of Vegetable and Flower Seeds for Export are offered as below. Where our customers, however, prefer to make their own selection of varieties from the body of the Catalogue an extra amount should be added to their remittance towards the cost of packing and postage. In the case of heavy seeds, such as Peas and Beans, the postage is an important item. All Vegetable and Flower Seeds can be supplied at any time or season.

PACKING OF PLANTS, TREES, Etc. :—All orders for these have special attention by our Export Packers, the plants being prepared and packed with the greatest care so as to ensure the best chances of successful transit, an important matter in dealing with perishable merchandise, and an extra amount should in all cases be remitted towards the cost of such special packing.

DAHLIAS, BEGONIAS, ROSES, FRUIT TREES & OTHER PLANTS :—Dahlias and Begonias are supplied for Export in *dry tubers only*, and must in all cases be left to our own selection of sorts. See pages 110 and 112. The Dahlias offered on pages 142 to 145, are as young green plants, and quite unsuitable for Export. Tubers of these, also Fruit Trees, Roses, Chrysanthemums, Pelargoniums, &c., can only be sent out late in the Autumn or during Winter, when they are in a dormant condition.

CUSTOMS OR POSTAL REGULATIONS :—Where special regulations or restrictions are in operation regarding the importation of Potatoes, Plants, Trees or Tubers, it will greatly help us if our customers will kindly make themselves acquainted with those which apply to their particular province, and give particulars of such at the time of ordering, to enable us to comply with them if possible, and thus prevent delay in delivery or confiscation.

VEGETABLE SEEDS.

These Collections which are made up from the most reliable and suitable varieties for Foreign and Colonial climates, are composed of the sorts mentioned below, in boxes containing proportionate quantities.

Price 10s. 6d., 15s., £1 1s., £2 2s., £3 3s., and £5 5s.

☞ *Post or Carriage Free to all countries included in the Parcel Post Union.*

Peas, Choice Sorts	Cucumber	Onion
Beans, Dwarf French	Kohl-rabi	Parsley
Beans, Runner	Capsicum	Radish
Beet, Garden	Cress	Herbs
Brussels Sprout	Leek	Marrow, Vegetable
Cabbages	Lettuce, Cos	Turnip
Cauliflower	Lettuce, Cabbage	Spinach
Carrot	Mustard	Tomato
Celery	Melon	

FLOWER SEEDS.

We offer liberal Collections from the list given below, and other choice sorts, at the following rates.

Price 5s., 7s. 6d., 10s. 6d., 15s., £1 1s., £1 11s. 6d., £2 2s.

☞ *Post or Carriage Free to all countries included in the Parcel Post Union.*

Asters	Dianthuses	Poppies
Antirrhinums	Gaillardias	Portulaca
Balsams	Godetias	Rhodanthe
Begonias	Larkspur	Salpiglossis
Calliopsis	Marigolds	Stocks
Candytuft	Mignonette	Sweet Peas
Canary Creeper	Nasturtiums	Sweet Williams
Celosias	Petunias	Verbena
Chrysanthemums	Phloxes	Wallflower
Cobœas	Pansy	Zinnias, &c., &c.

DANIELS BROS., Ltd., SEED MERCHANTS AND NURSERYMEN
NORWICH :: ENGLAND

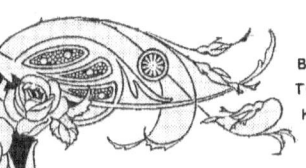

SEEDSMEN
BY APPOINTMENT
TO HIS MAJESTY
KING GEORGE V.

NURSERYMEN
BY APPOINTMENT
TO HER MAJESTY
QUEEN ALEXANDRA.

To·our·Customers

It is with much pleasure that we send you for the coming season, a copy of our ILLUSTRATED GUIDE FOR AMATEUR GARDENERS, and at the same time we beg to thank you for your very kind and liberal patronage during the past year, which has been a record, both for the number of customers on our books, and the volume of trade done. We also highly appreciate the many recommendations given by our customers to their friends, and shall at all times be pleased to forward catalogues free of charge, on receipt of the addresses of any who are interested in gardening.

THE SEED HARVEST. The very severe and protracted drought experienced during the Summer of 1911 was most disastrous to the growing crops of many kinds of kitchen garden seeds, the result being a great shortage of yield, especially of most varieties of Peas, Onions, Carrots, Broad and Runner Beans. On the other hand, we are glad to say that such seed as was saved proved to be of exceptionally high germinating power. Whilst we anticipate that we have sufficient stock of most varieties for our extensive trade, we strongly advise our customers to order early to prevent the possibility of disappointment.

SEED POTATOES. Proved an excellent crop, the tubers being of more uniform size, cleaner and more free from disease than for many years past. Our list contains a selection of the choicest varieties in commerce, including many fine sorts raised by ourselves. We would once again emphasize the importance of constant change of ground, and change of stock.

FLOWER SEEDS. We enjoy a very wide reputation for our magnificent strains of Choice Florists' and other Flower Seeds. In addition to our general list, we have added some splendid novelties in Sweet Peas and other subjects.

OUR NURSERIES. Contain a grand stock of the choicest in Fruit Trees and Roses, Clematises and other Hardy Climbers, Ornamental Trees and Shrubs, Forest Trees, Fencing Plants, Hardy Herbaceous Plants, Florists' Flowers, &c., a full list of which will be found on pages 116 to 159.

We have made every possible preparation for the prompt execution of orders, but as we are invariably very much pressed at the height of the sowing season, we venture to ask our regular customers to favour us with their orders as early as possible in the New Year, whatever may be the conditions of the weather.

January 1st, 1912. **DANIELS BROS., Ltd.**

DANIELS' SELECT VEGETABLE SEEDS FOR 1912.

CARROT, DANIELS' TELEGRAPH. This grand Carrot is one of the best forms of intermediate yet introduced, being far in advance of the old James' Scarlet, besides coming into use earlier than that variety. It produces a heavy crop of fine marketable roots, which are of splendid uniform shape, attractive colour, and very clear in the skin. Where sufficient depth of soil exists it will prove one of the most profitable sorts to grow. It is unequalled for exhibition purposes, having obtained more First Prizes than any Carrot with which we are acquainted. (See illustration opposite page.) per packet 4d.; per oz. 1s.

CARROT, DANIELS' SCARLET PERFECTION. A grand main crop variety of the intermediate type, and being stump-rooted, it is well adapted for growing on soils where deep culture is not possible. The roots are of a bright orange scarlet colour, very handsome and uniform in shape, with a fine clear skin, which makes it a most desirable sort for exhibition. It is one of the best flavoured and heaviest cropping varieties for general use, and one we can highly recommend. If grown for exhibition the roots should be thinned out 7 to 9 inches apart, but if for ordinary use they can be left much thicker in the row. (See illustration opposite page.) per packet, 4d.; per oz. 1s.

ONION, DANIELS' SELECTED AILSA CRAIG. This grand Onion has now taken its place as one of the largest and most useful varieties for all purposes. It is very good sown either in Spring or Autumn, and produces a heavy crop of fine handsome bulbs, which are unrivalled for exhibition purposes. They have been grown to the enormous weight of 26, 28, 30 and 34 lbs. per dozen bulbs. Our own selected stock grown from picked bulbs. (See illustration opposite page.) per packet, 1s.; per oz. 2s. 6d.

ONION, DANIELS' GOLDEN GLOBE. One of the finest types of Globe Onion in cultivation. The bulbs are of true globular shape with bright golden yellow skin; the flesh is very solid and of mild flavour. It produces a very heavy crop of fine, handsome bulbs, and is one of the best keepers. A most useful variety for all purposes. (See illustration opposite page.) per packet 6d.; per oz. 1s. 6d.

TOMATO, DANIELS' KING GEORGE V. This grand variety introduced by us last year has proved itself exceedingly popular. It is of robust constitution, short-jointed in habit of growth, and a very free setter. The fruit are produced mostly in racimes after the type of the well-known "Sunrise" but they are larger and of better colour than those of that variety. The fruit which are of a rich glowing scarlet colour are of perfect shape, and of the finest flavour. For exhibition purposes it will prove a great acquisition, whilst its handsome appearance and heavy cropping qualities will render it most valuable for all growers. (See illustration opposite page.) per packet. 1s. 6d. & 2s. 6d.

TOMATO, WISETON PROLIFIC (new). A grand variety raised by Mr. Musk, The Gardens, Wiseton Hall. The fruit, which are of good size, are of grand colour, very firm, and of excellent flavour. It is enormously prolific and will be found first-class for exhibition. per packet, 1s. 6d

RUNNER BEAN, DANIELS' WHITE EMPEROR. A fine new variety, bearing a heavy crop of long straight pods, quite equal to the Scarlet Emperor. The seed and flowers are white, and it has a good vigorous constitution. It will make a most valuable variety for exhibition, whilst its heavy cropping and fine quality render it most useful for all purposes. per pkt. 9d.; per half-pint 1s. 6d.; per pint 2s. 6d.

PEA, DANIELS' EXPRESS. A grand new first early Marrowfat variety, growing to the height of about 18 inches, and of great productiveness, bearing a profusion of handsome dark green pods 4½ to 5 inches in length, well filled with Peas of the most delicious marrow flavour. In habit of growth it somewhat resembles Competitor, but the pods are much darker in colour and better filled. We can strongly recommend this as one of the finest first early varieties yet introduced. (Stock limited.) per ½ pint 1s. 6d.; per pint 2s. 6d.

CUCUMBER, DISEASE RESISTER. A very prolific variety of similar type to the "Amateur" but a stronger grower. The plants are very robust and short-jointed, bearing a heavy crop of medium sized fruit of excellent shape and quality. The strong leathery leaves being impervious to disease it can be relied upon to keep in bearing for a longer period than most varieties. per pkt. 1s. 6d. & 2s. 6d.

COS LETTUCE, DANIELS' DREADNOUGHT. This is one of the largest Cos Lettuces in cultivation and at the same time the heads are very solid, crisp and of excellent flavour. It is self folding and requires no tying, and will be found invaluable for exhibition purposes. per pkt. 1s.; per oz. 2s. 6d.

CABBAGE LETTUCE, DANIELS' EXHIBITION GIANT. This grand variety is one of the largest Cabbage Lettuces yet introduced, and grows to an enormous size without becoming coarse. The heads are very firm, crisp, and of excellent flavour. For exhibition purposes it is unrivalled, and is one of the best for salads, especially where they are used in quantity. per pkt. 1s.; per oz. 2s. 6d.

RADISH, SPARKLER (new). A quite distinct variety, the upper half of the root is bright scarlet and the lower portion pure white. The two colours are sharply defined and do not merge into each other. Has a most dainty appearance on the table. per oz. 6d.

DANIELS'
TELEGRAPH

DANIELS'
SELECTED
STOCKS OF

CARROTS
& ONIONS

DANIELS'
GOLDEN
GLOBE

DANIELS'
SELECT
AILSA
CRAIG

DANIELS'
SCARLET
PERFECTION

A FINE COLLECTION OF VEGETABLES.

GROWN FROM SEEDS SUPPLIED BY DANIELS BROS. Ltd.

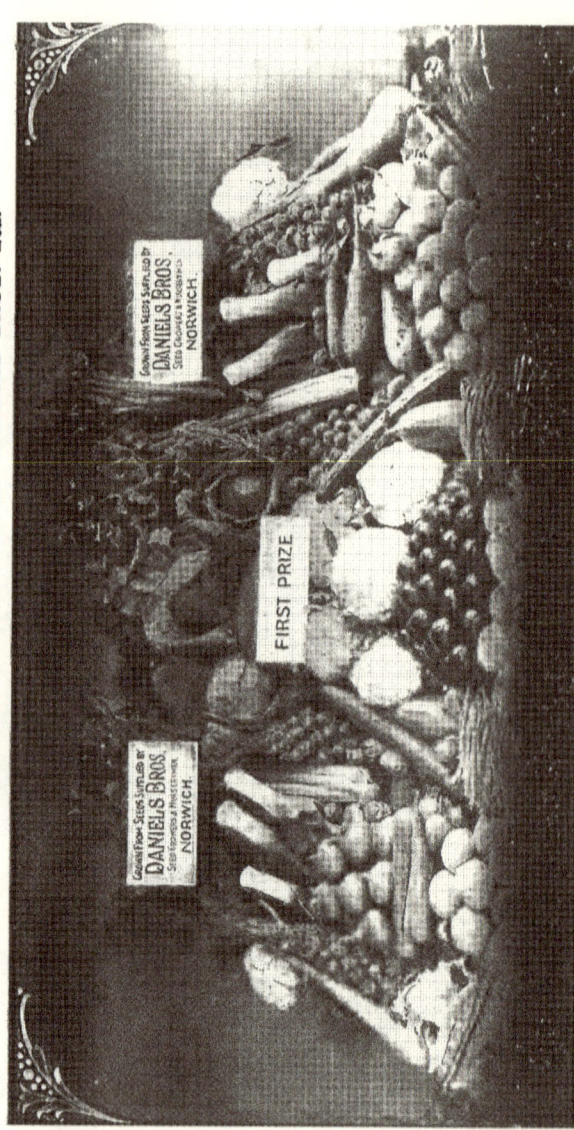

For many years past we have taken the greatest care to supply our customers with Seeds of the best possible stocks and growing quality, and true to name. It is, therefore, highly gratifying to note by our steadily increasing business and the large number of unsolicited testimonials we are constantly receiving from our patrons, that our efforts to supply them with really good and reliable Seeds are so fully appreciated.

UNSOLICITED TESTIMONIALS.

"I won 22 First and Special, also 14 Second Prizes with produce from your Seeds."—Mr. W. WRIGHT, Peterborough.

"Your Seeds have turned out wonderfully well. I took 20 Prizes at Fishtoft Show."—Mr. E. W. SCOTT, Grimsby.

"I may like to know that I did very well at the Shows. I exhibited at four Shows, winning forty-six First, seventeen Second, and at Third Prizes. I cannot speak too highly of your Seeds."—Mr. J. DEWE, Nuneaton.

"I might say that I have grown your Seeds for upwards of 12 years, and always had good results."—Mr. F. DEW, Romsey Hall.

"I am pleased to inform you that I won the 'Mayor of Wandsworth's Silver Challenge Cup at our Show, last year.—Mr. J. THOMSON, Wandsworth.

"I did very well with your Seeds last year, taking 50 Prizes out of 58 exhibits."—Mr. E. SPILLER, Welton.

KITCHEN GARDEN SEEDS.

Our large experience in this department has enabled us to select the finest possible stocks, the same being grown on our own grounds or under our personal supervision. The growth of all seeds is carefully tested before sending out, and customers ordering from us may thoroughly rely on being supplied with the best and newest varieties all of good growing quality,

DANIELS' COMPLETE COLLECTIONS.

All Package and Carriage Free.

These Collections, of which we annually sell immense quantities, are carefully made up with seeds of finest quality in best varieties from each class with a view of furnishing an ample supply of Choice Vegetables throughout the year, and will be found extremely valuable for those who have not sufficient time or experience for making their own selection.

As our Collections are made up on a most liberal scale, intending purchasers will kindly bear in mind that it is only by having Seeds specially grown, and by preparing the packets beforehand in large numbers, that we can be so liberal in the quantity of the Seeds supplied for the amount charged, and that by ordering our selections, instead of making their own, will reap an advantage of at least 25 per cent. below the general Catalogue prices. We therefore wish it to be understood that no reduction, alteration, or substitution can be allowed in any of the collections. When ordering please quote Number and Price of the Collection required.

No. 1.	Contains **26 quarts of Choice Peas**	And	-	£5	5	0
No. 2.	Contains **20 quarts of Choice Peas**	all	-	£4	4	0
No. 3.	Contains **16 quarts of Choice Peas**	other	-	£3	3	0
No. 4.	Contains **12 quarts of Choice Peas**	Seeds in	-	£2	2	0
No. 5.	Contains **9 quarts of Choice Peas**	proportion	-	£1	11	6

No. 6. Daniels' Complete Collection, £1 1s.

Package and Carriage Free. All the best kinds for succession.

12	pints	Peas, Early, Medium, and Late	2	pkts.	Cauliflower, Autumn Giant, &c.	
3	pints	Broad Beans				
1	pint	French Beans	2	pkts.	Celery, Giant Red and White	
1	pint	Runner Beans	1	pkt.	Couve Tronchuda	
1	pkt.	Beet, Crimson Perfection	8	ozs.	Cress, Plain and Curled	
1	pkt.	Borecole, Curled	2	pkts.	Cucumber, Frame and Ridge	
2	pkts.	Brussels Sprouts, Colossal and Defiance	1	pkt.	Endive, Curled	
			2	pkts.	Gourd or Pumpkin	
3	pkts.	Broccoli, Early and Late	1	pkt.	Leek, Giant	
3	pkts.	Cabbage, Defiance, &c.	3	pkts.	Lettuce, Cos or Cabbage	
½	oz.	Savoy, Drumhead	6	ozs.	Mustard, White	
2	ozs.	Carrot, Intermediate and Scarlet Horn	1	pkt.	Melon, Choice	
			1	oz.	Parsley, Fine Curled	

3	ozs.	Onion, White Spanish, &c.
2	ozs.	Parsnip, Hollow-crowned
4	ozs.	Radish, Long and Turnip
4	ozs.	Spinach, Summer and Winter
2	ozs.	Turnip, Snowball and Golden Ball
1	pkt.	Vegetable Marrow, Large Cream
4	pkts.	Herbs, Sweet and Pot
2	pkts.	Tomato, Scarlet Perfection and Open Air
1	pkt.	Capsicum, Long Red

No. 7. Daniels' Complete Collection, 12s. 6d.

Package and Carriage Free. All the best kinds for succession.

6	pints	Peas, Early, Medium, and Late	1	pkt.	Cauliflower, Choice
1	pint	Broad Beans	1	pkt.	Celery
½	pint	French Beans	4	ozs.	Cress, Plain and Curled
½	pint	Runner Beans	2	pkts.	Cucumber, Ridge and Frame
1	pkt.	Beet, Dark-leaved	1	pkt.	Endive, Curled
1	pkt.	Borecole, Curled	1	pkt.	Gourd or Pumpkin
1	pkt.	Brussels Sprouts	1	pkt.	Leek, Giant
2	pkts.	Broccoli, Choice Sorts	2	pkts.	Lettuce, Cos and Cabbage
2	pkts.	Cabbage, Choice Sorts	3	ozs.	Mustard, White
1	pkt.	Savoy, Drumhead	2	ozs.	Onion, White Spanish, &c.
2	pkts.	Carrot, Intermediate, &c.			

1	pkt.	Melon, Choice
1	pkt.	Parsley, Fine Curled
1	oz.	Parsnip, Hollow-crowned
2	ozs.	Radish, Long and Turnip
2	ozs.	Spinach, Round and Prickly
1½	oz.	Turnip, Snowball and Orange Jelly
1	pkt.	Vegetable Marrow
3	pkts.	Herbs, Sweet and Pot
2	pkts.	Tomato

DANIELS' SPECIAL COLLECTION
☛ FOR EXHIBITORS. ☜

The following Special Collection of our Choice Stocks of Vegetable Seeds has been carefully selected and arranged, and will be found especially useful to growers for competition, and at the same time for a good succession of Vegetables for general use. Customers ordering this Collection will effect a saving of quite 33% below our usual Catalogue prices.

OUR SPECIAL COLLECTION FOR EXHIBITORS.
Price 10s. 6d. Post Free.
CONTAINS THE FOLLOWING LIBERAL ASSORTMENT.

4	pkts.	Peas, Choice	1	pkt.	Cabbage, Dwarf Blood Red	1	pkt.	Onion, Golden Globe
1	pkt.	Broad Beans, Daniels' Selected Long-pod	1	pkt.	Cauliflower, Daniels' King	1	oz.	Parsnip, Daniels' Improved
			2	pkts.	Carrot, Telegraph and Scarlet Perfection	1	pkt.	Parsley, Daniels' Giant Curled
1	pkt.	Runner Beans				1	oz.	Radish, New Scarlet Turnip
1	pkt.	Dwarf Beans	1	pkt.	Celery, Exhibition Pink	1	oz.	„ Long Scarlet
1	pkt.	Beet, Crimson Perfection	1	pkt.	Cucumber, Improved Telegraph	1	pkt.	Tomato, Scarlet Perfection
1	pkt.	Brussels Sprouts, Colossal	1	pkt.	Leek, Champion	1	oz.	Turnip, Improved Snowball
1	pkt.	Broccoli, King	2	pkts.	Lettuce, Giant White Cos and Queen of Summer	1	pkt.	„ Golden Gem
2	pkts.	Cabbage, Defiance and Little Queen				1	pkt.	Vegetable Marrow, Large Cream

"I have again been very successful with your Seeds, taking three First, four Second, and seven Third Prizes at our Show. I can confidently recommend your 10s. 6d. Exhibitors' Collection of Vegetable Seeds."—Mr. J. THOMPSON, St. Bruvels.

"Please send me one of your 10s. 6d. Collections of Vegetable Seeds as I was well satisfied with the last I had."—Mr. S. WILLATT, Bromley.

"I received the Collection of Vegetable Seeds, and I am exceedingly pleased with it."—Mrs. L. HOPE, Musselburgh.

"The Collection of Vegetable Seeds I had from you last year gave me great satisfaction."—Mr. J. SMITH, Staindrop.

"Your Collection of Vegetable Seeds was very satisfactory last year and did well."—Mr. W. MURRELL, Almeley.

"I am very pleased with the Collection of Vegetable Seeds you have sent me."—Mr. A. KIDD, Willington.

"I am very pleased with the 10s. 6d. Collection of Vegetable Seeds you sent me."—Mr. E. WATTS, Shiplake.

"The 12s. 6d. Collection of Vegetable Seeds gave magnificent results. I have had things from you for over twenty years, and in no instance have I been disappointed."—Mr. A. WILLIAMS, Llandudno.

"I am well pleased with your 12s. 6d. Collection of Vegetable Seeds. My Celery is the best in the district."—Mr. M. BOLTON, Crathorne.

"I did extremely well with your 10s. 6d. Exhibitors' Collection of Vegetable Seeds. I took eight First, six Second, and one Special Prizes at our Show."—Mr. C. CORNISH, Yoxford.

"I am pleased to say the 10s. 6d. Collection of Vegetable Seeds turned out all that could be desired. I have won twenty Prizes and Bronze Shield for most points."—Mr. G. SPICER, Ashorne.

No. 8. Daniels' Complete Collection, 7s. 6d.

Package and Carriage Free. All the best kinds for succession.

3	pints	Peas, Early, Medium and Late	1 oz.	Carrot, Intermediate	1 pkt.	Parsley, Fine Curled
½	pint	Broad Beans	1 pkt.	Cauliflower, Autumn Giant	1 oz.	Parsnip, Hollow-crowned
½	pint	French Beans	1 pkt.	Celery, Red and White	1 pkt.	Pumpkin
½	pint	Runner Beans	2 ozs.	Cress, Plain	2 ozs.	Radish, Long and Turnip
1	pkt.	Beet, Dark-leaved	1 pkt.	Cucumber, Ridge	1 oz.	Spinach, Summer
1	pkt.	Borecole, Curled	2 pkts.	Lettuce, Cos and Cabbage	1 oz.	Turnip, Snowball
1	pkt.	Brussels Sprouts	1 pkt.	Leek, Musselburgh	1 pkt.	Vegetable Marrow
1	pkt.	Broccoli	1 oz.	Mustard, White	2 pkts.	Herbs
1	pkt.	Savoy, Drumhead	1 oz.	Onion, White Spanish	1 pkt.	Tomato
1	pkt.	Cabbage				

"I have done much better with your 7s. 6d. Collection of Vegetable Seeds than I did when I made my own selection, and find the Seeds cost me less. I have now dealt with you for thirty years."—Mr. F. WARNER, Shiplake.

"I received your 7s. 6d. Collection of Vegetable Seeds and was very pleased with it."—Mr. C. KIRBY, Weymouth.

"Please send me your 7s. 6d. Collection of Vegetable Seeds, the same as I usually have, and which has been so very satisfactory."—Dr. BIRTWHISTLE, Barton-on-Humber.

No. 9. Daniels' Cottager's Collection, 5s. 0d.

Package and Carriage Free. This collection is of exceptional value.

3	pkts.	Peas, for succession	1 pkt.	Savoy, Drumhead	½ oz.	Onion, White Spanish
1	pkt.	Broad Beans	½ oz.	Carrot, Intermediate	1 pkt.	Parsley, Fine Curled
1	pkt.	Runner Beans	1 pkt.	Cauliflower	½ oz.	Parsnip, Hollow-crowned
1	pkt.	French Beans	1 pkt.	Celery, Mixed	1 pkt.	Gourd or Pumpkin
1	pkt.	Beet, Dark-leaved	1 oz.	Cress	1 oz.	Radish, Mixed Turnip
1	pkt.	Borecole, Curled	1 pkt.	Cucumber, Ridge	½ oz.	Spinach, Round
1	pkt.	Brussels Sprouts	1 pkt.	Leek	1 pkt.	Tomato
1	pkt.	Broccoli	1 pkt.	Lettuce, Cos and Cabbage,	½ oz.	Turnip
1	pkt.	Cabbage, Nonpareil		Mixed	1 pkt.	Vegetable Marrow

"I am glad to give you praise for your 5s. Collection of Vegetable Seeds, everything turned out exceedingly good."—Mr. C. PICKESS, Burton-on-Trent.

"I had a 5s. Collection of Vegetable Seeds last year, and I had some very fine crops from the same."—Miss NIXON, Usk.

"I am very pleased with the 5s. Collection of Vegetable Seeds I had from you."—Mr. F. TOPLEY, Haverfordfraid.

No. 10. The Cottager's Packet, 2s. 9d. Post free.

Containing sixteen varieties of choice Vegetable Seeds, including fair quantities of
Peas, Broccoli, Cabbage, Carrot, Lettuce, Onion, Radish, Turnip, &c.

This is a very cheap collection which can be highly recommended.

"I consider your Cottager's Collection of Vegetable Seeds very good and bound to give great satisfaction."—Mr. H. HALE, Loughborough.

"I was delighted with your Cottager's Collection of Vegetable Seeds last year."—Mr. J. BOULTON, Knoddishall.

"Please send me a Cottager's Collection. I think every seed grew last year."—Mr. T. COOPER, Walsall.

COLLECTIONS OF VEGETABLE SEEDS FOR EXPORT.

These Collections which are made up from the most reliable and suitable varieties for Foreign and Colonial climates, are composed of the sorts mentioned below, in boxes containing proportionate quantities.

Price 10s. 6d., 15s., £1 1s., £2 2s., £3 3s. and £5 5s.

Post or Carriage Free to all countries included in the Parcel Post Union

Peas, Choice Sorts	Brussels Sprouts	Celery	Cress	Mustard	Herbs
Beans, Dwarf French	Cabbages	Cucumber	Leek	Melon	Marrow, Vegetable
Beans, Runner	Cauliflower	Kohl-rabi	Lettuce, Cos	Onion	Turnip
Beet, Garden	Carrot	Capsicum	Lettuce, Cabbage	Parsley	Spinach
				Radish	Tomato

"I am pleased to inform you that I had good results from the Seeds I obtained from you last season, and at our Show I gained sixteen First, eight Second, and six Third Prizes. Your King of the Cauliflowers is the first I have had to succeed out here, whilst your Defiance Cabbage is splendid."—Mr. S. ELSON, Marshall, Canada.

"I have the honour to acknowledge the receipt of your letter and to say the Seeds have arrived safely and seem to be germinating well. I appreciate the liberal manner in which you have treated me and the satisfactory way the order has been carried out."—Major H. W. COLE, Lushai Hills, India.

"I won every First Prize in the Adelaide big Show in five classes, so was very satisfied. I also did well in other classes. I believe a friend of mine has already sent you a list of the way Daniels' Seeds scored."—F. FAIREY Esq., Adelaide, Australia.

PEAS.

Cultivation.—Peas form one of the most valuable of garden crops, and when once started into growth, require, under favourable conditions, little attention beyond the staking of such varieties as need support, and mulching and watering in dry weather. Peas require a good rich soil, which should be well trenched, and should receive a liberal supply of well-decomposed manure early in the season. They are essentially a moisture loving plant, and only when the ground is well prepared can really satisfactory results be assured. Given these conditions, it is possible by a succession of sowings to have a continuous supply of Peas for the table from June till October, or even later.

First early varieties should be sown from the middle of January onwards, and the best sorts in this class are Daniels' Gem of the Season, Earliest of All, and The Pilot; if the seed is sown in boxes under glass in January, hardened off in a frame and planted out at the latter end of March or early in April, an advantage of ten days or a fortnight may be gained. Second early and main crop kinds should be sown in March and April, and for late use a succession of sowings at intervals from the beginning of May until the end of June should be made. For these sowings the tall varieties will be found more productive, and not so liable to mildew during hot weather. It should be borne in mind that although most of the **Wrinkled seeded** varieties may be sown in March, we do not recommend this unless the season is exceptionally favourable. We find from a careful record extending over ten years, that little if any advantage is gained by too early sowings, and that Peas sown at the beginning of April take less time to come to maturity than the earlier sown ones. If this rule was more generally followed, we should hear less about bad germination amongst this class of Peas especially in cold wet seasons. The seed should be sown in drills and covered about two inches deep; allow four or five feet between each row unless it is desired to grow some other crop between, when the rows may be 12 to 15 feet apart. Let the rows run from north to south thus allowing the plants to receive a maximum of light and air.

Peas suffer greatly from the depredations of all kinds of vermin, and it will always be found of advantage to give protection either by wire pea guards or some other means while the plants are growing. The rows should be earthed up before they are staked, and this should be done when the plants are about four inches high. If the tops of the sticks are cut evenly, and the pieces which are cut off placed between the large sticks at the base, they will prevent the plants from falling about, and give them an upward tendency from the start.

A good mulching of manure placed on each side of the row will help to retain the moisture in dry weather. Where this is not possible they must be regularly watered during dry periods, and liquid manure given once a week; a mixture containing four ounces Nitrate of Soda to one gallon of water will be found very useful for this purpose.

When it is desired to grow Peas for exhibition purposes the following points should be observed:—Sow the seed very thinly on ground that has been especially deeply trenched for the purpose, and which has been dressed with old farmyard manure or the remains of an old mushroom bed. If they are needed for early Summer Shows it may be desirable to raise the seed on turves in a greenhouse and transfer them bodily to the border when about four inches high, but, generally speaking, if the seed is sown in rows in March and April it will be found early enough.

When the plants have shown about four blooms, pinch out the leader or top of the haulm. As soon as the pods have formed, choose the best shaped, and remove the others, leaving only two or three on each plant. Always select the strongest and healthiest plants for this purpose. When ready to gather, do not handle the pods, but cut off with scissors so as to retain their bloom.

DANIELS' EXPRESS.

NEW PEA, DANIELS' EXPRESS.

A grand new first early Marrowfat variety, growing to the height of about 18 inches, and of great productiveness, bearing a profusion of handsome dark green pods, 4½ to 5 inches in length, well filled with peas of the most delicious marrow flavour. In habit of growth it somewhat resembles Competitor, but the pods are much darker in colour and better filled. We can strongly recommend this as one of the finest first early varieties yet introduced. Per ½ pint 1s. 6d. ; per pint 2s. 6d.

NEW PEA, THE PILOT.

This valuable introduction is rapidly taking a leading place amongst the most useful varieties, both for market and private garden purposes. It is a first early cropper producing deep green pods of the well-known Gradus type, and on account of its hardy constitution and the seed being round it may be sown very early with the certainty of a crop. It is a vigorous branching plant, growing three feet in height, bearing a large proportion of the pods in pairs, which contain fine deep green peas of excellent marrow flavour. Per pint 1s. 6d ; per quart 2s. 9d.

" I might mention that I had splendid results from your Seeds last year. The Gradus and Recorder Peas were especially fine."—Mr. E. MACAULAY, Bournemouth.

" I had a splendid crop of Peas last year, although in a town garden."—Mr. R. MACARTNEY, Liverpool.

" I had some excellent crops of Peas last year from your Seeds."—Miss CHITTENDEN, Broxbourne.

PEAS.

Section I.—Earliest Varieties.

☛ DANIELS' SELECTED GRADUS.

This large-podded early wrinkled variety, is without doubt the finest and most distinct early Pea yet introduced. The haulm which grows to the height of three to four feet is well covered with large dark green pods, averaging five inches in length, and well filled with eight to ten fine Peas of the most exquisite flavour ; indeed, amongst the early varieties it has no rival in this respect. It is an excellent cropper, this combined with its earliness and grand flavour, has made it a favourite with all growers.

Per pint 1s. 9d. ; per quart 3s.

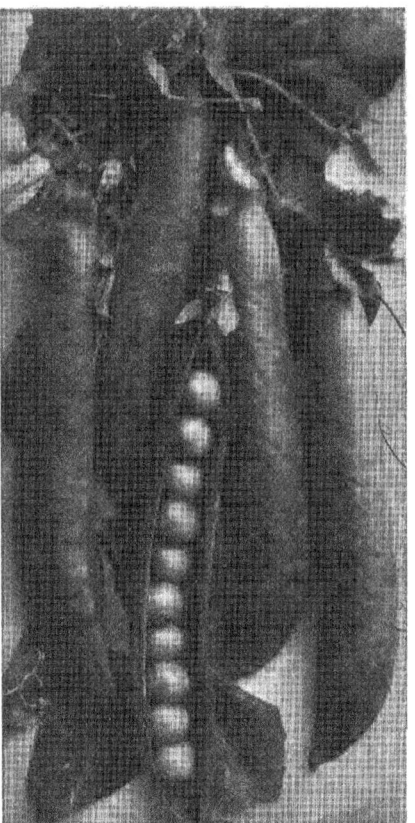

DANIELS' SELECTED GRADUS. *Reduced from a Photograph.*

per quart.
s. d

☛ **DANIELS' COMPETITOR.** This grand Dwarf Pea is of the true Marrowfat type, and as early as English Wonder or William the First, the haulm does not grow more than about a foot in height. It is exceedingly prolific, the numerous handsome pods are of large size, four to five inches in length, and well filled with large peas of good colour and excellent marrow flavour. This is, undoubtedly, the longest and largest podded, and finest quality of any Dwarf Pea of similar height ; and in consideration of its earliness, size, and superior quality, will prove of great value .. .. .. per pint 1s. 9d. —

☛ **DANIELS' BEST OF ALL.** A very fine dwarf Early Marrowfat variety, growing only about eighteen inches in height. It is an abundant cropper, bearing quite a profusion of handsome pods of 3½ to 4 inches in length, each with seven or eight large finely-flavoured peas. It is as early as English Wonder, and will prove a splendid and profitable Pea for the market or private grower .. ..per pint 1s. 6d. 2 6

DANIELS' GEM OF THE SEASON. The earliest Pea in cultivation, and very prolific. Is always the earliest, whether sown in Autumn, Winter, or Spring. Is also the hardiest, resisting frost better than any other kind, and is not affected by mildew. Being very prolific and of a most delicious flavour, will be found a most desirable variety for early work. Height 3 ft. Per pint 1s. 3d. 2 0
EARLIEST OF ALL. A round blue-seeded Pea of excellent and rich flavour ; very prolific, can be sown early. Height 2½ ft. Pt. 8d. 1 3
EARLY BOUNTIFUL. A grand first early round Pea. Pods nearly twice the size of Earliest of All, and comes in only a few days later, very hardy, useful for early sowings. Height 3½ ft. Pt. 1s. 1 9
ENGLISH WONDER. One of the most useful of the dwarf varieties, of good constitution and very prolific, may be sown earlier than some of the wrinkled sorts. Height 1 ft. .. per pint 1s. 3d. 2 0
KING EDWARD VII. A new early dwarf variety of great productiveness, bearing a profusion of dark green pods, well filled with peas of fine quality. It is a wrinkled marrow, and a great acquisition to our early dwarf varieties. Height 1½ ft. Pt. 1s. 6d. 2 6
THE SHERWOOD. A remarkably productive early variety, and is one of the best Dwarf Peas ever offered. It is an enormous cropper, the haulm being literally covered with pods containing eight to ten large peas of rich deep colour, and of exquisite flavour. Height 1 ft. .. .. per pint 1s. 6d. 2 6
THOMAS LAXTON. Award of Merit, Royal Horticultural Society. A large-podded first early Pea, coming in with Earliest of All but with pods of double the size, and rich dark green colour. It is a true wrinkled Marrow, a grand cropper, and the flavour is of the best. Height 3 ft. .. .. per pint 1s. 6d. 2 6
WILLIAM HURST. An early blue wrinkled variety of good hardy constitution, very prolific and of fine table quality. Height 1 ft. Per pint 1s. 3d. 2 0

EVIDENCE OF QUALITY.

" It might interest you to know that yesterday (June 5th) I gathered some of your Gem of the Season Peas, grown in an open field."—Mr. H. TIDD, Stanhoe.

" In spite of the dry weather your Gem of the Season Pea has been a grand crop, and very early."—Mr. H. A. TRUMAN, Meare.

PEAS.

Section II.—Second Early.

☛ DANIELS' DWARF PROLIFIC.

A grand second early dwarf wrinkled Marrow, of strong constitution and sturdy habit, growing about 1½ feet high; it is enormously prolific, bearing a profusion of dark green, slightly curved pods, four inches long, well filled with eight to nine peas of excellent flavour, at the same time it is an excellent variety for forcing, being quite as prolific under glass as in the open. It is a very compact grower, and will be an acquisition to all gardens where space is limited, on account of the little room it occupies as compared with its heavy cropping qualities.   Per pint 1s. 3d. ; per quart 2s.

DANIELS' DWARF PROLIFIC.

☛ **DANIELS' MIDSUMMER MARROW.** A grand early Marrowfat Pea of a good hardy constitution. It is an abundant bearer ; the pods, which somewhat resemble Gradus in shape, are about 4½ inches in length and well filled with nine or ten fine peas of excellent flavour. We can thoroughly recommend this as a first-class variety for all purposes. Height 3 to 4 ft.   ..   ..   ..   per pint 1s. 6d. 2 0

☛ **DANIELS' NORWICH WONDER.** Crop failed.

DUKE OF YORK. A fine wrinkled Marrow, of robust habit, pods five inches in length ; a very profitable bearer, coming in a few days earlier than Duke of Albany, and like that variety, A 1 for exhibition. Height 3½ to 4 ft. ..   .. per pint 1s. 3d. 2 0

LYE'S FAVOURITE. Improved Stock. A new selection of this fine second early variety, of hardy constitution and enormous productiveness, bearing a profusion of long, handsome, slightly curved pods, well filled with peas of excellent marrow flavour. Very useful for early sowing on account of its extreme hardiness. Height 3 to 4 ft. ..   .. per pint 1s. 3d. 2 0

PRODUCTIVE MARROWFAT. A fine second early variety, growing to the height of 1½ feet. The haulm is of good constitution, bearing a profusion of large pods mostly in pairs, and well-filled with fine peas of the true marrowfat flavour. Considering its dwarf habit and great productiveness it will prove of great value for small gardens. Height 1½ to 2 ft. per pint 1s. 6d. 2 6

THE DAISY. A dwarf second early wrinkled Marrow of great merit. The haulm which is very robust is well hung with handsome pods four to five inches in length, well filled with large peas of excellent flavour. On account of its numerous good qualities it has been awarded a First Class Certificate by the Royal Horticultural Society. Height 1½ ft. .. per pint 1s. 6d. 2 6

WILLIAM THE FIRST. Selected stock. One of the finest early green Marrows, combining flavour and earliness, and produces a very heavy crop of slightly curved dark green pods, well filled with peas of excellent colour and flavour, and is one of the best varieties for market purposes. Height 4 ft. per pint 1s. 3d. 2 0

SENATOR. A very prolific variety, bearing the pods mostly in pairs ; these are from four to five inches in length and well filled with peas of a fine marrow flavour. Height 3 ft. per pint 1s. 3d. 2 3

" I am pleased to tell you that the **Dwarf Prolific Peas** are splendid ; they deserve all the praise I can give them. The other seeds I had from you have done very well indeed."—**Mr. T. GRIMMER,** Beiminster.

" I am pleased to inform you that I secured a Prize with your **Lye's Favourite Pea.**"—**Mr. F. BODY,** Axbridge.

" I had some of your **Early Bountiful Peas** last year and they did very well."—**Mr. F. KENT,** Clayton.

" I have grown your **Peas** with great success. My friends said they were the finest they ever saw."—**Mr. H. PARKER,** Temple Ewell.

" The **Peas** are very fine notwithstanding six weeks without a drop of rain ; by far the best on all points in the district."—**Mr. H. J. BURGESS,** St. Breage.

" I have obtained excellent results in growing **Dwarf Prolific** and **Autocrat Peas** in the past."—**Mr. H. CASWELL,** Wotton-under-Edge.

" I have grown your **Matchless Marrow Peas** for the past two years and they have been greatly admired."—**Mr. A. BROWN,** Poole.

" I consider your **Matchless Marrow Peas** the very best in cultivation. It is now twenty years since I first grew them, and they are as good as ever."—**Mr. J. CUPIT,** Alfreton.

" The **Matchless Marrow Peas** I have grown this season have been the finest I have ever seen, quite up to the illustration in your Catalogue. My friends say they never saw anything to equal them."—**Mr. H. CATCHPOLE,** Brith.

MAINCROP PEA.

DANIELS' MATCHLESS MARROW.

This splendid maincrop variety continues to hold its position as first favourite, for all purposes, on account of its heavy cropping qualities and excellent flavour. It grows to the height of 4 to 5 feet, the haulm being well covered with fine dark-green pods 5 to 6 inches in length and of splendid appearance, each containing 10 to 12 large Peas of the most delicious marrow flavour. It is the leading variety for exhibition purposes, having obtained numerous First Prizes in all parts of the country.

Per pint 1s. 9d.
Per quart 3s. 0d.

MAINCROP PEA.

DANIELS' RECORDER

A grand long-podded maincrop variety, growing about three feet high. The haulm, which is very robust, is well hung with large pods, which are of a deep green colour, averaging from 5 to 6 inches in length, and contain 10 to 11 fine Peas of excellent colour and of the finest marrow flavour. Its great prolificness, combined with the large size of the pods, make it one of the most useful varieties, both for table and exhibition purposes. We can strongly recommend this fine variety to our customers.

Per pint 1s. 9d.
Per quart 3s. 0d.

PEAS.

Section III.—Main Crop.

☞ DANIELS' SELECTED DUKE OF ALBANY.

A fine selected stock of this useful Main Crop Pea. It grows between 4 and 5 feet in height. The haulm being covered with a very heavy crop of long handsome dark green pods, averaging five inches in length, which are well filled with 10 to 12 large peas of the true marrow flavour. A splendid variety for exhibition, whilst its fine cropping qualities combined with its excellent flavour will recommend it alike to the private grower and the market gardener. Per pint 1s. 3d. ; per quart 2s. 3d.

DANIELS' SELECTED DUKE OF ALBANY.

per quart.
s. d.

☞ **THE DANIELS'.** An extra large podded Main Crop variety of great merit. It is of robust constitution, the pods are long and handsome, averaging five to six inches in length, and well filled with ten to twelve large peas of the finest marrow flavour. It is a very heavy and reliable cropper, and a most useful sort for exhibition ; strongly recommended for general crop. Height 4 ft. .. **per pint 1s. 9d.** 3 0

ALDERMAN. Received the highest award from the Royal Horticultural Society after trial at Chiswick. In habit it is strong and branching, producing a few days later than Duke of Albany, very large handsome, straight, deep green and well-filled pods, which contain peas of the richest No Plus Ultra flavour and quality. Height 5 ft. per pint 1s. 6d. 2 6

CAPTAIN CUTTLE. A fine wrinkled main crop variety of strong constitution and robust habit, producing a heavy crop of long dark green pods containing 9 to 10 large peas of the finest marrow flavour. The pods are of the same shape as the well-known "No Plus Ultra," but are much larger. Very useful for exhibition purposes. Height 4 ft. .. per pint 1s. 6d. 2 6

DR. MACLEAN. A fine wrinkled Marrow, of vigorous growth, wonderfully productive, flavour of the first quality. Height 3½ ft. .. .. per pint 1s. 1 9

FILLBASKET. Very prolific. Height 3 ft. per pt. 1s. 3d. 2 0

GLADIATOR. The plant is very robust and vigorous, stem branched, growing about three feet in height, exceedingly productive, bearing in pairs an abundance of long, curved handsome pods, which are very closely filled with medium-sized peas of excellent quality. First-Class Certificate, R.H.S. Height 3 ft. pt. 1s. 3d. 2 0

MACLEAN'S WONDERFUL, or PRINCE OF WALES. Excellent cropping variety of superior flavour Height 3 ft. per pint 10d. 1 6

MAGNUM BONUM. This grand Pea is of a fine robust constitution, and resists mildew in dry seasons. The pods are of a deep rich green colour, measuring about 5 inches in length, and contain 10 to 11 peas of excellent marrow flavour. A very heavy cropper Height 3 to 4 ft. per pint 1s. 6d. 2 6

PEERLESS MARROWFAT. Crop failed.

" I was very successful with your **Duke of Albany Peas**, winning two First Prizes at our Show."—**Mr. J. HOWARD**, Robertsbridge.

" Your Recorder Pea is the best I have ever grown."—**Mr. B. NEWELL**, Saffron Walden.

" Your Recorder and Matchless Marrow Peas are the finest I have ever grown."—**Mr. D. BURREN**, Walton.

" I am pleased to tell you that I had a splendid crop of **Recorder** Pea last year, some of the pods containing from ten to twelve peas. I have never grown any kind so fine before."—**Mr. A. G. SHAW**, Frinton-ou-Sea.

" I have done very well with your Collection of Vegetable Seeds. I also took First Prize with your Recorder Pea."—**Mr. W. J. COOPER**, Plumstead.

" I must say that the Vegetable Seeds I had last Spring turned out well. The **Matchless Marrow Peas** were greatly admired."—**Mr. J. CHANCE**, Hendon.

" I am pleased to state that I took First Prize with your **Matchless Marrow Pea** last year against strong competition."—**Mr. P. HUGHES**, East Croydon.

" It may interest you to know that your **Matchless Marrow Pea** has never failed to secure First Prize at our Show."—**Mr. J. BOWEN**, Poulton.

PEAS.

Section III.—Main Crop.

☞ QUITE CONTENT.

This is undoubtedly the largest-podded pea yet introduced. It somewhat resembles Alderman, but with stronger growth and longer pods. It is exceedingly prolific, and the pods hang mostly in pairs. Grand exhibition variety. Height 5 to 6 ft.

Per pkt. 1s. ; half-pint 1s. 9d. ; pint 3s.

☞ DANIELS' COMMANDER. A fine dwarf Marrowfat of robust constitution, bearing a heavy crop of rich dark green pods, well filled with large peas of the finest flavour Height 1½ to 2 ft.   Per pint 1s. 6d. ; per quart 2s. 6d.

QUITE CONTENT.   *Reduced from a Photograph.*

per quart.
s. d.

☞ DANIELS' MAIN CROP MARROW. One of the finest Marrow Peas in cultivation, and of the same flavour as the old Ne Plus Ultra ; but the pods are longer. It is very prolific, bearing a profusion of dark green, well-filled pods, each containing eight to nine large peas of exquisite flavour ; as a Main Crop variety it should be in great demand on account of its numerous good qualities ..   ..   ..   per pint 1s. 6d.   2 6

DANIELS' IMPROVED CHAMPION OF ENGLAND. A great improvement on the well-known variety. It is very prolific, bearing a profusion of well-filled pods, twice the size of the old variety, at the same time retaining the fine rich marrow flavour for which that pea is celebrated. Height 5 to 6 ft.   per pint 1s. 3d.   2 0

HARRISON'S GLORY. A large blue-seeded variety of great productiveness. Height 3 ft.   ..   ..   per pint 10d.   1 6

STRATAGEM. This is a splendid variety, with pods five to six inches in length, containing eight to ten large fine-flavoured peas. First Class Certificate, R.H.S. Our own selected and improved stock. Height 2 ft.   ..   .. per pint 1s. 6d.   2 6

TELEGRAPH. A hardy variety of first-class quality and strong constitution, pods large and well-filled ; also fine for exhibition. Height 4 ft.   ..   ..   .. per pint 1s. 3d.   2 0

TELEPHONE. First Class Certificate, Royal Horticultural Society. This fine variety is good either for exhibition or market purposes. Height 4½ ft.   ..   ..   .. per pint 1s. 3d.   2 3

TRIUMPH. A blue wrinkled Marrow, of exquisite flavour ; the pods are long and well filled, each containing nine to eleven large peas. In constitution it is robust and hardy, Height 2 to 3 ft.   ..   ..   .. per pint 1s. 3d.   2 0

YORKSHIRE HERO. A fine dwarf Marrow Pea, of the Veitch's Perfection type, is very prolific, bearing a profusion of well-filled pods, containing six to eight large peas each ; flavour first-class. Height 3 ft. ..   ..   .. per pint 1s.   1 9

"I am pleased to tell you that I took First Prize with your Collection of Vegetables and First Prize for Quite Content Peas."—Mr. T. PEERS, Northop.

"I must tell you that your Matchless Marrow Peas were the talk of the Allotment Holders last season. They grow to an enormous size and could not be beaten."—Mr. W. BAYES, New Malden.

"I am pleased to say that I have grown your Matchless Marrow Pea for several years and find it quite up to your description."—Mr. W. TOMPSETT, West Farleigh.

"I have much pleasure in informing you that your Matchless Marrow Peas gained First Prize at our Show, and were greatly admired by all who saw them."—Mr. G. PRONGER, Horsham.

"All your Seeds have done remarkably well. I took First Prize with your Distinction Pea, and another First for a plate of three sorts, with Recorder, Distinction, and Matchless Marrow."—Mr. G. BERRY, Moreton Morrell.

"I might mention that I gained eight Prizes at our Show; I took First Prize with your Distinction Pea. It was said in the papers it was the finest that had ever been exhibited."—Mr. E. SIMMETT, Burton-on-Trent.

"I am pleased to say that your Sea is turned out well last year. The Distinction Peas were grand. I won two Prizes with them in very keen competition."—Mr. W. HADDON, North Petherton.

"I have enclosed a Postcard of your Autocrat Pea. I have had a good many admirers, who said the Peas looked lovely. I had four kinds altogether, and each has given me a splendid crop."—Mr. W. FLOYDD, Cheriton.

"The Telephone Peas I had from you were splendid."—Mr. G. ANDERSON, Long Sutton.

PEAS.

Section IV.—Late Varieties.

☛ DANIELS' DISTINCTION.

A very fine late variety which comes in about the same time as "Ne Plus Ultra," and which it rivals in its culinary qualities. The plants are of strong robust growth, attaining a height of about 3½ feet, and producing an abundance of handsome dark green, slightly-curved pods, five to six inches in length, filled with large peas of the finest and most delicate flavour. We can highly recommend this as one of the very best for exhibition ; for a late crop it is unrivalled. **Per pint 1s. 9d. ; per quart 3s.**

GLORY OF DEVON. Award of Merit, Royal Horticultural Society. A fine addition to our late varieties of Peas. It is of hardy constitution and a robust grower, the foliage being of a rich dark green. The haulm, which grows about four feet in height, is well laden with fine handsome pods, each containing eight to ten large peas of delicious flavour. For exhibition it is first-class. **Per pint 1s. 9d.; per quart 3s.**

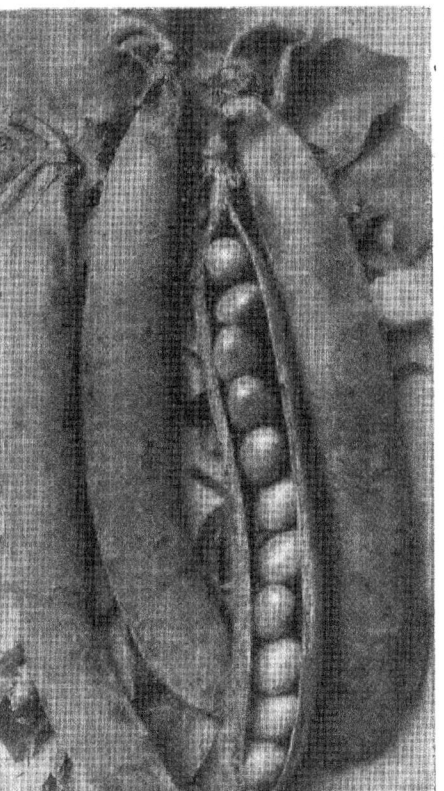

DANIELS' DISTINCTION. *Reduced from a Photograph.*

| | per quart. |
	s. d.
AUTOCRAT. First Class Certificate, Royal Horticultural Society. Is of exceedingly robust habit, much branched, foliage of a dark lustrous green. Owing to its strong constitution it is perfectly free from mildew, and is the best late Pea in cultivation. Height 4 ft. .. .. .. per pint 1s. 3d.	2 3
NE PLUS ULTRA. Extra select stock. Height 6 ft. per pint 1s. 3d.	2 0
NE PLUS ULTRA. Delicious Marrow Pea, very prolific, quality first-class, fine for general crop. Height 6 ft. per pint 10d.	1 6
QUEEN. Crop Failed.	
THE BELL. A grand late variety, with strong haulm, dark green foliage, long straight pods produced in pairs, containing ten to twelve peas of large size and exquisite flavour ; a heavy cropper, and one of the best for exhibition purposes. Award of Merit, Royal Horticultural Society. Height 3½ ft. per pint 1s. 3d.	2 3
VEITCH'S PERFECTION MARROW. Extra select stock One of the best-flavoured of our Marrow Peas. Height 3 ft. per pint 1s.	1 9

DANIELS' SPECIAL COLLECTIONS OF CHOICE PEAS FOR SUCCESSION.

We highly recommend these Collections to the notice of the Amateur. By successional sowings, in accordance with instructions, an excellent supply of fresh green Peas may be secured throughout the season.

| | per quart. |
	s. d.
DANIELS' BEST OF ALL. Fit to gather in about 12 weeks from time of sowing .. .. per pint 1s. 6d.	2 6
DANIELS' MATCHLESS MARROW. Fit to gather in about 13 weeks from time of sowing .. .. per pint 1s. 9d.	3 0
DANIELS' RECORDER. Fit to gather in about 15 to 16 weeks from time of sowing .. .. .. per pint 1s. 9d.	3 0
DANIELS' DISTINCTION. Fit to gather in about 17 weeks from time of sowing .. .. .. per pint 1s. 9d.	3 0

One pint each of the above, 6s.
One quart each of the above, 10s. 6d.

OTHER COLLECTIONS OF PEAS.

	s. d.
12 quarts for succession, our selection	21 0
6 ,, ,, ,, ..	12 0
4 ,, ,, ,, ..	8 6
12 pints for succession, our selection	11 0
6 ,, ,, ,, ..	6 6
4 ,, ,, ,, ..	5 0

SPECIAL COTTAGER'S COLLECTION.

4 varieties. One pint each for succession, our selection, 4s.
f 4 varieties. Half-pint each for succession, our selection, 2s. 3d.

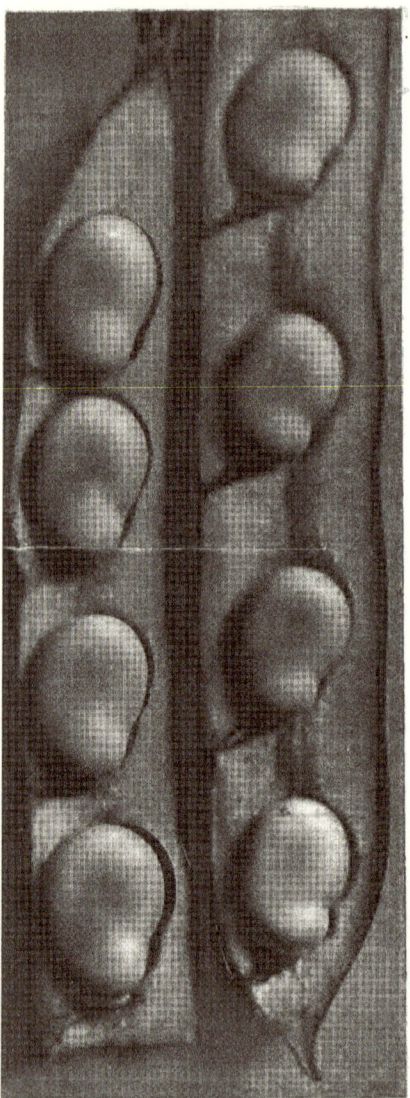

DANIELS' NORFOLK GIANT LONG-POD. *From a Photograph.*

BEANS—Broad.

Cultivation.—This highly nutritious vegetable grows well in any good garden soil, but responds readily to liberal treatment and should, therefore, when possible, be grown in well-prepared ground which has received a good supply of manure. The cultivation is of the easiest and everybody should be able to grow them successfully.

The earliest sowing should be made in February with our "**Selected Long Pod**," this being one of the earliest and best sorts. For the main crop, sow in March and for a succession in April.

The seed should be sown in double rows 6 inches apart, with an intervening space of 3 feet between the pairs of rows; place the seed 6 inches apart in the rows, earth up the plants by drawing the soil around them, when they are about 6 inches high, give a good covering of ashes to keep off the slugs.

When the plants have made a good growth and set a nice quantity of bloom, the centres should be nipped out, thereby throwing more vigour into the pods.

A liberal supply of liquid manure given at intervals during the bearing season will add much to the size of the pods, as also will a mulching of decayed manure, if put on before the hot weather comes.

The Windsor varieties whilst not giving such long pods are of excellent flavour; the best varieties for exhibition purposes are **Daniels' Norfolk Giant Long-pod**, which produces the finest pods of any of the long-podded sections, and **Daniels' Mammoth Windsor**, which is by far the best of its class.

WHITE-SEEDED VARIETIES.

per quart—s. d.

☞ **DANIELS' NORFOLK GIANT LONG-POD.** The longest-podded Bean known, has been grown up to 18 inches in length. The pods are of very handsome shape and excellent quality. First-class for exhibition, having obtained numerous First Prizes per pint 1s. 3d.   2 0

☞ **DANIELS' MAMMOTH WINDSOR.** The largest Broad Bean in cultivation. Very prolific, bearing a large quantity of fine broad pods, containing beans of exceptional size. These are of fine quality, and of flavour equal to the old Broad Windsor per pint 1s. 3d.   2 0

DANIELS' SELECTED LONG-POD. A grand selection of the Early Long-pod. Very prolific; pods larger and finer than the old variety; useful for exhibition .. .. per pint 10d. 1 6

BROAD WINDSOR. Fine selected stock .. per pint 7d. 1 0

HARLINGTON WINDSOR. Larger and finer pods than the old Windsor; very prolific .. .. .. per pint 10d. 1 6

JOHNSON'S WONDERFUL (Mackie's Monarch) per pint 7d. 1 0

MAZAGAN. Small, early, and hardy .. .. per pint 5d. 0 9

GREEN-SEEDED VARIETIES.

per quart—s. d.

☞ **DANIELS' IMPROVED GREEN WINDSOR.** An abundant bearer, pods large; a great improvement on the old variety per pint 1s. 0d. 1 9

☞ **DANIELS' MAMMOTH GREEN LONG-POD.** A very fine selection of this type, the pods being longer and much better filled than those of the old variety, and of excellent flavour per pint 1s. 0d. 1 9

BECK'S GREEN GEM. Excellent for small gardens per pint 10d. 1 6

EVIDENCE OF QUALITY.

"The Norfolk Giant Long-Pod Beans took First Prize at the Newmarket Show."—Mr. M. PEARSON, Newmarket.

"I was awarded First and Special Prizes for your Norfolk Giant Long-Pod Bean at our Show last year."—Mr. F. WHITCOCK, Ilkley.

"You will be pleased to know that I had such good Norfolk Giant Long-pod Beans last year that I was persuaded to show them and obtained First Prize."—Mr. W. HUMPHREY, Earlswood.

"Although my garden is small I appreciate quality, and I have always found your Seeds most excellent."—Mr. F. LIVINGSTONE, Northampton.

"I might say that I was highly pleased with the results obtained from your Seeds last year."—Mr. D. TAYLOR, Gillingham.

"I am pleased to tell you that I took several First Prizes last year with the produce from your Seeds."—Mr. W. BYFORD, Harlow.

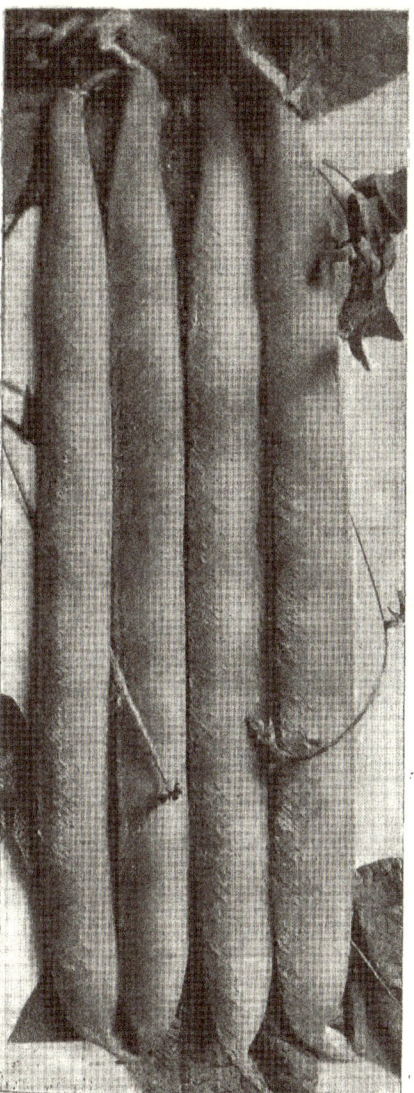

DANIELS' GIANT SCARLET. *Reduced from a Photograph.*

BEANS—Runner.

Cultivation.—Runner Beans form one of the most important and profitable of all garden crops grown for Summer and Autumn use, and yield a liberal supply of vegetables available for use after the main crop Peas are over.

They are easy of culture and may be grown as screens in small gardens, thus serving the double purpose of covering a trellis or wall and at the same time yielding a crop of delicious vegetables.

The ground should be prepared in the same manner as for other Beans, but Runners being somewhat tender the seed should not be sown until early in May.

Sow the seed in double rows 9 inches apart and, if possible, allow a space of 12 feet between each double row, cropping the intervening space with other vegetables.

For a succession make further sowings in June and July.

When the plants are about 9 inches high, draw the earth round them, and place tall, strong stakes to the rows, taking care to make them very firm and able to withstand the wind. A good mulching of rotted manure during the cropping season will lengthen the period of bearing and give quality to the beans.

Where it is impossible to procure tall stakes, it is the practice to take out the leading growths when the plants are about a foot high, thus encouraging a spreading habit and in this way good crops may be grown and space economised.

The best varieties both for exhibition and general purposes are **Daniels' Giant White** and **Daniels' Giant Scarlet.**

☞ IMPORTANT NOTICE.

Owing to the severe drought of the past summer the crop of Runner Beans was practically destroyed; only in a few instances have any been saved. The stocks are therefore the shortest on record. We have secured a limited supply of our special varieties which we offer below, and should strongly advise early orders.

per pint. s. d.

☞ **DANIELS' GIANT SCARLET.** A grand variety both for exhibition and the table, and is at the same time one of the most prolific varieties with which we are acquainted. The pods are long, straight, and of excellent quality. Our own selected stock

per pkt. 1s. 0d. ½ pint 1s. 9d.   3 0

☞ **DANIELS' GIANT WHITE.** This is without doubt the finest type of Runner Bean extant, bearing in profusion long, green, thick, fleshy pods, upwards of twelve inches in length, and nearly two inches in breadth. This variety, besides the best for culinary purposes, will also be found a grand exhibition kind

per pkt. 9d.   ½ pint 1s. 3d.   2 0

☞ **SCARLET EMPEROR.** A giant amongst Scarlet Runner Beans, producing fine straight pods fifteen inches in length, and is enormously productive. A grand sort for exhibition ..   .. per pkt. 1s. 0d. ½ pint 1s. 9d.   3 0

☞ **WHITE EMPEROR** (new). A fine white seeded variety bearing a heavy crop of long straight pods quite equal to the Scarlet Emperor. It will make a most valuable variety for Exhibition, at the same time it is enormously prolific.   per pkt. 9d.   ½ pint 1s. 6d.   2 6

BEST OF ALL. One of the longest-podded of the Scarlet Runners, very prolific. The pods, which are long, straight, and very handsome, are produced in large clusters. It is of excellent table quality, and one of the best for exhibition

per pkt. 9d.   ½ pint 1s. 6d.   2 6

NE PLUS ULTRA. A fine variety for exhibition and main crop, producing a large quantity of fine pods of splendid form, from ten to fourteen inches long, and quite straight. To grow it to perfection each bean should be planted one foot apart in the row ..   ..   .. per pkt. 9d. ½ pint 1s. 6d.   2 6

OLD SCARLET RUNNER. For general crop 0 10

PAINTED LADY. Crop failed.

VEITCH'S CLIMBING KIDNEY BEAN. First Class Certificate, Royal Horticultural Society. This Bean combines the best features of the two types, Dwarf French and Scarlet Runner. It crops earlier than the Runners and has all the delicate flavour and quality of the Dwarfs; height six to seven feet

½ pint 1s. 0d.   1 9

BEANS—Dwarf French.

Cultivation.—This useful vegetable may be grown by almost any one, as sufficient space for a row may be found in even the smallest garden. With attention to the preparation and manuring of the ground, there should be no difficulty in having a continuous supply of French Beans for a considerable portion of the Summer and Autumn.

The culture is of the simplest; the ground having been thoroughly dug and manured in early Spring, the Beans should be planted about the end of April; the rows should be 2½ feet apart and the Beans placed about 4 inches apart in the row, any gaps in the row may be filled up by transplanting the seedlings when just past the seed leaf.

The soil should be drawn round the plants to protect them from cold winds in Spring, and during the time of bearing occasional waterings with weak liquid manure will add much to the size of the produce and lengthen the period of bearing. Daniels' "Incomparable" can be highly recommended on account of its great prolificness and excellent quality.

Where greenhouses are available the earliest sowing may be made at the beginning of April and the young plants transferred to the outside border when large enough to handle. A crop may also be grown in the early months of the year in heated frames or greenhouses, the seed being sown in 8-inch pots half filled with good rich soil, and the pots gradually filled up with soil as the plants grow. It is most important that French Beans should be gathered as soon as ready, otherwise the plants will gradually give up blooming and the crop be much reduced.

DANIELS' INCOMPARABLE. *From a Photograph.*

per quart.

☞ **DANIELS' INCOMPARABLE** (new). This splendid dwarf Kidney Bean since its introduction has fully justified our high opinion of it, both as regards quality and prolificness. The pods are of great length, straight, and of a rich clear green colour, very tender, and of the best culinary quality. It is of strong constitution, sturdy habit, and wonderfully prolific. It is quite distinct in the seed and has proved a decided acquisition .. per pint 1s. 6d. 2 6

☞ **DANIELS' EARLY BLACK WONDER.** We can highly recommend this splendid variety as one of the hardiest and most prolific French Beans in cultivation. The pods are long, of a light rich green colour, tender, and of fine flavour .. per pint 1s. 1 9

DANIELS' WHITE QUEEN. Crop Failed.

CANADIAN WONDER. Abundant bearer, very fleshy and tender. The pods are long and of excellent shape and quality; one of the best for general crop 1 0

EARLY GOLDEN BUTTER. Pods thick and fleshy, nearly transparent, and of a bright yellow colour, which is retained when boiled; excellent flavour per pint 1s. 6d. 2 6

MAGNUM BONUM. A fine variety of recent introduction. The pods are long, straight, and of excellent quality, exceeding in size and productiveness the well-known Canadian Wonder; fine exhibition variety .. per pint 1s. 6d. 2 6

NEGRO LONG-FOD. Useful variety, heavy cropper 1 0

NE PLUS ULTRA. The finest Kidney Bean in cultivation for all purposes. First Class Certificate, R.H.S. 1 4

NEWINGTON WONDER (or NONSUCH). Early .. 1 4

PALE DUN OR BUFF. Very early; one of the most useful 1 2

ALL KINDS MIXED 1 0

"I should like to mention that the Seeds you sent me last year were the best I have ever grown, especially the Beans and Peas."—Mr. A. J. CLARKE, Leyton.

"The Seeds I had from you produced some splendid crops, especially the Beans and Peas. I obtained First Prize with your Incomparable Dwarf Bean."—Mr. G. E. HAYNES, Brewood.

"I had a splendid yield last year from your Beans and Peas."—Mr. A. HANNIBAL, Wouldstone.

"I have grown your Seeds for a good many years, and can truthfully say I can find none to equal them."—Mr. J. T. BRUMBY, Junr., Lincoln.

"I enclose a photo of my exhibits which I should like you to accept. I was fairly successful at the show, gaining nine Prizes. I think my success is due to the good quality of your Seeds."—Mr. T. BROOMFIELD, Totton.

"Out of twenty-three exhibits I gained twenty Prizes with Vegetables grown from your Seeds. I obtained First Prize for your Collection of four Vegetables."—Mr. W. BAKER, Stevenage.

BEET.

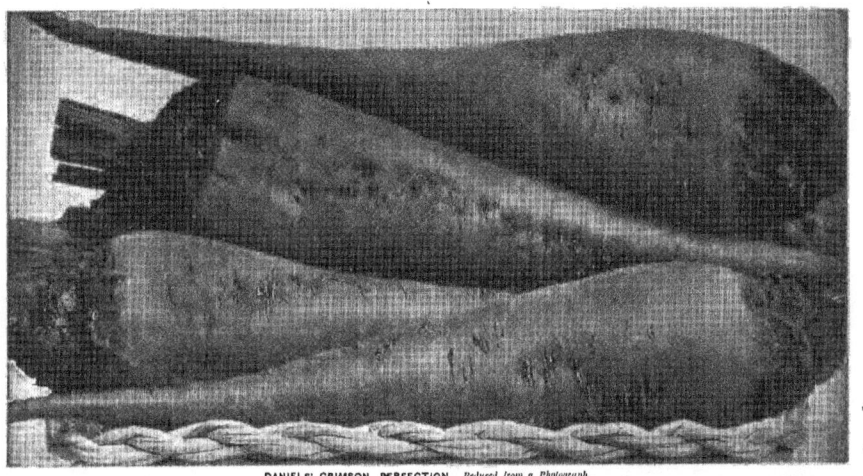

DANIELS' CRIMSON PERFECTION. *Reduced from a Photograph.*

Cultivation.—To ensure a crop of good Beetroot, it is of the highest importance that the seed should be of the very best strain procurable such as offered by ourselves. Another very important point to observe is that the ground must not be specially manured for this crop, a good plan being to select a plot that has been cropped during the previous season with French Beans, Potatoes, or Celery. The soil should be a good light loam where possible, and in an open part of the garden; the ground should be deeply trenched (the deeper the better) quite early in the season. Before sowing, the ground should be made firm and level.

Sow the seed any time from the middle of April to the end of May. For an early crop **New Red Globe** is one of the best. **Daniels' Crimson Perfection** and **Green Top** will be found the most useful for a general crop. The seed should be sown in drills one inch deep and about 18 inches from row to row. A liberal quantity of seed should be used to ensure a good plant, and when the seedlings are nicely up, they should be thinned out, leaving them about 9 inches apart. As a rule those sown at the end of May produce roots of better quality. Keep the beds regularly hoed and weeded so that the soil may be free about the plants.

When specimen roots are wanted for Exhibition, it is the usual practice to make holes about 2 feet deep in the bed with a crowbar, and fill them with fine soil. The seeds are sown in these and thinned out, one plant being left to each hole. In this way splendidly shaped roots are grown. The crop should be lifted in October and stored in dry sand in a shed or cellar for Winter use. Care should be taken that the roots are not injured in any way, or they will bleed and lose quality; also the leaves should not be cut but twisted off with the hand. In this way the roots may be kept until the following Summer.

	per oz.—s. d.
DANIELS' CRIMSON PERFECTION SALAD. A grand dark-leaved variety of medium size and very symmetrical. The flesh, which is of the finest texture, is deep crimson in colour and of excellent quality. A first-class sort for exhibition. Owing to the fine deep colour of its foliage it is very valuable for ornamental purposes .. .. per pkt. 6d.	1 6
DANIELS' BLACK QUEEN. Fine dark-leaved variety, roots medium in size, and of good shape and colour .. per pkt. 3d.	0 9
CHELTENHAM GREEN-TOP. Roots very dark, of excellent quality; one of the best for pickling .. .. per pkt. 3d.	0 9
DARK RED SALAD. A very useful variety, roots of a good deep colour	0 6
DRACÆNA-LEAVED. A highly ornamental variety for the Flower Garden. The leaves are fine, long, and of a deep rich crimson. The root is of fine quality and excellent colour per pkt. 4d.	1 0

	per oz.—s. d.
DANIELS' GREEN-TOP. This splendid Green-top Beet is chiefly remarkable for the fine deep colour of the roots, which are of excellent shape and of first-class quality and flavour .. .. per pkt. 4d.	1 0
DELL'S BLACK. A fine dark-foliaged variety, roots small, but of exceptionally fine shape and colour .. per pkt. 3d.	0 9
EGYPTIAN DARK RED TURNIP-ROOTED. One of the best for Summer Salads, as it comes to maturity very early ..	0 6
NEW RED GLOBE. A valuable variety, much superior to the Egyptian Turnip-rooted. The roots are of fine globular shape, of rich colour and excellent flavour; a fine variety for exhibition .. .. .. per pkt. 4d.	1 0
NUTTING'S DWARF RED. Fine dark foliage .. ,, 3d.	0 10
PRAGNELL'S EXHIBITION. A fine dark-leaved variety, roots very handsome and of good colour .. per pkt. 4d.	1 0
SILVER SEA KALE. The leaves make an excellent substitute for Spinach	0 6

"I am very pleased with the produce from the Seeds supplied by your Firm. Many thanks for your attention to my orders."—**Mr. A. B. ADRIMAR**, Colkirk.

"I should like to mention that the Seeds I had from you were very satisfactory and I hope to be a regular customer."—**Mr. H. WILSON**, East Galdeford.

"Everything I had from you last year did well."—**Mr. J. JACKSON**, Millom.

"I am pleased to inform you that your Seeds turned out very satisfactory last year."—**Mr. G. DIX**, Deane.

"I am pleased to say that I had a grand lot of Vegetables from your Seeds last year, and secured several Prizes."—**Mr. W. MOLLINGDALE**, Foynings.

"Seeds to hand this morning. I am delighted with them. Those I had from you last year yielded some splendid crops."—**Mr. G. HOPKINS**, Eastnor.

BROCCOLI.

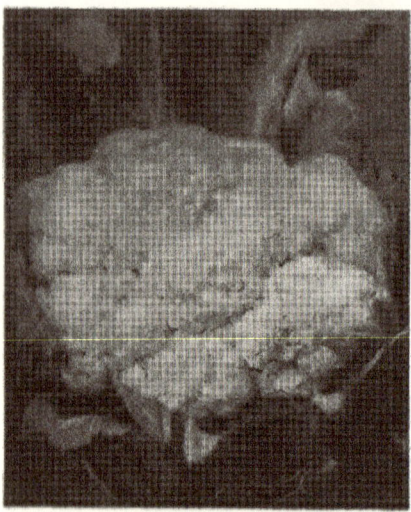

MICHAELMAS WHITE.

SECOND DIVISION.

Sow in April, May, and June, for cutting in January and February the following Spring.

	per pkt. s. d.	per oz. s. d.
DANIELS' NEW YEAR. A vigorous, compact, dwarf-growing variety, with self-protecting foliage over-lapping snow-white heads, of excellent quality and flavour; a most valuable variety	0 9	2 0
DANIELS' QUEEN OF SPRING. This splendid variety comes in for cutting during February, is of dwarf compact habit, producing large snow-white heads of the finest texture. Its earliness, combined with its excellent quality, makes it a valuable addition to our Spring Broccoli	0 9	2 0
ADAMS' EARLY WHITE. A strong growing variety of hardy constitution. Heads large pure white	0 3	0 9
DANIELS' SELECTED SNOW'S WHITE. A fine selected stock of this well-known Winter Broccoli. The heads are large, firm and beautifully white, one of the most useful of the Winter varieties	0 6	1 6
MAMMOTH WINTER WHITE. Large pure white heads of the finest quality, coming into use in mid-winter, well-protected with long over-lapping leaves	0 6	1 6
ST. HILARY. A splendid Broccoli of hardy, vigorous constitution. Dwarf, compact growth, and large white heads, coming into use in January	0 6	1 6

EVIDENCE OF QUALITY.

" I might say that at our Show last year I obtained eleven First and one Second Prizes out of fifteen exhibits."—Mr. A. BULLARD, Rochford.

FIRST DIVISION.

Sow in April and May for cutting in September, October, and November the same year.

	per pkt. s. d.	per oz. s. d.
MICHAELMAS WHITE. A grand variety for early use. It is of quick growth, forming large firm heads of fine texture and excellent quality ; if sown in March it will be fit to cut at Michaelmas	0 9	2 0
PENZANCE EARLY WHITE. Produces fine large heads of excellent quality. This variety is extensively grown in Cornwall	0 4	1 0
VEITCH'S SELF-PROTECTING AUTUMN. Extremely valuable to grow as a succession to " Autumn Giant " Cauliflower. The heads are well protected by the strong vigorous foliage, and it may be had in good condition till nearly Christmas	0 6	1 6
WALCHEREN. A useful variety for early Autumn use. Heads of good size and of fine even texture	0 4	1 0
WHITE CAPE. A valuable variety for Autumn, coming into use in August and September	0 4	1 0
WHITE SPROUTING. Produces a large crop of tender Sprouts of the most excellent flavour	0 6	1 0

EVIDENCE OF QUALITY.

" I have had some splendid heads from your King of the Broccoli Seed this year."—Mr. S. BROWN, Luton.

" I had a packet of your King of the Broccoli Seed last year and I have been cutting over a hundred very fine heads this month."—Mr. C. HAMMOND, Wood Green.

" I had some splendid results from your King of the Broccoli Seed. Some of the heads were fifty inches in circumference."—Mr. S. RAYNER, Cley.

" I must say that the Seeds I purchased from you last year were very satisfactory."—Mr. A. NICHOLLS, Woodstock.

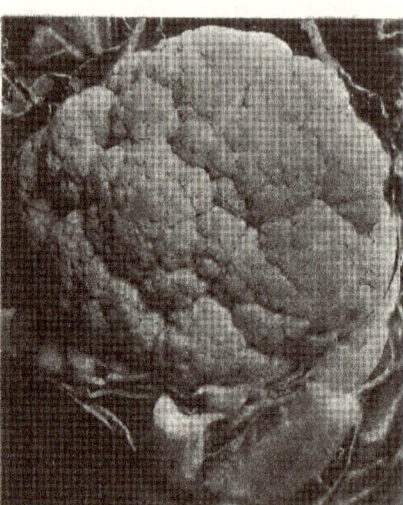

DANIELS' QUEEN OF SPRING.

BROCCOLI.

THIRD DIVISION.

Sow end of March and beginning of April for cutting in March and April the following season.

	per pkt. s. d.	per doz s. d.
DANIELS' NORFOLK GIANT. A magnificent variety of robust and compact habit, stem short, the flower heads are exceedingly large, beautifully white, and of the finest quality, being well protected by luxuriant, over-lapping foliage. The best and hardiest variety for general Spring use	0 9	2 0
EASTER DAY or SPRINGTIDE. A fine hardy variety of dwarf compact habit and vigorous growth, producing large, firm, white heads of excellent quality, which are well protected. One of the best kinds for maincrop in Spring	0 6	1 6
KNIGHTS' PROTECTING. One of the hardiest of our Spring Broccoli. The heads are well protected, large, and of fine quality	0 4	1 0
LEAMINGTON. Well-known hardy variety. Heads large and solid	0 4	1 0
PURPLE SPROUTING. Very hardy Winter variety, producing an abundant crop of Sprouts of excellent flavour	0 3	0 9

FOURTH DIVISION.

Sow in May and June for cutting in May and June the following season.

	per pkt. s. d.	per oz. s. d.
DANIELS' KING OF THE BROCCOLI. This splendid variety comes in for cutting from the beginning of May to the first week in June, and as a late kind cannot be surpassed. It is of a fine dwarf habit, and being well protected is exceedingly hardy. The heads are remarkably fine	0 6	1 6

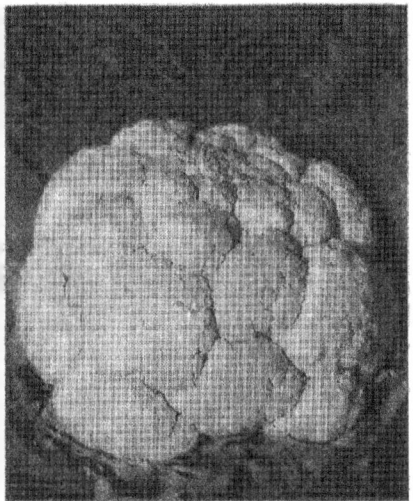

DANIELS' NORFOLK GIANT.

Fourth Division *(continued).*

	per pkt. s. d.	per oz. s. d.
DANIELS' LATEST WHITE. One of the best kinds for filling up the gap or period that occurs between Broccoli and Cauliflower	0 4	1 0
METHVEN'S JUNE. One of the latest Broccoli in cultivation, producing fine pure white heads till nearly the end of June	0 6	1 6
QUEEN. Very fine, heads well protected	0 4	1 0

Cultivation.—This excellent vegetable is of the greatest value during the Winter and early Spring, when Cauliflowers are not obtainable and vegetables generally are scarce. They like a good rich firm soil, which has during the previous Autumn been thoroughly trenched and liberally manured. If possible, choose a piece of land on which Celery has been grown.

The earliest sowing of seed should be made at the latter end of March, and the principal sowings during April, whilst May will be soon enough for the late varieties. Sow the seed either in a warm sheltered border or in a frame, in drills eight or nine inches apart and one inch deep. When the plants are large enough to handle, lose no time in pricking them out, as they quickly suffer if allowed to remain too long in the seed bed, becoming drawn and weak. The final plantings should be commenced in May, and followed on as opportunity occurs until the end of July, and as land becomes available. Choose the strongest plants first, as by this means a much better succession will be obtained.

The most important point in planting out Broccoli is to be quite sure that the ground is very firm; the harder it is the better it will be for the plants, as they will thereby be able to withstand the Winter, therefore if the land was trenched and manured during the past Winter, do not have it dug again just previous to planting out. Make the rows about 2½ feet apart and place the plants about two feet apart in the rows. Water the plants thoroughly after planting and keep the weeds down.

In severe Winters it is generally the practice to heel over the plants with their heads to the north, as soon as they are turning in, making the soil quite firm round the stem quite up to the neck, thus leaving only the head above the ground. In addition, a sprinkling of hay or bracken over each head will prevent any harm coming to them, and a very high percentage will be found to withstand the severest weather.

In the first division **Michaelmas White** and **Self-protecting Autumn** will be found most useful, followed by **Daniels' Queen of Spring** and **New Year.** For late crops **Daniels' Norfolk Giant** and **Daniels' King** are invaluable.

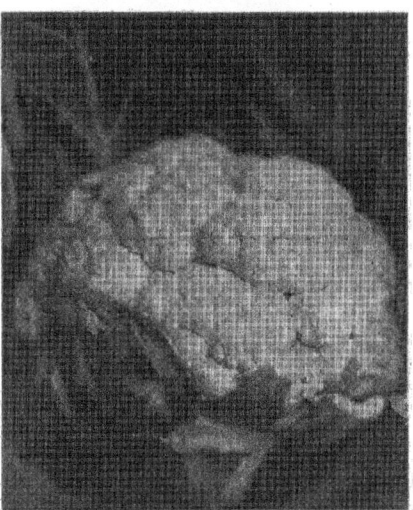

DANIELS' KING OF THE BROCCOLI.

BRUSSELS SPROUTS.

Cultivation.—To grow Brussels Sprouts successfully the seed should be sown at the latter end of February or early in March on a sheltered border or in a frame. Prick out the seedlings about four inches apart into seed beds as soon as they have made the first leaves, and directly the weather allows plant out permanently into well prepared ground, such as is used for general garden crops. For a later crop, a sowing should be made at the end of March, or early in April, and the seedlings planted as soon as possible; they cannot very well be planted out too early. Brussels Sprouts require plenty of room to develop, and therefore they should never be planted thickly. About 2½ feet apart in the row and 3 feet between the rows would be a suitable distance. Give a good supply of water when they are first planted, and keep the ground loose by frequent use of the hoe.

Brussels Sprouts thrive much better by themselves than when planted amongst other crops. In dry weather liberal supplies of liquid manure will be found of great advantage. Daniels' Colossal and Defiance are first-class stocks, and will be found the best for exhibition purposes and for general use.

DANIELS' COLOSSAL. *Reduced from a Photograph.*

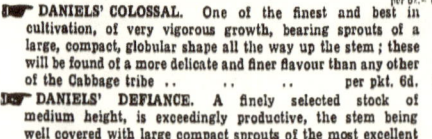

	per oz.—s. d.
DANIELS' COLOSSAL. One of the finest and best in cultivation, of very vigorous growth, bearing sprouts of a large, compact, globular shape all the way up the stem; these will be found of a more delicate and finer flavour than any other of the Cabbage tribe .. .. .. per pkt. 6d.	1 6
DANIELS' DEFIANCE. A finely selected stock of medium height, is exceedingly productive, the stem being well covered with large compact sprouts of the most excellent flavour. A very useful variety for exhibition purposes, and one of the best for general use .. per pkt. 6d.	1 6
AIGBURTH. A tall growing variety, of fine quality. The sprouts are of good size and very firm	0 8
DALKEITH. A fine selected stock of medium height, the stems being well covered with solid sprouts of fine flavour .. per pkt. 3d.	0 9
SCRYMGER'S GIANT. An excellent tall variety; stems well covered with fine sprouts, of first-class flavour .. per pkt. 3d.	0 9
IMPORTED. Good variety for general use	0 6

"I am pleased to tell you that I was very successful with your Seeds, taking many First and Second Prizes."—Mr. C. PAYNE, Wheathampstead.

"I have a few words of praise for your Seeds, having taken five First and two Second Prizes, out of nine exhibits."—Mr. A. LYON, Coventry.

"I beg to inform you that I have grown your Colossal Brussels Sprouts over four feet in height, and have been plucking for over a week (September 4th)."—Mr. F. EATES, Bexley Heath.

"I can find no Seeds to equal yours for exhibition purposes."—Mr. W. MUTIMER, Barley Green.

BORECOLE or KALE.

Cultivation.—Borecole is of great value for providing a supply of tender green heads from Christmas onwards, during the very severe weather when Cabbages and Broccoli are not available. Many varieties of Borecole are also quite ornamental and present most attractive objects in the kitchen garden. Sow the seed in April in seed beds, and when the plants are large enough transplant them into their permanent quarters about three feet apart. As an alternative they may be planted between Potato rows.

Borecole likes good soil, but does not require liberal treatment with liquid manure, etc., as many plants of the same family do. Give a thorough watering at the time of planting out. If there is any tendency to "clubbing" noticed in the garden, a dressing of lime applied in the Spring previous to planting will be found of great advantage. Daniels' Improved Drumhead can be highly recommended on account of its excellent flavour. It is much milder than some varieties. Daniels' Moss Curled Exhibition will be found invaluable for general purposes.

	per oz.—s. d.
DANIELS' MOSS CURLED EXHIBITION. The finest strain of curled Kale in cultivation. It is of medium height, foliage dark green, and beautifully curled, is very hardy, and may be relied upon to stand the severest Winters. For exhibition it is unsurpassed .. .. per pkt. 6d.	1 6
DANIELS' IMPROVED DRUMHEAD. A valuable variety for Winter use. Hearts up like a Drumhead Cabbage with broad leaves; very mild and tender when cooked, and of the true Kale flavour .. per pkt. 4d.	1 0
COTTAGER'S. Exceedingly hardy .. .. .. 3d.	0 8
DWARF GREEN CURLED. Very hardy, dwarf-stemmed, flavour very mild, colour dark green when cooked, the best for general crop ..	0 4
TALL GREEN CURLED. The Tall Scotch Kale	0 6
VARIEGATED or GARNISHING. A fine curled-leaved variety, beautifully variegated, very useful and ornamental for garnishing, also valuable for Winter gardening .. .. per pkt. 4d.	1 0
ASPARAGUS KALE. Fine for winter use	0 8

CELERY.

Cultivation.—This very important vegetable is one that fully repays a liberal outlay both of labour and manure. Being a moisture loving plant and a gross feeder, it should, if possible, be raised in soil where, during the growing period, copious supplies of water can be applied. For the earliest crop sow the seed about the middle of February, giving some heat, and when the plants have made their seed leaves, have them pricked off into boxes or frames, giving if possible a gentle bottom heat to keep them growing. Make a further sowing in March in a similar way, and, if necessary, another in April in an open border; these later sowings will give some useful Celery for cooking. It is an excellent plan to get the Celery trenches ready quite early in the season, so that advantage may be taken of the first favourable showery day to put out the plants when large enough.

In making the trenches throw out the soil 12 or 14 inches deep and 18 inches wide, and be careful to retain the top soil so that it may be placed in the bottom of the trench; mix with it a good dressing of farmyard manure and in this mixture the young plants should be placed; the rest of the soil taken out of the trench should be piled up on the sides and used, when the time comes, for earthing up the Celery; allow a space of three or four feet between the trenches.

In planting out the Celery in the trenches, place the seedlings about nine inches apart, in a single row for the earliest crop; for the main crop they are often planted in double rows. In dry weather give liberal supplies of water or liquid manure to keep the plants growing, as if they get a check they are liable to bolt.

It is a good plan to give a sprinkling of soot over the foliage, while damp with the early morning dew, in order to keep away the Celery fly and snails.

The greatest care should be taken in earthing up Celery. As soon as the plants are about nine inches high, go over them and thoroughly clean off all side shoots, and tie the growth loosely with Raffia. Choose a fine day, and gradually work down some of the finest soil round the bases of the plants, being most careful not to allow any of the soil to get between the leaves; do not make the soil too hard, or it will stop the growth. Continue to earth up as the plants grow. The final earthing should form a ridge as a protection. In very severe weather it will be found an advantage to give a slight covering of straw or bracken over the top of the row.

WHITE VARIETIES.

per pkt.—s. d.

DANIELS' EARLIEST WHITE. This fine white Celery has now firmly established its reputation as one of the very best for early work, and has become highly popular. Sown at the same time, it is ready for use quite six weeks earlier than any other variety. The heads which grow to a large size, are very firm and solid, and of a sweet nutty flavour   1 0

DANIELS' GIANT WHITE. This grand Celery is undoubtedly one of the largest and best white varieties in cultivation. The heads are very solid and of excellent flavour. Very fine for exhibition 1 0

SANDRINGHAM DWARF WHITE. Useful early variety   .. 3d. and 0 6
SEYMOUR'S SUPERB WHITE. Heads very solid, fine flavour 2d. and 0 6
SILVER PLUME. A fine, white-leaved variety. It blanches well by simply tying up the plants with matting   ..   ..   6d. and 1 0

RED VARIETIES.

per pkt.—s. d.

DANIELS' EARLIEST PINK (new). This grand new Celery is a useful companion to our Earliest White, and like that variety comes into use quite six weeks earlier than the old varieties. It grows to a large size, the heads being very solid and of excellent flavour. A most valuable variety for early shows 1 0

DANIELS' GIANT RED. The largest red variety grown. The heads are of splendid colour, very solid, and of fine nutty flavour, one of the very best for exhibition purposes. The seed offered is saved from carefully selected heads only   .. 1 0

DANIELS' EXHIBITION PINK. A very fine Celery, producing large solid heads of a delicate rosy pink colour. A fine variety for exhibition, and of excellent flavour 6d. and 1 0

CLAYWORTH PRIZE PINK. Heads very large, solid, and of a beautiful rosy pink colour. A most useful variety for general crop 6d. and 1 0
MANCHESTER FINE RED. Large, solid heads   ..   .. 3d. and 0 6
STANDARD BEARER. Heads firm, solid, and of an attractive nutty flavour; fine exhibition variety   ..   ..   .. 6d. and 1 0
MIXED RED AND WHITE. Useful for Cottagers   .. 3d. and 0 6
CELERIAC, or TURNIP-ROOTED CELERY. Very useful for flavouring soups, &c. 0 6

"I am pleased to say that I took First Prize with Celery in a very strong class."—Mr. J. J. SAUL, Garstang.

"The Seeds supplied by you have given grand results up to the present."—Mr. S. BARKER, Chiddingly.

DANIELS' GIANT WHITE. *Reduced from a Photograph.*

☞ DANIELS' DEFIANCE. ☜
THE FINEST CABBAGE IN THE WORLD.

We highly recommend this magnificent Cabbage, which we claim to be the finest in the world.   It is medium early, short-legged, and compact, and grows to a great size, at the same time retaining all the tenderness and delicacy of flavour of the smaller varieties.   First-class for the private grower or market gardener.   The seed we offer, which is our own true and original stock, has been carefully grown at our Seed Grounds from the stalks of fully developed and first-class Cabbages only, and owing to the many years of careful selection will be found of an unequalled and thoroughly reliable quality.   Per packet 6d. ; per oz. 1s. 6d.

DANIELS' DEFIANCE.   *Retured from a Photograph.*

EVIDENCE OF QUALITY.

" I have had much pleasure in recommending your Firm to my military friends. Your seeds have given me the greatest satisfaction especially your **Defiance Cabbage.** Mine were the best about here."— **Sergeant J. BAXTER,** Aldershot.

" I took a First Prize last year with your **Defiance Cabbage.**"—**Mr. J. CLARKE,** Rotherham.

" I am pleased to inform you that the **Defiance Cabbage** has been splendid.   In fact all the seeds have turned out well."—**Mr. C. JUDD,** Maidstone.

" I consider your **Defiance Cabbage** excellent, easily beating all others I have tried." —**Mr. W. HANNAM,** Stourton.

CABBAGES.

per oz.—s. d.

DANIELS' LITTLE QUEEN. The earliest Cabbage in cultivation. It is distinct in appearance and of dwarf compact habit, with very firm heads. A most useful variety both for Spring and Autumn sowing. Our own selected stock .. .. per pkt. 6d. — 1 6

ELLAM'S EARLY DWARF. A first-class Early Cabbage in all respects. Being very compact, they can be planted close together, thus growing double the quantity of plants on the same space than most kinds. A fine early market kind, and one of the best for Autumn sowing .. per pkt. 3d. — 0 9

DANIELS' IMPROVED ENFIELD MARKET. A first-class stock, earlier and larger than the ordinary variety per pkt. 4d. — 1 0

EARLY DWARF YORK. Dwarf and compact.. .. .. 0 4

LARGE YORK. Very useful variety for late crop 0 6

ENFIELD MARKET. Excellent main crop variety 0 4

EWING'S No. 1. A very fine, early, dwarf Cabbage 0 6

NONPAREIL IMPROVED DWARF. Early variety, dwarf and compact; very useful for market growers 0 6

OFFENHAM. A fine early variety of dwarf and compact habit, very useful; one of the best for Autumn sowing 0 8

ROSETTE COLEWORT. Very hardy 0 8

ST. JOHN'S DAY. A fine, dwarf, very early variety of the Drumhead type, but much smaller than that variety and of fine quality 0 6

WHEELER'S IMPERIAL. A fine variety of the Nonpareil type, heads very firm and compact 0 8

DANIELS' EARLY DRUMHEAD. This variety does not grow quite so large as the ordinary field varieties, is of dwarf compact habit, with solid heads, and of mild flavour 0 4

CHRISTMAS DRUMHEAD. A fine, dwarf, compact Cabbage of excellent flavour, of a dark green colour. A splendid variety for culinary purposes .. .. .. per pkt. 3d. 0 9

WINNINGSTADT. A most useful variety, with pointed heads, which are exceedingly firm and solid 0 6

" I am very pleased with the results of your Defiance and Little Queen Cabbages."
—Mr. A. POTTER, Porth.

" I might add that the Seeds I received have given the greatest satisfaction, especially the Little Queen and Defiance Cabbages."—Mr. E. WILLIAMS, Treharris.

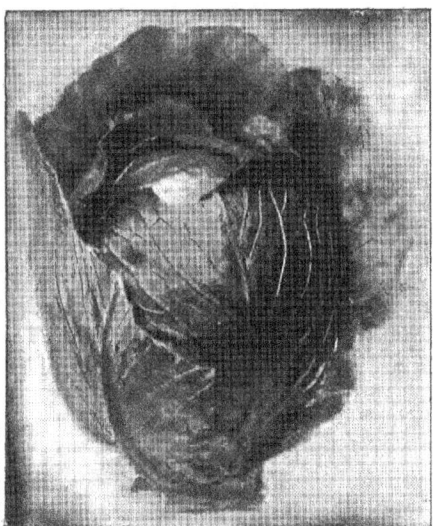

DANIELS' DWARF BLOOD RED. *Reduced from a Photograph.*

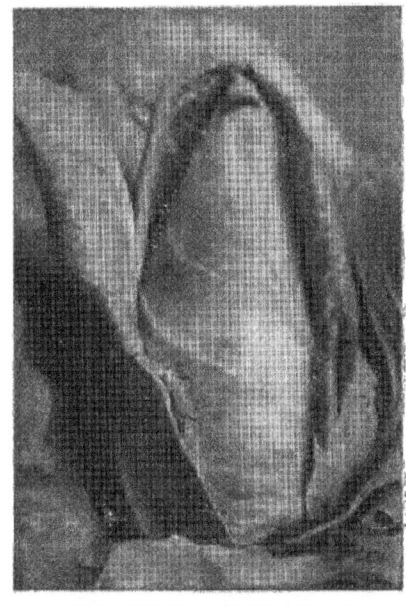

DANIELS' LITTLE QUEEN. *Reduced from a Photograph.*

RED OR PICKLING CABBAGES.

per oz.—s. d.

DANIELS' DWARF BLOOD RED. A dwarf, compact-growing variety, coming early into use; heads of a fine deep blood red colour, and very firm; can be planted much closer than the other sorts .. .. per pkt. 4d. 1 0

DANIELS' INTERMEDIATE RED. A fine type of Red Cabbage with medium sized heads, which are very firm and of a good deep colour. It is of medium height and very compact in growth; fine for exhibition .. .. per pkt. 4d. 1 0

DANIELS' GIANT RED DRUMHEAD. A fine variety, grows to a large size, very firm, and of fine deep colour, and is undoubtedly the finest Red Cabbage known .. .. per pkt. 4d. 1 0

COUVE TRONCHUDA, OR PORTUGAL CABBAGE.

Per packet 4d., per ounce 1s.

" Extensive trials of Autumn sown Spring Cabbages were made by the National Vegetable Society in 1909-10, from samples sent by nineteen leading Seed Firms. Three varieties only, including Daniels' Little Queen, were selected as excellent in every way, good hearts and even stocks, equal to the best of other varieties sown on the same date, August 11th."—From " The Garden," June 25th, 1910.

" I took two First Prizes with your Defiance Cabbage."—Mr. E. MASON, Leicester.

" I am pleased to tell you that I was successful in taking First Prize at our Show for Defiance Cabbage."—Mr. J. WILLIAMS, Lydbrook.

" I have had your Defiance Cabbage, weighing one stone this year when the outside leaves were cut off."—Mr. E. STEVENSON, Dogdyke.

" I took First Prize in the open class at Swanage Show with your Defiance Cabbage."—Mr. W. J. CROCKER, Swanage.

SAVOY CABBAGES.

SAVOY CABBAGE—DANIELS' SELECTED DRUMHEAD.

☞ **DANIELS' SELECTED DRUMHEAD.** A fine variety for general use, producing large firm heads of exceptionally good quality ; very hardy .. .. .. per oz.—s. d. 0 4

DANIELS' NONPAREIL. Splendid variety for early use, quite distinct ; the most delicately flavoured Savoy grown per pkt. 3d. 0 9

DANIELS' EXTRA EARLY. Fortnight earlier than Dwarf Ulm, very dwarf and compact .. .. per pkt. 4d. 1 0

DWARF GREEN CURLED. Very compact 0 4

DWARF ULM. Early, very dwarf .. .. .. per oz. 0 6

GOLDEN AUTUMN. A distinct and beautiful variety per pkt. 3d. 0 9

GREEN GLOBE. A good hardy variety 0 6

NORWEGIAN. Excellent variety for late use, and well suited for northern and cold climates .. .. per pkt. 4d. 1 0

ORMSKIRK. A fine hardy variety, heads very compact, and of excellent quality 0 6

TOM THUMB. Very early, dwarf and compact 0 6

VICTORIA. Large and of fine quality .. .. per pkt. 3d. 0 9

" I must say that the Seeds I had from you last year turned out excellent."—Mr. C. JEFFRIES, Beccles.

" I may say that I was successful in taking fourteen Prizes with the produce from your Seeds at the Cheshunt and Waltham Society Show."—Mr. H. HUBBARD, Waltham.

" I am pleased to tell you that I have again done well with your Seeds, taking ten Prizes with Vegetables."—Mr. T. HAWKES, Cropredy.

" The Seeds I obtained from you last year gave great satisfaction, taking five Prizes from six entries."—Mr. F. CROSS, Redhill.

" The Seeds I have had from you have given the greatest satisfaction, although the weather has been so dry."—Mr. W. T. ROGERS, Carmarthen.

" I have great pleasure in informing you that I have been very successful with your Seeds. I have obtained four First Prizes."—Mr. A. LAWLESS, Sheffield.

Cultivation.—Excellent Cabbages can be grown, without much outlay, by every one possessing a garden. They prefer a good rich loamy soil, a liberal supply of manure, and as open a position as possible. The hoe should be kept going every week on the beds, and an occasional application of Nitrate of Soda or Sulphate of Ammonia (at the rate of one ounce to the square yard) is recommended before the hearts form, when good succulent Cabbages are assured. For Summer and Autumn use, sow the seed in March, and a succession in April and May if required, and when the plants are large enough, prick out into seed beds, and finally plant out in rows two feet apart for the stronger growing varieties, such as **Daniels' Defiance** and **Enfield Market**, with two feet between each plant. For the smaller varieties such as **Little Queen, Ellam's Early, Nonpareil,** &c., rows 18 inches apart, and 15 inches from plant to plant fulfil requirements. Cabbages are highly appreciated in early Spring. For this crop the seed should be sown in the Northern districts in July, and in the Midland and Southern districts during August.

RED CABBAGES.—Seed may be sown either in Spring or Autumn ; if sown in the middle of August and planted out late, splendid heads will be produced the following Autumn.

CARROTS.

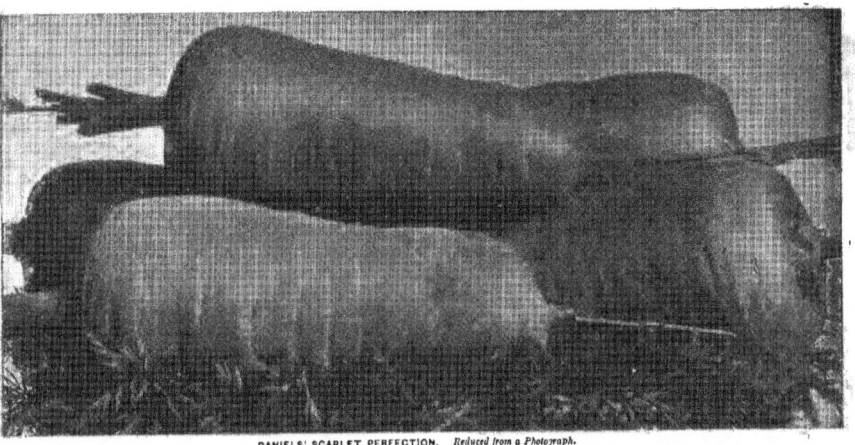

DANIELS' SCARLET PERFECTION.   *Reduced from a Photograph.*

Stump-rooted Varieties.

per oz.—s. d.

☞ **DANIELS' SCARLET PERFECTION.** A grand main crop variety of the intermediate type, and being stump-rooted, it is well adapted for growing on soils where deep culture is not possible. The roots are of a bright orange colour, very handsome and uniform in shape, with a fine clear skin, which makes it a most desirable sort for exhibition. It is one of the best flavoured and heaviest cropping varieties for general use, and one we can highly recommend   ..   ..   ..   **per pkt. 4d. 1 0**

DANIELS' NEW EARLY FORCING HORN. One of the earliest Carrots yet introduced. In shape it is nearly round. They can be left thickly in the row, and drawn for use as required per pkt. 4d. 1 0

DANIELS' HARBINGER. A fine Carrot for early exhibition; the roots are of good shape and excellent quality, averaging four to five inches in length, and three inches in diameter. It is a distinct and useful Carrot   ..   ..   **per pkt. 4d. 1 0**

DANIELS' LONG RED WITHOUT HEART. Flesh bright red, without the core usually found in the Carrot   ..   0 9

EARLY FRENCH NANTES. A medium-sized, stump-rooted variety of very fine quality 0 9

EARLY SCARLET HORN. A stump-rooted variety. Very useful for first early crops 0 8

Long Varieties.

per oz.—s. d.

☞ **DANIELS' TELEGRAPH.** This grand Carrot is one of the best forms of intermediate yet introduced, being far in advance of the old James' Scarlet. It produces a heavy crop of roots, which are of uniform shape, attractive colour, and very clear in the skin. Where sufficient depth of soil exists it will prove one of the most profitable sorts to grow. It is unequalled for exhibition purposes, having obtained more First Prizes than any Carrot with which we are acquainted

     ..   ..   ..   **per pkt. 4d. 1 0**

ALTRINCHAM IMPROVED LONG RED. A fine stock, and stores well 0 6

DANIELS' GIANT WHITE. Much larger and of finer quality than Belgian White. Highly recommended 0 6

JAMES' SCARLET (Intermediate). Excellent for shallow soils. One of the heaviest cropping and most useful for general use 0 6

LONG RED ST. VALERY. A very choice stock, producing clean handsome roots and a great improvement on the Long Surrey. Fine for exhibition 0 8

LONG RED SURREY or LONG ORANGE. Roots long, of good shape, and fine quality; on a deep soil it will produce a very heavy crop 0 6

Cultivation.—By attention to a few points of importance, splendid clean straight Carrots can be cultivated without great delay. It is not necessary to manure the land for a Carrot crop, in fact, freshly manured land is a drawback; the soil should be (where possible) of a deep light nature, and the land should, the Autumn previously, be deeply trenched two to three feet, and a quite light dressing of manure given at the same time; land which has been recently used for Celery is excellent, and will not need specially manuring.

For the earliest crop, make a sowing on the hotbed in frames between the rows of early Potatoes, and pull the Carrots quite small. The first sowing of the outdoor crop should be made early in April on a warm border, Daniels' "Harbinger" or "Forcing Horn" being excellent kinds; make other sowings in succession through the Summer until August, when the best kind to sow is "Scarlet Horn." For main crop, "Daniels' Scarlet Perfection" and "Telegraph" can be highly recommended.

Carrot seed should be sown on borders of finely worked soil, in drills about a foot apart. When the plants are nicely up, thin out gradually, leaving the smaller growing kinds, such as "Forcing Horn," to be pulled as required, and the larger kinds seven to nine inches apart. Keep the hoe going between the sows to ensure cleanliness, and nothing more is needed until the end of October, when the crop should be lifted, the tops carefully twisted off, and the roots stored in dry sand in a cellar, for use as needed during the Winter.

When specimen roots are wanted for exhibition, it is the practice to make holes with a crowbar, and fill with fine soil, sowing the seeds on the top and thinning out to one plant in each hole, as advised for Parsnips.

"I have much pleasure in sending you my order for Seeds. They always turn out so well. I took First Prize for Scarlet Perfection and Telegraph Carrots last year."—Mr. J. PENNELLS, Burwash.

"I am pleased to tell you that your Telegraph Carrot cannot be beaten. I took seven First and three Second Prizes last year."—Mr. T. DODD, Wye.

CAULIFLOWERS.

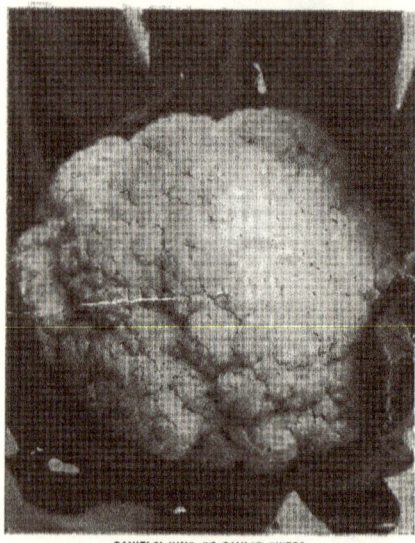

DANIELS' KING OF CAULIFLOWERS.

per oz.—s. d.

☞ DANIELS' KING OF CAULIFLOWERS. The earliest variety in cultivation, of very dwarf and compact habit, the heads beautifully white and of the finest texture. Seed raised in frames in February, and planted out as soon as the weather permits, will produce some fine heads in June. One of the best to sow for succession through the Summer .. per pkt. 1s. 6d. and 2s. 6d. —

DANIELS' SNOWBALL. An invaluable early variety of dwarf compact habit, producing fine white heads of excellent quality. Ready to cut in four months from time of sowing
per pkt. 1s. 6d. and 2s. 6d. —

DANIELS' DWARF MAMMOTH. A very superior dwarf early variety, grows to a larger size than Daniels' King, and forms a good succession to that variety, heads large, white, and compact. Also useful for forcing .. .. per pkt. 1s.   2 6

ECLIPSE. This is an excellent large Autumn variety, and very useful for Market purposes. By successional sowings it can be had from August to Christmas .. .. per pkt. 6d.   1 6

EARLY LONDON WHITE. Useful variety, growing to a large size, heads very white and firm .. .. per pkt. 4d.   1 0

SELF-PROTECTING AUTUMN GIANT. A fine late variety coming into use directly after Veitch's Autumn Giant. The heads are well-protected by luxuriant over-lapping foliage. May be had in good condition up to Christmas .. per pkt. 6d.   1 6

VEITCH'S AUTUMN GIANT. The most useful of our Autumn Cauliflowers and most valuable for general crop. It is very distinct in appearance, producing splendid large heads, beautifully white and firm, and of the finest texture   per pkt. 6d.   1 6

WALCHEREN. Sow under glass in February, to succeed the Spring Broccoli, and in beds from May to July for succession
per pkt. 4d.   1 0

☞ DANIELS' AUTUMN QUEEN. A grand variety, coming in fit for use three weeks earlier than Veitch's Autumn Giant, is very short-legged and compact ; the heads are beautifully white and of the finest quality
per pkt. 1s.   3 0

Cultivation.—The Cauliflower is one of the choicest of our vegetables, and requires much care and very liberal treatment. Cauliflowers are very liable to bolt if any check occurs in their growth, and therefore every care should be taken that they grow on from start to finish without a break. It does not much matter whether the soil on which Cauliflowers are grown is light or heavy, so long as it is thoroughly trenched, and a very liberal quantity of farmyard manure applied. To get the earliest Cauliflowers, the seed should be sown in September in the open, and transferred when big enough to cold frames for the Winter months. Early in March select a warm border and plant them out when a very early crop will be secured.

The earliest Spring sowing should be made in February in boxes on a hot bed, and the plants moved to frames and gradually hardened so as to be ready to plant out in May. A succession of sowings should be made in March in frames and in the open during April, May, and June, so as to secure an unbroken supply. Cauliflowers are most highly prized in Autumn when the Summer crops are over, and it is as well to have more than one batch. When planting and also during dry weather, great care should be given to watering. Frequent applications of liquid manure will give size to the heads for exhibition purposes.

Cauliflowers are particularly subject to white fly which causes the plant to become blind, and any suspicion of this should be met with a dressing of soot upon the leaves in the early morning. The beds should be regularly gone over to ensure the heads being cut before they get too old as they soon get past their best. For early work, **Daniels' King** is undoubtedly the best, followed by **Dwarf Mammoth** and **Autumn Queen.** For general crop, **Autumn Giant** will be found the most useful.

" I may say that I had splendid results from your King of the Cauliflowers last year. I could wish for nothing better."—Mr. H. TONGE, Earls Colne.

" I have only a small garden, but I took twenty-one First, eleven Second, and one third Prizes last year."—Mr. C. TAYLOR, Lowdham.

" I was delighted with your Seeds last season. All the crops being a success."—Mr. E. BROOKER, Crawley.

" I am very pleased indeed to inform you that I had wonderful success with your Seeds last year."—Mr. W. R. PEACHEY, Romford.

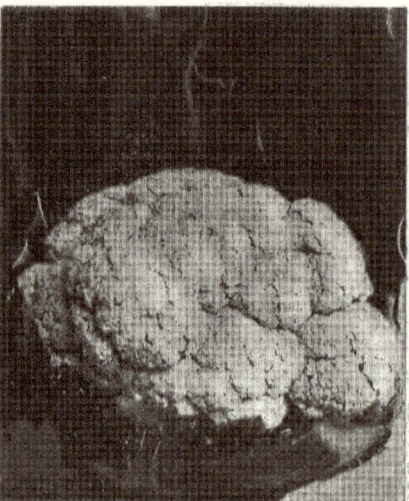

VEITCH'S AUTUMN GIANT.

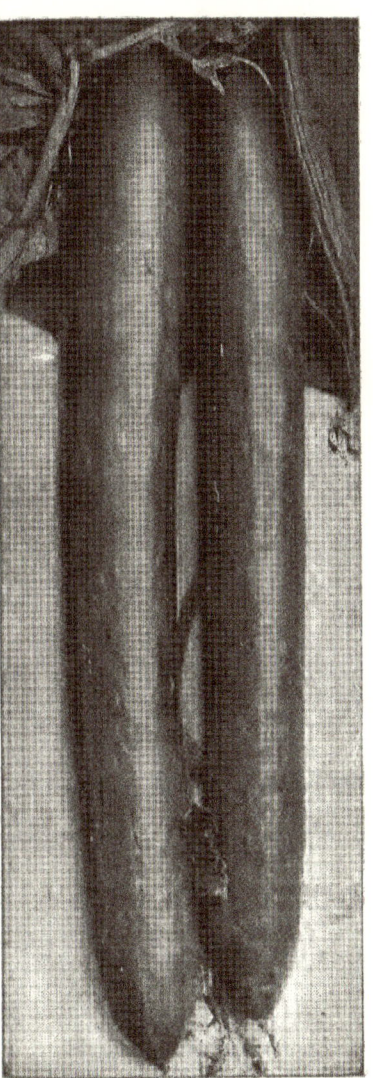

LORD ROBERTS *Reduced from a Photograph.*

CUCUMBERS.

per pkt.—s. d.

LORD ROBERTS. An exceedingly handsome variety raised by Mr. W. H. Apthorpe, Cambridge ; the result of a cross between Royal Osborne and Lockie's Perfection. The fruit which are longer than the last named variety, are of a rich dark green colour, of splendid shape, with no neck, and are borne in the greatest profusion. It is useful for Winter or Summer cultivation, and on account of its prolificness and beautiful appearance, will prove a most valuable variety for the private or market grower per pkt. 1s. 6d. and **2 6**

DISEASE RESISTER. A very prolific variety of similar type to the Amateur, but a stronger grower. The strong leathery leaves resisting all kinds of disease much better and it keeps in bearing for a long period .. 1s. 6d. and **2 6**

THE AMATEUR. This can perhaps be best described as a very finely selected stock of The Rochford or Covent Garden type. It is enormously productive, bearing 3 to 4 fruit at a joint. The fruit, which are of handsome shape, average about 20 to 24 inches in length, are slightly spined and of fine colour, whilst the neck is very short. As its name implies, it will prove one of the best for the amateur grower for all purposes .. .. per pkt. 1s. 6d. and **2 6**

DANIELS' IMPROVED TELEGRAPH. A great improvement on the old Telegraph, bearing clean, straight fruit twenty to twenty-four inches long, an abundant bearer. Our own selected stock, all saved from picked fruit per pkt. 1s. 6d. and **2 6**

DANIELS' DEFIANCE (early prolific). A variety of hardy, robust constitution, producing in great abundance very short-necked and elegant fruit of a rich dark green colour, from eighteen to twenty-four inches in length, straight and uniform .. .. .. 1s. and **2 0**

DANIELS' DUKE OF ALBANY. This is the finest Cucumber ever introduced for exhibition, having obtained numerous First Prizes. The fruit are long, straight, and of a beautiful dark green colour, very handsome, and of the finest quality .. .. .. 1s. and **2 0**

DANIELS' DUKE OF EDINBURGH. A beautiful, white-spined variety of fine, robust constitution and habit, its fruit growing rapidly to the length of thirty to thirty-six inches .. .. .. 1s. and **2 0**

EVERY-DAY. This fine Cucumber is of medium size, the fruit being dark-skinned, very handsome in shape, most prolific, and of splendid flavour. First Class Certificate, R.H.S. **1 0**

THE ROCHFORD. A most prolific bearer. The fruit are slightly spined, eighteen to twenty inches in length, of a beautiful fresh green colour, and of the most handsome form **1 0**

LOCKIE'S PERFECTION. The fruit are produced in great abundance 1s. and **2 0**

ROLLISSON'S TELEGRAPH .. .. 6d. and **1 0**

TENDER AND TRUE. Superior quality and flavour **1 0**

SPECIAL NOTICE.

One of the great causes of failure in raising Cucumber Seed is too much moisture at starting. To begin with, the soil should be warm and not over moist ; plant in small pots three or four Seeds in each ; place in heat of from 80° to 90°. Be sure and give no water until the Seeds are well up, and then water but sparingly for a day or two. We have adopted this plan for many years past with the greatest success.

RIDGE CUCUMBERS.

per pkt.—s. d.

DANIELS' PERFECTION RIDGE. The longest and best out-door variety in cultivation, is very hardy and prolific, bearing a heavy crop of nice shaped fruit, averaging fifteen to twenty inches in length and of superior flavour 6d. and **1 0**

JAPANESE CLIMBING. A most useful variety for growing on trellis work, &c., being very ornamental. It produces a good crop of fruit, averaging from ten to twelve inches in length .. .. .. 6d. and **1 0**

LONG PRICKLY. A very useful variety of fine flavour **0 4**

SHORT PRICKLY. Very hardy, fine for pickling **0 3**

STOCKWOOD. Fine selected stock .. .. .. 3d. and **0 6**

PROLIFIC PICKLING. The most prolific out-door variety ; very hardy .. **0 4**

CRESS.

CRESS, GROWING IN BOX.

		per oz.—s.	d.
PLAIN. The best for early salads	per qt. 1s. 6d., per pint 10d.	0	2
CURLED. For salads in the second leaf ,, 1s. 8d., 1s.		0	2
AUSTRALIAN or GOLDEN. This valuable Cress is a most desirable			
addition to all salads	.. ..	0	4
DANIELS' GARNISHING or PARSLEY-LEAVED. Useful alike for			
salads and garnishing	.. .. ..	0	6
AMERICAN or LAND. Eaten as Water Cress in Winter ..		0	4
SORREL-LEAVED. The largest-leaved of all, dark green colour,			
and good flavour. A most useful salad	.. ..	0	6
WATER. Sow in a moist, shady place	per pkt. 6d. and 1s.	—	

Cultivation.—Cress is one of the most useful salads grown, and it is quite easy to keep up a continual supply, as no expensive appliances are needed. If a greenhouse is available, fill boxes with good soil to within about half inch of the top, pressing the soil firmly, then sow the seeds thickly and evenly but do not cover them with soil. Put the boxes in a dark place and give a good watering; in about a fortnight the cress will be ready to cut. By repeating this process a succession can be maintained throughout the early Spring.

During Summer a shady border should be selected, and the soil raked fine and pressed firm. Sow the seeds and press down with a board, giving good waterings and protection with mats until the seed has germinated. To keep up a constant supply a sowing should be made every week.

American or Land Cress is most useful for mixed salads, and is quite easy to grow; sow the seeds from March onwards on a north border and thin out to allow about four inches between each plant, using the outside leaves only.

Water-cress can be grown in ordinary garden soil provided a shady border is chosen and copious waterings given. The seed should be sown in April, and the plants thinned out, leaving about six inches between each. Keep the plants pinched to prevent them from flowering. In Autumn fill pans half full of soil and place some of the plants therein. Put them in a greenhouse and keep thoroughly watered, and a supply of good tender Water-cress will be available all the Winter.

MUSTARD.

		per oz.—s.	d.				per oz.—s.	d.
WHITE. For early salads	..	per quart 1s. 9d., per pint 1s.	0	2	**CHINESE.** Fine salad variety	per quart 3s., pint 1s. 9d.	0	4

Cultivation.—The Common or White Mustard is much used for saladings, and is generally used with Cress. Out of doors, any cool, moist place is suitable for sowings, which should be made at frequent intervals during Spring and Summer. When sown under glass in Winter and early Spring, no better way exists than that recommended for Cress.

CAPSICUM.

Very valuable as decorative plants for the conservatory, besides being exceedingly useful for stews, pickles, &c.

			per pkt.—s.	d.			per pkt.—s.	d.
RUBY KING	..	..	6d. and	1 0	**LONG YELLOW** ..	..	0	6
CELESTIAL	..	..	6d. and	1 0	**PROCOPP'S GIANT** ..	..	0	6
CHILI or BIRD	..	..	..	0 3	**MONSTREUSE**	..	0	6
ELEPHANT'S TRUNK	..	..	6d. and	1 0	**SWEET GOLDEN DAWN**	..	0	6
LONG RED	..	..	..	0 4	**MIXED, all kinds** ..	..	0	4

CHICORY.

		per pkt.—s.	d.
IMPROVED LARGE-LEAVED. Excellent for blanching	..	0	6
LARGE-ROOTED or COFFEE	.. ..	0	6
WHITLŒF. Equally good as a salad or boiled. Sow in June	..	0	6

CORN SALAD (Lamb's Lettuce).

		per oz.—s.	d.
GREEN CABBAGING. A fine variety, rosette-shaped per pkt. 4d.	0	9
LETTUCE-LEAVED	.. ..	,, 4d.	0	9
LARGE ROUND-LEAVED DUTCH	.. ..	,, 4d.	0	9

ENDIVE.

		per oz.—s.	d.
☛ **DANIELS' SUPERB CURLED. The best of all**			
the Curled Endives, it bleaches well, is of first-class			
quality	.. .. ..	per pkt. 6d.	1	6
DANIELS' PRIZE MOSS CURLED. A splendid variety for			
exhibition, leaves beautifully curled, is very hardy, and bleaches			
well	.. .. ..	per pkt. 4d.		
GREEN CURLED. Extra	.. ..		1	0
BATAVIAN GREEN. Broad-leaved, very hardy, and desirable		0	8
for Winter cultivation, tie up for blanching	..		
EXTRA BROAD-LEAVED. An excellent variety, highly recom-		0	8
mended	.. .. ..	per pkt. 4d.	1	0
WHITE CURLED. Useful variety	.. ..	,, 3d.	0	9

GOURD or PUMPKIN.

Large Varieties.

		per pkt.—s.	d.
☛ **DANIELS' YELLOW MAMMOTH. Seed from large,**			
handsomely netted fruit, weighing one hundredweight			
or more	.. ..	6d. and	1	0
POTIRON JAUNE or MAMMOTH. A giant variety	6d. and	1	0
COMMON PUMPKIN. Very useful for pies and preserves in Winter	0	3
VARIEGATED TURK'S CAP. Striped orange, green, and white	0	6

Smaller Ornamental Varieties.

			d.
SMALL ORANGE. Strongly resembling an orange	..	0	4
PEAR-SHAPED. Green and yellow, pretty	..	0	4

Twelve varieties, one packet of each, 2s. 6d.

LEEKS.

Cultivation.—The Leek is one of the most nutritious vegetables cultivated, and although to produce exhibition specimens much care and attention is needed, still a thoroughly good crop for cooking purposes can be grown quite easily. Leeks are gross feeders and therefore require well tilled and liberally manured ground; the best plan is to give the land a thorough dressing of well decayed manure in Autumn and trench it deeply, allowing it to remain rough for the Winter. The seed should be sown in drills in March for the main crop, and care must be taken to keep the ground thoroughly clean from the outset in order to give the seedlings a good start.

The easiest mode of culture is to dibble the young plants when about six inches high into holes made about twelve inches deep, giving occasional dressings of liquid manure. In September draw the earth round the plants. It is best to defer using Leeks till as late as possible in the Autumn, as the flavour improves.

When it is desired to grow Leeks for exhibition, a good plan is to grow them in trenches in the same way as Celery, allowing two feet between the trenches; for this purpose the seed should be sown on a gentle hotbed in February, and the seedlings pricked off into boxes when big enough; it is important that the young plants be thoroughly hardened, as they will not stand coddling, but cold draughts should be avoided; When the plants have made about six inches of growth, plant them into trenches, allowing about 15 inches between each plant; lift the plants out of the box with a trowel, to ensure getting a good lot of roots. As the plants grow, the soil must be carefully and firmly worked round the roots and this process continued all the Summer at intervals, giving frequent waterings of liquid manure. Some growers place collars of brown paper round the stems before commencing to earth up the plants as this excludes all light and is a great aid to blanching.

There is every encouragement to grow Leeks to a large size, as the flavour of the finest specimens is superior to the smaller ones. This is not so in most vegetables, but is certainly the case with Leeks.

	per oz.—s.	d.
☞ **DANIELS' CHAMPION.** This is undoubtedly one of the finest Leeks in cultivation. It grows to a large size, and is unsurpassed for exhibition purposes, having produced specimens with 18 inches of blanched stem, and of perfect shape. It comes early into use, and is of exceptionally mild flavour. It has obtained First Prize at a great number of Shows on account of its extraordinary clearness of skin and handsome appearance. We strongly recommend this variety to intending exhibitors, as one likely to give the greatest satisfaction .. .. .. **per pkt. 1s.**	2	6
AYTON CASTLE GIANT. Remarkably large and good, may be grown ten to twelve inches in circumference, and with one foot of blanched stem per pkt. 4d.	1	0
CONQUEROR. First-class; very superior either for competition or culinary purposes. It is of large size and blanches for considerable distance up the stem; highly recommended .. .. .. per pkt. 1s.	2	6
HENRY'S PRIZE. Exceedingly large, blanches well, flavour mild, fine for exhibition .. .. per pkt. 4d.	1	0
LONDON FLAG. Large, broad-leaved. A good old variety possessing many excellent qualities	0	6
LYON. One of the largest kinds grown and excellent in every way. A kind much in demand for exhibition purposes .. .. per pkt. 6d.	2	0
MUSSELBURGH. Extra broad-leaved, blanches to a large size, flavour mild, highly esteemed for soups. A well-established kind of considerable merit and hardiness; grand stock .. .. per pkt. 4d.	1	0

EVIDENCE OF QUALITY.

" I am pleased to tell you that the Seeds I had from you last year came up to the mark in every respect."—Mr. J. BUDGE, Drummore.

" I may say that your Seeds did extremely well last year although a very poor season."—Mr. R. ARMSTRONG, Skelton.

" I am pleased to say I took four First, five Second, and three Third Prizes with the produce from your Seeds last year."—Mr. R. WING, High Wycombe.

" I took First Prize for Leeks grown from the Seed had from you last year; they were splendid, with 18 inches of blanched stem."—Mr. V. BURLEY, Sandwich.

" At our Show last year I took First Prizes with produce from your Seeds."—Mr. L. UZZELL, Fairford.

" I had splendid results from your Seeds last year."—Mr. G. WORKMAN, Cwmdows.

" I am pleased to say that I took several Prizes (17 in all) with Vegetables grown from your Seeds."—Mr. E. MOUNTFORD, Bovey Tracey.

" I have much pleasure in saying that your Seeds have given me the greatest satisfaction. I showed two Collections of Vegetables and took First Prize with both. I also took First Prize with your Ailsa Craig Onion."—Mr. R. GILLETT, Robertsbridge.

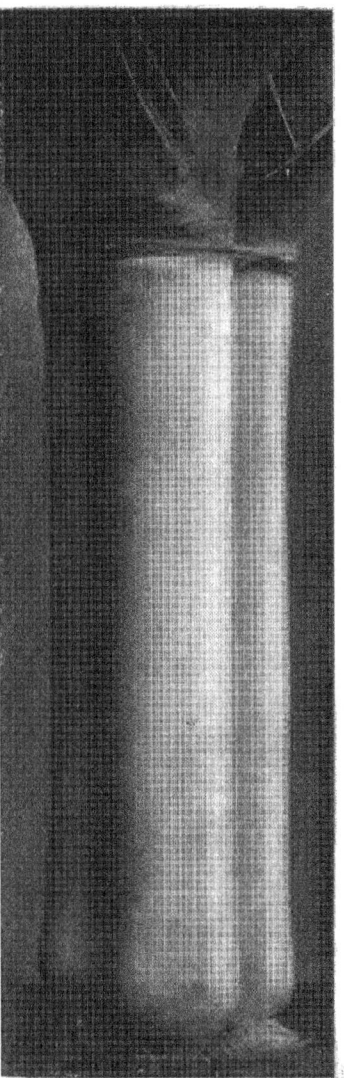

LEEK, DANIELS' CHAMPION.

Reduced from a Photograph.

LETTUCES—Cabbage Varieties.

DANIELS' CONTINUITY LETTUCE.

Daniels' Continuity.

The Longest Standing Cabbage Lettuce in the World.

This fine Cabbage Lettuce is remarkable from the fact that not even in the hottest and driest season does it ever run to seed, the heads remaining firm and crisp long after all others have bolted or decayed. A bed of these sown or planted will keep up a supply of good Lettuces for a long period, one sowing of these being equal to three or four sowings of other varieties Per pkt., 6d. ; oz., 1s. 6d.

	per pkt. s. d.	per oz. s. d.
DANIELS' QUEEN OF SUMMER. This is one of the finest Summer Lettuces yet introduced. It is remarkable for its large size, splendid appearance, and for withstanding the drought. It produces fine, crisp, and tender Lettuces in the driest season ..	0 4	1 0
DANIELS' GIANT WHITE. An exceedingly large and fine variety, crisp and tender and of fine flavour, stands a long time without running to seed	0 4	1 0
DANIELS' BLACK-SEEDED TEXTER. Large, compact, and solid, one of the most splendid varieties in cultivation, first-class for market gardeners ..	0 4	1 0
ALL THE YEAR ROUND. One of the best for general use ; very hardy ..	0 4	1 0
BROWN DUTCH. Very large and hardy	0 3	0 8
DRUMHEAD or MALTA. Well known	0 3	0 8
LARGE WHITE WINTER. The best for Winter use ; heads large and solid	0 4	1 0
STANSTEAD PARK. A fine variety for sowing in Autumn to stand the Winter	0 4	1 0
NEW YORK. A very superior American variety. The heads attain a large size, and are very crisp and tender ; grand variety for exhibition ..	0 4	1 0
NEAPOLITAN. Leaves beautifully curled and tender, one of the finest Summer sorts	0 3	0 9
WHEELER'S TOM THUMB. The earliest variety grown, heads small, and very solid and tender ..	0 4	1 0
MIXED CABBAGE VARS. All the best kinds for succession ..	0 2	0 6
MIXED. All kinds, Cos and Cabbage	0 2	0 6

" I am pleased to say that I have done well this year at our shows with the produce from your **Seeds**, obtaining several First, Second, and Third Prizes, also the Silver Challenge Shield for excellence in horticulture."—**Mr. G. H. SPICER**, Warwick.

"The Seeds I had from you last Spring have done splendidly. I obtained four First Prizes with Lettuce and First Prize for Peas."—**Mr. J. H. BELTON**, Little Weighton.

"I am pleased to inform you that I took a Prize for your Continuity Lettuce at our Show."—**Mr. H. E. FOOTER**, Uxbridge.

"I have now had your **Seeds** for many years and can testify to the absolute satisfaction they always give."—**Mr. E. WIDE**, Hemyock.

	per pkt. s. d.	per oz. s. d.
DANIELS' EXHIBITION GIANT (new). One of the largest Cabbage Lettuces yet introduced, and grows to an enormous size without becoming coarse. The heads are very firm, crisp, and of excellent flavour. For exhibition purposes it is unrivalled, and is one of the best for Salads	1 0	2 6
DANIELS' MAGNUM BONUM. A splendid Cabbage Lettuce growing to a large size, the heads being very firm and crisp and of excellent flavour, stands well ; a useful variety for exhibition	0 6	1 6
DANIELS' GOLDEN BEAUTY. A grand Summer Lettuce of fine appearance ; the leaves are of a light golden colour, very crisp and solid, stands the drought well	0 4	1 0
DANIELS' MAMMOTH GREEN. A fine large Cabbage Lettuce. The heads although large are very firm and crisp ; an excellent variety for Autumn sowing	0 4	1 0

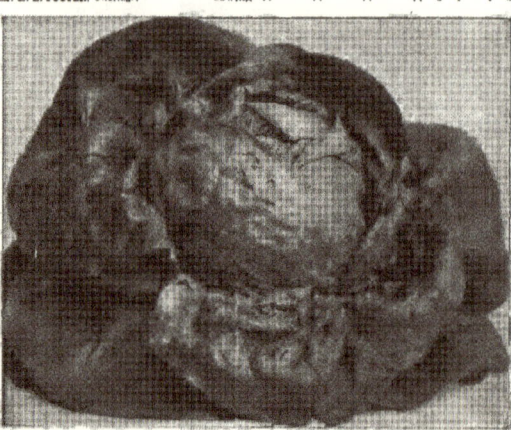

DANIELS' QUEEN OF SUMMER.

LETTUCE—Cos Varieties.

DANIELS' GIANT WHITE COS LETTUCE, *Reduced from a Photograph.*

	per pkt. s. d.	per oz. s. d.
☛ **DANIELS' GIANT WHITE.** The finest and largest Cos Lettuce in cultivation, very tender and crisp, with fine solid hearts, and will stand a long time without running to seed ; should be grown in all gardens ; unrivalled for exhibition purposes ..	1 0	2 6
☛ **DANIELS' DREADNOUGHT.** One of the largest Cos Lettuces in cultivation, the heads being very solid, crisp, and of fine flavour. An invaluable variety for exhibition ..	1 0	2 6
☛ **DANIELS' ALL HEART.** A fine Cos Lettuce growing to a large size, the leaves folding well over the hearts, which are very solid and of fine flavour	0 6	1 6
DANIELS' MONSTROUS BROWN. Tender and crisp, the largest grown ; fine variety for exhibition	0 4	1 0
DANIELS' SELECTED PARIS WHITE. Self-blanching, tender, and mild flavour ; useful exhibition variety	0 4	1 0
DANIELS' BLACK-SEEDED BATH	0 4	1 0
DANIELS' GREEN WINTER. An excellent and hardy kind, valuable for Winter and early Spring	0 4	1 0
DANIELS' SOLID BROWN. A medium-sized Lettuce, outer leaves brown, hearts very solid and of a beautiful creamy yellow ; very crisp, requires no tying. An invaluable variety for Winter use	0 4	1 0
HICKS' HARDY WHITE. A superior variety both for Summer and Winter use ..	0 4	1 0
PARIS WHITE. Best for general use ..	0 3	0 10
MIXED COS VARS. All the best for succession	0 2	0 6
☛ **DANIELS' LITTLE GEM.** A very early Cos Lettuce, coming into use at the same time as the Cabbage varieties. It is very dwarf and compact, the heads, which are self-folding, require no tying	0 6	1 6

" I obtained First Prize last year with your Giant White Cos Lettuce."—Mr. J. STEVENSON, Southall.

DANIELS' LITTLE GEM.

Cultivation.—It is often necessary that a practically continuous supply of Lettuces should be maintained throughout the year, and by a succession of sowings this may be done. For the earliest crop the seed should be sown in boxes under glass during January, and when big enough to handle prick out the plants about three inches apart into frames, there to be hardened off ready for planting out in a south border when the weather permits. Early in March a sowing may be made out of doors, preferably on a south border. Sow the seeds in drills, cover lightly with soil and protect from the birds if possible ; when the plants are big enough prick them out six inches apart. By cutting some of the plants early, space will be left which will allow the remainder to develop.

A succession of sowings may be made until the beginning of September, and the plants which are to stand the Winter should be finally pricked out in October, the most sheltered position in the garden being chosen. In a severe Winter it will be found necessary to give some protection to these plants ; a slight covering of straw or bracken being suitable. To secure crispness and succulence in Lettuces, liberal supplies of water should be given, and the hoe kept going regularly between the rows. For Spring and Summer use we recommend in the Cos varieties, "Daniels' Giant White" and "Daniels' All Heart" ; in the Cabbage varieties, "Daniels' Queen of Summer" and "Daniels' Continuity," the latter is a kind which very rarely runs to seed even in the hottest weather. For Autumn and Winter work "Daniels' Solid Brown" and "Daniels' Green Winter," both very hardy Cos Lettuces, and "All the Year Round" and "Large White Winter," and "Daniels' Mammoth Green" in Cabbage Lettuces, are to our mind the pick of the List.

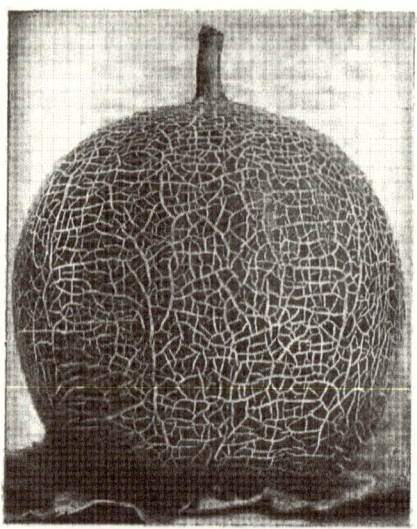

NEW MELON, EMINENCE. *Reduced from a Photograph.*

MELON, GUNTON SCARLET. *Reduced from a Photograph.*

MELONS.

Cultivation.—This delicious fruit is widely cultivated by all who can command sufficient heat. Melons are raised from seed in a similar way to Cucumbers, and their general treatment is much the same in the early stages of their growth.

Sow the seeds singly in a pot of fine loam and leaf mould, and place on a hot-bed ; as soon as the plants are in the rough leaf, pot on into six-inch pots ; keep at an even temperature to avoid checking the plants, meanwhile have the beds prepared by forming a mound of good rich turfy loam and well-decayed manure on the border of the greenhouse stage, or in the frame. When planting make the soil quite firm round the stem, and give liberal waterings of clear water.

When the fruits are set, they should be thinned out to about two or three fruits on each plant, and occasional waterings of weak liquid manure given. As they ripen keep the bed a little drier ; the temperature for Melon growing should be about 75° to 80° in the day, and 65° to 70° at night.

per pkt.—s.　d.

☞ **NEW MELON. EMINENCE.** A fine variety, raised by Mr. A. McKellar, the Royal Gardens, Windsor. Received an Award of Merit from the Royal Horticultural Society. The fruit are rather large, roundish oval, skin bright yellow and beautifully netted, flesh white, thick. Very melting and of delicious flavour.
1s. 6d. and 2 0

☞ **NEW MELON. IDEAL.** This is undoubtedly a very valuable and desirable variety. It is the result of crossing Ingestre Hybrid and Royal Favourite. The flesh is thick and of a pale green colour, very luscious, and of delicious flavour. The fruit is of medium size, rich yellow, and well netted. It is a free setter, and the fruit matures rapidly 1 0

GUNTON SCARLET (S.F.). A very superior scarlet-fleshed Melon of medium size, oval in shape, and finely netted. The flesh is very deep and the finest flavour of any Melon with which we are acquainted. Highly recommended .. .. .. 1s. 6d. and 2 6

*****BLENHEIM ORANGE (S.F.).** A grand scarlet-fleshed variety, very prolific and a fine setter 1 0

DANIELS' IMPROVED GOLDEN PERFECTION. A splendid green-fleshed variety, regularly and beautifully netted ; thin skin, flesh very thick, firm, of the most exquisite flavour ; the plant is of fine robust constitution and a free setter ; we confidently recommend this .. .. .. 1s. and 2 0

DUCHESS OF YORK. A very useful variety, both for table and exhibition purposes, having gained numerous first prizes. It is a cross between Best of All and Hero of Lockinge ; fruit medium-sized, white-fleshed, colour golden, and beautifully netted, sets freely, of robust constitution, thick in the flesh, and of delicious flavour 1 0

HERO OF LOCKINGE (W.F.). Fine exhibition variety ; very prolific.. .. .. 1 0

MELTON HYBRID (S.F.). This choice variety will be found a valuable addition to our list of good Melons. The fruit is large and handsome, and nicely netted. The flesh is thick, of rich salmon colour, juicy and melting, and of fine flavour .. 1 6

MUNRO'S LITTLE HEATH (S.F.). A well-known variety of excellent flavour 1 0

*****ROYAL SOVEREIGN.** A grand variety. Raised at The Royal Gardens, Windsor ; has received Award of Merit from the R.H.S. It has a robust constitution, and is a free setter, the average weight of the fruit being about five pounds. The skin is of a beautiful golden colour, slightly netted, flesh white, faintly tinged with green, and very deep ; flavour first-class .. 1 6

ROYALTY. A new variety of strong constitution, vigorous growth, and a free setter. The fruit is very handsome, round, yellow, and beautifully netted. The flesh, pale green, melting, and juicy. The fruit never cracks, and will keep in perfect condition eight or ten days after being ripe 1 0

*****READ'S SCARLET-FLESH.** One of the best red-fleshed varieties, a free setter ; flesh thick, solid, and of excellent flavour
6d. and 1 0

*****THE COUNTESS (W.F.).** A cross between American Musk and Cashmere ; of strong constitution, and enormously prolific ; clear yellow skin, beautifully netted ; flesh thick, tender, juicy, and melting 1 0

Abbreviations.—Those marked with an (*) have received a First Class Certificate from the Royal Horticultural Society. S.F. scarlet flesh, G.F. green flesh, W.F. white flesh.

PARSLEY.

DANIELS' QUEEN OF THE PARSLEYS GROWING AT OUR SEED GROUNDS. *From a Photograph.*

	per oz.—s. d.
☞ ¡ **DANIELS' QUEEN OF THE PARSLEYS.** An extra selected stock carefully grown on our own Seed Farm. The most useful for garnishing, and extremely valuable as an ornamental plant for the flower-border .. per pkt. 4d.	1 0
GIANT CURLED. A very handsome variety, leaves finely curled, grows to a large size, and is very ornamental ; this is the best sort to grow where Parsley is required in large quantities .. .. per pkt. 3d.	0 9
COVENT GARDEN GARNISHING. A splendid variety, beautifully curled	0 4
EXTRA-FINE CURLED. Fine for garnishing	0 4
FERN-LEAVED. Distinct foliage, useful for garnishing .. .. per pkt. 3d.	0 3

Cultivation.—Parsley being a deep-rooting plant pays well for liberal cultivation ; it likes a good rich soil in a cool but not too shady position. Parsley is often grown as an edging to other kitchen garden crops and has a pleasing effect when thus used, and as it is in demand the whole year round it is an excellent plan to make a succession of sowings during the year to ensure a continuous supply. Make the first sowing in a box in February and when the plants have been gradually hardened off they should be planted out during April in the permanent border, allowing about twelve inches between each plant. Another sowing at the end of March will be of value for a succession.

☜ For a Winter supply, a sowing should be made in June or July, choosing a sunny aspect on a south border. The plants should be thinned out to prevent over-crowding ; those taken out may be potted up and placed in a cold frame or greenhouse and will yield an excellent supply of leaves for Winter garnishing. In the event of severe weather it will be found advisable to cover the outside beds with mats or an old frame, and a sprinkling of soot in the early morning during the growing season will be found to have an excellent effect.

HERBS (Sweet and Pot).

Per packet 3d.   Per dozen packets, 2s. 6d.

‡ **ANGELICA.** The mid-rib may be eaten as Celery, or when candied makes an excellent perfection.

* **ANISE.** The seeds are much used for medicinal purposes ; the leaves for garnishing or seasoning.

‡ **BALM.** For making balm tea, which is invaluable in cases of fever ; makes also a fine-flavoured wine.

* **BASIL, Bush.** The leaves and tops impart the flavour of Cloves to soups, and are much used for seasoning.

* **BASIL, Sweet.** For flavouring salads and soups.

* **BORAGE.** The young leaves used as salad or pot herb.

‡ **BURNET.** The young leaves have the flavour of Cucumbers.

‡ **CARAWAY.** For flavouring soups.

* **CHERVIL, Green Curled.** Very fine for salads.

* **CORIANDER.** The tender leaves are used for soups or salads.

† **DILL.** The leaves are used in soups, sauces, and pickles.

‡ **FENNEL.** Used in sauces for fish and for garnishing.

‡ **HOREHOUND.** Makes an esteemed well-known beverage.

* **HYSSOP.** Young shoots used as pot herbs.

* **MARIGOLD, Pot.** The flowers impart a beautiful colour to broths and soups.

* **MARJORAM, Sweet or Knotted** ⎫ Aromatic and sweet flavour, used in
‡ **MARJORAM, Pot** •▮▮ ⎬ soups and stuffings.

‡ **LAVENDER.** Cultivated for its flowers, which are very aromatic.

* **PURSLANE, Green** ⎫ The shoots and succulent leaves are cooling when
* **PURSLANE, Golden** ⎬ used in Spring as salads.

* **RAMPION.** The leaves used as salads ; the roots, which have a pleasant nutty flavour, used as Radish.

‡ **ROSEMARY.** The leaves make a drink esteemed for relieving headache.

‡ **RUE, Broad-leaved.** Leaves used medicinally ; also used as a remedy for croup in fowls.

‡ **SAGE.** Used in stuffing and sauces.

* **SAVORY, Summer** ⎫ The tops being very aromatic are used in salads
‡ **SAVORY, Winter** ⎬ and soups ; they improve the flavour if boiled
   with Peas or Beans.

‡ **SKIRRET.** The tubers when boiled and served up with butter are most delicious.

‡ **SORREL, Broad-leaved** ⎫ The leaves are used in salads, soups, and
‡ **SORREL, Lettuce-leaved** ⎬ sauces.

‡ **TANSY.** Used for colouring and flavouring confections.

‡ **TARRAGON.** The leaves are excellent when pickled.

‡ **THYME, Broad-leaved.** Used in stuffings, soups, and sauces.

‡ **WORMWOOD.** Fine tonic when taken as tea ; and imparts bitterness to drinks.

Annuals marked thus (*)   *Biennials (†).*   *Perennials (‡).*   *For Plants of most of the Perennial sorts, see page 61.*

ONIONS FOR SPRING SOWING.

DANIELS' SELECTED AILSA CRAIG. *Reduced from a Photograph.*

☞ **DANIELS' SELECTED AILSA CRAIG.** This grand Onion has now taken its place as one of the largest and most useful varieties for all purposes. It is very good sown either in Spring or Autumn, and produces a heavy crop of fine handsome bulbs, which are unrivalled for exhibition purposes. They have been grown to the enormous weight of 26, 28, 30, and 34 lbs. per dozen bulbs. Our own selected stock grown from picked bulbs.   **Per pkt. 1s. ; per oz. 2s. 6d.**

	per oz.—s. d.
ROUSHAM PARK HERO. A magnificent variety of the White Spanish type. The bulbs, which are very solid, grow to a large size, producing a heavy crop of excellent quality and fine appearance. It is a grand sort for exhibition purposes, and an extra good keeper .. .. per pkt. 4d.	1 0
CRANSTON'S EXCELSIOR. A superior variety of fine globular shape, very deep, with fine skin ; a good keeper and excellent exhibition variety .. .. .. per pkt. 1s.	2 6
DANIELS' LONGLASTER. Crop failed.	

	per oz.—s. d.
DANIELS' NEW RED GLOBE. The finest Red Onion in cultivation. The bulbs are large, of a fine globular shape, and of a beautiful dark crimson. Besides being very attractive in appearance, it has the mild flavour and good keeping qualities of the very best of the White Spanish type .. .. .. per pkt. 4d.	1 0
UP-TO-DATE. A fine new variety of globular shape. It is very solid, and has a well developed shoulder, and will therefore produce a heavier crop than the older sorts. The skin is a bright straw colour. It is an excellent keeper, and will be found a useful variety for exhibition .. .. per pkt. 4d.	1 0

EVIDENCE OF QUALITY.

" Your Ailsa Craig Onion is splendid. I am pleased with it. It has grown to an enormous size."—Mr. H. W. KIRK, Oundle.

" I am pleased to tell you that I have had a splendid crop of Ailsa Craig Onions."—Mr. C. CLARK, Bedford.

" I have taken First Prize with Ailsa Craig Onion and Telegraph Carrot."—Mr. A. G. PICK, Newport.

" I am glad to say that I have had a fine crop of your Ailsa Craig Onion this year, and am more than pleased with the same."—Mr. G. DAVIES, Llandilo.

" I obtained three First Prizes last year with your Ailsa Craig Onion. Your Defiance Cabbage and Improved Hollow-crowned Parsnip continue to give every satisfaction."—Mr. J. FINEGAN, Oldcastle.

" The Ailsa Craig Onions I had from you last year were excellent. I took three Prizes with them."—Mr. W. COYLE, Dublin.

" Your Ailsa Craig and Golden Rocca Onions are doing splendidly again this year."—Mr. W. H. STURGESS, South Wigston.

" The Seeds I had from you last year turned out very satisfactory, especially the Onion. I have Onions now from 13 to 14 inches in circumference grown without any special manure."—Mr. S. PEACHEY, Kidlington.

ONIONS FOR SPRING SOWING.

DANIELS' IMPROVED WHITE SPANISH. *Reduced from a Photograph.*

☛ DANIELS' IMPROVED WHITE SPANISH. This grand stock of Onion has been carefully selected by us for a great many years, and we have no hesitation in recommending it to our customers as one of the very best of its type ; grows to a large size, very even, and it is unequalled for mildness of flavour. It is a very heavy cropper, a grand variety for Exhibition purposes, and is sure to give satisfaction.

Per pkt. 9d. ; per oz. 2s.

	per oz.—s. d.
JAMES' KEEPING. An excellent keeper of fine globular shape, producing a very heavy crop of bulbs of the finest quality	0 10
NUNEHAM PARK. Much recommended, bulbs of fine globular shape and of good keeping quality	0 9
BEDFORDSHIRE CHAMPION. A well-known variety, producing a very heavy crop of good sized bulbs. Keeps well	0 10
BROWN GLOBE. Very useful, heavy cropper	0 9
DANIELS' BLOOD RED. Fine rich colour, very hardy	0 9

	per oz.—s. d.
WHITE SPANISH. Ordinary stock. A heavy cropper, flesh very firm, and keeps well	0 8
WHITE SPANISH, Portugal or Reading. A finely selected stock, producing a very heavy crop of handsome bulbs, of first-class keeping quality	0 10

	per oz.—s. d.
ZITTEAU GIANT YELLOW. A magnificent variety with fine yellow skin, and grows to a large size, the bulbs are of handsome appearance and excellent quality, remains sound till June. May also be sown with advantage in Autumn	1 0
STRASBURGH or DEPTFORD. Well known	0 8
MIXED, all sorts for Spring sowing	0 7

DANIELS' GOLDEN GLOBE. One of the finest types of Globe Onion in cultivation. The bulbs are of true globular shape with bright golden yellow skin ; the flesh is very solid and of mild flavour. It produces a very heavy crop of fine, handsome bulbs, and is one of the best keepers. A most useful variety for all purposes. **Per pkt. 6d. ; per oz. 1s. 6d.**

DANIELS' GOLDEN GLOBE.

EVIDENCE OF QUALITY.

" I would like to say a few words about the New Golden Globe Onion. I consider it the best all-round Onion that can be grown, and for keeping there is none to beat it. I have some as hard as when first lifted."— Mr. S. HARPER, Burton-on-Trent.

" I am very pleased with your Golden Globe Onion, they are grand, both as an exhibition and a keeping variety. I have grown it for several years and taken numerous prizes with it."—Mr. A. WOODHOUSE, The Gardens, Letheringsett Hall.

" I am pleased to tell you that I took two First Prizes last year and two First Prizes this year with your Onions ; they were the best I ever grew."—Mr. J. HOOPER, Grimsby.

" I have had some splendid bulbs of Onion from Seed supplied by you last year."—Mr. G. BRINKLECOMBE, Oakhampton.

" I have been very successful with your Onions this year, taking twelve Prizes."—Mr. R. W. STEEL, Spilsby.

" Your Onion took First Prize at our Show last week."—Mr. J. DOWRICK.

" I am pleased to inform you that I took First Prize with your Onions at the Colwyn Bay Show."—Mr. J. MARSAN, Rhos.

" I have the best bed of Onions in the Allotments from your Seed."— Mr. J. HOWE, West Hartlepool.

ONION—Allan's Reliance.

ALLAN'S RELIANCE. *From a Photograph.*

☞ **ALLAN'S RELIANCE.** This fine Onion has been grown and selected by Mr. Allan, of Gunton Park Gardens, for many years past, and, as will be seen from our illustration, is now brought up to the very highest type of a White Spanish Onion ; besides being of splendid size and keeping quality, it is unsurpassed for exhibition. **Per pkt. 6d. ; per oz. 1s. 6d.**

ALL THE YEAR ROUND. A new type of Onion growing to a large size, but having the advantage over many of the present exhibition varieties of being a grand keeper. The bulbs ripen off well, and from seed sown early in Spring have been grown to over 1¼ lb. each. Per pkt. 6d. ; oz. 1s. 6d.

COCOANUT. This fine Onion has been grown to the weight of three pounds each. The skin is a very delicate pale straw colour, flesh white and mild ; one of the best for exhibition. Per pkt. 1s. ; per oz. 2s. 6d.

Silver Skinned or Pickling Varieties.

	per oz.—s. d.
EARLY WHITE GEM. One of the earliest in cultivation, three weeks earlier than the Queen, and comes to maturity from eight to ten weeks from time of sowing. Very useful for pickling ... per pkt. 4d.	1 0

	per oz.—s. d.
EARLY QUEEN. Remarkably quick-growing, may be sown in July and will ripen the same year ...	0 9
SILVER SKIN. Of very quick growth, best for pickling	0 10

Cultivation.—There are few vegetable crops upon which so much care is expended as the Onion, and during recent years its culture has received much more attention than was formerly the case. When the seed can be raised in January in heat (thereby obtaining an early start) it is possible to grow bulbs of equal size to those grown from seed sown the previous Autumn ; about the last week in January is the time for the earliest sowing.

Sow the seed in boxes or pots in fine soil, a good mixture being two parts of good loam to one part of decomposed manure, or leaf soil. When the young plants are about three inches high prick them off into boxes, and give all the light possible, gradually admitting air, and hardening as the days lengthen, until the time arrives for planting out in the beds about the middle of April. The earliest sowing out of doors should be made in February, and the main sowing of all kinds in March.

The greatest care should be taken in preparing the Onion bed, the ground being thoroughly raked over, all the stones cleared off, and a perfectly fine surface obtained and the soil made quite firm. Sow the seeds very evenly in shallow drills about eighteen inches apart and carefully cover the seed by putting the soil from the side of the drills with the feet. The whole bed should then be well trodden down both down the bed and across as well, after this, again rake the soil level and little further work is necessary beyond keeping the hoe going and thinning out the plants when the time arrives. Unless specially fine bulbs are required it is not advisable to thin too much. To prevent an attack of Onion Maggot in a dry season, a good watering with lime water will be found to be of much service.

Great care is necessary in harvesting the Onion crop. It is a good plan to bend over the tops of the plants in August by going over the plants individually, this will assist the ripening of the bulbs. Onions require to be thoroughly ripened before being taken off the ground and should, therefore, be pulled about the middle of September and turned over on the ground every two or three days for a fortnight, when they should be gathered into an airy shed in readiness for roping together, this being the best method of storing them for Winter use.

ONIONS FOR AUTUMN SOWING.

CANIELS' GOLDEN ROCCA. *Reduced from a Photograph.*

☞ **DANIELS' GOLDEN ROCCA.** One of the largest and finest Onions ever introduced. Fine globular shape, golden yellow skin, mild flavour, and with careful cultivation comes equal to the imported Portugal Onions, and keeps sound till June This variety is the best exhibition kind known, and has obtained more Prizes than any other Onion. If sown in Autumn, and kept under first-class cultivation, will grow bulbs two to three pounds each ; may also be sown in Spring, and will produce some fine bulbs. **Per packet 9d. ; per ounce 2s. 0d.**

	per oz.—s. d.		per oz.—s. d.
DANIELS' GIANT ROCCA. A splendid large globular variety of delicate flavour, grows to a large size 0 9		**TRIPOLI ITALIAN RED.** Fine dark red skin ; a well-known and popular sort 0 9	
DANIELS' WHITE ELEPHANT TRIPOLI. The largest and best of the Tripoli sorts .. .. .. per pkt. 4d. 1 0		**TRIPOLI ITALIAN WHITE.** Similar to the above, but milder .. 0 9	
SILVER SKIN. Very early, excellent for Spring use 0 10		**LISBON WHITE.** Very useful for pulling green for salads early in Spring 0 7	

PLANTS.

Strong Autumn sown, to plant out for show purposes, can be supplied in Spring of the following kinds only :—

White Elephant Tripoli, Golden Rocca, Giant Rocca .. .. ..)
Improved White Spanish, Ailsa Craig, and Allan's Reliance. All Carriage Paid) .. .. each sort 2s. per 100.

The Autumn sowing of these, which offers many advantages to the cultivator, has very much grown in favour of late years. When sown in Autumn, Onions grow to a much larger size, and are milder in flavour than those sown in Spring, especially when transplanted, and being much less liable to attack from fly, are rarely destroyed by maggot. They are besides exceedingly valuable for the supply of fresh green Onions in early Spring which can always be relied on.

Cultivation.—For securing specially fine Onions there is no doubt that it is much better to sow the seed in the Autumn. The ground should be prepared as for the Spring crop, except that the drills should be made a little deeper. Sow the seed any time from the middle of July to the end of August and treat in the same manner as advised for Spring sowing. Keep the ground clear of weeds, and give good soakings of water, if the Autumn is a dry one. If cooking size only is needed it will merely be found necessary to thin out the Onions and a good crop will be obtained, but if exhibition bulbs are required, the strongest must be selected in Spring, lifted carefully with a trowel, and transplanted nine inches apart on to a specially prepared bed of rich soil. Water thoroughly, at the same time making the soil firm round the bulbs. Keep the hoe going and excellent Show specimens should be produced without further trouble.

Potato Onions are a very useful crop and produce a heavy yield of underground bulbs ; they are grown from bulbs (see page 52) and should be planted out in February in rows about 1½ feet apart, allowing ten inches between each bulb in the row. Draw the earth round them as for Potatoes and gather the crop in June.

PARSNIPS.

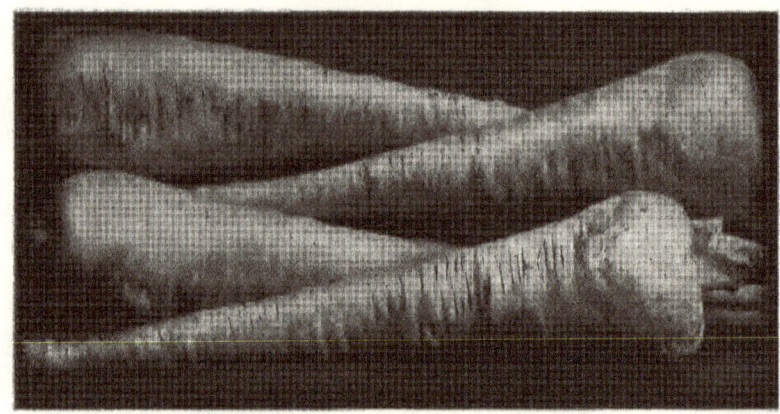

DANIELS' IMPROVED HOLLOW-CROWNED. *Reduced from a Photograph.*

per oz.—s. d.

DANIELS' IMPROVED HOLLOW-CROWNED. A finely selected stock of the Hollow-crowned variety. It grows to a very large size without becoming coarse. The roots are of grand symmetrical shape and very clear in the skin. It produces a heavy crop of even-sized Parsnips, and is the best variety for exhibition purposes   ..   per lb. 6s.   0   8

ELCOMBE'S IMPROVED. Very choice stock, of fine flavour, much esteemed for exhibition   ..   per lb. 6s.   0   8

GUERNSEY or JERSEY MARROW. A fine, large, and heavy cropping variety   0   4

HOLLOW-CROWNED. Largest and best for general use ; a fine selected stock   ..   ..   per lb. 3s. 6d.   0   4

THE STUDENT. A first-class variety, but requires a good depth of soil   0   6

TURNIP-ROOTED. Excellent for shallow soils   0   6

Cultivation.—Parsnips are amongst the most nutritious of vegetables, and are quite easy to grow ; a good loamy soil free from stones being the most suitable. Have the ground thoroughly trenched (at least two feet deep) in the Autumn, and give a good dressing of farmyard manure, leaving it rough for the Winter. Early in February the bed should be levelled, forked down, and the seeds sown in drills about 1½ feet apart ; thin the young plants out to about 12 inches apart as soon as it is possible to handle them, and be sure to keep the ground thoroughly clean between the rows by frequent hoeing.

When specimen roots are being grown for exhibition, holes should be bored three or four feet deep with a crowbar, and filled with specially mixed soil, leaf mould, and wood ashes ; sow four or five seeds in each hole and thin out the plants, leaving one to each ; weed the ground carefully and give a sprinkling of soot to keep away pests.

Parsnips are always better when allowed to remain in the ground and lifted when required for use, but when it is necessary to lift and store them, they should be placed in dry sand in a dark shed or cellar.

"I obtained First Prize in open class and First Prize in local class at the Troedyrhiw Show with your Improved Hollow-crowned Parsnip. Also First Prize in open class at Merthyr Tydvil Show."—**Mr. T. PICTON,** Troedyrhiw.

"I lifted one of your Improved Hollow-crowned Parsnips last week measuring 3 feet 4 inches in length and 16 inches round the crown."—**Mr. F. TOPLEY,** Llansaintffraid.

"The Seeds turned out remarkably well last year ; the Parsnips and Carrots were excellent. None in this district to touch them."—**Mr. W. BINNY,** Badock.

"I won First and Second Prizes at our Show with your Improved Hollow-crowned Parsnip last year."—**Mr. J. V. GWYTHER,** Milton.

"I have pleasure in saying that I have taken the First Prize with your Improved Hollow-crowned Parsnip for several years."—**Mr. W. JONES,** Clydach.

"I think it is only fair that I should let you know how well I did with your Seeds last year. I had Parsnips 44 inches in length."—**Mr. W. WILSON,** Todholls.

SPINACH.

per oz.—s. d.

LONG STANDING. A most valuable variety for Summer use, as it stands the dry weather and keeps longer fit for use than any other sort   per qt. 2s. ; per pt. 1s. 3d.   0   4

MONSTROUS ITALIAN or VIROFLAY. Large and superior ; leaves dark green, and extremely thick and fleshy .. per qt. 2s. ; per pt. 1s. 3d.   0   4

NEW ZEALAND. Large and succulent   0   6

PERPETUAL or SPINACH BEET. Produces an abundance of green leaves close to the ground, as soon as these are cut fresh leaves appear, producing a supply during the Autumn and Winter   0   6

PRICKLY. For Winter use   ..   ..   per qt. 1s. 9d. ; per pt. 1s.   0   3

ROUND. For Summer use ; best for general crop   ..   ..   ..   per qt. 1s. 9d. ; per pt. 1s.   0   3

Cultivation.—All kinds like a good rich soil ; for the Summer Spinach select a warm border and sow the seeds in rows, where a little shade can be given ; it is often grown between the rows of Peas and Beans. It is important that the plants should be thinned out so as to allow plenty of room for each to develop, and that the crop should be kept well gathered while young.

Winter Spinach should be sown in July or August in drills one inch deep, and twelve inches apart in a well-drained border, care being taken to thin out well, otherwise the leaves will decay, as they will also if grown on heavy water-logged soil. New Zealand Spinach is a useful vegetable for the Summer, but will not stand the frost. Sow it on a warm border in April, and thin out the plants to about two feet apart.

RADISHES.

WHITE TURNIP.   DANIELS' BEST OF ALL. FRENCH BREAKFAST.   DANIELS' EARLY SCARLET TURNIP.

LONG VARIETIES.

per oz.—s. d.

DANIELS' BEST OF ALL. A new and distinct long variety ; colour, beautiful bright scarlet, flesh pure white, very tender and crisp. It comes into use very early ; and will be found a most useful variety, its bright colour making it very attractive both for the table and market purposes .. per pint 2s. 6d. 0 6

DANIELS' LONG WHITE. A new variety of excellent quality. It is the same shape as the Wood's Frame, and pure white in colour. The flesh is exceedingly firm and crisp, and it keeps solid and in good condition a long time 0 6

DANIELS' LONG SCARLET. A fine select Stock, beautiful colour, and very crisp, best for general crop per qt. 3s. ; per pt. 1s. 9d. 0 4
WOOD'S EARLY FRAME. The best for early crop, forces well
per qt. 3s. ; per pt. 1s. 9d. 0 3
SCARLET SHORT-TOP. Best for general crop and market purposes
per qt. 2s. ; per pt. 1s. 3d. 0 3

OLIVE-SHAPED VARIETIES.

FRENCH BREAKFAST. Scarlet, tipped white, oval shaped, forces useful market variety per qt. 3s. ; per pt. 1s. 9d. 0 4
OLIVE-SHAPED SCARLET. Early, good forcer, very tender and mild .. .. .. per qt. 3s. ; per pt. 1s. 9d. 0 4
OLIVE-SHAPED WHITE. Of quick growth, mild and crisp, handsome shape .. per qt. 3s. ; per pt. 1s. 9d. 0 4
OLIVE-SHAPED MIXED .. per qt. 3s. ; per pt. 1s. 9d. 0 3

" I may say this is the twenty-ninth year that I have used your Seeds, and up to now I have never had a failure."—Mr. R. TUCKER, Lynton.

TURNIP VARIETIES.

per oz.—s. d.

DANIELS' EARLY SCARLET TURNIP. A very early variety, the roots are firm, solid, and of true globular shape. Colour, rich glowing crimson scarlet. This is unquestionably the earliest forcing Radish extant. It grows very rapidly, is of delicate flavour, and is fit to use in three weeks from time of sowing per pint 2s. 6d. 0 6

CRIMSON GIANT. A new Radish of fine colour, and the same shape as our Early Scarlet Turnip, but attains more than twice the size in the same period of growth ; it also remains quite firm and crisp for a much longer time 0 6

SPARKLER (new). A quite distinct variety, the upper half of the root is bright scarlet and the lower portion pure white. The two colours are sharply defined and do not merge into each other. Has a most dainty appearance on the table 0 6

TURNIP, Scarlet, White-tipped. Delicious and handsome
per pint 1s. 9d. 0 4

TURNIP, Scarlet { For Summer }
" White and } qt. 2s. 6d. ; pt. 1s. 9d. 0 3
" Mixed { Autumn use }

WINTER RADISHES.

CHINESE ROSE-COLOURED. Of oblong shape and mild flavour ;
for Winter use .. .. per pint 2s. 0 4
BLACK SPANISH. For Winter salads ; sown in Autumn for Spring use .. .. per pint 2s. 6d. 0 6

Cultivation.—The Radish is one of the most popular of all salads, and to be crisp and mild in flavour should be quickly grown. It requires a good rich soil and liberal supplies of water during hot dry weather. Care should be taken in making the sowings to ensure a continuous succession rather than a great quantity at one time. The earliest sowing (for which our new variety, "Best of All," is most suitable) should be made between the rows of early Potatoes or other vegetables grown in frames on the hot-bed. Be sure to admit plenty of air as they will not bear excessive heat.

From February onwards sowings may be made about every fortnight in a warm sheltered bed out of doors, making provision for covering the beds with mats or straw on cold nights. This covering must always be removed in the day-time. It is most important, however, that protection from birds be made in the day-time, and fish netting is generally used for this purpose. In the middle of Summer a north-east border will be found a most suitable position for Radishes. Sow the seed broadcast and evenly, so that they are not too crowded. For Winter work the varieties "Chinese Rose" and "Black Spanish" are the best ; they should be sown in August and the plants thinned out about four inches apart.

TOMATOES.

TOMATO—DANIELS' KING EDWARD VII.
Reduced from a Photograph.

per pkt.—s. d.

☞ **DANIELS' KING GEORGE V.** This grand variety introduced by us last season has proved itself one of the most useful sorts for all purposes. It is of strong constitution and a free setter. The fruit which are of a rich glowing scarlet colour, are of perfect shape a id of excellent flavour. For exhibition purposes it will prove a great acquisition .. Per pkt. 1s. 6d. and 2 0

☞ **DANIELS' KING EDWARD VII.** This fine Tomato is a decided advance on most existing varieties, and certainly one of the best yet sent out. It is a free setter, and an abundant bearer. The large, splendidly coloured fruits, which are produced in handsome clusters of eight to ten or twelve, are very deep, almost round in form, and very solid and heavy, whilst in flavour it is all that can be desired. This fine Tomato is admirably suited for growing in pots, and will be found a really first-class variety, alike for the market grower or amateur exhibitor 1 0

☞ **DANIELS' No. 1.** A grand Tomato, which we have every confidence in recommending as one of the finest. The plant is of a sturdy habit and a robust constitution ; a free setter and exceedingly heavy cropper. The fruit are of good size, of the most beautiful form and perfectly smooth, and of splendid colour 1 0

☞ **WISETON PROLIFIC** (new). A grand variety raised by Mr. Musk, The Gardens, Wiseton Hall. The fruit, which are of good size, are of grand colour, very firm, and of excellent flavour. It is enormously prolific and will be found first-class for exhibition 1 0

Cultivation.—One of the chief things which has contributed to the great popularity of the Tomato is the fact that it is so very easily grown. It is now generally recognised that Tomatoes can be quite successfully cultivated without such heavy dressings of manure as were used at one time, although there are certain periods when good liberal dressings of manure are necessary ; but when the plants are young they do not need it.

For the earliest Spring crop the seed should be sown in January or early in February in pots or pans of light rich soil, and these should be placed on a shelf in the greenhouse ; the vessel should be covered with a sheet of glass to hold the moisture and kept at an even temperature until the seed has germinated. As soon as the plants have formed the seed leaf, have them potted off singly into three-inch pots and grow them on in a warm house, potting on into six-inch pots later, in which size they should remain until permanently planted out in the borders, or potted into the fruiting pots.

Many people prefer to grow their early crops in pots ten inches to twelve inches in diameter, claiming (we believe rightly) that they are better able to attend to the careful watering of the plants and thus avoid any injury to the roots. The treatment of young Tomato plants is pretty much the same as would be given to early Cucumbers, they should have a temperature of 60° during the day, and not less than 50°—55° at night. For a main crop sow the seed in February or March, then transfer into pots as before advised ; it is of great importance that the plants be kept sturdy and therefore air should be given on all favourable occasions. The drainage of both the pots in which the young plants are grown on and the borders or boxes in which they are to fruit should be very carefully looked to, so as to allow of their receiving copious supplies of water, especially during the fruiting period. When planted out in the greenhouse border, the plants should be placed about 18 inches apart and supported either by means of a stake or tied up with soft string to the roof, all side growths should be cleared off as they appear, and only the main stem allowed to grow away, this being stopped when it reaches the glass, or when three or four trusses of fruit have been set.

The best soil for Tomatoes is a good rich loam to which has been added a light dressing of farmyard manure, say one-fifth of the bulk ; many growers do not put any manure in the soil at the time of planting, leaving the feeding until the first truss of fruit has set, when they apply regular dressings of artificial manure, or give a mulching of well-decayed manure and water the same thoroughly in. In no case must the manure used be taken from a heap that is heated or the result will be disastrous.

TOMATOES—RED VARIETIES.

<small>per pkt.—s. d.</small>

☞ **THE DANIELS.** The fruit are of good size, rather above the medium, smooth, brilliant scarlet in colour, of beautiful form, exquisite flavour, and remarkably solid. It is a robust grower, and a marvellously profuse and continuous bearer. A first-class variety for cultivation under glass 1 0

***SUNRISE, NEW.** This grand variety has received a First Class Certificate from the Royal Horticultural Society for its numerous good qualities. It is very early, a free setter, and enormously prolific, bearing ten to eleven even sized fruit in one bunch. Colour rich scarlet. It is equally prolific either in the open air or under glass 1 0

***DANIELS' SCARLET PERFECTION.** Very handsome, perfectly round and smooth, firm and solid, flavour first-class and of a beautiful glossy scarlet colour; obtains first prize wherever exhibited 1 0

***DANIELS' HARBINGER.** This variety, being very early and a prolific bearer, will be found extremely valuable for growing in the open air. The fruit are round, smooth, solid, and of a bright red .. .. 6d. and 1 0

UP-TO-DATE. One of the heaviest cropping varieties, the smooth round fruit are of medium size and produced in clusters, bearing as many as twenty fruit at a joint, and of a bright crimson .. 1 0

<small>per pkt.—s. d.</small>

☞ **DANIELS' SELECTED OPEN AIR.** The heaviest cropping out-door variety with which we are acquainted. It is of hardy constitution, bearing large clusters of bright crimson fruit of medium size and good shape. Its distinct and delicate flavour will make it a favourite with all lovers of the Tomato 1 0

***FROGMORE SELECTED.** A very free setter .. .. 6d. and 1 0

***KING HUMBERT or CHISWICK RED** 0 6

***EARLY RUBY.** Very prolific, is of dwarf habit, good shape, colour bright scarlet, flesh solid, succeeds well in the open air .. 0 6

SUPREME. Awarded Highest Marks, R.H.S. The fruit are medium sized, round, very smooth, and of a beautiful scarlet 6d. and 1 0

***LAXTON'S OPEN-AIR.** Very early and hardy 1 0

***LARGE RED.** Very prolific and useful 0 6

MIXED. All sorts 0 3

YELLOW VARIETIES.

DANIELS' GOLDEN BEAUTY. A new and beautiful variety of splendid flavour. The fruit, which are freely produced in large clusters, are of good size, round, smooth, and of a rich bright golden yellow, occasionally flushed with a pale red .. 1 0

***GOLDEN EAGLE.** This is the most prolific variety that we know, and there is none to equal it in flavour .. .. 6d. and 1 0

***LARGE YELLOW IMPROVED.** A fine variety 0 4

Those marked thus * are the best for open-air cultivation.

"I am writing to you to tell you how pleased I am with your King Edward VII Tomato. I have been picking for the past fourteen days, and will, no doubt, be well supplied with fruit for the next eight or ten weeks. I have sent a photograph of them to the Amateur Gardening paper."—Mr. F. ONION, Colchester.

"I am well pleased with your Seeds, especially the King George V. Tomato."—Mr. L. WILLIAMS, Terdreth.

"I have grown your King Edward VII Tomato for three years, and can find nothing better."—Mr. W. BENTLEY, Tipton.

VEGETABLE MARROWS.

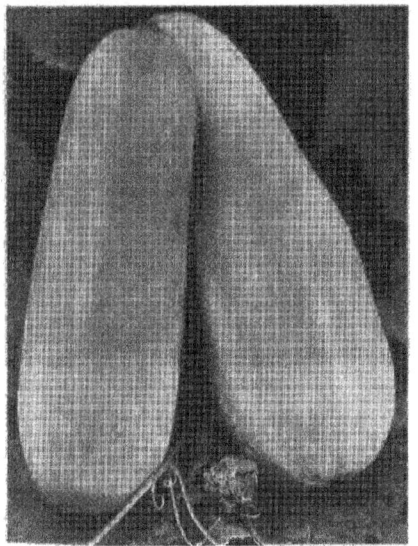

DANIELS' LARGE CREAM.

<small>per pkt.—s. d.</small>

☞ **DANIELS' LARGE CREAM.** One of the best Marrows in cultivation, grows to a large size, very handsome, and is an immense cropper, unequalled for general crop .. 0 6

☞ **DANIELS' GOLDEN CREAM.** A very prolific variety, fruits medium size, and of a beautiful pale cream colour, flavour first-class 0 6

PEN-Y-BYD (The best in the World). Awarded two First Class Certificates. This distinct variety is enormously prolific and a continuous bearer. The vine is extremely short-jointed, setting a fruit at every joint. The fruit is of handsome appearance, almost globular in form, sometimes very slightly ribbed, averaging about six inches in diameter 0 6

CUSTARD-SHAPED. Prolific, ornamental-shaped variety .. 0 4

GREEN BUSH. Very prolific; compact habit of growth .. 0 4

LONG GREEN. Good variety, forms a striking contrast with other kinds 0 4

LONG WHITE-RIBBED, or BUSH. Good; a prolific kind .. 0 4

MOORE'S CREAM. Very prolific, delicious flavour 0 3

VEGETABLE MARROW and SQUASH. Various sorts mixed } .. 0 3

Cultivation.—Vegetable Marrows are easy to grow, and it is possible in every garden to find a corner in which to grow two or three plants; they are often planted on old heaps of refuse, etc. It is not, however, essential that they should be planted on manure heaps, as they will grow quite well in the open garden in a hole which has been well manured, and in fact, they continue to fruit longer when so grown.

Copious supplies of water are necessary for Vegetable Marrows, and the fruits should be cut when young, as otherwise they become tough, and the plants cease bearing sooner. Sow the seeds singly in small pots, and plant out when about a foot high, giving protection for the first few nights. Another plan is to sow the seeds in the mound, where they are to grow, and to cover the plants with a hand-light, or some similar covering until frost has disappeared. Frequent waterings with liquid manure at the time of fruiting will add much vigour to the plants and size to the fruits.

"You will be pleased to know that the Seeds I had from you this spring have done splendidly; nothing better could be desired."—Mr. S. DODD, Shrewsbury.

"I am pleased to say that I took several Prizes with vegetables grown from your Seeds—seventeen Prizes in all."—Mr. E. MOUNTFORD, Bovey Tracey.

GARDEN TURNIPS.

WHITE-FLESHED VARIETIES.

DANIELS' IMPROVED SNOWBALL. *Reduced from a Photograph.*

	per oz.—s. d.
☞ **DANIELS' IMPROVED SNOWBALL.** An early and distinct variety of perfect shape, having only a single tap root. It is small, very solid, sweet and crisp, and of remarkably quick growth, flesh snow white and juicy, one of the very best for exhibition purposes, having obtained numerous first prizes per pint 2s.	0 6
☞ **DANIELS' GREEN TOP STONE.** One of the most useful varieties for late sowing, being very hardy will stand well into the Winter. The roots are of splendid shape, and the flesh firm, crisp, and juicy per pint 1s. 6d.	0 4
EARLY WHITE MILAN. Of similar shape and quality to the Red-top Milan, quite as early, but pure white in colour ..	0 6
CHIRK CASTLE (Black Stone). Very hardy, one of the most useful varieties for Winter	0 6
EARLY MILAN RED-TOP. One of the earliest varieties in cultivation, roots flat, of medium size and quite smooth. First-class Certificate, Royal Horticultural Society	0 4
EARLY WHITE STRAP-LEAVED. One of the earliest grown ..	0 4
EARLY WHITE STONE, or DUTCH SIX WEEKS per pint 1s.	0 2
SCARLET GEM. This is quite distinct; in shape, round and flat, the colour is a rich glowing scarlet; top small and neat; flesh white and of excellent flavour	0 6
VEITCH'S RED GLOBE. Useful variety	0 4

YELLOW-FLESHED VARIETIES.

	per oz. s. d.
DANIELS' GOLDEN GEM. A distinct variety. The top is small and neat; the roots are very handsome, with very fine tap-root. The skin and flesh are of a rich golden-yellow, and of excellent quality per pint 3s.	0 6
GOLDEN BALL. Fine stock.. .. .. per pint 1s. 6d.	0 4
ORANGE JELLY. Fine for late sowing .. per pint 1s. 6d.	0 4
ORANGE RED-TOP. Red top and golden yellow flesh	0 4

Cultivation.—This most wholesome vegetable is a lover of moisture, and to be crisp and juicy (as it should be) must be grown quickly and not checked in its growth. Choose good rich soil which has been dug over some time previously, and if possible, in a slightly shady position, as during the Summer months Turnips become stringy and hard if exposed to the hot sun.

For the first crop sow **Daniels' "Snowball"** on a very warm border early in March, and a succession of varieties onwards until July. Thin out the plants when in the seed leaf, leaving the single roots twelve inches apart. Give occasional dustings with wood ash and soot in the early morning to ward off the deadly Turnip fly.

For Autumn and Winter use sow in August and September either broadcast or in rows. Keep the hoe going and all weeds cleared off to hasten the growth and ensure crisp tender roots.

" I have always had such good results from your **Seeds**, and have been very fortunate with Prizes, having gained eleven last year."—**Mr. H. HAINES,** Southam.

DANIELS' GREEN TOP STONE.

SALSAFY.

	per oz.—s. d.
SANDWICH ISLAND MAMMOTH. Splendid variety per pkt. 6d.	1 6
COMMON .. .. " 3d.	0 9

Cultivation.—Salsafy is a vegetable which deserves to be more grown, as it has quite a rich and distinct flavour. Being a deep rooting plant, it must have well-worked land. The seed should be sown early in May in drills about fifteen inches apart, and the plants thinned out to about nine inches in the row. If specimen roots are desired for exhibition, they may be grown in holes made by a crowbar and filled with fine soil as recommended for Parsnips and Beetroot; a liberal supply of water should be given in dry weather and the soil kept loose between the rows by hoeing during the Summer. Salsafy should be lifted and stored in dry sand in a cellar for Winter use.

Scorzonera is a vegetable resembling Salsafy, being purple in colour. It requires similar treatment, but is somewhat hardier and requires a little more space in the drill.

SCORZONERA.

	per oz.—s. d.
RUSSIAN IMPROVED .. .. .. per. pkt. 4d.	1 0
COMMON .. .. 3d.	0 9

SEED POTATOES.

The accompanying photograph illustrates a corner of a plot of some acres in extent of DANIELS' "SENSATION" POTATO being lifted at the Royal Gardens, Windsor. Mr. MacKellar, to whose courtesy we are indebted for the photograph, has grown "Sensation" since its introduction with most satisfactory results, as the picture shows.

As a heavy cropper, giving beautiful pebble-shaped tubers, and possessing unusual powers for resisting disease, "Sensation" stands in the very first rank among Potatoes. The stock we offer this season is very carefully selected and possesses the same high qualities as that distributed in past years. Should any of our customers not yet have grown this variety, we confidently recommend them to add it to their order.

LIFTING A CROP OF DANIELS' "SENSATION" AT THE ROYAL GARDENS, WINDSOR.

HINTS ON POTATO CULTURE, &c.

Cultivation.—The varieties quoted in our list are the best in cultivation. It is most important that frequent changes of seed should be made, as Potatoes deteriorate if repeatedly saved from the same soil and district. For those growing for exhibition it is necessary to select varieties which are not only handsome in appearance, but also of known good quality for cooking purposes, such as "Southern Queen," "Duchess of Norfolk," "Sensation" and "President." For early work, "Duke of York," the well-known variety introduced by ourselves is still pre-eminent, and the increasing demand for this kind proves its superiority over all others as a first early.

Much depends upon the selection and treatment of the "sets," it is therefore necessary to secure good moderate sized Potatoes which should be set up on end in shallow boxes or trays, and allowed to sprout before being planted, as when this is done much advantage is gained both in the development of the plants and in the weight of the crops. Potatoes like a good open position in the garden and the most suitable soil is a medium to light soil in a well-drained position, the ground should be deeply dug and manured in the Autumn. Where stable manure is available a good dressing should be given at the time of planting, placing a layer on the bottom of the trenches; well-decayed leaf-mould, or the remains of an old mushroom bed are also excellent for this purpose.

When planting it is important that an abundance of room be left between the rows and the sets in the row; allow a distance of two feet between rows for the early, and three feet for the late strong-growing sorts, and twelve to eighteen inches between the sets in the rows. Where the land is naturally low and wet it is a capital plan to elevate the rows by forming ridges and so planting the sets on about a level with the natural soil; it is also good to keep the surface soil constantly stirred with the hoe until the earthing up commences.

When the young growths begin to push through the soil care must be taken to protect them from the frost by continually earthing up the soil round them. (Neglect of this has often resulted in the loss of a complete crop of Early Potatoes,) and when it is desired to grow exhibition specimens only, one haulm should be left to a plant, all the weakest ones being drawn out as they appear. Slight dressings of soot or of "Norwich Fertilizer" during the growing season will be of much advantage. Immediately the growth is completed, the crop should be lifted; choose fine weather for the work and store them after having had a few hours' sun on them.

Where small quantities only are grown it is much better to store Potatoes in a cool dry place where they can be easily got at, as they are not so liable to disease as when stored in a pit or trench.

IMPORTANT NOTICE.—Seed Potatoes procured during the Winter and early Spring, when not required for immediate planting should be taken out of the bag or package in which they are received and laid out in a dry, airy place protected from frost, or they will begin to sprout and a weakly growth will be the result.

TWO GRAND FIRST EARLY POTATOES

Daniels'
Defiance
Ashleaf.

Daniels'
Duke of York.

POTATOES.

FIRST EARLY VARIETIES.

DANIELS' DUKE OF YORK. This grand variety still holds its own as one of the best heavy-cropping Earlies in cultivation. In habit of growth, it is very compact, the haulm being only a foot high. The leaves are smooth and of a rich glossy green colour, whilst the tubers cluster compactly round the stem, and are very easy to raise. The tubers are large, oval, smooth and handsome, and distinct in appearance, the eyes are few and quite even with the surface, ensuring a minimum of waste ; the flesh is dry and mealy when cooked, and of the most excellent flavour. (See illustration, opposite page.) **Per 14 lb. 2s. 6d. ; 56 lb. 8s. 6d. ; cwt. 15s.**

A POTATO CENSUS.

Reprinted from THE GARDENERS' CHRONICLE.

"We now present a list of the most popular early and mid-season varieties of Potatoes. These details have been furnished us, in reply to our enquiries, by our correspondents in all parts of Great Britain and Ireland. It must be borne in mind that the votes have been given by cultivators in no way commercially interested in the Potato. Whatever differences there may be in individual opinions and in other circumstances, the very large proportion of votes cast for a few varieties shows quite clearly the high opinion generally entertained as to their merits. In the list of early varieties, Duke of York (*distributed by Messrs. Daniels Bros. of Norwich, in 1893*), heads the list with 78 votes and this variety is followed by Sharpe's Victor with 61 votes."

DANIELS' DEFIANCE ASHLEAF. This variety has now been several years before the public and still holds its place as one of the best of the first earlies, and in most seasons it can be lifted before the disease makes its appearance. It is one of the heaviest cropping varieties of this class, producing a full crop of good sized tubers of first-class table quality, having the exceptional flavour found only in the best Ashleaf sorts. (See illustration, opposite.) **Per 14 lb. 3s. 6d. ; 56 lb. 12s.**

OLD ASHLEAF. A fine old variety, noted for its good table quality (scarce) **Per 14 lb. 3s. 6d. ; 56 lb. 12s.**

MYATT'S ASHLEAF, IMPROVED. This will be found a heavier and more reliable cropper than the old variety, and of exceptionally good table quality. **Per 14 lb. 2s. 6d. ; 56 lb. 8s. 6d.**

EARLY ASHLEAF KIDNEY. Useful variety. **Per 14 lb. 2s. 6d. ; 56 lb. 8s. 6d.**

SOUTHERN QUEEN. An early White Kidney of handsome appearance, the tubers being of a beautiful kidney shape, and is an abundant cropper of the best table quality. The haulm is dwarf and of good constitution. The grower says, "I think I never lifted such a handsome lot as the Southern Queen, not a mis-shaped tuber." This was awarded First Prize in the Cooking Competition at the National Potato Society's Exhibition on December 13th, 1906.
Per 14 lb. 2s. 6d. ; 56 lb. 8s. 6d. ; cwt. 15s.

EARLY ECLIPSE. A handsome first early white kidney of great productiveness, with white skin and flesh, it cooks well early and late, and during the past season it has again yielded a very heavy crop of nice clean tubers free from disease.
Per 14 lb. 2s. 6d. ; 56 lb. 8s. 6d. ; cwt. 15s.

LADY LLEWELYN. A fine early potato, similar in appearance and growth to the well-known Sir J. Llewelyn, but of stronger constitution and a much heavier cropper, and of first-rate cooking quality.
Per 14 lb. 3s. ; 56 lb. 10s. 6d. ; cwt. 18s.

MAY QUEEN. A first early White Kidney of exceptional productiveness. The tubers are kidney shaped, with white skin and flesh, and of first-class table quality. This is one of the best of the early kidney varieties.
Per 14 lb. 3s. ; 56 lb. 10s. 6d. ; cwt. 18s.

	per 14 lb.	per 56 lb.			
SIR JOHN LLEWELYN. This splendid White Kidney, in consideration of its earliness, heavy cropping, good quality, and disease resisting properties, has become highly popular. The tubers are of good size and shape, and when cooked, white and floury.			s. d.	s. d.	
Award of Merit, R.H.S. This is a really first-class early Potato.	per cwt. 15s.		2 6	8 6	
RECORDER. A splendid first early variety. A cross between the Ashleaf and Beauty of Hebron. The very handsome tubers are of good size, with very shallow eyes, whilst the flesh is white and of first-rate quality when cooked. It is a strong grower and enormously productive	per cwt. 15s.		2 6	8 6	
EXPRESS (Sharpe). A fine early White Kidney of handsome appearance and excellent cooking quality, and is at the same time a very heavy and sure cropper	per cwt. 15s.		2 6	8 6	
EARLY PURITAN. Awarded First Class Certificate, R.H.S. An early variety of great excellence, and a good cropper	per cwt. 15s.		2 6	8 6	
SHARPE'S VICTOR. A specially selected and improved stock of this well known early variety, of fine appearance, and producing twice the weight of the old sort	per cwt. 18s.		3 0	10 6	

EVIDENCE OF QUALITY.

"I might say that I consider your **Duke of York Potato** the best I have ever grown."—Mr. C. MANN, Aldeburgh.

"The Duke of York is the best Potato in the world, and ought never to run out."—Mr. A. MARSINGALL, Poughkeepsie.

"I must tell you that I took First Prize for your **Duke of York Potato.**"—Mrs. SUMTERS, Chesham.

"I am very pleased to say that the **Recorder Potatoes** I had from you turned out splendidly this season, after having been planted only eight weeks."—Mr. G. M. STONE, Birchover, Winster.

"Your **Duke of York Potato** took First Prize."—Mr. H. GARWOOD, Writtle.

"I took these First Prizes with your **Recorder Potatoes.**"—Mr. G. W. STONE, Birchover.

SECOND EARLY VARIETIES.

DANIELS' DUCHESS OF NORFOLK.

DANIELS' DUCHESS OF NORFOLK. *Reduced from a Photograph.*

DANIELS' DUCHESS OF NORFOLK. A grand second early variety of handsome appearance and a heavy cropper. It is a second early, growing about 2 feet high, the foliage being quite distinct. The tubers, which are pebble-shaped or round, with shallow eyes, are of good size, producing a nice even crop of marketable tubers with a minimum of small. The skin and flesh are white and of the finest table quality ; very useful for exhibition.

Per 14 lb. 3s. ; 56 lb. 10s. 6d. ; cwt. 18s.

DANIELS' PRINCE EDWARD. This grand new Potato is a seedling from our celebrated Duke of York, crossed with The Factor. It is a second early of enormous productiveness, having produced 32 times its own weight. It shows the character of both its parents, and is a nice upright grower (about 2 feet in height) with strong leathery dark green foliage and white flowers. The tubers, which are kidney-shaped, with clear white skin and flesh, are of the finest table quality.

Per 7 lb. 1s. 9d. ; 14 lb. 3s. ; 56 lb. 10s. 6d.

		per 14 lb.		per 56 lb.	
		s.	d.	s.	d.
DANIELS' EARLY QUEEN. A grand early variety of extra fine quality and enormous productiveness. It is kidney-shaped, somewhat inclined to oblong ; the eyes few and almost even with the surface. The flesh is white and mealy when cooked	per cwt. 15s.	2	6	8	6
BEAUTY OF HEBRON. A well-known excellent variety, of good table quality	„ 15s.	2	6	8	6
EARLY ROSE. A well-known variety. Fine for early use on light soils	„ 15s.	2	6	8	6
EARLY WHITE HEBRON. A well known variety of fine cooking quality	„ 15s.	2	6	8	6
BRITISH QUEEN. A second early variety of great merit. The skin and flesh are white, and of extra fine table quality ; this, combined with its great productiveness and good keeping qualities, make it a most desirable variety for all purposes	per cwt. 15s.	2	6	8	6
KING EDWARD VII. A very fine Main Crop variety ; the haulm grows to the height of two feet and is fairly robust, producing a large crop of handsome tubers. The skin is white, with a blotch of pink about the eyes, which gives it a very pleasing appearance. It is a good cooker and free from disease ; for exhibition it is first class	per cwt. 14s.	2	6	8	6
MAIRSLAND QUEEN. A second early white round of very hardy constitution, the haulm being of medium height and very robust. The tubers are almost round in shape, with fleet eyes, skin and flesh white, the latter being beautifully white and floury when cooked, and of first-class flavour. It is a heavy and sure cropper	per cwt. 15s.	2	6	8	6
SNOWDROP. Tubers well formed, eyes shallow, skin clear, and flesh beautifully white and mealy when cooked; an abundant cropper, and very distinct. First Class Certificate, R.H.S.		3	0	10	6
WINDSOR CASTLE. An excellent second early variety. Tubers oblong or pebble-shaped, skin white, very heavy cropper; flesh firm, white, and of splendid quality. First Class Certificate, R.H.S.		3	0	10	6

" I bought two pounds of Prince Edward Potatoes from you last Spring, and I have just lifted them. I have got just seventeen pounds, and not one diseased."—**Mr. H. STONE,** Morpeth.

" I have just dug up a root of Early Puritan Potato, and on it I had thirty-three tubers, weighing 8½ pounds."—**Mr. A. PANGBOURNE,** Weymouth.

A GRAND MAIN CROP POTATO,

RADIUM.

RADIUM. *Reduced from a Photograph.*

RADIUM. This is a Main Crop variety, and has again proved itself one of the heaviest croppers in our trial grounds. The tubers are oval in shape, with beautifully netted skin, and of the finest table quality. The haulm which grows to about two feet in height is very robust, and of a fine dark green, and the flowers which are produced in abundance are white. As a cropper and cooker we consider it one of the best introductions of recent years. **Per 14 lb. 2s. 6d. ; 56 lb. 8s. 6d. ; cwt. 15s.**

COLOURED VARIETIES FOR EXHIBITION.

The following varieties will be found first-class for exhibition, and are at the same time heavy croppers of good table quality.

	per 14 lb.	per 56 lb.
	s. d.	s. d.
DANIELS' EMPEROR FREDERICK. The tubers are large, handsome, kidney-shaped; skin rich purple, mottled with crimson. A good cropper and cooks well. First class for exhibition purposes	3 0	10 6
PEERLESS ROSE. A flat, smooth, very handsome kidney-shaped Potato; skin of a delicate pink colour, eyes even with the surface; fine quality, and excellent for exhibition	3 0	10 6
PURPLE PERFECTION. A heavy cropping purple round variety, of strong constitution and excellent quality, fine for exhibition	3 0	10 6
QUEEN OF THE VELDT. A handsome purple kidney, of extra fine cropping and cooking qualities. A most useful exhibition variety	3 6	12 0
READING RUSSET. A handsome red round variety of good quality. Fine for Exhibition	3 0	10 6
THE SUTTON FLOURBALL. A red round variety of extra good cropping qualities, and good table quality; very useful for exhibition purposes, and a good disease resister	3 0	10 6
VICAR OF LALEHAM. A handsome round variety, with rich dark purple skin, a good cropper, cooks well, and fine for exhibition	3 0	10 6
WONDERFUL RED KIDNEY. A heavy cropping and handsome red kidney, with clear smooth skin; fine for exhibition	2 6	8 6

EVIDENCE OF QUALITY.

" I am very pleased to say that I generally take First Prize with your Potatoes, and hope to do so again."—**Mr. T. HAWKES,** Cropedy.

" I am very pleased to inform you that I won four First, two Second, and one Third Prize with your Potatoes; also a Special Prize for a Collection of Vegetables."—**Mr. H. J. BRAKE,** Preston Plucknett.

" I was very pleased with the **Radium** Potatoes, which turned out very well."—**Mr. A. E. DENNY,** Leiston.

" I planted seven pounds of your **President** Potatoes, and have to-day dug up 175 pounds, none small, and the quality A1."—**Mr. W. MIZEN,** Codford.

MAIN CROP AND LATE VARIETIES.
DANIELS' SENSATION.

DANIELS' SENSATION. *Reduced from a Photograph.*

DANIELS' SENSATION. This grand Main Crop Potato is one of the heaviest-cropping and best varieties we have ever grown. It is of a good, robust constitution, the haulm growing about two feet high. The tubers are of good size, thick pebble-shape, with very shallow eyes, almost level with the surface; the skin is white and slightly netted—a sure indication of good cooking qualities—the flesh being white, mealy, and of the finest texture. Its splendid cropping and good culinary qualities, combined with its very handsome appearance, have made this variety a great favourite alike with the cook and exhibitor.   Per 14 lb. 2s. 6d. ; 56 lb. 8s. 6d. ; cwt. 15s.

MILLION MAKER. A grand Main Crop White Kidney of exceptionally heavy cropping quality and a good disease resister. It is of true kidney shape with white skin and flesh, and of superb cooking quality. On account of its handsome shape will be found invaluable for Exhibition purposes.   Per 14 lb. 3s. ; 56 lb. 10s. 6d. ; cwt. 18s.

PRESIDENT. This is without doubt the heaviest cropping late potato yet introduced, and has, during the past season, resisted disease better than any other variety. It resembles the Up-to-date in growth, and is of a strong hardy constitution. The tubers are somewhat oblong in shape, with white skin and flesh, and is of grand table quality.
      Per 14 lb. 2s. 6d. ; 56 lb. 8s. 6d. ; cwt. 15s.

THE FACTOR. A fine oval-shaped White-skinned Potato of robust habit, and a splendid cropper, the tubers being of good size and handsome appearance. It is one of the best keepers, and will cook splendidly quite into May. One of the very best Main Crop varieties of recent introduction ..   ..   per cwt. 15s.

DUCHESS OF CORNWALL. A Main Crop variety of exceptional merit, the tubers are of good size and thick pebble-shaped with a white skin. The haulm is dwarf, strong, and quite distinct. It is a grand cropper, remarkably free from disease, and of excellent table quality ..   ..   per cwt. 16s.

ELECTRIC SPARK. A fine new Main Crop variety of vigorous constitution and an enormous cropper. The tubers are kidney shaped and somewhat inclined to oblong with very deep eyes ; skin and flesh white. It is a strong grower with bushy haulm and dark green leaves, flowers pink. We can strongly recommend this variety both on account of its great productiveness and fine table quality ..   ..   per cwt. 16s.

UP-TO-DATE. A large handsome Kidney of very heavy cropping qualities, skin roughly netted, flesh white, dry, and mealy when cooked ..   ..   per cwt. 12s.

	per 14 lb.	per 56 lb.
	s. d.	s. d.
THE FACTOR	2 6	8 6
DUCHESS OF CORNWALL	2 6	8 6
ELECTRIC SPARK	2 6	8 6
UP-TO-DATE	2 0	7 6

" You will be pleased to hear I again won First Prize in the open class with your **Sensation Potato.** I also won First Prize for two Red Cabbages."—Mr. A. BARNESBY, Beverley.
" I might say that the **Sensation Potatoes** were excellent last year ; two of the tubers weighing 5½ lbs."—Mr. J. BOWEN, Poulton.

" I have taken two First Prizes at our show with your **Sensation** and Royal Norfolk Potatoes."—Mr. T. B. MILNE, Basingstoke.
" I have grown some excellent crops from your **Sensation Potatoes.**" Mr. A. SINGLETON, Langrish.

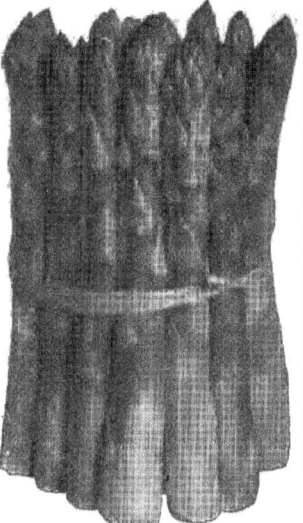

ASPARAGUS—CONNOVER'S COLOSSAL.

MISCELLANEOUS PLANTS & ROOTS

ASPARAGUS PLANTS.

An abundance of fine Asparagus may be grown with less than half the expense usually incurred in making costly "beds," and will succeed admirably on most soils when planted in lines or clumps on the Kitchen Garden borders, or amongst dwarf-growing Fruits where the space will admit, a liberal cultivation being all that is required to ensure the best results. The roots are liable to injury if removed during severe weather in Winter. They are best planted when growth has commenced in Spring, and when they can be carefully taken up and packed so as to travel a long journey, without injury. They should, however, in all cases be planted as quickly as possible after receiving them. We consider March and April the best months for planting in the open ground.

CONNOVER'S COLOSSAL. Two and three years old .. .. per 100, 6s. and 7s. 6d.
TRUE-GIANT. Two and three years old .. .. .. per 100, 3s. 6d. and 5s.

ASPARAGUS SEED.

per oz.—s. d.
TRUE GIANT. A fine variety, producing large heads of excellent quality per lb. 4s. 0 4
CONNOVER'S COLOSSAL. A very large variety, very prolific, and of fine flavour
per lb. 6s. 0 6
EARLY GIANT PURPLE (Argenteuil). As grown by the celebrated French growers for
Paris Market; robust variety of the most delicious flavour .. .. per lb. 7s. 0 8

RHUBARB.

One of the most useful, wholesome, and profitable of garden plants. The ground for this should be well broken up and manured, and the plants should be 2½ to 3 feet apart. March is the best month for planting, but it is not advisable to pull any of the stalks the first season for fear of unduly weakening the growth. A top-dressing of well-decayed manure in Winter is very beneficial.

DAWS' CHAMPION. A fine new variety of great size and splendid colour. Very productive.
each 1s.; per doz. 10s. 6d.
CHAMPAGNE. Deep red stems, early, one of the very best for general use.
each 1s.; per doz. 10s. 6d.
PARAGON (Kershaw). The most prolific kind known .. each 1s.; per doz. 10s. 6d.
NEW CRIMSON QUEEN. A fine new and very early Rhubarb. The stalk is of a beautiful bright red quite through, whilst it is also of a very superior and delicate flavour.
each 2s.; per doz. 21s.

Two-year Seedlings, strong transplanted roots of the following, per doz. 6s.

MYATT'S LINNÆUS. ROYAL ALBERT. MYATT'S VICTORIA.

SEA KALE.

This valuable esculent is easily forced if care is taken only to apply heat gradually, as it will not succeed if placed in too high a temperature at starting. Place several crowns a few inches apart in large pots, and stand them in a temperature of about 45 degrees, with an inverted pot placed over each to exclude light and insure blanching; a mushroom house, pit or cellar, will do well for this purpose. Sea Kale may also be easily forced in the open ground by covering it over with large specially made pots, and applying fermenting material. The heads should be cut when in about the condition shown in illustration, and taken off in the same way.

STRONG PLANTING ROOTS .. .. .. per doz. 1s.; per 100, 7s. 6d.
GOOD STRONG ROOTS, for forcing .. .. per doz. 1s. 6d.; per 100, 10s. 6d.
EXTRA STRONG ROOTS, for forcing, very fine .. .. per doz. 2s.; per 100, 15s.

SWEET AND POT HERBS.

We have a fine collection of these, including the following useful sorts :—

		per doz.—s. d.			per doz.—s. d.
BALM	—	.. 4 0	ROSEMARY	.. each 8d.	6 0
CHAMOMILE	..	.. 4 0	RUE	..	.. 4 0
CHIVES	..	.. each 6d. 5 0	SAGE, Common	.. each 6d.	4 0
HOREHOUND	..	.. 4 0	SAVORY, WINTER	..	.. 4 0
HYSSOP	..	.. 4 0	SORREL, GIANT FRENCH	.. each 6d.	5 0
LAVENDER	..	.. each 6d. 5 0	TARRAGON	.. each 6d.	4 0
MARJORAM, POT	..	.. 4 0	THYME, LEMON	.. each 6d.	5 0
MINT, LAMB	..	.. 4 6	„ COMMON	..	.. 4 0
„ PEPPER	..	.. 4 0	WORMWOOD	—	.. 1 0
PENNYROYAL	..	.. each 6d. 5 0			

The most useful varieties assorted, our selection, per doz. 4s.; per 100, 25s.

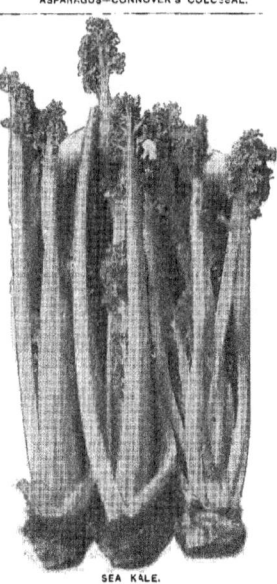

SEA KALE.

MISCELLANEOUS PLANTS, ROOTS, AND SEEDS.

ARTICHOKE—DANIELS' WHITE MAMMOTH.

ARTICHOKES.

DANIELS' WHITE MAMMOTH. This is a pure white skin variety of the Jerusalem Artichoke. The tuber, which is are more regularly formed than those of the old variety, are somewhat globular in shape, and of excellent quality.
Per 14 lb. 2s. 6d. ; 56 lb. 8s. 6d.
JERUSALEM. Good sound tubers
per peck (14 lbs.) 2s. ; bush. (56 lbs.) 7s.
GLOBE. Strong plants ..   .. per doz. 1 s.

CARDOONS.

per pkt.—s. d.
SMOOTH SOLID. Cultivated for the mid-rib of the leaf
LARGE SPANISH 0 6

SEA KALE (Seed).

ORDINARY   ..   .. per pint 2s. ; per oz. 6d.
LILY WHITE (Special) ..   per pint 3s. 6d. ; per oz. 1s.

For Plants, see page 51.

FRUIT SEEDS.

CURRANT, GOOSEBERRY, GRAPE, STRAWBERRY, RASPBERRY, APPLE PIPS, PEAR PIPS   ..   each 6d. and 1s. per pkt.

RHUBARB (Seed).

	per pkt.—s. d.		per pkt.—s. d.
CHAMPAGNE	.. .. 0 6	MYATT'S LINNÆUS	— 0 6
MONARCH. Excellent new		MYATT'S VICTORIA	— 0 6
sort	.. .. 0 6	MIXED	— 0 4
ROYAL ALBERT	.. 0 6		

CROSNES (Stachys tuberifera). First Class Certificate, Royal Horticultural Society. This is a new tuberous vegetable introduced from Japan. It is a hardy plant, producing a large quantity of tubers in the same way as the Potato. Its culture is very easy, as it grows well in any good garden soil, and is readily propagated by means of its numerous tubers. They may be left in the ground until required for use, as the severest frost does not injure them in any way. The best and simplest way of cooking this vegetable is to boil in water with a pinch of salt, then fry them. They are of delicate flavour, somewhat resembling boiled Chestnuts.

FINE ENGLISH GROWN TUBERS   ..   —   per lb. 1s. ; 7 lb. 6s.

CHIVES AND GARLIC.

CHIVES. Fine strong clumps   ..   .. each 6d. ; per doz. 5s.
GARLIC BULBS   ..   .. per lb. 1s.

POTATO ONIONS.

BULBS. Fine select stock   ..   ..   .. per lb. 6d. ; 12 lb. 5s.

MERCURY (Good King Henry).

(Chenopodium Bonus Henricus.)

A hardy and useful vegetable, much grown in Lincolnshire ; it forms an excellent substitute for Spinach ..   ..   .. per pkt. 6d.

SHALLOTS.

(Sow and Cultivate as Onions.)

Far superior to Onions for pickling.

BULBS. Fine sound bulbs   ..   ..   .. per lb. 1s. ; 7 lb. 6s.
SEED. New Jersey. Extra large   ..   .. per pkt. 6d. and 1s.

DANDELION.

Very valuable for Winter Salads when blanched.

per pkt.—s. d.
IMPROVED LARGE-LEAVED 0 6
THICK-LEAVED CABBAGING 0 6

EGG PLANT OR AUBERGINE.

(Solanum Esculentum.)

Till comparatively recent times these handsome plants have only been grown for decorative purposes. They are now, however, coming into great favour as a delicious esculent, and when generally known will be in great demand, and we should advise all who have not yet grown these to give them a trial.

per pkt.—s. d.
DANIELS' IMPROVED LARGE PURPLE. Fine handsome fruit ; very prolific   ..   .. 6d. and 1 0
BLACK CHINESE. Very effective   .. 6d. and 1 0
LARGE WHITE. A very useful variety .. 6d. and 1 0

"Your Seeds have given me the greatest satisfaction this year, and I can recommend you to many of my friends."—Mr. T. BAINBRIDGE, Hesto .

SHALLOTS, NEW JERSEY.

HOME-GROWN FARM SEEDS.

MANGELS.

Our stocks of these are all English grown, and can be fully relied on as really first-class. All growers of Mangels should give our Seeds a trial, as we feel sure the result would be most satisfactory.

	s.	d.
☞ **DANIELS' CORONATION GLOBE.** A new variety carefully selected by ourselves. It is of large size, perfect form, very solid, and of a feeding quality rivalling the famous Golden Tankard; a very heavy cropper	1	3
DANIELS' INTERMEDIATE or GATE-POST. A grand stock; one of the finest Mangels ever introduced, grows to a great size, with a uniform crop of very heavy, handsome, and clean roots	1	3
DANIELS' RED INTERMEDIATE. Our stock is very fine, and can be highly recommended	1	6
DANIELS' GOLDEN TANKARD. Specially selected for its yellow or golden flesh, its richness in saccharine matter, and handsome shape	1	6
DANIELS' CHAMPION ORANGE GLOBE. Highly recommended for its neat top, fine clear skin, and tap root; a heavy cropper	1	3
YELLOW GLOBE. Good stock	1	3

Price per Cwt. on application.

SWEDE TURNIPS.

	per lb.—s.	d.
DANIELS' NORFOLK GIANT PURPLE-TOP. The roots are somewhat oval, and of a deep rich purple. It is a heavy cropper and excellent keeper. All farmers should give it a trial	0	9
DANIELS' IMPROVED PURPLE-TOP. Selected Stock	0	8
DANIELS' DEFIANCE GREEN-TOP. A first-class keeper	0	9

WHITE-FLESHED TURNIPS.

DANIELS' NORFOLK GREEN ROUND. Excellent for main crop, hardiest of the Globe varieties	0	8
DANIELS' PURPLE-TOP MAMMOTH. Early Turnip, very heavy cropper, large and handsome roots	0	10
BELL or DECANTER. Extra selected stock	0	10

YELLOW-FLESHED TURNIPS.

DANIELS' GREEN-TOP YELLOW SCOTCH. Grows a heavy crop, flesh solid and juicy, much relished by cattle	0	9
DANIELS' PURPLE-TOP YELLOW SCOTCH	0	10

Price per Bushel on application.

CABBAGES.

	per lb.—s.	d.
DANIELS' CHAMPION DRUMHEAD. Produces large solid heads per oz. 4d.	4	0
DANIELS' EARLY DRUMHEAD. Comes into use some weeks before the larger varieties per oz. 4d.	4	0
ROBINSON'S DRUMHEAD 4d.	3	6
THOUSAND-HEADED KALE. Selected stock 3d.	2	0

CARROTS.

	per lb.—s.	d.
DANIELS' GIANT YELLOW INTERMEDIATE. Our own stock; grown from selected roots, and the heaviest cropper we know of		6 0
GIANT WHITE BELGIAN. Very large and of fine quality	All	6 0
YELLOW BELGIAN. Best for general crop, roots large and of good shape	Clean	5 0
JAMES' SCARLET or INTERMEDIATE. A heavy cropper, one of the best for shallow soils	Seed	6 0
ALTRINCHAM. A fine long Red variety		6 0

KOHL RABI.

EARLY WHITE VIENNA. Best for garden pkt. 4d.; per oz. 1s.		
DANIELS' SHORT-TOP GREEN. For field culture	2	6

CLEANED GRASS SEEDS & CLOVERS,

For all Soils and Situations, for Pasturage, Ensilage, &c.
Samples and Special Quotations on Application.

DANIELS' MIXTURES.

FOR ALTERNATE HUSBANDRY OR ROTATION CROPS.

DANIELS' SPECIAL PERMANENT PASTURE.

FOR LIGHT, MEDIUM, AND HEAVY SOILS.

DANIELS' SPECIAL RENOVATING MIXTURES.

RYE GRASSES AND CLOVERS OF THE FINEST QUALITIES

Orders for Farm Seeds not less than 20s. Carriage paid to any Station in England and Wales. £2 and upwards free to any Railway Station in Scotland or Shipping port in Ireland.

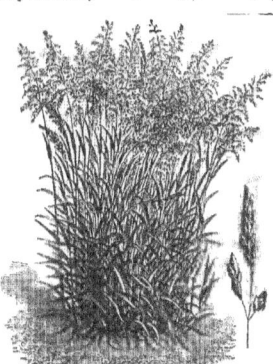

ROUGH-STALKED MEADOW GRASS.

OUR FARM SEED CATALOGUE FOR SPRING, 1912,

Will be published on March 1st, and will be sent gratis and post free on application. If you are interested, let us register your name at once.
It contains a complete list of the choicest sorts of Mangels, Swedes, Turnips, and other Root Seeds, Clovers, Grasses, and other Forage Plants, besides many valuable hints on cultivation.

DANIELS' SUPERIOR GRASS SEEDS FOR LAWNS.

☞ For many years we have given close attention to the selection of the most suitable Grasses for producing the best Lawns, Tennis Courts, Cricket Grounds, Golf Links, &c., and we have much pleasure in recommending the splendid mixtures we offer as the very best procurable for the purposes named. March and April are the best months for sowing in Spring, and September for Autumn sowing. These Grass Seeds are usually supplied without Clover, but in all cases Clover will be added if desired.

No. 1. DANIELS' SPECIAL MIXTURE FOR LAWNS.

This is a special mixture of the finest leaved dwarf evergreen Grasses, and will produce an extra fine close velvety turf. First-class for making new lawns or for renovating. Highly recommended.   Per lb. 2s., per bushel, 30s.

No. 2. DANIELS' FINE MIXTURE OF DWARF GRASSES.

A splendid mixture of fine Grasses, suitable for Tennis Courts, Croquet Grounds, &c., also a most useful mixture for renovating bare and weak patches.
Per lb. 1s. 6d., per bushel 25s.

No. 3. DANIELS' MIXTURE OF DWARF GRASSES.

A good cheap mixture for producing a fine close turf.
Per lb. 1s., per bushel 20s.

No. 4. DANIELS' MIXTURE FOR SHADY LAWNS AND UNDER TREES.

A useful mixture for producing a fine turf in enclosed and shady places.   Per lb. 1s. 6d., per bushel 25s.

No. 5. DANIELS' PEERLESS MIXTURE

Without Perennial Rye Grass.
FOR GARDEN LAWNS.

This mixture is composed of the finest dwarf-growing Grasses for producing a fine velvety Turf of extra good quality.
Per lb. 1s. 6d. and 2s., per bushel 25s. and 30s.

No. 6. DANIELS' PEERLESS MIXTURE.

Without Perennial Rye Grass.
FOR TENNIS LAWNS.

A mixture of fine Grasses for producing a close, dwarf, springy Turf, most suitable for this purpose.
Per lb. 1s. 6d. and 2s., per bushel 25s. and 30s.

Where larger quantities than those mentioned are required we shall always be pleased to make special quotations.

N.B.—Where no definite instructions are given, we shall supply our Special Mixtures, containing Perennial Rye Grass.

DANIELS' SUPERIOR GRASS SEEDS FOR GOLF LINKS, &c.

A GOLF GREEN, SOWN WITH OUR SPECIAL MIXTURE.

No. 7. DANIELS' SPECIAL MIXTURES FOR GOLF LINKS.

For Putting Greens. A selection of the finest Grasses for producing a smooth even surface. Per bushel 30s.

Other mixtures for Golf Courses, 15s. to 25s. per bushel.

No. 8. DANIELS' SPECIAL MIXTURES FOR BOWLING GREENS.

A selection of fine Grasses, specially adapted for hard wear and at the same time producing a fine even turf.

Per lb. 1s. and 1s. 6d., per bushel 20s. to 25s.

No. 9. DANIELS' SPECIAL MIXTURES FOR CRICKET & FOOTBALL GROUNDS.

Per bushel 15s. to 20s.

No. 10. DANIELS' SPECIAL MIXTURES FOR PARKS, RECREATION GROUNDS, &c.

Per bushel 15s. and 18s.

Where larger quantities than those mentioned are required we shall always be pleased to make special quotations.

Hints on Lawns.—There is no part of a garden which requires such careful and regular attention as the lawn, and certainly there is nothing more delightful than a well-kept lawn in proximity to a residence. It is quite possible for even the smallest cottage to have its plot of grass, providing sufficient care is taken at the outset in forming it. The following hints will be found of help to those about to form or renovate a lawn.

Choose an open space as level as possible, and naturally well drained; if the ground is at all uneven it must be levelled by removing the higher to the lower parts. The whole of the ground should be well dug and pulverized to a depth of eighteen inches, giving a good dressing of manure at the same time, after digging rake the surface level and very carefully remove all stones, rolling it quite firm all over. Care must be taken not to allow any carting or wheeling upon the ground after being dug unless boards are laid down for the purpose.

The best time for sowing Grass Seeds is the Spring, during March and April, although satisfactory results are often obtained when sown in September. To ensure the securing of a good thick even turf, it is imperative that the seed be sown very thickly, in fact it is much better to sow a liberal quantity at first than to have to renovate at the end of the season. Four or six bushels per acre is not too much, generally speaking about one to two lb. to a rod of ground is a good dressing.

Remove all weeds as they appear and as soon as the grass is three or four inches high it should be mown with a scythe and well rolled. Frequent rolling and cutting must be done if a really fine turf is desired, and an occasional dressing of Daniels' Lawn "Manure," applying about two to three ounces to the square yard, will be found to promote a healthy growth of the young sward.

The renovating and improving of old lawns is most important work and may be done either in March or September. The seed should be sown evenly over all bare places and in all holes, using the finest lawn mixture; cover the seeds with a slight sprinkling of finely sifted soil and roll the whole surface down evenly and firmly. The sowing of Lawn Seeds should always be done in calm fine weather when there is no fear of either the seed being blown about or of the soil adhering to the roller. Small birds are very fond of grass seeds, and it is therefore most advisable to give some protection (when convenient) until the young grass gets hold.

HORTICULTURAL MANURES, &c.
DANIELS' NORWICH FERTILIZER.

Without doubt the finest Manure for Fruit, Chrysanthemums, and all general Garden Crops; the sales have again more than doubled those of any previous year, and we strongly recommend our customers to give it a trial.

EVIDENCES OF QUALITY

From Mr. C. FOX,
Gardener to Lady Mansel,
Catton, Norwich.

"Having again this year given your Norwich Fertilizer a thorough trial for growing Black Hambro Grapes on inside borders, I beg to say it has proved satisfactory in every respect; a grand crop, good bunches, and well finished berries of fine flavour. I can, therefore, again testify to the good properties of your Manure for Grape growing."
Nov. 24th, 1909.

From Mr. J. HEATON,
Gardener to H. O. Barclay, Esq.,
Colney Hall, Norwich.

"I have used Daniels' Norwich Fertilizer for the past few years, and find it an excellent Manure for all kinds of Flowers, Fruit, and Vegetables. No garden should be without it."
May 16th, 1907.

From A. GRAY, Esq.,
How Barnet.

"The Norwich Fertilizer you sent to Sheringham for me acted beautifully. My Zonal blooms were lovely."
Jan. 16th.

House containing 263 Bunches Black Hambro Grapes, grown by Lady Mansel, Catton House, fed with Norwich Fertilizer only.

NORWICH FERTILIZER
IS SENT

Carriage Paid on orders of 56 lbs. and upwards to any Railway Station in England and Wales, and to Edinburgh, Glasgow, and Irish Ports.

PRICES.

7 lbs.	...	1s. 9d.
14 lbs.	...	3s. 0d.
28 lbs.	...	5s. 6d.
56 lbs.	...	9s. 6d.
112 lbs.	...	17s. 6d.

Copies of a special article on "Manures for Vegetable Crops," by Mr. J. Gibson, F.R.H.S., Head Gardener to His Grace The Duke of Portland, Welbeck Abbey, may be had on application.

DANIELS' DAISY DESTROYER.

This preparation has become an immediate success having given great satisfaction in every instance.

We have made arrangements for an increased demand during the coming Spring, all who value a velvety clean lawn should use it if troubled with Daisies or Plantains. We have every confidence that it will give entire satisfaction wherever used. It will be found to thoroughly eradicate all Daisies, and at the same time, as a fertiliser, give renewed vigour to the finer grasses.

A dressing of about 4 ounces to the square yard will be found sufficient, and the best time to apply it is in April, choosing dry weather for the work; where the lawn is badly infested with Daisies it should be carefully applied to the plants individually.

Prices—7 lb. 2s. 6d.; 14 lb. 4s. 6d.; 28 lb. 7s. 6d.; 56 lb. 12s. 6d.; 112 lb. 25s. Carriage Paid on 1 cwt. and ½ cwt. lots.

OTHER GARDEN MANURES.

*CANARY GUANO. Tins, 6d. and 1s.; 14 lb., 4s. 6d.; 28 lb., 7s. 6d.; 56 lb., 12s. 6d.; 1 cwt., 20s.

CLAY'S FERTILIZER. In tins, 6d. and 1s. each. In bags, 7 lb., 2s. 6d.; 14 lb., 4s. 6d.; 28 lb., 7s. 6d.; 56 lb., 12s. 6d.; 1 cwt., 20s.

ICHTHEMIC GUANO. In tins, 1 lb., 6d.; 2 lb., 1s.; 7 lb., 2s. 6d. In bags, 14 lb., 4s. 6d.; 28 lb., 7s. 6d.; 56 lb., 12s. 6d.; 1 cwt., 20s.

*THOMSON'S VINE, PLANT, AND VEGETABLE MANURE. In tins, 1s.; 7 lb., 2s. 6d.; 14 lb., 3s. 6d.; 28 lb., 6s.; 56 lb., 10s.; per cwt., 20s.

*THOMSON'S CHRYSANTHEMUM MANURE. Of great value in growing Chrysanthemums for exhibition. 7 lb., 3s. 6d.; 14 lb., 6s.; 28 lb., 11s.; 56 lb., 20s.

WATSON'S LAWN SAND. In tins, 1s. and 2s. 6d.; 14 lb., 5s. 6d.; 28 lb., 9s. 6d.; 56 lb., 18s.; per cwt., 34s.

* Carriage paid on orders of 28 lbs. and upwards on the G.E.R. and Mid. & G.N.R.

POTTING MATERIALS.

CHARCOAL. In Lumps. Used very extensively for Orchids, &c. Per bushel, 2s. 6d.

COCOA-NUT FIBRE. 1s. 6d. per bushel; 5s. per sack.

JADOO FIBRE. Peck bag, 1s.; bushel bag, 3s. 6d.

LEAF SOIL. 1s. 6d. per bushel. LOAM. Fibrous, 1s. 6d. per bushel. PEAT. Best Orchid, 5s. per bushel. Ordinary Potting. 2s. 6d. per bushel.

SILVER SAND. Fine and coarse, 4s. per bushel. SPHAGNUM MOSS. 2s. 6d. per bushel.

RAW MANURES.

BASIC SLAG. An excellent dressing for lawns. 14 lb., 1s.; 28 lb., 1s. 9d.; 56 lb., 3s.; 112 lb., 5s. 0d.

BONES. ½-in., ½-in., and 1 in. 9s. per cwt. These should be used liberally when forming Vine borders.

BONE MEAL. 10s. per cwt. Excellent for all crops, forms a splendid Manure for Lawns; this should be applied in February.

GUANO, Peruvian. Price, 18s. cwt. Highly concentrated. First-rate for Tomatoes and other quick-growing crops.

KAINIT. 14 lb., 1s. 6d.; 28 lb., 2s. 6d.; 56 lb., 4s.; 112 lb., 6s. 6d.

MURIATE OF POTASH. 4d. per lb., 2s. 6d. per 14 lb.

NITRATE OF SODA. A most powerful assistant in the Vegetable Garden. Per lb., 6d.; per stone, 3s. 6d.

SULPHATE OF AMMONIA. Specially adapted for Chrysanthemum growing. Per lb., 6d.; per stone. 3s. 6d.

SUPERPHOSPHATE. 14 lb., 1s.; 28 lb., 1s. 9d.; 56 lb. 3s.; 112 lb., 5s. 6d.

STERILISED SOIL.

Per Bushel 2s. Special Quotations for large quantities.

It has been found that when the soil is sterilised and thus cleaned of all hurtful agencies the ammonia producing Bacteria increases rapidly, and there is a corresponding greater production of plant food from the soil, followed by an increase of crop of a more healthy character.

DANIELS' SWEET PEA FERTILIZER.

An excellent stimulant for applying to Sweet Peas. We have thoroughly tested it and can thoroughly recommend it. About 4 ounces to each plant about once a fortnight, or if applied as a liquid, about the same quantity to a gallon of water (see page 108).

3½ lb., 1s. 6d.; 7 lb., 2s. 6d.; 14 lb., 4s. 6d.; 28 lb., 7s.; 56 lb., 12s.; 112 lb., 20s. Carriage Paid.

INSECTICIDES AND FUMIGATORS.

INSECTICIDES, &c.

"ABOL" INSECTICIDE. Most effectual, and may be used by any amateur. Pints, 1s. 6d. ; quarts, 2s. 6d. ; half-gallons, 4s. ; one gallon, 7s. 6d.

"CARMUM." A certain cure for rust in Carnations and Chrysanthemums. Price, 1s. 6d., 3s., and 5s. per bottle.

EWING'S MILDEW COMPOSITION. 1s. 6d. per bottle.

FIR TREE OIL. An excellent Insecticide. In bottles, 1s. 6d., 2s. 6d., and 4s. 6d. each.

FORMICACIDE. Ant destroyer. 1s. 6d. per bottle.

FOWLER'S GARDENERS' INSECTICIDE. A preparation we recommend. In jars, 1s. 6d.

GISHURST COMPOUND. Especially useful for the winter cleansing of fruit trees. In boxes, 1s. and 3s. each.

GISHURSTINE. An excellent dressing for gardeners' boots. 6d. and 1s. per tin

HELLEBORE POWDER. 8d., 1s., and 2s. per tin.

LETHORION VAPOUR CONE. 6d., 8d., and 1s. each.

LEMON OIL INSECTICIDE. Pints, 1s. 6d. ; quarts, 2s. 9d. each.

McDOUGALL'S CARBOLIC SOFT SOAP. Tins, 1s. and 2s. 6d. each.

MEALY BUG DESTROYER. 1s. per jar.

QUASSIA CHIPS. 6d. lb. ; 7 lbs. 3s. ; 14 lbs. 5s. 6d.

QUASSIA EXTRACT (THE BEST). Per gallon, 3s. 8d. ; half-gallon, 2s. 6d. ; and in 6d. and 1s. tins.

SLUGENE. A certain exterminator of Slugs. Tins, 6d. and 1s. each.

SULPHUR, YELLOW. 6d. per lb. Excellent remedy for Red Spider.

TOBACCO JUICE. 1s. 6d. per quart ; 2s. 9d. per half-gallon.

TOBACCO POWDER. 6d., 1s., and 2s. 6d. per tin.

V. I. FLUID. For winter spraying of fruit trees. Per quart, 2s. 6d. ; gallon, 7s. 6d.

VAPORITE. For destroying Wireworms, &c., in soil. Tins, 9d. and 2s. ; 28 lbs., 4s. 6d. ; ½-cwt., 6s. 6d. ; 1 cwt., 10s.

WEED KILLER, McDOUGALL'S NON-POISONOUS. 1 gallon tin, 3s. ; 5 gallon drums, 2s. 6d. per gallon ; 40 gallon casks, 2s. gallon. *All packages free.*

TRADE MARK REG?

"ABOL" INSECTICIDE.

FUMIGATORS.

DANIELS' RELIABLE COMPOUND TOBACCO PAPER.

1-lb. and 2-lb. Packets, 1s. and 2s. *Every packet is accompanied with full instructions for use.*

CAMPBELL'S FUMIGATING INSECTICIDES—

		s. d.
No. 3 Roll, sufficient for 1,000 cubic feet ..	.. each	0 8
No. 4 „ „ 2,000 „	.. „	1 2

McDOUGALL'S INSECTICIDE FUMERS. Sufficient for 1,000 cubic ft., 8d. each ; per doz., 8s. ; for 2,000 ft., 1s. each ; 12s. per doz.

McDOUGALL'S SELF-ACTING INSECTICIDE SHEETS, each sufficient for 1,000 cubic ft., 8d. each ; per doz., 8s.

NICOTICIDE VAPORISING COMPOUND. An excellent Compound for vaporising greenhouses, &c., for the destruction of insects.

No. 1 bottle.—1 pint containing sufficient for 40,000 cubic ft., each 15s.		
No. 2 bottle.—½ „ „ „ 20,000 cubic ft., each 7s. 6d.		
No. 3 bottle.—6 oz. „ „ 12,000 cubic ft., each 4s. 6d.		
No. 4 bottle.—4 „ „ „ 8,000 cubic ft., each 3s.		
No. 5 bottle.—1 „ „ „ 2,000 cubic ft., each 10d.		

FUMIGATORS for above (will last for years). These are made in one size only, large enough for 6,000 cubic feet, each 1s.

McDOUGALL'S FUMER.

XL ALL SPECIALITIES.

XL ALL VAPORISING COMPOUND, in solid dry cake. This cake when used in the XL All Fumigator first melts, and then passes entirely away as vapour and is as effective and safe as XL All Liquid Vaporising Compound. These cakes, each of which is sufficient for 1000 cubic feet, are packed in boxes to correspond with the liquid contained in the various sizes of bottles, viz. :—Boxes for 40,000 feet, 20s. ; 20,000 ft., 10s. 6d. ; 10,000 feet, 5s. 6d. ; 5000 feet, 2s. 10d. ; 2000 feet, 1s. 2d. per box.

BOX OF 10 CAKES, EACH FOR 1000 CUBIC FEET OF SPACE

IN SOLID DRY CAKE.

XL ALL VAPORISING FUMIGATOR—

								s. d.
No. 4 bottle contains Liquid Compound for 5,000 cubic feet of space ..					..	..	..	2s. 10d.
No. 3 bottle „ „ „ 10,000 cubic feet „			..			..	..	5s. 6d.
No. 2 bottle „ „ „ 20,000 cubic feet „			..			..	..	10s. 6d.
No. 1 bottle „ „ „ 40,000 cubic feet „			..			..	..	20s. 0d.

Fumigators complete for above, each 1s. 9d. and 2s.

RICHARDS' PATENT FUMIGATOR.

XL ALL WASH FOR MILDEW. A certain cure for mildew, killing insects at same time. Pints, 2s. 6d. ; quarts, 4s. ; half-galls., 6s. 6d. ; galls., 12s. 6d.

XL ALL INSECTICIDE. The safest and most effectual Insecticide. Pints, 2s. ; quarts, 3s. 6d. ; half gallons, 5s. ; gallons, 10s.

XL ALL WINTER WASH (non-poisonous). The most effectual wash for applying to all kinds of Fruit Trees and Bushes. Must be used in Winter when the trees are dormant. Price, 1s. per tin ; 12 tins for 10s.

HORTICULTURAL SUNDRIES.

TOOLS AND IMPLEMENTS.

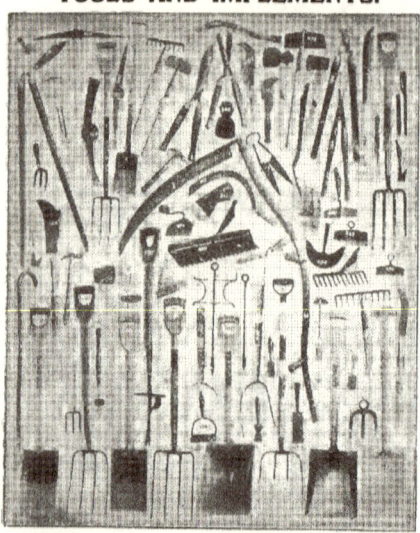

SCYTHE BLADES. 4s. and 4s. 6d. each.

GRASS SHEARS.

SHEARS, GRASS. 3s. 6d. and 4s. 6d. per pair.
  ,,   EDGING. 6s. 9d. per pair.
  ,,   SHEEP. 3s. per pair.
  ,,   SLIDING PRUNING. 6s. 6d., 8s. 6d., and 11s. per pair.
SHOVELS. Improved London, 3s. each.
SPADES, GARDEN. Half bright, 3s. 6d. and 3s. 9d. each.
  ,,   ,,   "The Sword," all bright, 4s. each.
  ,,   ,,   All bright, "The Norfolk," 3s. 9d., 4s. and 4s. 9d. ea.
  ,,   LADIES'. 2s. 6d. each.
SPUDS, CAST STEEL. 1s. 3d. each; with walking stick handles, 2s. each.
STANDARD TREE PRUNER. 8 ft., 7s. 6d.; 10 ft., 8s. 6d.; 12 ft., 10s. 6d.
TOOLS (GARDEN), LADIES'. In sets of four, very best manufacture,
  Spade, Rake, Hoe, and Fork, 7s. 6d. and 11s. per set.
TROWELS, BRIGHT STEEL. 6 in., 1s. 6d.; 7 in., 1s. 9d.; 8 in., 2s. 3d. each.
WATER CANS (HAWES' PATTERN). With two roses. 3 quarts, 4s. 3d.;
  4 qts., 5s.; 6 qts., 6s.; 8 qts., 6s. 9d.; 10 qts., 7s. 9d.; 12 qts., 9s. each.

KNIVES.

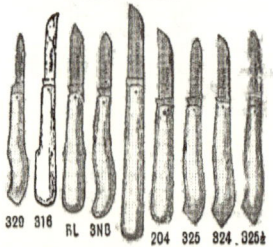

329 316   RL 3NB   204 325 324 325½
207

ASPARAGUS KNIVES. 3s. 6d. each.
BUDDING KNIVES. No. 329, 3s. 6d.; 316, 3s.; 3NB, 3s.; 207, 3s. 6d.;
  204, 3s.; 323, 2s. 6d.; 324, 3s.; 325½, 3s. 6d.
BUDDING KNIVES. No. 204B, "The Gardener's Favourite," brass
  bound, 3s. 6d. each.

AVERUNCATORS, PATENT TREE PRUNERS. 5s. 6d., 7s. 6d., and
  10s. 6d. each. Handles any length can be supplied extra.
BROOMS, BIRCH. 4d. each; 3s. 6d. per doz.
DAISY GRUBS. 2s. 6d. each. Extra strong with long handles, 3s. 6d. each.
EDGING IRONS, CAST STEEL. 3s. 6d. each; with handle, 4s. 6d. each.
FORKS, GARDEN. 3s. 6d., 4s. 6d. Four or five prongs.
  ,,   LADIES' DIGGING. 2s. 6d. each.
GOOSEBERRY PRUNERS, STRAIGHT. 2s. 6d. each; with hook, 3s.
HAMMERS. No. 1, 2s.; No. 3, 2s. 6d.
HOES, DUTCH. 5 in., 1s.; 6 in., 1s. 3d.; 7 in., 1s. 6d.
  ,,   DRAW. 5 in., 10d.; 6 in., 1s.; 7 in., 1s. 2d.; 8 in., 1s. 4d.
RAKES, DAISY. 6s. 6d. and 7s. 6d. each.
  ,,   IRON. 8 teeth, 10d.; 10 teeth, 1s.; 12 teeth, 1s. 3d.
  ,,   AMERICAN STEEL, WITH ASH HANDLES. 8 teeth, 3s. 6d.;
  10 teeth, 4s.; 12 teeth, 4s. 6d.; 14 teeth, 5s. each.
REELS, GARDEN. 2s. each; Lines (30 & 60 yds. long), 1s. 6d. & 2s. 6d. ea.
  ,,   PRUNING, CAST STEEL. 3s. each.
SAWS, PRUNING, WITH BILL HOOK. 6s. each.
SCISSORS, FLOWER-GATHERING. 6 in., 3s.; 7 in., 3s. 6d.; 8 in., 4s.
  ,,   PRUNING. 6 in., 2s. 6d.; 7 in., 3s. 3d.; 8 in., 3s. 9d.
  ,,   PRUNING. With slide, 5s. 6d. per pair.
  ,,   VINE. 6 in., 2s. 6d.; 7 in., 3s. 6d.; 8 in., 4s. per pair.
  ,,   SHRED. 2s. 6d. per pair.

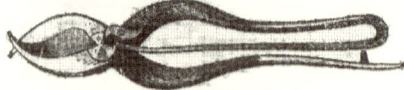

SECATEURS.

SECATEURS. With Aubert's Spring. *See Illustration.* 6¼ in., 3s. 6d.;
  7½ in., 4s.; 5½ in., 4s. 6d.
  ,,   All bright, 7 in., 3s. 9d.; 8 in., 4s. 3d.
  ,,   Not bright, 7 in., 3s.; 8 in., 3s. 9d.
  ,,   HERCULES PATENT. Spiral Spring, 8 in. 4s.

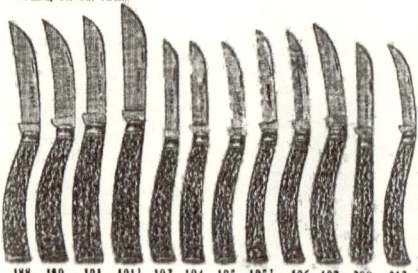

188   189   191   191½   193   194   195   195½   196   197   200   312
3/-   3/3   3/3   3/6   3/6   3/-   3/6   3/6   4/-   3/6   2/-   2/6

PRUNING KNIVES. No. 188, 3s.; 189, 3s.; 187, 3s.; 188, 3s.; 189,
  3s. 3d.; 191, 3s. 3d.; 191½, 3s. 6d.; 193, 3s. 6d.; 194, 3s.; 195, 3s. 6d.;
  195½, 3s. 6d.; 196, 4s.; 197, 3s. 6d.; 200, 2s.; 312, 2s. 6d.; 312NB,
  2s. 6d.; 313, 2s.; 938, 3s. 6d.

HORTICULTURAL SUNDRIES.

SYRINGES AND DISTRIBUTORS.

"ABOL" NEW PATENT. For distributing Insecticides and for ordinary Syringing. Each, 8s. 6d., and 10s. 6d. and 14s. 6d. Bends for any size, 1s. 6d. extra. Postage 4d. extra.

THE "ABOL" SYRINGE.

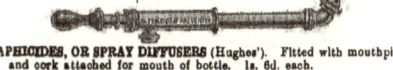

APHICIDES, OR SPRAY DIFFUSERS (Hughes'). Fitted with mouthpiece and cork attached for mouth of bottle. 1s. 6d. each.
THE FOUR OAKS UNDENTABLE SYRINGE. A great improvement on the old types. 12s. 6d., 17s. 6d., 21s., 25s. each.
REID'S PATENT SYRINGE, with extra Roses. Superior make, 19s. each.
USEFUL GARDEN SYRINGE, with Rose, 5s. each.
ALPHA SPRAYING MACHINES. The most simple and efficient sprayer yet introduced. No constant pumping; once charged the machine empties automatically. Charged with compressed air by means of any ordinary bicycle foot-pump. Any tree-spraying solution may be used in these machines, and the spray can be maintained at will until the whole of the contents are discharged.
Knapsack Machine, 3½ gals., complete, with powerful foot-pump. 60s.
Hand Sprayer, 3 quarts. 17s. 6d. *See illustration.*

THERMOMETERS & BAROMETERS.

THERMOMETERS, BOXWOOD (SPIRIT OR MERCURY), 1s., 1s. 6d., and 2s. 6d. each.
,, BOXWOOD, WITH STORM GLASS, 2s. 6d. & 3s. 6d. each.
,, WHITE JAPANNED SCALES ; especially adapted for the garden (Negretti and Zambra), 3s. 6d. each.

CAST METAL THERMOMETER 3/6

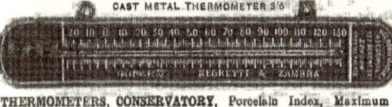

THERMOMETERS, CONSERVATORY, Porcelain Index, Maximum and Minimum combined, 10s. 6d and 15s. each.
,, MINIMUM AND MAXIMUM REGISTERING ; japanned case, 6d., 7s. 6d., and 10s. 6d. each.
PLUNGING THERMOMETERS, for hot beds, 4s. 6d., 7s. 6d., and 10s. 6d. each.
BAROMETERS (ANEROID). 12s. 6d., and upwards.

GARDENING GLOVES.

GLOVES, Strong Norfolk Hedging. 1s. 9d. per pair, Postage extra.
,, Men's Drummonds'. 1s. 9d. and 2s. per pair.
,, Best Oxfords. 2s. per pair.
,, Cape Oxfords. 2s. 6d. per pair.
,, Ladies' Gardening. Dark Tan. 1s. 6d. and 2s. per pair.
,, Housemaid's. 1s. and 1s. 6d. per pair.
,, Gentleman's Best. 2s. 6d. and 3s. 6d. per pair.

SHADING MATERIALS.

SCRIM CANVAS, GREEN, 54 in. wide, 1s. 2d. per yd., 36 in. wide, 9d.
SCRIM CANVAS, BROWN. 36 in. wide, 6d. per yd. ; 54 in. wide, 9d. per yd. ; 72 in. wide, 1s. per yd.
SUMMER CLOUD, "ELLIOTT'S." For shading greenhouses. In ½-lb. packets, 1s. each.
SUMMER SHADING, "THE PERFECT." 1 lb. tins, 1s.
TANNED NETTING (FOR PROTECTING FRUIT TREES, &c.). 2 and 4 yards wide. 3d. and 6d. per yard run. In pieces 50 by 4, or 100 by 2, 10s. per piece.
TIFFANY. A thin material for shading. 20 yds. long by 38 ins. wide, 5s. per piece.

GENERAL SUNDRIES.

APHIS BRUSHES. 2s. each.
BASKETS (TRUCK). Made of strong wood, and are indispensable to every garden. No. 2, 11½ in. by 6 in., 1s. ; No. 3, 13½ in. by 7½ in., 1s. 3d. ; No. 4, 15 in. by 8½ in., 1s. 6d. ; No. 5, 17½ in. by 9½ in., 1s. 9d. ; No. 6, 20½ in. by 10½ in., 2s. 3d. ; No. 7, 23 in. by 12 in., 2s. 6d. ; No. 8, 26 in. by 14 in., 3s. ; No. 9, 28 in. by 15 in., 3s. 6d.
BOUQUET WIRE. 7 in. lengths 1s. to 2s. per lb.
BOWLS. Japanese, suitable for growing bulbs in, a great variety. Price, each 9d., 1s., 1s. 3d., 1s. 6d., 2s., and upwards.
CLOTH SHREDS. Per lb., 6d. ; per stone, 5s. 6d.
DEANS' MEDICATED SHREDS in Boxes of 100. 2 in., 6d. ; 2½ in., 7½d. ; 3 in., 8d. ; 3½ in., 9d. per box.
FLORAL AID. A useful arrangement for dinner-table decoration. 1s., 1s. 6d., and 2s. 6d. each.
FLORAL CEMENT OR GUM. 1s. and 2s. per bottle.
GARDENERS' APRONS. Shaloon, 4s. 6d., 4s. 9d., and 5s. each. Serge, 3s., 3s. 3d., and 3s. 9d. each.
GRAFTING WAX. 6d., 1s., and 2s. per tin.
LAYER PEGS (ZINC). In boxes of 100. 1s. each.
LAWN SPRINKLERS. 4 arm spray, 16s. 6d. each ; 8 arm spray, 19s. 6d. each.
MARTIN FLOWER RACK. An ingenious and simple contrivance for the easy arranging of cut flowers in bowls 6d., 9d., 1s., 1s. 3d., and 1s. 6d. each.
MELON NETS (STRING). Per doz., 3s. 6d.
NAIL BAGS. Leather, best quality. 5s. each.

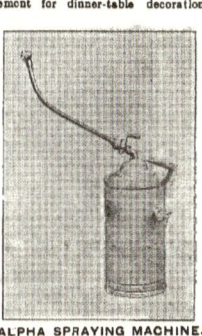
ALPHA SPRAYING MACHINE. PRICE 17s. 6d.

PENCILS, WOLFF'S GARDEN. 3d. each.
SPRINGTHORPE CUPS AND TUBES, for exhibiting Roses and Chrysanthemums. 9s. per dozen.
STYPTIC. For preventing bleeding in vines, 1s. 6d. and 2s. 6d. per bottle.
"TAM O'SHANTER" HONES. The best, each 1/- ; in case, 3s. each.
TOBACCO POWDER DISTRIBUTORS, INDIA-RUBBER WITH BRASS NOZZLE, 2s. 6d. each; BELLOWS, 9d. per pair.
VERBENA PINS (GALVANIZED WIRE). For pegging down Verbenas, &c. Per box of 1 gross (3 inches long), 1s.
VIRGIN CORK. 3s. per stone. Quarter-cwt., 6s. ; half-cwt., 11s. ; cwt., 20s. Carriage Paid on 1 cwt. and upwards.
WALL NAILS. Square cast, 3d. per lb. ; per stone, 2s. 6d. French, 4d. per lb. ; 3s. per stone.
WALL NAILS, CHANDLER'S PATENT. A useful invention. Shreds not required. Boxes of 100, 1½ in., 1s. 9d. ; 1½ in., 2s.
WATSON'S LAWN SAND DISTRIBUTOR. For applying the sand to individual weeds. 10s. 6d. each.
WIKEHAM WEED ERADICATOR (PATENT). An excellent instrument for destroying Dandelions, Docks, &c., on Lawns. Fill with Weed Killer, stab the crown of the weed and it will soon perish. 9s. 6d. each.
WIRE ALUMINIUM. 1s. per coil of 40 feet.
WREATH AND CROSS TROUGHS, for holding Cut Flowers; the very best made. 2s., 2s. 3d., 2s. 9d., and 3s. 6d each.

DANIELS' SUPERIOR MUSHROOM SPAWN.

This Illustration (from a Photograph) represents a group of Mushrooms in all stages of growth taken while growing at Ashwellthorpe Hall.

In Bricks, each 6d., 4 bricks 1s. 6d., one bushel of 16 bricks, 5s.

COMPLETE INSTRUCTIONS FOR CULTIVATION WILL BE SENT WITH EVERY ORDER.

From Mr. R. STEWARDSON, Whiteindwell.

July 7th.
"I am pleased to tell you that the Mushroom Spawn I had from you has done wonderfully well. This is the first time I have tried growing them, and the bed has been a picture for weeks."

From Mr. C. PAGE, Bexleyheath.

Sept. 20th.
"The Mushroom Spawn I had from you has done remarkably well and has produced the finest lot of Mushrooms I ever saw and in such large quantities."

PACKING AND TYING MATERIALS, Etc.

BAMBOO CANES. 4 ft. Thin. Medium. Thick. 5 ft. 6 ft. 7 ft.
2s. 6d.   3s.   4s.   6s.   7s.   9s. per 100.

BAMBOO POLES. Suitable for forming arches, &c., 8 to 10 ft. long (tapering), 2s. per doz.; 16s. per 100.

BAMBOO TIPS. For tying Carnations, 2s. 3d. per 100.

CARNATION COIL STAKES. Galvanized and painted green. 20 in., 1s. per doz., 7s. 6d. per 100; 25 in., 1s. 6d. per doz., 10s. 6d. per 100; 30 in., 2s. per doz., 13s. 6d. per 100; 36 in., 2s. 6d. per doz., 17s. 6d. per 100.

DAHLIA STAKES.—Painted Green, with tarred ends.
per doz.   2 ft.   2½ ft.   3 ft.   4 ft.   4½ ft.   5 ft.
  1s.   1s. 3d.   1s. 6d.   2s.   2s. 6d.   2s. 9d.

FLOWER STICKS.—Unpainted Deal.
1 ft.   1½ ft.   2 ft.   2½ ft.   3 ft.   3½ ft.   per 100
9d.   1s. 3d.   1s. 6d.   2s.   2s. 6d.   3s.

FLOWER STICKS.—Painted Green. Per 100, 1 ft., 1s. 3d.; 1½ ft., 1s. 9d.; 2 ft., 2s.; 2½ ft., 2s. 6d.; 3 ft., 3s.; 3½ ft., 3s. 9d.; 4 ft., 4s. 6d.; 5 ft., 5s. 0d.

LABELS, WOOD.—Painted, in boxes of 100.
4 in.   5 in.   6 in.   7 in.   8 in.   9 in.   12 in.
7d.   9d.   10d.   1s.   1s. 3d.   1s. 6d.   2s. 6d.

LABELS, WOOD.—Plain.
4 in.   5 in.   6 in.   7 in.   8 in.   9 in.   12 in.
5d.   6d.   8d.   10d.   1s.   1s. 3d.   2s.

LABELS, ZINC, IMPERISHABLE for Roses and Fruit Trees, 2s. and 3s. 6d. per 100.

METALLIC INK, for writing on above, 6d. and 1s. per bottle.

LABELS, ACME GARDEN. For Roses, 1s. 3d. per doz.; for Fruit Trees, 1s. 9d. per doz.
Please give names of varieties wanted.

MATS. Archangel, large, new. 2s. each, 21s. doz.

MATS. St. Petersburg. 1s. to 1s. 6d. each; 10s. 6d. to 15s. doz.

PUNNETTS. ½ lb., 7d. per doz. ⎱ Either square or
PUNNETTS. 1 lb., 9d. per doz. ⎰ round.

RAFFIA. Very best quality for tying. In bundles, 6d.; per lb., 1s. 6d.

RAFFIA.—GREEN. 2s. per lb.

RAFFIA TAPE. 1s. 6d. per reel.

TAR TWINE. In balls, thin, medium, and thick, ½-lb., 9d.; 1 lb., 1s. 3d.

WADDING, BLEACHED. For packing, in sheets measuring about 36 in. by 18 in., 3s. 6d. per doz. sheets.

WHITE OR BLUE TISSUE PAPER. 3s. 6d. to 5s. per ream.

WOOD WOOL. Finest quality for fruit packing. 6d. per lb.; 5s. 6d. per stone.

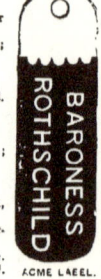

BARONESS
ROTHSCHILD

ACME LABEL.

FLOWER SEED DEPARTMENT

For many years past we have given very careful attention to the growth and selection of our choice strains of Florists' and other Flower Seeds, and as a consequence of this we are pleased to note the steady increase in our very large Business in this Department.

We have again carefully revised our fine List of Flower Seeds, and several interesting and valuable additions have been made, whilst some fine Novelties in Sweet Peas and other choice flowers have been introduced, for which we anticipate a great demand.

Our very fine strains of Asters, Stocks, Pansies, Primulas, Petunias, &c., have again been specially grown for our Retail Trade, and can be confidently recommended as the finest procurable.

Owing to the severe and long protracted drought of last Summer, many of the newer kinds of Sweet Peas and other Flower Seeds, although of excellent growing quality, are very scarce, and to prevent disappointment we strongly advise our Friends to send us their Orders as early as convenient after receiving this Catalogue.

RELIABLE ANNUALS, &c., SPECIALLY RECOMMENDED.

To assist customers who only require a comparatively small selection of the choicest Annuals, &c., we give below a list which contains a few of the varieties that we would specially recommend, and all of which are worthy of a place in the garden.

See Page		Pat. No.	Price.
	ANTIRRHINUM—		
78	Daphne (new)	351	6d.
78	Golden Queen	353	6d.
78	Black Prince	343	6d.
78	Niobe	345	6d.
78	Aurora	347	6d.
78	Tom Thumb, 6 brilliant varieties	356	1s. 6d.
78	Tom Thumb, choicest mixed	361	6d. & 1s.
	ASTER—		
75	Daniels' Dwarf Perfection, 6 varieties	226	2s. 6d.
75	Daniels' Giant Ostrich Plume, 8 varieties	215	3s. 6d.
75	Daniels' Giant Ostrich Plume, choice mixed	224	1s.
	Peerless Pink (See Novelties)		1s.
	CALLIOPSIS—		
81	Tom Thumb, Beauty	423	4d.
	CANDYTUFT—		
82	Daniels' Mammoth Spiral	433	6d. & 1s.
82	Daniels' Rose Cardinal	434	4d.
	CARNATION—		
84	Marguerite, new large-flowered, mixed	405	6d. & 1s.
	CHRYSANTHEMUM—		
84	Daniels' Choicest Mixed	507	6d.
84	Morning Star	501	6d.
84	Northern Star	501	6d.
	CLARKIA ELEGANS—		
85	Carmine Queen	515	6d.
	DIANTHUS—		
87	Fireball	566	6d.
87	Heddewigi, mixed, double	569	6d. & 1s.
87	**DIMORPHOTHECA AURANTIACA**	565	1s.
	ESCHSCHOLTZIA—		
88	Carmine King	593	1s.
	GAILLARDIA—		
88	Large-flowered single, mixed	606	6d. & 1s.
	GYPSOPHILA—		
89	Elegans grandiflora alba	626	6d.
	GODETIA—		
89	Daniels' Dwarf Carmine	635	4d.
89	Daniels' Dwarf White	636	6d.
89	Crimson Glow (new)	627	6d.
89	Large-flowered, mixed	637	4d.
	LAVATERA—		
92	Rosea Splendens	702	4d.
	LUPINUS—		
92	Hybridus atrococcineus	717	3d.

See Page		Pat. No.	Price.
	MIGNONETTE—		
94	Aurea magnifica	750	6d. & 1s.
94	Daniels' Crimson King	740	6d. & 1s.
94	Giant White	762	6d. & 1s.
	NASTURTIUM, TOM THUMB—		
95	Empress of India	786	4d.
95	Queen of Tom Thumbs	788	1s.
95	Golden King	792	4d.
	NEMESIA—		
94	Strumosa grandiflora, choice mixed	820	1s.
	PANSY—		
97	Daniels' Exhibition Giant	831	1s. 6d.
	PENTSTEMON—		
101	Large-flowered hybrids	977	1s.
	PETUNIA—		
98	Grandiflora, brilliant rose	888	1s.
	PHLOX DRUMMONDI GRANDIFLORA—		
90	6 Brilliant varieties	909	2s. 6d.
90	Choice mixed	917	1s.
	PHLOX, DWARF COMPACT—		
99	Fireball	910	6d.
	POPPIES—		
102	Selected Shirley	992	3d. & 6d.
	SALPIGLOSSIS—		
103	6 Beautiful varieties	1025	1s. 6d.
103	Choicest mixed	1026	6d. & 1s.
	SCHIZANTHUS—		
104	Wisetonensis	1051	1s.
	STOCK—		
72	Daniels' Large-flowered Ten-week, 6 varieties	172	2s.
72	Daniels' Large-flowered Ten-week, choice mixed	187	1s.
	SWEET PEAS—		
65	Exhibition, 12 varieties	2	5s.
65	Exhibition, 6 varieties	3	2s. 6d.
	SWEET SCABIOUS—		
103	Choicest mixed	1045	3d. & 6d.
	SWEET SULTAN—		
103	Giant Flowered, hybrids	1083	6d. & 1s.
	VERBENA—		
106	Large-flowered, mixed	1128	1s.
	ZINNIA—		
107	Fire King	1162	1s.
107	Large-flowered double, choicest mixed	1158	3d. & 6d.

SEEDS OF NEW AND VERY CHOICE FLOWERS.

ANTIRRHINUM, Venus. A very beautiful new tall growing variety of just the shade of colour hitherto required in this popular class, the blooms being of pink on a white ground, set off by a pure white throat. The long stems are thickly studded with the large flowers, which are of the finest form, the spikes of bloom being exceedingly handsome.
Per pkt. 1s.

ASTER, Peerless Pink. *(See Plate.)* An exceedingly beautiful variety of the tall late-flowering section, growing about two feet high and branching almost to the base of the stem. The numerous blooms, which are four to five inches across, are of the most delicate and charming pale satiny rose pink colour, and being borne on long wiry stems are of great value as cut flowers. Highly recommended.
Per pkt. 1s.

CLARKIA ELEGANS, Scarlet Queen. The most striking colour yet produced in Clarkia Elegans. The plant grows about 2½ feet high and produces its beautifully coloured double blooms quite to the top. The flowers are very double and open a fiery orange colour, turning later to salmon scarlet. This is a splendid variety and will be in great demand for garden decoration.
Per pkt. 1s.

COSMOS, New Early Flowering. Rose Queen. *(See Plate.)* The flowers of this beautiful variety are from 2 to 3 inches in diameter, of a charming soft rose shade, and are produced in the greatest abundance. Sown under glass in March and planted out in May will commence blooming by the end of June and continue till killed by the frost in Autumn. A.M., R.H.S.
Per pkt. 6d. and 1s.

DIMORPHOTHECA AURANTIACA HYBRIDA. Similar in habit and size of bloom to the beautiful D. aurantiaca, but range in colour from pure white to blush, with salmon-glow and orange-salmon reverie, creamy white with lemon reverse, blush with chrome and brown reverse, lemon with deep brown reverse, canary yellow, soft salmon, and salmon orange. The flowers have mostly a central zone of some other colour, and all have a dark centre. This is one of the prettiest novelties sent out for several years.
Per pkt. 1s

MIGNONETTE, Daniels' Giant White. *(See Plate.)* A beautiful compact growing variety about one foot high, throwing up a profusion of very large, stout, almost pure white spikes of bloom, which are of the most delicious fragrance. This is by far the finest of all the White Mignonettes, and should be found in every garden.
Per pkt. 6d. and 1s.

NASTURTIUM TOM THUMB, Fireball. A new and distinct variety. A decided advance in dwarf bedding Nasturtiums and one of the finest yet introduced. The plant is of a dwarf compact habit of growth, about 9 inches high, with small dark green foliage, the deep orange scarlet flowers showing well above.
Per pkt. 6d. and 1s.

PENTSTEMON, New Large-flowered Hybrids. A magnificent strain of beautiful flowers, of great size and of the most charming colours, including the most delicate shades of pink and rose to crimson and scarlet. Sown in a gentle heat in February or March, and planted out in May, they will commence blooming in July and continue to throw up their handsome spikes of flowers until late Autumn.
Per pkt. 1s. and 2s. 6d.

PRIMULA MALACOIDES. A beautiful little plant from the forest of Yunnan, China. The plants grow about 9 inches high and branch and bloom very freely. The flowers, which are of a pleasing pale lilac, are borne in whorls on strong, graceful stems. Sown in February or March, in a slight heat, will bloom profusely in the greenhouse within four or five months from sowing.
Per pkt. 1s.

SCHIZANTHUS GRANDIFLORUS MAXIMUS. A very fine new class of beautiful varieties, of a more robust habit of growth, and with much larger blooms than those of the class hitherto offered. The plants grow from 1½ to 2 feet in height, and the blooms, which are of great substance, measure from 1 to 1½ inches across, with an almost endless variety of beautiful colours. The foliage is bright-green, fern-like and handsome. The lighter coloured varieties have a ground colour of white, pink, buff, red, or yellow, marked and surrounded by a deeper shade. The darker varieties have a ground of purple, mauve, or red, with beautiful centre lines of yellow or white, surrounded by a deeper shade. This will be found a splendid plant for pots in the greenhouse, and planted out in May will make a beautiful display in the garden throughout the Summer.
Per pkt. 1s.

SUNFLOWER, Starlight. *(See Plate.)* This fine new variety of annual Sunflower marks a distinct advance in this interesting group; the flowers are of good size with petals beautifully twisted like a fine form of Single Cactus Dahlia. The colour is a beautiful canary yellow, and the blooms being on long stems are excellent for cutting purposes and lend themselves admirably to decorative work. They also have the great merit of lasting a long time in water.
Per pkt. 6d. and 1s.

ZINNIA ELEGANS NANA, Fire King. An exceedingly brilliant and splendid variety of a compact habit of growth and very free flowering. The deep rich scarlet flowers measure from 3 to 4 inches across and are perfectly double. This comes quite true from seed.
Per pkt. 6d. and 1s.

COSMOS
"ROSE QUEEN"

SUNFLOWER
"STARLIGHT"

DANIELS
FLORAL
NOVELTIES
FOR 1912

NEW ASTER
"PEERLESS PINK"

MIGNONETTE
DANIELS
"GIANT WHITE"

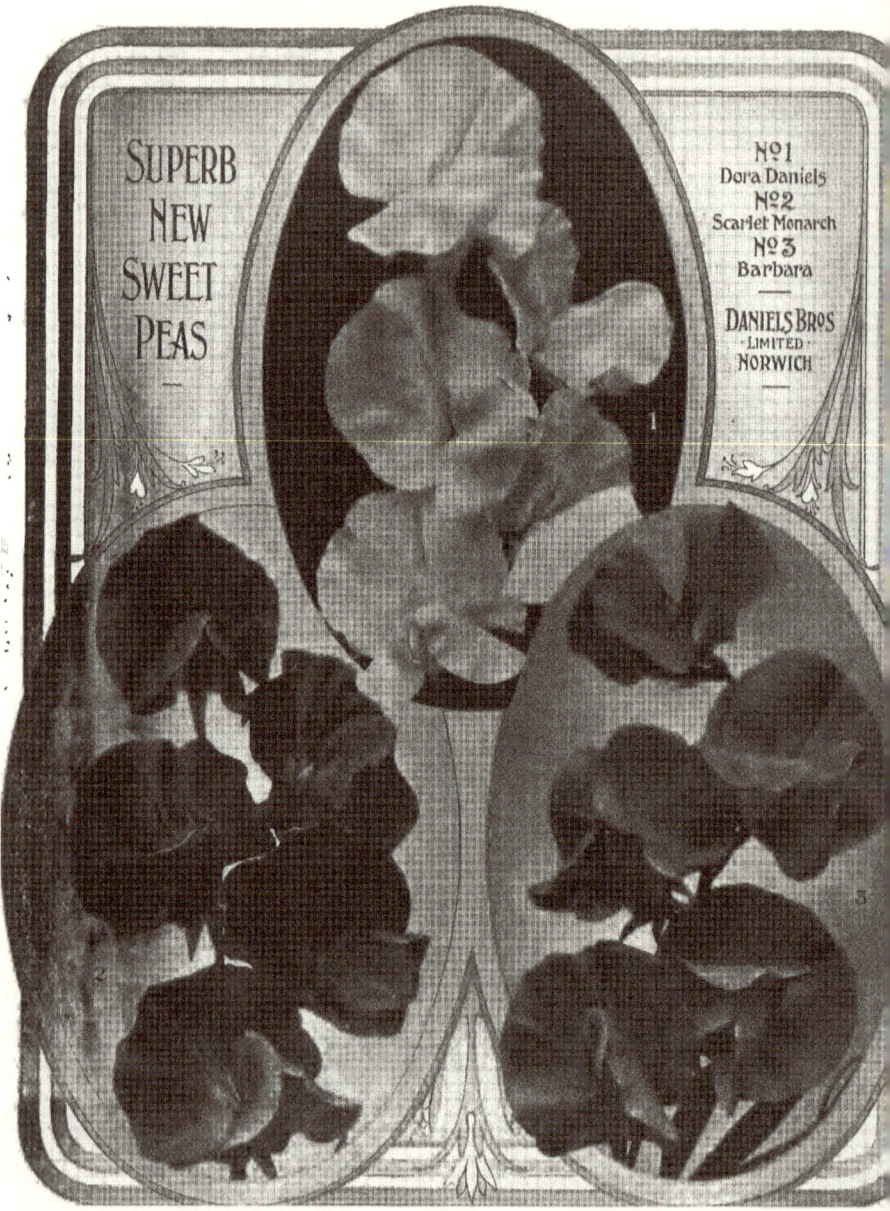

SUPERB
NEW
SWEET
PEAS
—

Nº 1
Dora Daniels
Nº 2
Scarlet Monarch
Nº 3
Barbara

DANIELS BROS
· LIMITED ·
NORWICH

SWEET PEAS.

☞ The seeds of Sweet Peas generally are this season well-ripened, large, and of splendid growing quality, but owing to the severe drought of last Summer, many of the new and choicer sorts are very scarce. We therefore strongly advise all who wish to secure special varieties, to send us their orders as early as convenient after receiving this Catalogue.

SUPERB VARIETIES OF RECENT INTRODUCTION.

The following list includes the finest and most beautiful of the new varieties. Most of these have been grown and selected at our Nurseries during the past season and can be highly recommended as really first-class for garden decoration or exhibition.

	per pkt.—s. d.
44 AFTERGLOW. A most distinct and telling novelty. The base of the standard is a bright violet blue, shading to glowing rosy amethyst ; wings electric blue. The flowers are large, of true Spencer form, and mostly four on a stem	1 0
28 ARTHUR UNWIN. A vigorous grower, with splendid large flowers. Standards rosy pink, wings creamy-blush. Very telling .. .. 6d. and	1 0
83 BARBARA. A lovely salmony-orange self, with large, beautifully waved flowers of true Spencer type, mostly produced four on a stem. May be called an improved Earl Spencer, but withstands the sun better than that variety. F.C.C., N.S.P.S., 1911	1 0
8 BEATRICE STEVENS. Pure white, slightly waved, and of good substance. The flowers are of enormous size. The largest of any known variety, and quite distinct ..	1 0
57 BERYL TATHAM (Daniels Bros., Ltd.). Large, beautifully waved flowers, three and four on a stem ; colour a charming clear rose pink self. One of the finest of the Countess Spencer type and a superb exhibition flower	
40 BERTRAND DEAL. A lovely pale, rosy lilac of immense size, standard beautifully waved. A very pleasing shade of colour and a grand exhibition flower. Should be grown by all exhibitors .. .. 6d. and	1 0
47 CHARLES FOSTER. A peculiar and charming combination of lavender and rosy pink, very distinct and attractive ..	
21 DORA DANIELS (Daniels Bros., Ltd.). Very large, beautifully waved flowers, three and four on a stem. The standards are a clear bright rose shading to white at the base. This is a fine exhibition variety, quite distinct, and of the most dainty and charming appearance	1 0

	per pkt.—s. d.
85 EDNA UNWIN IMPROVED. A brilliant, deep orange-scarlet self. This variety withstood the sun far better than any other of the class at our seed grounds last season. A fine exhibition flower and one of the best of its colour. We offer a fine selected stock .. .. 6d. and	1 0
71 ETHEL ROOSEVELT. Large, beautiful flowers of the most perfect Spencer form. The colour is a soft primrose overlaid with dainty flakes and splashes of blush crimson 6d. and	1 0
48 FLORENCE NIGHTINGALE. A magnificent variety, undoubtedly the finest of its class. The flowers are of great size, beautifully waved and often produced four on a stem. The colour is a charming soft, clear, rich lavender blue, with a faint sheen of rose pink. An exhibition flower of the highest merit .. .. 6d. and	1 0
55 MAY FARQUHAR. A deep, rich, bronzy-blue Spencer with large waved flowers. A distinct and striking colour that is very effective on the exhibition stand .. .. 6d. and	1 0
32 MRS. C. MASTERS. Standard bright rosy pink, wings white ; large beautiful flowers on long stems. Undoubtedly the finest of the bicolors .. .. 6d. and	1 0
72 MRS. W. J. UNWIN. A beautiful flower of splendid size, white ground heavily flaked with orange scarlet. Very fine, much superior to Aurora Spencer .. .. 6d. and	1 0
81 SCARLET MONARCH. A deep, rich, scarlet Spencer, equal in colour to "Queen Alexandra," but much larger and of better form. First-class for exhibition .. .. 6d. and	1 0
80 THOMAS STEVENSON. Brilliant orange-scarlet, almost a self with large waved flowers. A superb variety. First-class for exhibition, garden decoration, or cut flowers. Highly recommended. F.C.C., N.S.P.C., 1911 .. 6d. and	1 0

1A One Packet of each above sixteen superb varieties, 9s. 6d.

DANIELS' SPECIAL COLLECTIONS OF SWEET PEAS FOR EXHIBITION.

We highly recommend these special collections to the notice of intending exhibitors. All the varieties included are first-class exhibition sorts, and have been carefully selected and arranged to give the best possible variety of colours.

* † Arthur Unwin, cream and rose
* † Asta Ohn Spencer, mauve
† Clara Curtis, primrose yellow
  Countess Spencer, pale rose
* † Constance Oliver, creamy rose
† Earl Spencer, orange salmon

* † Etta Dyke, pure white
  Frank Dolby, lavender blue
  King Edward Spencer, crimson
* † Marie Corelli, brilliant rose
* † Sunproof Crimson, crimson scarlet
  Mrs. Townsend, white, edged blue

  Mrs. Andrew Ireland, rose and white
  Nora Unwin, pure white
† Picotee, white, edged rose
* † Thomas Stevenson, orange scarlet
† Tom Bolton, maroon
† Winsome, rosy heliotrope

		s. d.
1	EIGHTEEN SUPERB VARIETIES, one packet of each as above	6s. 6d.
2	TWELVE SPLENDID VARIETIES, marked (†)	5s. 0d.
3	SIX FINE SELECTED SORTS, marked (*)	2s. 6d.

DANIELS' SPECIAL COLLECTIONS OF SWEET PEAS.

The following liberal collection include what we consider the best selection of varieties for garden decoration or for cut flowers :—

* Black Knight, maroon
† * Countess Spencer, pink
† * Constance Oliver, rose and cream
† * Colleen, crimson and white
* Dorothy Eckford, pure white
* Evelyn Byatt, orange scarlet
* Evelyn Hemus, cream, edged rose
† * Florence Morse Spencer, blush

† Helen Lewis, rosy orange
† * Helen Pierce, marbled blue
† * Hon. Mrs. Kenyon, primrose
† * John Ingman, brilliant rose
† * King Edward VII., crimson
† * Lady Grisel Hamilton, lavender blue
  Lord Nelson, dark blue
* Lord Rosebery, magenta

† Miss Willmott, orange pink
* Mrs. Townsend, white, edged blue
† Nora Unwin, pure white
† Picotee, white, edged rose
* Primrose Spencer, primrose
  Queen Alexandra, scarlet
* Winsome, heliotrope rose
* Zoe, bright blue

		s. d.
4	TWENTY-FOUR SPLENDID VARIETIES, one packet of each as above	6s. 0d.
5	EIGHTEEN SELECTED VARIETIES, marked (*)	4s. 6d.
6	TWELVE SUPERB VARIETIES, marked (†)	3s. 0d.
7	SIX FINE VARIETIES, Dorothy Eckford, Constance Oliver, Evelyn Hemus, King Edward VII., Lady Grisel Hamilton, John Ingman	1s. 9d.

SWEET PEAS—Select Varieties.

We no longer catalogue the older and inferior varieties of Sweet Peas, and the following list only includes those which we consider the most beautiful and distinct in each class. To assist our Customers in making their selection, we have classified the varieties in their prevailing shades of colour.

☞ All Flower Seeds quoted in 3d. packets may be had at 2s. 6d. per dozen.

PURE WHITE.

per pkt.—s. d.

8 **BEATRICE STEVENS. (See Novelties)**   1 0
9 **DOROTHY ECKFORD.** One of the finest pure white Sweet Peas yet raised. First-class for cutting   0 3
10 **ETTA DYKE.** Very large beautiful pure white flowers with bold wavy standards, on long wiry stems, undoubtedly the finest of all the pure whites. A splendid exhibition flower   0 6
11 **NORA UNWIN.** A magnificent pure white, which easily takes its place in the front rank. The flowers are of great size, with the same bold wavy standard as Gladys Unwin   0 3

CREAM AND YELLOW SHADES.

12 **CLARA CURTIS.** Beautiful primrose yellow, one of the best in this section   0 4
13 **DORA BREADMORE.** Pale yellow delicately tinged with rosy pink. A very beautiful large flowered variety of charming effect   0 3
14 **GIANT CREAM WAVED.** A superb variety, with very large beautifully waved flowers. The colour is a deep rich cream   0 6
15 **HON. MRS. KENYON.** Large beautiful flowers of a delicate primrose yellow   0 3
16 **MRS. A. MALCOLM.** Beautiful rich creamy yellow. Large splendid flowers borne three and four on a stem. Very free-flowering and first-class for exhibition   0 4
17 **PRIMROSE SPENCER.** Large flowers of a beautiful primrose or creamy yellow, with three and sometimes four blooms on a stem   0 3

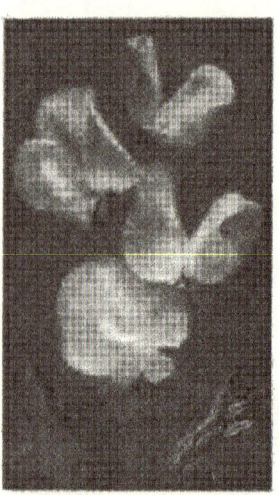

MRS. HARDCASTLE SYKES. (No. 26.)

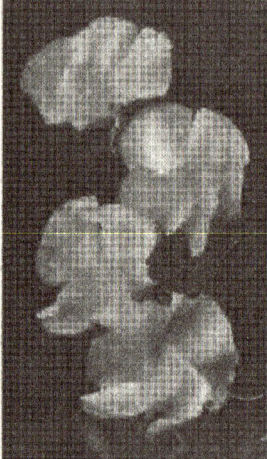

MIRIAM BEAVER. (No. 31.)

PALE ROSE AND PINK.

per pkt.—s. d.

18 **BOBBY K.** Large beautiful flowers, with bold wavy standards of the true Spencer type. The colour is a lovely pale apple-blossom blush. Fine Exhibition variety   0 6
19 **BOLTON'S PINK.** A beautiful erect pink-self, with very large flowers. The standard shaded delicate rose   0 3
20 **COUNTESS SPENCER. (True.)** A lovely shade of pink, with large wavy standards. The flowers are of splendid size   0 4
21 **DORA DANIELS. (See Novelties)**   1 0
22 **FLORENCE MORSE SPENCER.** Delicate blush with pink margin. A most beautiful variety of splendid size   0 4
23 **GLADYS UNWIN.** The flowers are large, bold, with a crinkled or wavy standard and broad wings. The colour is a lovely pale rosy pink   0 3
24 **HERCULES.** Pale rosy pink, very large flowers, of splendid substance   0 6
25 **MRS. ALFRED WATKINS.** Very large flowers, produced three and four on long stems; the colour is a beautiful pale rose, with bold wavy standards.   0 3
26 **MRS. HARDCASTLE SYKES.** Rosy pink, with white at base of standards. A superb flower.   0 4

BICOLORS.

27 **APPLE BLOSSOM SPENCER.** Standard rosy pink, wings blush rose. Large beautiful flowers on very long stems   0 4
28 **ARTHUR UNWIN. (See Novelties)**   6d. and 1 0
29 **COLLEEN.** A magnificent new bicolor. The bold standard is of an intense deep carmine, and the wings a faint blush   0 6
30 **JEANNIE GORDON.** Standards bright rose, shaded cream, wings creamy suffused with rose : most beautiful variety   0 3
31 **MRS. ANDREW IRELAND.** Rosy-pink and blush waved ; a very attractive and beautiful bicolor   0 4
32 **MRS. C. MASTERS. (See Novelties)**   6d. and 1 0

CREAM-PINK.

per pkt.—s. d

33 **CONSTANCE OLIVER.** Cream, suffused with delicate rose. Flowers large with waved standards ; one of the most beautiful varieties yet raised   0 4
34 **MIRIAM BEAVER.** Large beautifully waved flowers, three and four on a stem. The colour is a bright soft pinkish salmon on a primrose ground. A variety of the most charming effect   0 6
35 **MRS. HENRY BELL.** Beautiful pale rosy-pink, suffused with apricot cream at base of standards. A most lovely flower   0 3
36 **MRS. HUGH DICKSON.** A beautiful pale salmon pink self, one of the finest of recent introduction   0 4
37 **MRS. ROUTZAHN.** Very large beautiful flowers, with broad, deep, wavy standards. The colour is a rich apricot, shaded with salmon pink. A distinct and lovely variety   0 4
38 **W. T. HUTCHINS.** Apricot and lemon overlaid with blush. Flowers three and four on a stem. A true Spencer and one of the most superb varieties yet raised   0 6

MAGENTA, MAUVE, HELIOTROPE.

39 **A. J. COOK.** Deep bright mauve. A fine variety   0 3
40 **MENIE CHRISTIE.** A superb new variety. The standards are a beautiful bright purplish carmine, with rosy magenta wings, beautifully waved. A very distinct and splendid flower   0 6
41 **MRS. WALTER WRIGHT.** A beautiful shade of mauve, with bright shaded mauve wings   0 3
42 **THE MARQUIS.** Rosy heliotrope. A charming flower. First-class for exhibition   0 4
43 **WINSOME.** A quite distinct and lovely flower that should be in every collection. The colour is a bright heliotrope-rose with white at the base. *(See illustration)*   0 4

MRS. ROUTZAHN. (No. 37.)

KING EDWARD SPENCER. (No. 77.)

BLUE AND LAVENDER.

per pkt.—s. d.

44 **AFTERGLOW.** (See Novelties) .. 1 0
45 **ASTA OHN SPENCER,** Lavender tinted mauve, a magnificent variety with large splendid flowers three and four on a stem 0 6
46 **BERTRAND DEAL.** (See Novelties) 6d. and 1 0
47 **CHARLES FOSTER.** (See Novelties) 1 0
48 **FLORENCE NIGHTINGALE.** (See Novelties) .. .. 6d. and 1 0
49 **FLORA NORTON SPENCER.** Beautiful bright blue self, large waved flowers 0 4
50 **FRANK DOLBY.** A lovely pale blue, resembling Lady Grisel Hamilton, but the flowers are much larger .. 0 3
51 **HELEN PIERCE.** Pale blue front, with darker back, marbled and mottled with a darker shade of blue .. 0 8
52 **LADY GRISEL HAMILTON.** A grand variety of the large-flowered type, with flowers of a beautiful shining pale lavender 0 3
53 **LORD NELSON.** (Brilliant Blue.) Deep bright blue self. A very fine and distinct variety 0 3
54 **MASTERPIECE.** Very large flowers of true Spencer type, borne three and four on a stem; colour a beautiful clear lavender blue. A fine exhibition variety 0 6
55 **MAY FARQUHAR.** (See Novelties) 6d. and 1 0
56 **ZOE.** Clear blue self. Very fine and distinct.. .. ... — 0 3

DEEP ROSE AND CARMINE.

per pkt.—s. d.

57 **BERYL TATHAM.** (See Novelties) 1 0
58 **E. J. CASTLE.** Magnificent variety, with large wavy, rosy carmine standard, and bright rosy shades; the flowers produced three and four on a stem 0 3
59 **JOHN INGMAN.** (True.) A grand flower, very large and of good substance. Colour a bright rich rosy carmine. The blooms are produced three and four on a long wiry stem, and are splendid for cutting or exhibition 0 4
60 **LORD ROSEBERY.** A self-coloured rosy magenta, of large size and the most perfect form; one of the best 0 3
61 **MARIE CORELLI.** Brilliant rosy carmine, showing a little white at the base. A strikingly beautiful variety either for garden decoration or for Exhibition 0 4
62 **PRINCE EDWARD OF YORK.** Large flowers, standards scarlet, wings of a beautiful deep rose 0 3
63 **ROSE DU BARRI.** Deep rich carmine-rose and orange, quite a novel shade 0 6

PICOTEE EDGED.

64 **DAINTY.** Large beautiful flowers of splendid form, a lovely white, delicately edged with pink 0 3
65 **EVELYN HEMUS** (syn. Mrs. C. W. Breadmore). Rich cream shading to yellow with a picotee-edging of bright terra-cotta red. Very large flowers of Spencer form. Superb .. 0 4
66 **MAID OF HONOUR.** White, edged with pale blue; charming variety 0 3
67 **MRS. TOWNSEND.** Large white flowers edged and flushed with pale lilac blue. A most charming variety 0 3
68 **PICOTEE.** Large, splendidly waved flowers, three and four on a stem; colour pearly white, distinctly edged bright carmine 0 4

STRIPED OR FLAKED VARIETIES.

69 **AMERICA SPENCER.** Deep blood-red striped; handsome .. 0 3
70 **AURORA SPENCER.** Large beautiful waved flowers, white ground, striped with bright salmon-red 0 4
71 **ETHEL ROOSEVELT.** (See Novelties) .. 6d. and 1 0
72 **MRS. W. J. UNWIN.** (See Novelties) .. 6d. and 1 0
73 **PRINCE OLAF.** Blue striped and flaked 0 4
74 **SENATOR SPENCER** (new). Rosy heliotrope striped chocolate Large flowers. A distinct and fine variety 0 6

SCARLET AND CRIMSON.

per pkt.—s. d.

75 **CHRISSIE UNWIN.** Light clear cherry scarlet, flowers of splendid form and substance, very beautiful and quite distinct .. 0 6
76 **DORIS BURT.** Brilliant glowing scarlet shaded cerise, a very fine variety, placed by the N.S.P.S. as first in the scarlet section 0 6
77 **KING EDWARD SPENCER.** Splendid flowers of a deep rich crimson scarlet colour, borne on long wiry stems. The blooms, which are produced three and four on a stem, are of immense size, and the standards are beautifully waved in the true Spencer style 0 6
78 **KING EDWARD VII.** A grand variety. The blooms are large, of splendid form, and borne on long robust stems .. 0 3
79 **QUEEN ALEXANDRA.** Brilliant pure scarlet; one of the very best 0 3
80 **SUNPROOF CRIMSON** (Maude Holmes). Flowers of great size, borne three and four on a stem; the colour is deep rich crimson scarlet. An improvement on King Edward Spencer .. 0 6
81 **SCARLET MONARCH.** (See Novelties) .. 6d. and 1 0

SALMON & ORANGE-RED SHADES.

82 **ANGLIAN ORANGE.** Large splendidly formed flowers, three and four on a stem; colour a beautiful bright salmon pink.. 0 6
83 **BARBARA.** (See Novelties) 1 0
84 **EARL SPENCER.** Flowers of great size, waved, three and four on a stem; colour a brilliant orange-rose, magnificent variety 0 6
85 **EDNA UNWIN IMPROVED.** (See Novelties) .. 1 0
86 **EVELYN BYATT.** The richest orange-coloured Sweet Pea yet introduced. The standard is rich bright salmon, and the falls a trifle deeper in colour; splendid variety .. 0 3
87 **HELEN LEWIS** (The Orange Countess) (true). The flowers are very large, the standards wavy and of a rich orange colour, the wings rosy. A very beautiful and indispensable flower .. 0 4
88 **MISS WILLMOT.** Beautiful bright orange pink, shaded with rose; one of the largest and most beautiful varieties .. 0 3
89 **THOMAS STEVENSON.** (See Novelties) .. 6d. and 1 0

MAROON, CLARET, CHOCOLATE.

90 **ANNA LUMLEY.** A very fine deep maroon Spencer; large, richly coloured waved flowers, three and four on a stem .. 0 3
91 **BLACK KNIGHT.** Deep maroon self; one of the very finest .. 0 3
92 **OTHELLO SPENCER.** Deep brown chocolate red, very large waved flowers; fine 0 4
93 **TOM BOLTON.** Very deep maroon, large waved flowers, the finest of its class 0 6

SWEET PEAS.

SPENCER SWEET PEAS IN VASE.

DANIELS' LARGE-FLOWERED.
In Selected Colours.

		per oz.—s.	d.
94 DANIELS' BRILLIANT SCARLET		1	0
95 DANIELS' LIGHT BLUE		1	0
96 DANIELS' BRIGHT ROSE		1	0
97 DANIELS' PURE WHITE		1	0
98 DANIELS' DARK BLUE		1	0
99 DANIELS' PRIMROSE YELLOW		1	0
100 DANIELS' DELICATE ROSE		1	0
101 DANIELS' ROSE AND WHITE		1	0

Beautiful large-flowered varieties, specially selected for cut flowers or garden decoration.

New Large-flowered Varieties in Collections.

The sorts given in these collections are carefully selected to ensure the best possible variety.

		s.	d.
102 12 CHOICE VARIETIES, 100 seeds of each		2	6
103 6 " " " " "		1	6

DANIELS' SPECIAL MIXTURE OF GIANT-FLOWERED SPENCERS.

We highly recommend this splendid mixture which we feel sure will give great satisfaction. The varieties included are all of the true Giant-flowered Spencer type, and the colours include all the most brilliant and beautiful shades of scarlet, crimson, magenta, orange, salmon, pink, mauve, cream and primrose to the purest white. This will prove a first-class mixture where really good Sweet Peas are required for cut bloom.

104 Per quart, 10s.   105 Per pint, 5s. 6d.   106 Per oz., 9d.

Large-flowered in Mixture.

Splendid varieties in choicest mixture, including a good proportion of the light and delicately coloured sorts. Very highly recommended.

107 Per quart, 6s.   108 Per pint, 3s. 6d.   109 Per oz., 6d.

SWEET PEAS—Ordinary Class, Choice Mixed.

110 Per quart, 3s. 6d.   111 Per pint, 2s.   112 Per oz., 4d.

☛ NEW TOM THUMB SWEET PEAS—CUPID. ☚

Charming and highly interesting new varieties growing only four or five inches high, and of a compact, spreading habit of growth; when fully grown the plants are about a foot across, the foliage being dark green, and the flower-stems about four inches long.

			per pkt.—s.	d.					per pkt.—s.	d.
113	CUPID—APPLE BLOSSOM.	Rose, shaded blush	0	3	120	CUPID—LOTTIE ECKFORD.	Rose and white, edged blue	0	3
114	"	BEAUTY. Rosy crimson and white	0	3	121	"	MAUVE QUEEN. Pinkish mauve	0	3
115	"	BOREATTON. Deep maroon	0	3	122	"	PINK. Rose and white, very pretty	0	3
116	"	CAPTAIN OF THE BLUES. Deep blue	0	3	123	"	PRIMROSE. Delicate pale yellow	0	3
117	"	FIREFLY. Dazzling scarlet	0	3	124	"	PURE WHITE. Beautiful	0	3
118	"	HER MAJESTY. Deep rose crimson	0	3	125	"	SALOPIAN. Deep crimson	0	3
119	"	LADY MARY CURRIE. Orange pink	0	3	126	"	STELLA MORSE. Primrose, flushed pink	0	3

127 One Packet of each fourteen varieties, 2s. 6d.

128 NEW DWARF SWEET PEAS, in mixture, containing many pretty varieties   per oz. 8d.; per pkt. 3d.

Cultivation.—To grow really fine Sweet Peas, the ground should be deeply dug or trenched and plenty of well-decayed manure, with some coarse bone meal worked well in and to the bottom of the trench. This should be done in Autumn if convenient, or as early as possible in Spring, so as to allow of the ground settling down firmly before planting out.

For early blooming, sow the seeds thinly in pots or pans in January or February, and place in a gentle heat; harden off as soon as the plants are well up, and plant out as soon as convenient in March. If intended to be grown for exhibition, we should recommend planting in clumps four feet apart, six or eight plants in a clump, or they may be planted in single or double rows six feet apart; but in any case the plants should be not less than six or eight inches apart in the row or clump. Stakes should be placed as soon as the plants are three or four inches high. The ground should be kept free of weeds, and water given if the weather is dry.

As growth advances some weak liquid manure should be given once or twice a week, and if the weather continues dry, a mulching of some short, well-decayed manure should be placed on the surface about the roots. This will be of great benefit in stimulating a healthy growth, and some splendid flowers will be produced.

An excellent liquid manure can be made by dissolving Daniels' Sweet Pea Fertiliser, about four ounces to the gallon of water, or guano, about two ounces to the gallon, with the addition of some soot. Either of these are splendid stimulants for promoting growth and improving the size and brilliancy of the flowers. Drainings from a cowshed or manure heap, mixed with five or six times its bulk of clear water, also forms a very good liquid manure.

For later successive blooming the seeds may be sown out of doors at intervals from early March to the middle of May, giving them a similar treatment to that recommended above. Excellent results may also be had by sowing in October or November in a sheltered position in the garden. These, with a slight protection, will survive a moderately severe Winter and furnish some nice blooms for cutting earlier than those sown in spring.

If the blooms are closely gathered and seed pods not allowed to develop, the plants will continue in bloom for a much longer period.

DANIELS' COMPLETE COLLECTIONS OF

Choice Flower Seeds for Amateurs

Carefully arranged to ensure a fine display of flowers throughout the Summer and Autumn, and specially adapted to the requirements of the Cottage, Villa, or large Garden.

Collection A.—Price 5s. 6d. Post Free.

Contains the following choice selection.

6 Distinct vars. Aster, Ostrich Plume
6 „ „ Stock, large-flowered Ten-week
1 Packet Phlox Drummondi Grandiflora

6 Choice vars. Sweet Peas, new large-flowered
1 Packet Petunia, large-flowered
1 „ Zinnia, finest double

12 Packets Choice Hardy and Half-hardy Annuals, including Godetias, Shirley Poppy, Candytuft, Dwarf Nasturtiums, Mignonette, Salpiglossis, Marigold, &c.

Collection B.—Price 7s. 6d. Post Free.

6 Choice vars. Comet Aster
1 Packet Ostrich Plume Aster
6 Choice vars. Large-flowered Ten-week Stock
8 Choice Hardy Annuals

1 Packet Balsam, choice double
6 Half-hardy Annuals, including Phlox, Marigold, Portulaca
9 Distinct varieties Sweet Peas, new large-flowered

1 Packet Petunia, finest mixed
1 „ Zinnia, finest double
1 „ Helichrysum, mixed
1 „ Rhodanthe maculata
1 „ Salpiglossis, mixed

Collection C.—Price 10s. 6d. Post Free.

8 Choice vars. Victoria Aster
6 „ „ Large-flowered Ten-week Stock
6 Varieties Zinnia elegans, double
6 Choice Half-hardy Annuals for bedding out, &c.

12 Choice Hardy Annuals, the most useful and showy kinds
3 Choice varieties Everlasting Flowers
2 Choice Ornamental Grasses
1 Packet Petunia, choice mixed

1 Packet Camellia-flowered Balsam
1 Packet Verbena, choice
1 Ounce Mignonette
12 Choice varieties Sweet Peas, new large-flowered

Collection D.—Price 21s. Carriage Free.

6 Choice vars. Ostrich Plume Aster
6 „ „ Dwarf Peony Aster
12 „ „ Victoria Aster
12 „ „ Ten-week Stock Large-fld
6 „ „ Double Zinnia
12 „ „ Phlox Drummondi
12 „ „ Showy Hardy Annuals, for borders, &c.

3 Choice Ornamental Grasses
6 „ varieties Half-hardy Annuals, for bedding out, pots, &c.
6 Hardy Perennials and Biennials
3 Choice varieties Everlasting Flowers
18 Choice varieties Sweet Peas, new large-flowered

1 Packet Petunia, choice mixed
1 „ Verbena, fine mixed
1 „ Calceolaria, choicest mixed
1 „ Cineraria, choice mixed
1 „ Primula, choice fringed
1 Ounce Nemophila insignis
1 „ Mignonette, Giant

Other Collections of Choice Flower Seeds, 31s. 6d., 42s., 63s., 84s., and 100s.

THE AMATEUR'S PACKET OF CHOICE FLOWER SEEDS.

(REGISTERED.)

Price 2s. 6d. Post Free.

Contains the following Choice Assortment in full-sized packets, with cultural directions. This is a very cheap and splendid collection, which we can highly recommend.

Sweet Peas, New Large-flowered
  Six distinct and beautiful varieties, one packet each.
Aster, "Ostrich Plume," choicest mixed

Stock, Large-flowered Ten-week, mixed
Phlox Drummondi, mixed
Shirley Poppy, selected strain
Nasturtium, Empress of India

Sweet Sultan, Giant mixed
Godetia, Large-flowered, mixed
Mignonette, Giant Machet
Night-scented Stock

Biennials and Perennials.			Everlasting Flowers.			Ornamental Grasses.		
	s.	d.		s.	d.		s.	d.
12 Selected Hardy Varieties ..	3	6	12 Very Fine Varieties ..	2	6	12 Fine Annual Varieties ..	2	6
6 „ „ „ ..	2	0	6 „ „ „ ..	1	6	6 „ „ „ ..	1	6

GIANT ENGLISH BROMPTON STOCKS.

An exceedingly fine and useful class of Spring flowering plants of the old cottage garden type, producing large, handsome spikes of beautifully coloured and deliciously scented flowers in April and May. The seeds should be sown in May or early in June; sow thinly, and soon as the young plants are large enough to handle, prick them out about six inches apart on nursery beds in a sheltered position where they can remain during Summer. In September or October they should be planted out where intended to bloom in Spring. For this purpose some sheltered spot, as on a sunny border or under a South wall, should always be selected, as the plants are liable to suffer from severe frosts in early Spring if too much exposed. The plants grow about two feet high and should be planted eighteen inches or more apart.

				s. d.					s. d.
129	SIX CHOICE VARIETIES, Separate		..	2 0	133	BRILLIANT ROSE, Splendid variety	..	.. per pkt.	0 6
130	DARK BLOOD RED, Splendid colour	..	.. per pkt.	0 6	134	DARK PURPLE, Fine colour ..	..	.. ,,	0 6
131	SNOW WHITE, Very fine	..	.. ,,	0 6	135	CHOICEST MIXED } In beautiful variety	..	.. ,,	1 0
132	CARMINE, A beautiful colour ..	..	.. ,,	0 6	136	,, ,, }		smaller pkt.	0 6

Cultivation of Stocks.—These deliciously-scented half-hardy annuals are amongst the most popular of all Summer bedding plants and they are deservedly given a place in both large and small gardens.

Ten-Week Stocks are easily raised from seed, but require careful treatment when in the seedling stage, as they are liable to damp off if over-watered and kept close, but if they are given an abundance of air and kept moderately moist, nothing need be feared and sturdy plants are assured.

During recent years much care has been devoted to the improvement of Stocks, both with regard to increasing the size of the individual flowers as well as the spike, and to the introduction of much clearer colours. It is now possible to grow them in every shade of colour from pure white to deep crimson and purple.

When planted in clumps of distinct colours on borders or in separate beds, Ten-Week Stocks form most attractive subjects, and the perfume is so delicious that after a shower of rain a bed in full bloom will fill the garden with its delightful odour.

The seed may be sown at any time from February to June, according to the time the plants are required to bloom; they are best raised in a frame or greenhouse. Either shallow wooden seed boxes or pans may be used, and the seed can be sown either in drills lengthwise down the boxes or (in the case of pans) sprinkled lightly over the surface, the seed being spread as evenly as possible.

The soil used should be rich potting mould finely sifted, and after sowing, the seed should be thinly covered with the same, keep the frame close and shaded until the seeds have germinated, when a little air should be given and the amount gradually increased as the plants gain strength.

When the plants are large enough to handle with safety they should be transplanted into boxes, allowing nine inches between each plant.

They can then be gradually hardened off, but should be at first carefully protected at night from the frost.

Give abundance of air during the daytime, and after about three weeks or a month they should be ready for planting out in the positions in which they are to bloom in the border or beds.

When a succession of flowers is desired, a sowing of Stocks should be made in the open border when strong sturdy plants will be raised; these will follow on in succession after those raised inside.

Always be careful that the borders are thoroughly trenched and given a liberal supply of decomposed manure before the Stocks are planted.

If possible, select showery weather for planting out, and be sure that the plants are thoroughly watered into the ground and kept shaded during the middle of the day for the first few days.

In planting out seedling Ten-Week Stocks, with a view to securing the largest number of double flowers, preference should always be given to those with a good share of *fine fibrous* roots, even if the plants are somewhat weaker; we have found from long experience that those having coarse forked roots invariably produce the largest percentage of single blooms.

By sowing the seed in July and potting the seedlings in single pots and growing on in a frame, a good display of bloom may be had in the greenhouse during the Winter months.

WINTER FLOWERING STOCK—BEAUTY OF NICE.

WINTER-FLOWERING AND INTERMEDIATE STOCKS.—This is a very useful class for Winter blooming. The seed should be sown in July and the plants potted on into 5 inch pots, placing 3 plants in each pot; no artificial heat is needed, but the plants may be grown on, and placed in a greenhouse or conservatory, where they will provide a splendid show of bloom in the early part of the year.

From Mr. R. PRATCHELL, Leytonstone.

March 20th,
"I enclose a photo of our bed of Stocks which were grown from your Seeds; I thought you would be interested to know what can be done by amateurs. We had a grand display and numerous enquiries as to the reedsmen."

From Mr. J. GILBERT, London.

March 21st.
"I should like to tell you that the Giant Stocks were the finest round here last year, and could not be beaten."

DANIELS' SUPERB TEN-WEEK AND OTHER STOCKS.

PERPETUAL PERFECTION TEN-WEEK.

A new and exceedingly valuable class growing to the height of about eighteen inches, and blooming profusely from July till late in Autumn. If sown in July or August and potted up may be wintered in a cool frame, and will bloom splendidly under glass in early Spring.

		per pkt.—s.	d.
137	SIX CHOICE VARIETIES	2	6
138	CRIMSON	1	0
139	PURE WHITE	1	0

		per pkt.—s.	d.
140	LIGHT BLUE	1	0
141	CANARY YELLOW	1	0
142	CHOICEST MIXED	6d and 1	0

INTERMEDIATE STOCKS.

EAST LOTHIAN AUTUMNAL—
Splendid for late blooming on the open border or for Winter decoration in the greenhouse.

		per pkt.—s.	d.
143	AN ASSORTMENT OF 4 DISTINCT VARIETIES	2	0
144	SCARLET	1	0
145	CRIMSON	1	0
146	PURPLE	1	0
147	WHITE	1	0
148	CHOICEST MIXED	1	0
149	" "	smaller pkt. 0	6

LARGE-FLOWERED EMPEROR—
Remarkable for their large flowers and vigorous habit. If sown in March will produce a magnificent effect in Autumn.

150	AN ASSORTMENT OF 8 SPLENDID VARIETIES	2	0
151	FINEST MIXED	0	6

AUTUMN FLOWERING INTERMEDIATE—
A fine class for late flowering.

152	AN ASSORTMENT OF 6 SPLENDID VARIETIES	2	0
153	CHOICEST MIXED	0	6

IMPROVED WALLFLOWER-LEAVED TEN-WEEK.

A very distinct and beautiful class, growing about nine inches high, with rich glossy dark green foliage, which contrasts admirably with the bright colours of the flowers.

		per pkt.—s.	d.
154	SIX CHOICE VARIETIES, DISTINCT	1	6
155	DARK BLOOD RED	0	6
156	PURE WHITE	0	6
157	DARK BLUE	0	6
158	CHOICEST MIXED	1	0
159	" "	smaller pkt. 0	6

DWARF GERMAN TEN-WEEK.

Useful compact growing class. Height nine inches.

			per pkt.—	
160	SIX CHOICE VARIETIES, DISTINCT		1	6
161	SCARLET	per pkt.	0	3
162	PURPLE	"	0	3
163	WHITE		0	3
164	CHOICE MIXED		0	3

From Mr. E. WALLIS, Neithrop.

June 28th.
"We had a fine show of **Brompton Stocks** from your Seed last year. Everybody remarked what fine blooms they were."

From Mr. G. NEEDLE, Byfield.

May 27th.
"The **Winter Stocks** I had from you last year are now making a splendid show; they could not be finer."

ALMOND BLOSSOM.

WINTER-FLOWERING STOCKS.

A splendid race of tall growing varieties, producing magnificent spikes of very large deliciously-scented double-flowers. Sown in July or August and potted up in Autumn, these will furnish some beautiful flowers under glass in Winter and early Spring, the long flower-stems making them of especial value for cutting. If sown in February or March and planted out in good soil, some grand spikes of bloom may be had during the summer and autumn.

	per pkt.—s.	d.
165 **ALMOND BLOSSOM** (new). Long central spikes and numerous side branches of lovely white flowers delicately shaded with carmine. Height 2 feet	1	0
166 **BEAUTY OF NICE.** Large spikes with very large blooms of a delicate satiny flesh colour. Height 2 feet 6d. and	1	0
167 **CRIMSON KING.** Brilliant fiery crimson, large blooms and spikes. Finely scented. Beautiful variety. 2 feet 6 and	1	0

	per pkt.—s.	d.
168 **NAVY BLUE** (new). Fine spikes of rich dark purplish blue, double flowers	1	0
169 **MAUVE BEAUTY** (new). A superb variety with noble spikes of large double flowers of the most beautiful pale bluish mauve. Quite distinct. Height 2 feet 6d. and	1	0
170 **QUEEN ALEXANDRA.** Magnificent spikes of very large sweet-scented flowers of a lovely soft rosy-lilac colour. 2 feet	1	0

DANIELS' SUPERB TEN-WEEK STOCKS

Our splendid strains of Ten-week and other Stocks are especially grown for our retail trade by one of the most famous growers, and may be thoroughly relied on to produce the largest percentage of fine double flowers procurable from seed.

DANIELS' LARGE-FLOWERED TEN-WEEK.

This is incomparably the finest strain of Ten-week Stocks in existence, and, where space is limited, should always be grown in preference to others. The plants which attain about one foot in height are of the same compact habit as the dwarfer varieties, but the flowers when well grown are nearly double the size of those of the old variety. The seeds of this always produce a high percentage of double flowers, whilst in substance of petal, brilliancy of colouring and richness of fragrance they are unrivalled.

			s.	d.
171	A COLLECTION OF 12 SUPERB VARIETIES. The most distinct and beautiful colours		3	6
172	,, 6 ,, ,,		2	0

		per pkt.—s.	d.				per pkt.—s.	d.				per pkt.—s.	d.
173	DANIELS' SPECIAL MIXTURE of			178	PURE WHITE		0	6	184	BRIGHT ROSE		0	6
	the most brilliant varieties	1	6	179	LIGHT BLUE ..		0	6	185	DARK PURPLE		0	6
174	DARK BLOOD RED ..	0	6	180	FLESH COLOUR		0	6	186	ROSY LILAC ..		0	6
175	DARK VIOLET ..	0	6	181	SALMON ROSE		0	6	187	CHOICEST MIXED		1	0
176	SULPHUR YELLOW ..	0	6	182	BRILLIANT CARMINE..		0	6	188	,, ,, smaller pkt.		0	6
177	BRILLIANT ROSE ..	0	6	183	ASH GREY ..		0	6					

FINE NEW VARIETIES.

The following splendid new varieties of our superb strain of Large-flowered Ten-week Stocks bloomed magnificently at our Seed Grounds last Summer, and were greatly admired by our many visitors. The colours of these will be found distinct and beautiful, with exceptionally large spikes of fine double blooms, and a decided advance on most of the older sorts.

			per pkt.—s.	d.
189	DANIELS' SPECIAL WHITE ..			1	0
190	DANIELS' SPECIAL SCARLET	Producing very fine spikes of large perfectly double flowers of the most delicious fragrance.		1	0
191	DELICATE FLESH COLOUR			1	0
192	NEW SALMON ROSE			1	0
193	NEW LIGHT BLUE			1	0

194   One Packet of each above 5 Superb Varieties, 4s.

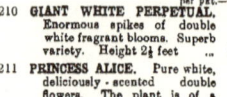 ## DANIELS' GIANT PERFECTION TEN-WEEK.

A grand class of tall-growing, beautiful varieties. The plants attain a height of from 15 to 18 inches, are of a handsome pyramidal form with branching habit, and throw up long central spikes of large, beautifully double flowers. This is an exceedingly fine strain that we can highly recommend.

			s.	d.					s.	d.					s.	d.
195	SIX CHOICE VARIETIES, distinct	1	6	198	LIGHT BLUE ..		per pkt.	0	6	201	ROSE		.. per pkt.	0	6
196	CRIMSON ..	per pkt.	0	6	199	DARK BLUE ..	..	,,	0	6	202	CHOICEST MIXED	.. ..	,,	1	0
197	CANARY YELLOW	.. ,,	0	6	200	PURE WHITE	..	,,	0	6	203	,, ,, smaller pkt.			0	6

DANIELS' MINIATURE TEN-WEEK.

A very beautiful class of dwarf-growing German Ten-week Stock, height about eight inches, and producing a large percentage of fine double flowers, which are carried well above the foliage.

			s.	d.					s.	d.					s.	d.
204	SIX CHOICE VARIETIES	..	1	6	206	PURE WHITE	— per pkt.		0	6	208	CHOICEST MIXED	.. per pkt.		1	0
205	DARK BLOOD RED	.. per pkt.	0	6	207	DARK PURPLE	..	,,	0	6	209	,, ,, smaller pkt.			0	6

SUMMER FLOWERING STOCKS.

	per pkt.—s.	d.
210	GIANT WHITE PERPETUAL. Enormous spikes of double white fragrant blooms. Superb variety. Height 2½ feet ..	1	0
211	PRINCESS ALICE. Pure white, deliciously - scented double flowers. The plant is of a branching habit. Height 18 inches ..	1	0
212	PRINCESS MAY. A beautiful early-flowering variety with double primrose yellow flowers. Wallflower leaved. Height only 8 inches ..	1	0

STOCK—MAUVE QUEEN.

	per pkt.—s.	d.
213	SCARLET QUEEN, DWARF TEN - WEEK. A charming variety, growing only 6 inches high and literally covered by its numerous spikes of deep blood crimson flowers. Splendid for beds, edgings, or pots ..	1	0
214	MAUVE QUEEN (Heliotrope). A beautiful variety, growing about 1 foot high, with finely scented double flowers of a pale bluish mauve colour, quite a distinct and novel shade of colour amongst Stocks —	1	0

From Mr. F. HALLIS, Bournbrook.
March 19th.
  " I am glad to say I was very successful with my Flowers last year; I took three Firsts and one Second at the Clipston Show."

From G. B. KILMINSTER, Esq., Coleford.
Oct. 26th.
  " I beg to express my entire satisfaction with the Seeds you supplied, and trust to do more business with you in future."

DANIELS' SUPERB STRAIN OF

LARGE-FLOWERED TEN-WEEK STOCKS

DANIELS'
GIANT OSTRICH PLUME ASTERS

DANIELS' SUPERB PRIZE ASTERS.

☞ We have long been famous for our magnificent strains of Asters, which form an important branch of our Flower Seed business, and we would mention that our seeds of these having been grown especially for our retail trade may be relied on as the very finest procurable.

PLEASE NOTE.—We do not as a rule count the seeds contained in our packets, but customers may in all instances rely on liberal quantities of good seeds being given for the prices charged.

DANIELS' GIANT OSTRICH PLUME.

☞ We have much pleasure in recommending this grand new strain of beautiful varieties which we have every confidence in saying will give the highest satisfaction amongst our customers.

The plants are of a strong bushy habit of growth, and attain a height of 18 to 24 inches. The very large handsome flowers, which are borne on long wiry stems, are of the true Ostrich Plume type, and of immense size—when well grown, frequently measuring six inches and even seven inches in diameter, whilst the colours embrace the most beautiful and delicate shades known in Asters. These will prove a splendid class alike for garden decoration, as cut flowers or for exhibition.

		s.	d.				s.	d.
215	A COLLECTION OF 8 BEAUTIFUL VARS., DISTINCT	3	6	221	DANIELS' ROSY LILAC	.. per pkt.	1	0
216	DANIELS' BRILLIANT ROSE .. .. .. per pkt.	1	0	222	DANIELS' BRILLIANT CRIMSON	.. ,,	1	0
217	DANIELS' LILAC BLUE .. .. .. ,,	1	0	223	DANIELS' DARK BLUE	.. ,,	1	0
218	DANIELS' PURE WHITE .. .. .. ,,	1	0	224	DANIELS' CHOICEST MIXED	.. ,,	1	0
219	DANIELS' AZURE BLUE .. .. .. ,,	1	0	225	,, ,, ,,	smaller pkt.	0	6
220	DANIELS' DELICATE ROSE .. .. .. ,,	1	0					

DANIELS' DWARF PERFECTION.

This grand Aster, introduced by us, has proved itself by far the finest and best dwarf variety hitherto sent out. The plants grow only about eight or ten inches high, with stiff, upright stems and branches, and form handsome, circular, bushy plants. The flowers are of large size, perfectly double, beautifully imbricated, and of the most splendid form. This is a superb variety for garden decoration or for exhibition, whilst the beautiful and distinct colours of the different varieties render them especially valuable for bedding out.

		s.	d.				s.	d.
226	AN ASSORTMENT OF 6 SUPERB VARIETIES	2	6	230	DANIELS' BRIGHT ROSE	.. per pkt.	0	6
227	DANIELS' BRILLIANT CRIMSON .. per pkt.	0	6	231	DANIELS' LIGHT BLUE	.. ,,	0	6
228	DANIELS' DARK BLUE .. .. ,,	0	6	232	DANIELS' CHOICEST MIXED ..	.. ,,	1	0
229	DANIELS' PURE WHITE .. .. ,,	0	6	233	,, ,, ,, ..	smaller pkt.	0	6

ASTER—NEW TALL BRANCHING.

A splendid new class of beautiful late blooming varieties, growing about 2 feet high and branching almost from the base of the stem. The blooms, which are produced in the greatest profusion, are of medium size and are borne on very long wiry stems, rendering them of especial value for cut flowers.

		s.	d.				s.	d.
234	SIX VARIETIES AS FOLLOWS, one packet of each	2	6	238	LIGHT BLUE ..	.. ..	0	6
235	PURE WHITE .. .. per pkt.	0	6	239	SHELL PINK ..	.. .. ,,	0	6
236	SALMON ROSE .. .. .. ,,	0	6	240	CRIMSON	.. .. ,,	0	6
237	DARK BLUE .. .. .. ,,	0	6	241	VERY CHOICE MIXED	.. 6d. and	1	0

DWARF VICTORIA.

A beautiful, compact-growing class, with the same form of flower as Victoria, but growing only one foot in height. An excellent variety for bedding.

		s.	d.
242	SIX BEAUTIFUL VARIETIES ..	2	6
243	WHITE. Splendid .. .. per pkt.	0	6
244	BRILLIANT CRIMSON .. .. ,,	0	6
245	INDIGO BLUE .. .. .. ,,	0	6
246	VERY CHOICE MIXED .. .. ,,	0	6

DANIELS' IMPROVED PRIZE QUILLED.

A fine strain of splendid varieties, producing beautifully formed perfectly double flowers of the most charming colours. Being on long wiry stems the flowers are very useful for cutting, but the plants are too straggly for bedding.

		s.	d.
247	AN ASSORTMENT OF 6 CHOICE VARIETIES	1	6
248	CHOICEST MIXED .. .. per pkt.	1	0
249	,, ,, ... smaller pkt.	0	6

DANIELS' IMPROVED PÆONY-FLOWERED PERFECTION.

These Asters are of the greatest perfection, producing large flowers of the most perfect Pæony form, and in a great variety of beautiful colours.

		s.	d.				s.	d.
250	AN ASSORTMENT OF 6 SPLENDID VARIETIES ..	2	0	256	DARK PURPLE VIOLET	.. per pkt.	0	6
251	BRILLIANT CRIMSON .. .. per pkt.	0	6	257	PURE WHITE ..	.. ,,	0	6
252	SKY BLUE .. .. .. ,,	0	6	258	SPLENDID MIXED ..	.. ,,	1	0
253	DELICATE ROSE .. .. .. ,,	0	6	259	,, ,,	smaller pkt.	0	6
254	LIGHT BLUE AND WHITE .. .. ,,	0	6	260	,, ,,	smallest pkt.	0	3
255	DARK SCARLET AND WHITE .. .. ,,	0	6					

RAY ASTER—New Giant White.

A fine new robust growing variety, attaining the height of eighteen inches or two feet. It is of a free branching habit, is a splendid drought resister, and blooms freely in the hottest weather. The very large pure white flowers are composed of long, straight, needle-like petals which radiate from a yellow centre, giving the blooms a most handsome appearance. The flowers being produced on long wiry stems will be found of great value to cut for decorative purposes.

261 Per packet .. .. ..   6d. and 1s.

DANIELS' SUPERB PRIZE ASTERS.

ASTER, GIANT WHITE COMET.

COMET ASTERS,
New Large-flowered or Giant.

An elegant strain of highly improved and beautiful varieties, growing about fifteen inches high, the individual flowers resembling those of the Japanese Chrysanthemum, and are of great size. The blooms are very useful for cutting, the pure white and the delicately-striped flowers being extremely beautiful.

		s.	d.
262	SIX BEAUTIFUL VARIETIES	2	6
263	LIGHT BLUE AND WHITE per pkt.	0	6
264	WHITE. Very fine variety	0	6
265	THE BRIDE. White, shading to delicate rose; beautiful	0	6
266	DARK BLUE, with white centre. Splendid variety	0	6
267	RUBY Rich scarlet; fine	0	6
268	ROSE. Beautiful.	0	6
269	DARK VIOLET. Fine colour	0	6
270	MAUVE or ROSY-LILAC	0	6
271	CHOICEST MIXED	0	6
272	,, ,, smaller pkt.	0	3

GIANT VICTORIA.

A very fine class of splendid flowers. The plants grow about fifteen inches high, and produce extra large double flowers of the most beautiful colours.

		s.	d.
273	SIX DISTINCT VARIETIES	2	0
274	CHOICEST MIXED per pkt. 6d. and	1	0

ASTERS, "Ostrich Plume."
(ORDINARY CLASS.)

Charming varieties of exquisite beauty. The large flowers are borne on long stems, sixteen to eighteen inches in length, and the long petals are beautifully curled and twisted, giving them somewhat the appearance of Japanese Chrysanthemums. Very useful for bedding, besides being of great value for cut flowers or for exhibition.

		s.	d.
275	AN ASSORTMENT OF SIX BEAUTIFUL VARIETIES	2	6
276	PURE WHITE. Splendid for cutting per pkt. 6d. and	0	6
277	ROSE. Beautiful per pkt.	0	6
278	CRIMSON. Very fine ,,	0	6
279	DARK BLUE ,,	0	6
280	WHITE, CHANGING TO ROSE ,,	0	6
281	REDDISH LILAC ,,	0	6
282	CHOICEST MIXED per pkt. 3d. and	0	6

DWARF, PÆONY-FLOWERED.

A beautiful class of Pæony-flowered Aster, with the same form of incurved, perfect flowers as the older varieties but with a much more compact and handsome growth.

		s.	d.
283	SIX BEAUTIFUL VARIETIES	2	0
284	DARK CRIMSON per pkt.	0	6
285	PURE WHITE ,,	0	6
286	LIGHT BLUE ,,	0	6
287	ROSE ,,	0	6
288	CHOICEST MIXED ,,	0	6

SINGLE-FLOWERED ASTERS.

per pkt.—s. d

SINGLE MAUVE (Sinensis)—
This is well described as the best and grandest of the Single-flowering Asters. The plants form elegant branching bushes about 16 inches high, well furnished with rich dark green foliage, and produce an abundance of large, handsome single flowers three to four inches across, having a single row of delicate pale mauve florets with golden central disc. It is a plant of great beauty, quite distinct from the Single German, and far away the most beautiful of all the Single Asters. First-class as border plant or for cut flowers.

289		6d. and	1	0

GIANT SINGLE—
A fine, showy class for garden decoration, and very effective when grown in large beds of separate colours. The flowers are produced on long wiry stems and are very useful to cut for decoration.

290	,, Bright rose	0	6
291	,, Pure white	0	6
292	,, Dark blue	0	6
293	,, Choice mixed 6d. and	1	0

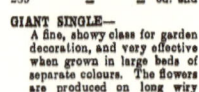

ASTER, SINGLE MAUVE.

We beg to intimate that we cannot "break" packets quoted in this list.

DANIELS' SUPERB PRIZE ASTERS.

IMPROVED VICTORIA ASTER.

DANIELS' IMPROVED VICTORIA.

A magnificent class, growing about fifteen inches high, and producing an abundance of large, perfectly double and beautifully imbricated flowers, four to five inches across. This is one of the most splendid Asters for garden decoration, and a first-class variety for exhibition.

				s.	d.
207	AN ASSORTMENT OF 12 BEAUTIFUL VARIETIES	..		3	6
298	,, ,, 8 ,, ,,			2	6
299	DARK CRIMSON	..	per pkt.	0	6
300	PURE WHITE ..	..	,,	0	6
301	DARK CRIMSON AND WHITE	..	,,	0	6
302	BRIGHT ROSE	..	,,	0	6
303	RICH PURPLE	..	,,	0	6
304	LIGHT BLUE ..	..	,,	0	6
305	FINEST MIXED, In beautiful variety	..	,,	1	0
306	,, ,, ,,	..	smaller pkt.	0	6

DWARF CHRYSANTHEMUM-FLOWERED.

This fine class is a decided acquisition. It commences blooming when many other Asters are off, and is invaluable for a late display; its height is only nine inches, and in consequence of its fine dwarf habit of growth it is admirably suited for beds, edgings, pots, &c.

				s.	d.
307	AN ASSORTMENT OF SIX FINE VARIETIES	..		1	6
308	FIERY SCARLET	..	per pkt.	0	6
309	PURE WHITE	..	,,	0	6
310	BRILLIANT ROSE	..	,,	0	6
311	DARK BLUE	..	,,	0	6
312	LIGHT BLUE AND WHITE	..	,,	0	6
313	CARMINE	..	,,	0	6
314	VERY CHOICE MIXED	..	,,	1	0
315	,, ,, ,,	..	smaller pkt.	0	6

ASTER—Salmon Queen.

A new and beautiful variety growing about 18 inches high and producing a profusion of large beautiful flowers on long wiry stems. The colour of the flower is a beautiful bright salmon-rose, quite a new colour amongst Asters. A splendid variety for cut flowers.

316 Per Packet .. .. .. 6d. and 1s.

DWARF COMET.

A charming strain of beautiful colours. The plants grow only about nine inches high, and the numerous double flowers have the elegant form and lovely colours of the larger growing varieties.

						s.	d.
204	PURE WHITE, Beautiful	—	—	—	6d. and	1	0
205	CHOICEST MIXED	—	—	—	..	1	0
206	,, ,,	—	—	smaller pkt.		0	6

ASTER—Hercules.

A grand new variety growing 15 to 18 inches high and of a robust branching habit of growth. The pure white blooms are of immense size and under good culture will attain as much as six or even seven inches diameter, the long curly petals giving them the appearance of well-grown Japanese Chrysanthemums. The plant is of vigorous growth, and the very handsome flowers are borne on long stout stems, useful for cutting.

317 Per Packet .. .. 1s.

CULTIVATION OF ASTERS.

Cultivation.—Asters form one of the chief attractions in all gardens in which annuals are grown. They are procurable in every colour from white to deep crimson, are very easy to raise from seed, and give a glorious display of bloom in Autumn after many other plants have ceased to flower.

Asters are alike useful for borders and as cut flowers; the single kinds being of especial value for the latter purpose. The seed should be sown in March or April in boxes of good rich soil, and treated in the same manner as other half-hardy annuals; give plenty of room between the plants, and place the boxes in a sunny position under glass, allowing abundance of air and water; after about three weeks remove the boxes to a frame where the lights can be lifted off during the day, and so gradually harden the plants in readiness for their removal to the borders. The greatest care should be exercised in transplanting from the boxes, so as to ensure the seedlings getting a good start. For a succession of flowers seed may be sown at the latter end of April in the open border where they are to bloom. Good sturdy plants may be raised by this method, and will give a supply of late flowers, until the frost cuts them off.

Asters respond readily to liberal treatment although they will thrive in any good garden soil. An excellent position for them is on beds or borders which have been well trenched and liberally manured early in the season. Occasional waterings with weak manure water will be found of great benefit when the plants are developing their blooms. Such treatment gives substance to the flowers and extends the period of blooming. Where the space is available, it is an excellent plan to grow beds in the kitchen garden of separate colours of Asters specially for cutting purposes. Such varieties as Giant Ostrich Plume, Improved Comet, and the Single Sinensis will be found admirable for this purpose, and a supply for the house will be at hand without spoiling the effect of the beds. When only one kind can be grown we should strongly recommend our customers to try our Giant Ostrich Plume as being in our opinion the most delightful of all the doubles. The flowers which are very large, are borne on tall graceful stems often 18 inches long, and the colours are most distinct and varied. Ostrich Plume are quite as easily grown as the ordinary sorts.

Our Large-Flowered Comet, while not growing quite so tall as the former, gives large, beautiful flowers, and is of great value both for bedding and cutting purposes. The perfect type of Dwarf Bedding Aster is found in our Dwarf Perfection, which forms an ideal edging to a bed of taller kinds, or is equally effective in a bed by itself.

From Mr. R. JONES, Coychurch.
March 27th.
"I was so very pleased with the Aster Seed I had last year. It was undoubtedly the finest show of Asters I have ever had."

From Mr. A. DUNNING, Wargate.
March 6th.
"I have much pleasure in saying your Ostrich Plume Aster gave me every satisfaction last year. I think they were the finest Asters I have ever seen. Many people were of the same opinion."

ALPHABETICAL LIST OF FLOWER SEEDS.

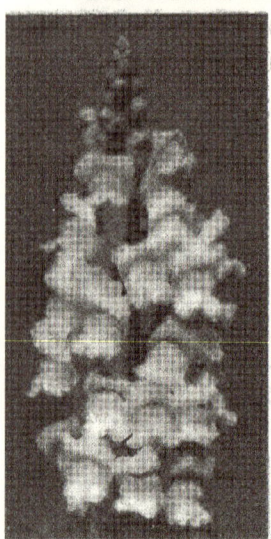

ANTIRRHINUM, DAPHNE.

ANTIRRHINUM, NIOBE.

ABUTILON.
Choice Mixed Hybrids.
per pkt.—s. d.
318   Very useful for training on the wall in conservatory or greenhouse .. 1 0

ACACIA LOPHANTHA.
319   A beautiful greenhouse shrub, growing about 6 feet high. A fine pot plant   0 4

ACROCLINIUM.
Beautiful free-flowering everlastings, succeed well sown and grown as hardy annuals.
320   ROSEUM.   Bright rose 0 3
321   ALBUM.   White 0 3
322   DOUBLE-FLOWERED.   Mixed   .. 0 6

AGERATUM.
Very useful and effective half-hardy annuals. Excellent for bedding out.
323   IMPERIAL DWARF BLUE} Fine for 0 4
324   IMPERIAL DWARF WHITE} Bedding. 0 4
325   PRINCESS VICTORIA LOUISE (new).
   Pale, with white centre, very pretty   0 6

AGROSTEMMA ATROSANGUINEA.
326   ROSE CAMPION.   A fine showy hardy perennial, blooming in Summer and Autumn. Flowers dark crimson .. 0 3

AGROSTIS PULCHELLA.
327   An elegant hardy annual ornamental grass, growing about 9 inches high .. 0 3

ALONSOA.
Beautiful pot plant for the greenhouse or for planting on the mixed border. Hardy biennials. Height about 1 foot.
328   LINIFOLIA.   Orange scarlet   .. 0 3
329   MYRTIFOLIA.   Scarlet   .. 0 3

ALYSSUM.
per pkt.—s. d.
330   COMPACTUM "LITTLE GEM."   A charming little dwarf-growing annual only 4 or 5 inches high, and bearing quite a profusion of pretty white flowers. A splendid little plant for edgings, beds, or rockwork, blooming throughout the Summer and well into Autumn 0 4
331   MARITIMUM (Sweet Alyssum). A free-flowering hardy annual of great value as an edging to large beds, &c. Flowers white.   Height about 9 inches 0 3
332   SAXATILE COMPACTUM.   A fine hardy perennial, growing about 6 inches high and quite covered with bright yellow flowers in Spring. First-rate for rockwork or borders .. 0 4

AMARANTHUS.
A brilliant class of ornamental foliaged plants, excellent for greenhouse decoration or in a warm spot out of doors.
333   MELANCHOLICUS RUBER, 1 foot   .. 0 3
334   TRICOLOR SPLENDENS.   Beautiful variety, very superior to the old *tricolor.*   18 inches .. .. 6d. and 1 0

AMMOBIUM ALATUM.
335   A pretty everlasting, growing about 2 feet high and bearing white flowers in May and June.   Hardy perennial .. 0 3

ANAGALLIS.
Beautiful showy half-hardy annuals growing only about 6 inches high.
336   GRANDIFLORA COCCINEA.   Scarlet   .. 0 4
337   ,,   CÆRULEA.   Blue   .. 0 4

ANCHUSA ITALICA.
338   DROPMORE VARIETY.   A splendid hardy perennial growing about 4 foot high with large gentian blue flowers 6d. and 1 0

ANEMONE.
339   SINGLE.   Choice Mixed.   Garden Anemones, well known, 1 foot   0 3
340   ST. BRIGID.   Very fine strain of beautiful colours, 1 foot .. 0 6

ANTIRRHINUMS.
These fine hardy perennials make a beautiful display during the Summer and Autumn, and are very attractive. The Tom Thumb varieties, which grow only about 6 inches high, are very useful and pretty for dry banks and rockeries, and form a splendid edging for large beds or borders, continuing in bloom for a long time. Sow the seeds in February or early in March in light, rich soil and place in a gentle heat, prick out in pans or boxes to strengthen and plant out where intended to flower as soon as large enough. These will bloom during the Summer and Autumn. The tall varieties grow 2 to 3 feet in height, the semi-dwarf, 12 or 18 inches.   per pkt.—s. d.
341   TALL VARIETIES, 6 brilliant sorts, with names 1 6
342   ,,   Coral Pink, bright rosy pink, beautiful ..   0 6
343   ,,   Black Prince, dark maroon crimson 0 6
344   ,,   Pure white, beautiful variety   .. 0 4
345   ,,   Niobe, dark crimson, white throat   .. 0 6
346   ,,   Roseum, delicate rose 0 4
347   ,,   Aurora, cinnabar scarlet with white throat .. 0 4
348   ,,   Fire King, scarlet and orange   .. 0 6
349   ,,   Golden yellow, very fine 0 4
350   ,,   Choicest mixed, in beautiful variety ..   3d. and 0 6
SEMI-DWARF, OR INTERMEDIATE—
351   ,,   ,,   Daphne, carmine rose and white   .. 0 6
352   ,,   ,,   Pure white, beautiful 0 6
353   ,,   ,,   Golden Queen, rich yellow, splendid .. 0 6
354   ,,   ,,   Pink Empress, deep rose pink ..   0 6
355   ,,   ,,   Choicest mixed, in fine variety ..   0 6
356   TOM THUMB, 6 brilliant varieties, with names   .. 1 6
357   ,,   ,,   Pure white 0 6
358   ,,   ,,   Scarlet } Beautiful varieties, for edging 0 6
359   ,,   ,,   Yellow } large or small beds.   0 6
360   ,,   ,,   Rose   ..   0 6
361   ,,   ,,   Choicest mixed   ..   .. 6d. and 1 0

ARABIS ALPINA.
362   A very useful hardy perennial for early Spring flowering. The plant grows only about 6" high, and the pure white flowers afford an excellent contrast to most Spring flowering plants   0 3

AQUILEGIAS.

AQUILEGIAS—LONG SPURRED VARIETIES.

An exceedingly beautiful class of hardy perennials that will thrive in almost any position where they are not disturbed. Sow in Spring in pots or pans of light sandy soil, and place in a cool pit or frame, and plant out in Autumn, or early in the following Spring, where the plants are intended to remain. The New Long-spurred Hybrids are very elegant, and are highly recommended for cut flowers.

per pkt.—s. d.

363 **MRS. SCOTT-ELLIOT'S LONG-SPURRED HYBRIDS.** The result of many years' careful selection and hybridising, this is undoubtedly the finest strain in existence of these charming hardy plants. The large beautifully-formed flowers vary in colour through all the delicate shades and tints of white lavender, salmon, mauve, pink, yellow, &c., with the most exquisite blendings .. .. .. — 6d. and 1 0
364 **ALPINA SUPERBA.** Blue and white, 18 inches 0 3
365 **CALIFORNICA HYBRIDA.** Yellow and orange, 2 feet .. 0 6
366 **CHRYSANTHA.** Golden yellow, 2½ feet 0 6
367 **GLANDULOSA VERA.** Dark blue and white, 1½ feet .. 1 0
368 **SKINNERI.** Scarlet and yellow 0 6
369 **CHOICE MIXED,** in many charming colours, garden varieties 0 3

ARALIA SIEBOLDI.

370 This beautiful plant, a native of the far East, forms a handsome pot plant for the greenhouse or for table decoration. Grown outside in a sheltered place it makes a handsome shrub and is quite hardy. New seed supplied end of April .. 1 0

ARCTOTIS GRANDIS.

371 A pretty free-flowering, half-hardy annual, about 2 feet in height. White, Marguerite-like flowers with mauve centre 0 6

ASPARAGUS.

372 **PLUMOSUS.** A beautiful greenhouse climber, with finely divided, fern-like foliage. Useful for cutting 1 0
373 **SPRENGERI.** Very handsome foliage. Splendid as a pot plant or for hanging baskets in the greenhouse 1 0

AUBRIETIAS.

These charming dwarf-growing hardy perennials are amongst the most beautiful and useful of all plants for Spring gardening, they are of a dwarf-spreading habit of growth, only about 6 inches high and for a long period in Spring are quite covered with bloom, forming perfect cushions of flowers, grown in association with Spring flowering bulbs as edgings to beds, etc., they are very effective and are also admirably suited for growing on rockeries.

per pkt.—s. d.

374 **LEICHTLINI ROSEA,** Carmine rose, a beautiful Spring bedder. v
 Height 6 inches 1 0
375 **GRÆCA.** Bright blue, height 6 inches 0 6
376 **VIOLACEA.** Violet blue, height 6 inches.. .. .. 0 6

AURICULAS.
(PRIMULA AURICULA.)

These deliciously-scented, fine old hardy perennials are worthy of extensive cultivation. Sow the seeds in March or April, in pots or pans of firmly pressed, light rich soil, giving them but a slight covering, and place in a cool pit or frame. Prick the young seedlings off into pots to strengthen soon as large enough to handle, and pot off when large enough, for blooming under glass, or plant out of doors early in Autumn where intended to bloom. The best soil for Auriculas in pots is composed of about four parts loam with about one part leaf soil, and one part well-rotted cow dung. They should be kept comparatively dry during Winter, but have plenty of moisture when growth commences in Spring, and bloom best in a cool pit or frame close to the glass and facing the north. The Alpine varieties are the hardiest and best for out-door growing, and will do well planted on a well-drained, fairly sheltered border, and give a charming display of beautiful flowers in Spring. A position facing west or north-west is preferable.

377 **DANIELS' PRIZE MIXED,** From a fine collection of choice named flowers, including the green-edged and grey-edged sorts; highly recommended 2 6
378 " " " smaller pkt. 1 0
379 **"ALPINE,"** From a superb collection, including all the most beautiful shades of colour; very hardy and desirable .. 1 0
380 " " " smaller pkt. 0 6
381 **STORRIE'S GIANT YELLOW.** A fine strain of Giant Yellow Auriculas, remarkable alike for their all-round vigour as hardy border plants, and their large trusses of handsome and deliciously fragrant flowers 1 0

ALPINE AURICULA.

All Flower Seeds quoted in 3d. packet may be had at 2/6 per dozen.

BALSAMS.

CAMELLIA-FLOWERED BALSAM.

These beautiful flowers are well worthy of cultivation, and when well-grown in good-sized pots form handsome objects for the decoration of the greenhouse or conservatory, where they will make a fine display for a long period. Balsams also succeed admirably when planted out of doors in good soil, and in a sheltered position, and besides making a fine show of bloom will produce some pretty sprays of flowers for table decoration. Sow the seeds in March or April in pots or pans of light rich soil, and place in a gentle heat. Pot off singly into small pots as soon as the young plants have made a second pair of leaves, using a compound of turfy-loam, leaf mould and well-rotted manure. Shift into larger pots as the plants advance in growth, and gradually harden off those which are intended for planting outside. The end of May or the beginning of June will be early enough for this, and the plants should not be less than 18 inches apart. The fine varieties of the Camellia-flowered class, mentioned below, are undoubtedly the best, and we highly recommend the splendid strain which we offer.

DANIELS' CAMELLIA-FLOWERED.

		per pkt.—s.	d.
382	AN ASSORTMENT OF 6 SPLENDID VARIETIES, 20 seeds each	2	6
383	SALMON QUEEN (new). Brilliant salmon-rose, with large, perfectly formed imbricated double flowers. One of the finest yet sent out	0	6
384	SNOW QUEEN. Pure white. Splendid double Camellia-like flowers	0	6
385	CRIMSON. Very brilliant	0	4
386	PURE SCARLET. Spotted white	0	4
387	WHITE, SHADING TO BLUSH..	0	4
388	CHOICEST MIXED	0	4
388	CHOICEST MIXED 6d. and	1	0
389	CAMELLIA-FLOWERED GERMAN. Double; fine mixed	0	3
390	ROSE-FLOWERED. Double; fine mixed	0	3

From Mr. J. SPRATT, Ash.

May 8th.
"The Begonias I had from you last year were very beautiful, and quite the best I have ever seen."

BEGONIAS.

Sow the seeds in February on the surface of well-drained pots or pans of light rich soil, press the surface firm before sowing and sprinkle with tepid water, cover the pot or pan with a sheet of glass and retain the moisture and place in a heat of about 65°. The plants from this sowing if grown on freely will commence blooming in July, and will make fine tubers for the following year.

		per pkt.—s.	d.
391	DANIELS' PRIZE SINGLE. Carefully saved from a grand collection of the choicest English varieties, will produce some splendid flowers..	2	6
392	,, ,, smaller pkt.	1	0
393	DANIELS' PRIZE DOUBLE. A superb strain, carefully hybridised, saved from finest varieties. Will produce some grand flowers	2	6
394	,, ,, smaller pkt.	1	6
395	CRESTED, SINGLE. Beautifully crested or bearded flowers of great size and many handsome colours	1	6
396	FRINGED, DOUBLE. Handsome, double flowers with elegantly fringed petals, splendid for pot culture	1	6

FIBROUS-ROOTED BEGONIAS.

		per pkt.—s.	d.
397	GRACILIS RUBY (new). Bright metallic brown foliage, with rosy carmine flowers. Height about 10 inches. A splendid variety for bedding	1	0
398	SEMPERFLORENS ALBA. Useful for bedding out or edging. Highly recommended..	1	0
399	SEMPERFLORENS ROSEA. Useful for bedding out or edging. Highly recommended	1	0
400	SEMPERFLORENS VERNON COMPACTA (new). Brilliant red flowers and deep red foliage; splendid bedder	1	0
401	SCHMIDTI. White, shaded with rose. Very free bloomer. Sown in heat in February may be had in bloom throughout the Summer and Autumn	1	0
402	REX, VARIETIES. Beautiful plants for the stove or greenhouse. Saved from choicest sorts	1	6

For Begonia Tubers see page 110.

DOUBLE-FLOWERED BEGONIA.

BARTONIA AUREA.

per pkt.—s. d.

403 A free-flowering showy hardy annual, growing about 18 inches high, with rich golden yellow flowers — — — 0 3

BEET.

404 **DARK-LEAVED BEDDING.** Fine dark crimson leaves — 0 3
405 **CHILIAN.** Variegated. First rate for large beds, &c. The colours are very fine in Autumn .. — 0 6

BRACHYCOME IBERIDIFOLIA.

406 The Swan River Daisy, very pretty, small, cineraria-like flowers of a light blue colour. Height 1 foot. May be sown in Spring as a hardy annual — — — — — 0 3

BRIZA MAXIMA.

407 The Giant Maiden Hair Grass. Very pretty for vases in Winter if gathered green. Hardy annual, height 1 foot — 0 3

BROOM.

408 **CRIMSON AND YELLOW (G. Andreanus).** A beautiful hardy shrub, which commences blooming the second year from seed 0 6
409 **WHITE PORTUGAL.** Well-known beautiful hardy shrub, producing long sprays of white flowers in early Summer .. 0 6

BROWALLIA ELATA GRANDIFLORA.

410 Dark green glossy foliage with bright blue flowers. Makes a pretty pot plant for the greenhouse. Half-hardy annual, Height 18 inches 0 3

CACALIA COCCINEA.

411 A very useful and pretty hardy annual, growing about 1 foot high, with brilliant scarlet flowers. Excellent for bouquets or decoration 0 3

CALANDRINIA.

412 **SPECIOSA.** A dwarf growing, spreading hardy annual, 6 inches high, with bright rosy-crimson flowers. Excellent for rockwork or sunny places.. .. .. .. 0 3
413 **GRANDIFLORA.** Showy hardy annual, about 2 feet high, with bright rosy purple flowers. Succeeds well in a sunny position 0 3
414 **UMBELLATA.** A splendid dwarf growing hardy perennial, only 6 inches high, and producing a profusion of brilliant magenta-crimson coloured flowers. It blooms the first year from seed, and is excellent for dry rockeries, &c. — 0 6

CALENDULA OFFICINALIS FL. PL.

(Pot Marigolds.)

Free-flowering showy hardy annuals, growing about 1 foot high, and continuing in bloom for quite a long period in Summer. The blooms are pleasantly scented, and very useful for cutting.

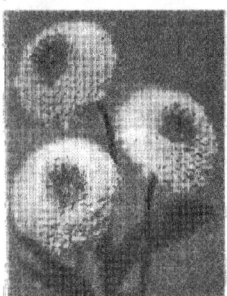

CALENDULA SULPHUREA PLENA.

415 **PRINCE OF ORANGE.** Rich orange yellow double flowers, striped with lemon-yellow. Very free-flowering and useful 0 3
416 **METEOR.** Beautiful double orange-coloured flowers, striped with pale yellow, very pretty 0 3
417 **SULPHUREA FL. PL.** Handsome double flowers of a pale sulphury yellow. Will remain in bloom until late in Autumn — 0 3
418 **CHOICE MIXED, DOUBLE.** A beautiful variety of orange, yellow, primrose, striped, and other varieties 0 3

CALLIOPSIS OR COREOPSIS.

CALLIOPSIS TINCTORIA.

These beautiful free-flowering hardy Annuals are exceedingly valuable for garden decoration. They succeed almost anywhere, but are of especial value for growing in town gardens, where they thrive better than most annuals. They remain in bloom for a long period during the Summer and Autumn, and the blooms of all the taller growing varieties will be found very useful for cutting. The beautiful golden-yellow C. stillmanni blooms within five weeks of the seeds being sown. The Tom Thumb varieties are exceedingly pretty.

per pkt.—s. d.

419 **DRUMMONDI.** Golden yellow, with brown centre. Fine. 18 inches 0 3
420 **TINCTORIA.** Yellow and chestnut brown, very showy. 2 feet 0 3
421 **CARDAMINIFOLIA NANA.** Dark crimson brown. 18 inches 0 3
422 **STILLMANNI.** Clear golden yellow, very early bloomer. 18 inches 0 4
423 **TOM THUMB, BEAUTY.** Very pretty, free-flowering variety. 1 foot high, bright golden yellow with rich brown centres .. 0 4
424 **TOM THUMB, CRIMSON KING.** Dark brownish crimson flowers. 1 foot 0 4
425 **TOM THUMB.** Beautiful dwarf-growing varieties, about 1 foot high, and producing quite a profusion of pretty flowers as large as those of tinctoria; very useful for cutting and excellent for town gardens 0 4
426 **TALL VARIETIES.** Choice mixed, including all the prettiest varieties. A useful selection for cutting 0 3

CALLIOPSIS GRANDIFLORA.

427 A very handsome perennial variety, quite hardy and growing about 3 feet high. The beautiful golden yellow flowers, 3 inches across, are borne on long wiry stems making them of great value for cutting. Seeds sown in March or April will bloom freely in the summer and autumn following. This is a fine showy plant for the garden 0 6

From Mr. W. WHITCHER, Christchurch.

Feb. 21st.
"The Seeds arrived safely and everything is very satisfactory. I have had your Seeds over twenty years."

CALCEOLARIAS.

☞ We have much pleasure in offering our splendid strain of Calceolaria hybrida, which has been carefully saved from a magnificent collection during the past season, and been awarded many First Prizes. The flowers will be found of large size, beautiful form, and tigred and spotted with the most exquisite and brilliant markings.

DANIELS' CALCEOLARIA HYBRIDA. *From a Photograph.*

Sow the seeds of these in May, June, or July, in well-drained pots or seed-pans; cover the drainage with rough fibrous loam, and fill up the surface with fine light sifted mould and silver sand; water with a fine rose water-pot, after which sow the seed, placing a piece of glass over the pot to retain the moisture, no covering of soil being required. Place the pots in a cool frame or under a handlight, taking care to shade from the sun. Remove the piece of glass as soon as the plants are up, and when large enough to handle, prick off one inch apart into pots or pans made up as before, placing in a somewhat close situation, and when of sufficient size pot off singly, and treat in a similar manner to that recommended for tender annuals. Calceolarias should however be always kept in a cool, moist position, a dry heated atmosphere being very prejudicial to their growth, and they should be kept well supplied with fresh air.

CALCEOLARIA HYBRIDA   per pkt.—s. d.
428 DANIELS' CHOICEST MIXED. Beautifully spotted and marked flowers 2 6
     ,,   ,,   smaller pkt.   1 6
429
430 NEW DWARF. A beautiful strain of handsome varieties growing only about ten inches high, and bearing a profusion of large, brilliantly marked and spotted flowers   2 6
431   ,,   ,,   ,,   ,,   smaller pkt.   1 6

CALCEOLARIA—Golden Glory.

432 This is a beautiful new hardy hybrid, with bright golden yellow flowers that are produced for a long period. It is an excellent plant for the greenhouse, a capital bedder, and sufficiently hardy for the herbaceous border, where it forms a very attractive object 1 0

CANDYTUFT.

An exceedingly useful and showy class of hardy annuals that should be grown freely wherever a good display is desired. The beautiful variety "Rose Cardinal" is particularly fine, as are also those of the new dwarf large-flowered section. "Little Prince" is distinct and charming with its numerous trusses of pure white flowers.

			per pkt.—s.	d.
433	DANIELS' MAMMOTH SPIRAL. Immense spikes of large pure white flowers, very fine .. .. .. 6d. and		1	0
434	ROSE CARDINAL. Brilliant carmine rose, very showy, and most beautiful colour. 6 inches		0	4
435	CREAMY WHITE. Large creamy flowers, beautiful. Height 1 foot		0	3
436	DARK CRIMSON. Selected, very fine colour. Height 1 foot		0	3
437	LILAC. Pale lilac-purple. 1 foot		0	3
438	CHOICEST MIXED		0	3
439	LITTLE PRINCE. Only 6 inches high, and producing large spikes of pure white flowers. Very pretty and quite distinct		0	6

LARGE-FLOWERED DWARF (new). A splendid new class of large-flowered beautiful varieties of a dwarf, compact habit of growth. Highly recommended for edgings of large beds or borders. Very showy. Height 9 inches.

440	,,	,,	PURE WHITE. Very fine ...	0	4
441	,,	,,	BRIGHT ROSE. Soft bright rose ..	0	4
442	,,	,,	DARK CRIMSON. Very rich colour ..	0	4
443	,,	,,	LILAC. Pale purplish lilac	0	4
444	,,	,,	CHOICE MIXED ..	0	4

CANDYTUFT, DANIELS' MAMMOTH SPIRAL.

CANNA.

A splendid race of handsome foliaged plants suitable for the sub-tropical garden or for greenhouse decoration. The seeds of these, being extremely hard, should be soaked in tepid water a day or two before sowing.

445	NEW DWARF LARGE-FLOWERED. A superb strain of large, brilliantly-coloured flowers. Highly recommended for pot culture. Height 3 feet	1	0
446	VARIEGATA. Beautiful variegated foliage and brilliantly coloured flowers. Very handsome. Height 2 feet	1	0
447	CHOICE MIXED VARIETIES	0	6

All Flower Seeds quoted in 3d. packets may be had at 2/6 per dozen.

CAMPANULAS.

Campanulas pyramidalis and p. alba form very useful pot plants for the cool greenhouse, whilst C. fragilis is an excellent trailer and very suitable for suspended pots or baskets. Amongst others mentioned, the beautiful persicifolia varieties are very fine and greatly prized for garden decoration, whilst Turbinata is excellent for borders and rockeries. The Campanulas form a splendid group of plants for the garden, and are well worthy of cultivation. They are easily grown, and when in bloom are very charming. They will succeed almost anywhere, but generally speaking thrive best in a light rich sandy soil. Seeds sown from April to end of June.

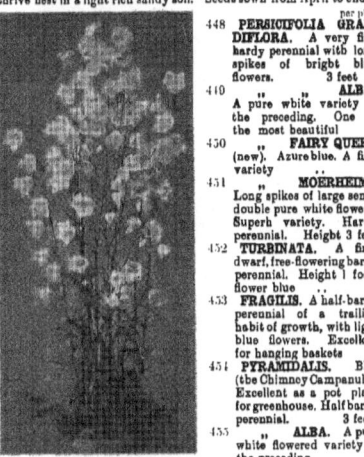

PERSICIFOLIA GRANDIFLORA.

		per pkt.—s. d.
448	PERSICIFOLIA GRANDIFLORA. A very fine hardy perennial with long spikes of bright blue flowers. 3 feet	1 0
449	,, ALBA. A pure white variety of the preceding. One of the most beautiful	1 0
450	,, FAIRY QUEEN (new). Azure blue. A fine variety	1 0
451	,, MOERHEIMI. Long spikes of large semi-double pure white flowers. Superb variety. Hardy perennial. Height 3 feet	1 6
452	TURBINATA. A fine, dwarf, free-flowering hardy perennial. Height 1 foot, flower blue	0 4
453	FRAGILIS. A half-hardy perennial of a trailing habit of growth, with light blue flowers. Excellent for hanging baskets	1 0
454	PYRAMIDALIS. Blue (the Chimney Campanula). Excellent as a pot plant for greenhouse. Half-hardy perennial. 3 feet	0 4
455	,, ALBA. A pure white flowered variety of the preceding	0 4

CANNABIS GIGANTEA.

456 THE GIANT HEMP. A very fine, tall, vigorous growing plant, 6 to 8 feet high, with dark green foliage. Hardy annual 0 3

CATANANCHE.

Useful hardy perennials, growing about 2½ feet high with everlasting flowers.

457	BICOLOR. Blue and white	0 3
458	CÆRULEA. Pale blue	0 3

CELOSIA PLUMOSA
(FEATHERED COCKSCOMB).

These beautiful greenhouse annuals produce long brilliantly coloured plumes of flowers, and are exceedingly useful for decorating the greenhouse or conservatory during the Summer. They may also be planted out of doors towards the end of May on a sheltered border, and will have a very pretty effect.

		per pkt.—s. d.
459	CELOSIA PLUMOSA COCCINEA. Brilliant crimson	0 6
460	,, ,, AUREA. Golden yellow, height two feet	0 6
461	,, ,, CHOICEST MIXED. All shades of yellow and rose to brilliant crimson, &c. 6d. and	1 0
462	,, ,, DWARF MIXED. Beautiful	1 0
463	,, ,, THOMPSONI. Dark bronze foliage, handsome	0 6

CENTAUREA CYANUS MINOR.
(CORNFLOWER.)

Highly popular showy hardy annuals; very useful to cut for bouquets and table decoration. The plants grow about 3 feet high. per pkt.—s. d.

464	EMPEROR WILLIAM. Bright blue	0 3
465	PURE WHITE. Large flowers, white	0 3
466	BRIGHT ROSE. Beautiful colour	0 3
467	CHOICE MIXED. All colours	0 3
468	DWARF ROSE (new). Height 1 foot. Bright rose	0 4
469	,, Very choice mixed, all colours	0 4

CANTERBURY BELLS.
(Campanula Medium.)

A beautiful class of free-flowering hardy biennials for garden decoration. The large bells of pure white varieties are very handsome and should be freely grown for the fine contrast they afford with most other flowers. The double-flowered and Calycanthema varieties are exceedingly fine. Young plants potted up in early Autumn and stored in a cool pit for the Winter, may be brought into the greenhouse or conservatory in Spring, and will bloom beautifully without forcing. It should be borne in mind that all the varieties have a tendency to sport and cannot be depended on to come absolutely true from seed, the best selected strains of doubles always producing some single flowers. All the sorts grow about 2 feet high.

per pkt.—s. d.

470	SINGLE, ROSY CARMINE (new). Beautiful bright rose	0 6
471	,, Pure white, very fine	0 3
472	,, Blue, large-flowered	0 3
473	,, Rose, large-flowered	0 3
474	,, Choicest Mixed	0 3
475	DOUBLE, Pure white, fine	0 6
476	,, Blue	0 6
477	,, Rose	0 6
478	,, Choice Mixed	0 6

Beautiful showy varieties, splendid for garden decoration.

Large massive blooms, very fine.

CALYCANTHEMA VARIETIES.
Cup and Saucer.

479	BLUE. Very large flowers	0 6
480	PURE WHITE. Very beautiful	0 6
481	ROSE. Handsome rose-coloured flowers of great size	0 6
482	CHOICE MIXED	0 6

DOUBLE CANTERBURY BELLS.

CENTAUREA RAGUSINA.

483 Handsome, broad silvery foliage, much prized as a bedding plant. Half-hardy perennial. Height 1 foot 1 0

CERASTIUM TOMENTOSUM.

484 A capital hardy perennial for dry rockeries, banks, &c. Produces an abundance of white flowers and silvery white foliage. Height 9 inches 0 6

CHELONE BARBATA COCCINEA.

485 Very pretty hardy perennial for borders, &c., with long racemes of scarlet pentstemon-like flowers. Height about 3 feet 0 3

CARNATIONS.

SEEDLING CARNATIONS, FROM OUR COLLECTION OF CHOICE VARIETIES.

Carnations are easily raised from seed, and give a profusion of delightfully scented blooms.

The "Marguerite" Section is a special favourite with amateurs, as the plants when raised from Seed early in the Spring, produce an abundance of flowers during the Summer, if sown in June, carefully lifted in Autumn and potted up, they will continue to bloom right into the Winter. Carnation seed may be sown from March to May in well-drained pans of good rich soil, and these should be kept shaded until the seeds have germinated, when the plants should be gradually hardened off by admitting air and light. Prick off the seedlings about nine inches apart in boxes or prepared borders, and let them stay there until the Autumn, when they may be permanently planted in the positions they are to occupy.

The Perpetual or Tree varieties are a very valuable class, giving as they do a charming display in Winter, when flowers are so much valued.

		per pkt.—s. d.
486	AN ASSORTMENT OF 25 CHOICE VARIETIES, including some of the finest selfs, flakes, and yellows	6 0
487	SIX CHOICE VARIETIES	2 6
488	DANIELS' CHOICEST MIXED. From stage flowers, will produce a high percentage of choice double flowers	2 6
	Smaller pkt.	1 6
489	AMERICAN PERPETUAL. A fine class for pot culture, very choice mixed	1 6
491	YELLOW GROUND VARIETIES. Very fine shades	2 6
492	PURE WHITE. Beautiful	1 6
493	DANIELS' PERPETUAL or TREE. A fine strain of beautiful flowers. Fine for pot culture	2 6
	Smaller pkt.	1 6
494	MARGUERITE, NEW LARGE-FLOWERED. Handsome, double, fringed flowers, deliciously scented. Sown early will bloom freely the first year from seed; splendid for pots; a highly improved strain. Very choice mixed 6d. and	1 0
496	MARGUERITE, PURE WHITE. Very useful for cut flowers	1 0
497	PICOTEES. Very choice mixed from stage flowers	2 6
498	Smaller pkt.	1 6
499	GARDEN PINK, "ARGUS." A splendid strain of beautiful double, sweet-scented flowers; bloom first year from seed	1 0

ANNUAL CHRYSANTHEMUMS.

An exceedingly useful and showy class of hardy annuals for garden decoration. The single-flowered varieties are especially valuable to cut for vases and large bouquets, and will last for a long time in water. Sow the seeds in March or April in the open ground and thin out to 6 or 8 inches.

		per pkt.—s. d.
500	MORNING STAR. Beautiful large pale yellow flowers, a gem for cutting. Height 18 inches	0 6
501	NORTHERN STAR (new). Very large flowers, with soft yellow centres, clear white edges, and black disc. Fine for cutting	0 6
502	EVENING STAR. Large, rich golden yellow flowers, 18 in.	0 6
503	CORONARIUM PRINCESS MAY. Large, beautiful single white flowers with primrose centre, very handsome	0 4
504	CARINATUM ATROCOCCINEA. Crimson. 2 feet	0 3
505	„ BURRIDGEANUM. Beautiful flowers with bands of crimson yellow, &c. 2 feet	0 3
506	„ CHAMELEON. Very handsome flowers, with variously coloured bands. 2 feet	0 3
507	DANIELS' CHOICEST MIXED. A beautiful strain of handsomely coloured flowers, splendid for garden decoration or cut flowers 3d. and	0 6
508	DUNNETTI FL. PL. ALBA. Double white flowers. 2 feet	0 3
509	„ Double yellow	0 3
510	SEGETUM GLORIA (new). Pale yellow centre with pure white edge. Large flowers, splendid variety. Height 18 inches	0 6
511	INODORUM, "BRIDAL ROBE" (new). Large double snow-white flowers, very fine. Height 9 inches	1 0

CHRYSANTHEMUM FRUTESCENS.
(Parisian Daisy.)

512	Exceedingly pretty starry white flowers, very useful for pots or window boxes, or for bedding out. The seeds should be sown in March on a gentle heat, and the young plants potted singly into small pots for planting out towards the end of May	0 6

ANNUAL CHRYSANTHEMUMS, CHOICEST MIXED.

DANIELS' SUPERB CINERARIAS.

☞ Carefully saved from a fine collection of named and choicest seedling flowers, which we have every confidence in recommending as unsurpassable. The colours will be found varied and brilliant, combined with a faultless habit of plant and form of flower.

DANIELS' LARGE-FLOWERED CINERARIAS.

CINERARIAS FOR BEDDING.

per pkt.—s. d.

513 **CINERARIA CANDIDISSIMA.** Beautiful silvery elegantly-cut foliage. Very useful as a bedding plant. Half-hardy perennial, height 1 foot 0 6
514 **CINERARIA MARITIMA "DIAMOND."** A very handsome variety with almost pure white foliage, a great improvement on the preceding. Half-hardy perennial, height 1 foot .. 1 0

CLARKIA.

A beautiful fine-flowering class of hardy annuals that should be found in every garden. The new varieties of Elegans, which grow about two feet high, are splendidly effective. The Pulchella and Integripetala varieties grow only about one foot in height.

per pkt.—s. d.

515 **ELEGANS CARMINE QUEEN** (new). Fine sprays of brilliant carmine-red double flowers; splendid 0 6
516 **ELEGANS SALMON QUEEN.** Long sprays of double flowers of a bright salmon colour, magnificent variety 0 4
517   ,,   **DOUBLE WHITE.** Very fine 0 4
518   ,,   **PURPLE KING.** Rich purple sprays of double flowers 0 4
519 **INTEGRIPETALA, DOUBLE ROSE.** Bright rose 0 3
520   ,,   **ALBA.** Double white 0 3
521   ,,   **MARGINATA.** Rose edged with white, very pretty 0 3
522 **PULCHELLA, DOUBLE CRIMSON.** Bright crimson purple .. 0 3
523   ,,   **SINGLE WHITE.** Pure white .. .. — 0 3
524   ,,   Choice mixed .. .. .. — 0 3

CLIANTHUS DAMPIERI.
(The Parrot-beak Plant of Australia.)

525 A very handsome greenhouse annual, growing about 3 feet high, with singularly formed scarlet and black flowers 1 0

CINERARIA HYBRIDA.

per pkt.—s. d.

526 **DANIELS' CHOICEST MIXED** .. .. 1s. 6d. and 2 6
527 **PURE WHITE.** Very useful 1 6
528 **BLUE.** Fine dark colour 1 6
529 **NEW DWARF.** A fine compact-growing class, with large, handsome flowers, height 4 to 6 inches, exceedingly floriferous. Choicest mixed .. .. 1s. 6d. and 2 6
530 **DOUBLE-FLOWERED.** Very fine, will produce a large percentage of handsome, double flowers. Choicest mixed .. 2 6
531   ,,   ,, Pure white, very fine 2 6

Cultivation.—When required for a general display in early Spring, the seed should be sown in July or early in August, and when for Winter blooming, a few should be sown in March or April. Where the quantity of glass available is somewhat limited, the July sown will, however, be found the most useful. Sow in well-drained pots or pans of light rich soil, giving the seeds but a very slight covering, and place in a cool frame or under a hand-light in a shady spot, pot off singly into small pots as soon as the young plants are large enough, and shift as required. Good Cinerarias may also be easily raised by sowing in July or August in a moist, shady situation in the open air, taking care to pot up in September. Cinerarias will bear a great amount of cold, but should never be exposed to frost. Green fly, damp, excessive waterings, and extreme dryness should also be carefully guarded against.

CINERARIA STELLATA.
(New Star Cinerarias.)

A magnificent plant for the conservatory or for corridor decoration during the Winter and Spring months. The immense heads of flowers are borne on long stalks, and well above the foliage. The blooms are star-shaped and smaller than the ordinary form, and the colours run all through the various combinations of white, violet, lilac, almost to red shades. The plants, which grow from 2 to 4 feet in height, are remarkably free-flowering. Will become very popular.

532 Per packet .. .. 1s. 6d. and 2s. 6d.

CINERARIA STELLATA.

COBÆA SCANDENS.

per pkt.—s. d.

533 Well-known useful climber for the conservatory or sheltered
walls. It is a half-hardy perennial, but blooms the first year
from seed and is easily raised in a gentle heat 0 6

COCKSCOMB (Celosia cristata).

Sow the seeds in February or March in pots or pans of light rich soil
and plunge in a good heat. The object being to keep the plants in free
growth without a check, the young plants should be carefully pricked out
into small pots as soon as they can be handled, and as these fill with roots
they should be shifted into larger pots.

534 DANIELS' GIANT PRIZE. A splendid strain, saved from
combs of the richest crimson colour _ _ 1 0

SEEDLING COLEUS.

COLEUS.

These beautiful and highly interesting ornamental-foliaged plants are
easily raised, and grown from a really good strain of seed will produce
plants of great beauty. Sow the seeds in February or March in light rich
soil and place in a good heat. When the young plants are large enough,
pot off singly into small pots, keeping near the light, and shift into larger
pots as required. Those of about six or seven inches diameter being ample
for a final potting.

535 NEW LARGE-LEAVED HYBRIDS, Choicest Mixed. This is
a grand strain of large-leaved and brilliantly coloured
varieties, invaluable for the decoration of the greenhouse
or conservatory. The seed offered will produce a splendid
variety of beautiful foliage .. 1s. 6d. and 2 6
536 SALICIFOLIUS. A beautiful and quite distinct class, with
long narrow willow-like foliage and a great variety of handsome colours 1 0

From Mr. A. BOOTY, Park Superintendent, Belle Vue Park, Lowestoft,
Oct. 8th.

"I write to say that the Seeds supplied by you to this Corporation (Lowestoft)
have given very great satisfaction; the Coleus were very beautiful; the Salpiglosis
were much admired by hundreds of visitors; and the Tuberous Begonias have been a
perfect sight, and are still at the time of writing."

From Mr. E. QUICKENDEN, Dormans.

Feb. 9th.

"The Cyclamen I had from you are very good, and I am very pleased with them."

CYCLAMEN.

A beautiful class of plant for the greenhouse, blooming freely in
Winter and early Spring. The seed should be sown in January or
February in a gentle heat, for blooming the following year. For earlier
flowering sow in November.

per pkt.—s. d.

537 DANIELS' GIANT, MIXED. A magnificent strain of a highly
improved type, having large, beautifully mottled coriaceous
leaves and stout flower-stalks. The blooms, which are
carried well above the foliage, are of splendid size, each
flower frequently measuring from two and a half to three
inches in length 2 6
538   Smaller pkt. 1 6
539 SALMON KING. Large beautiful flowers of a clear salmon-
pink colour. A very fine variety 1 0
540 DANIELS' GIANT WHITE. Pure white, large flowers. Splendid 1 6
541 PURE WHITE CRESTED. Beautifully crested, pure white
flowers, very handsome, and quite novel .. 1 6
542 FRINGED. A beautiful class of handsomely fringed or crested
flowers, choicest mixed 1 6
543 PERSICUM. Choice mixed 0 6

CONVOLVULUS MAJOR.

A fine class of well-known beautiful annual climbers for covering walls,
trellis work, &c. Although only half-hardy, may be sown out of doors
in April and May with perfect safety.

544 CRIMSON. Fine colour 0 3
545 WHITE. Pure white 0 3
546 ROSE. Bright rose 0 3
547 PURPLE. Dark purple 0 3
548 CHOICEST MIXED. All colours.. .. .. 0 3

CONVOLVULUS MINOR.

Beautiful hardy annuals, growing about 1 foot high and continuing in bloom for a long time.

549 CRIMSON VIOLET. Splendid colour, quite distinct .. 0 3
550 DARK BLUE OR PURPLE. Fine .. _ .. 0 3

COSMEA.

Showy half-hardy annual growing about 3 feet high. The flowers
which somewhat resemble those of Single Dahlias, are borne on long wiry
stems, and are very useful for cutting.

551 BIPINNATA ALBA. Large pure white 0 4
552   CHOICEST MIXED. All colours 0 3
553 ROSE QUEEN (New). Soft rose, beautiful early-flowering
variety, continues in bloom from July till killed by the frost 0 6

DAHLIA.

Sow the seeds of these in February or March in a gentle heat, pot the
young plants singly into small pots and plant out towards the end of May.
In a favourable season an abundance of fine bloom will be produced from
July till the plants are killed by the frost.

554 LARGE-FLOWERED SHOW AND FANCY. Saved from our
fine collection of choice named flowers 1 6
555 CACTUS-FLOWERED. From named flowers, very choice .. 1 6
556 POMPONE. Fine dwarf varieties from choicest named
flowers 1 6
557 SINGLE-FLOWERED. From a very fine collection of named
sorts _ .. .. .. 6d. and 1 0

DAISY, Double-flowered.

(Bellis perennis.)

Well-known useful hardy perennial plants for Spring bedding,
edgings, &c. The plants grow only about 3 inches high and are exceedingly pretty when in bloom. Sow in March or April for blooming
the same year, and sow in June for blooming the following Spring.

558 NEW GIANT WHITE. Large double pure white flowers ;
very fine _ 0 6
559 DARK ROSE. Double 0 6
560 CHOICEST MIXED. Double 0 6

DIANTHUS.

DIANTHUS HEDDEWIGI—SNOWDRIFT.

These constitute one of the most brilliant and splendid groups of hardy biennials in cultivation. The large, beautifully coloured flowers vary from pure white to the darkest crimson, some of the double flowers being almost equal to carnations in size. All the varieties are easily raised from seed, and sown in March under glass and transplanted they will bloom freely the first season and make charming beds during the Summer and Autumn. The Heddewigi section produces the largest flowers and are perhaps the most beautiful, but all are deserving of extensive cultivation. The plants vary in height from 8 inches to 1 foot.

DIANTHUS HEDDEWIGI, Double-flowered.

VERY USEFUL FOR CUT FLOWERS. | er pkt.—s. d.

		s.	d.
566	FIREBALL. Dark crimson, splendid	0	6
567	SNOWDRIFT. Pure white, beautifully fringed flowers, charming	0	6
568	FRINGED, DOUBLE. Splendid mixed. The petals of these are elegantly laciniated. Excellent for cutting	0	6
569	DANIELS' CHOICEST MIXED, DOUBLE. A charming variety of beautiful colours .. .. 6d. and	1	0

DIANTHUS HEDDEWIGI, Single-flowered.

		s.	d.
570	PURE WHITE. Large flowers, very freely produced..	0	6
571	SALMON QUEEN. Brilliant salmon pink, one of the most beautiful, makes a splendid bed	0	6
572	DARK CRIMSON. Very rich colour	0	6
573	CHOICEST MIXED SINGLE. Very showy and beautiful varieties	0	6
574	CHINENSIS (Indian Pink). Finest double mixed. Very choice .. .. 3d and	0	6
575	,, ALBA FL. PL. White, double _ ..	0	6

DIGITALIS—FOX-GLOVE.

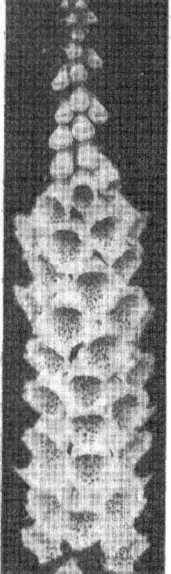

FOX-GLOVE—LARGE SPOTTED.

A very beautiful and showy class of hardy perennials, of fine effect for shrubbery borders, and first class for planting in any odd corner of the garden. The large-spotted varieties, of which we give illustration, are exceedingly handsome. They grow about 5 to 6 feet in height, with long spikes of beautiful Gloxinia-like flowers that continue for a long period when the plants are partially shaded by trees, &c. The seeds should be sown somewhat thinly out of doors in May or June, and the young plants should be planted out where intended to bloom, in Autumn or early Spring.

per pkt.—s. d.

		s.	d.
561	DANIELS' SUPERB SPOTTED. Magnificent varieties with large, gloxinia-like spotted flowers	0	6
562	MONSTROSA. Splendid mixed. Beautiful shades of rose and white	0	4
563	LARGE WHITE. Very fine	0	3

DIASCIA BARBERÆ.

564	A beautiful little half-hardy annual growing about 9 inches high and bearing a profusion of pretty terra-cotta red flowers. Excellent for pots in the greenhouse or for borders ..	1	0

DIMORPHOTHECA AURANTIACA.

565	A beautiful and showy half-hardy annual growing about a foot high with brilliant orange yellow Marguerite-like flowers. Sow in Spring under glass and transplant	1	0

DELPHINIUM.

These beautiful hardy border Perennials, when grown in clumps on the herbaceous border are strikingly effective when in bloom. Their handsome spikes of flowers ranging in colour from white through all the richest shades of blue and purple, furnish some rare colours not found in any other class of plant. The new Dwarf Hybrids and the Formosum varieties are very fine, whilst the scarlet Nudicaule and the pale yellow Sulphureum, provide some novel colours amongst these charming flowers.

per pkt.—s. d.

		s.	d.
576	CARDINALE. Bright scarlet. 18 inches ..	0	6
577	FORMOSUM. Rich dark blue. Very fine. Height 4 to 5 feet	0	4
578	FORMOSUM CŒLESTINUM. Beautiful sky blue	0	0
579	NUDICAULE. Bright scarlet flower. Height 1 foot. Very pretty	0	0
580	SULPHUREUM. Long spikes of beautiful clear yellow flowers. Height 3 feet ..	1	0
581	NEW DWARF HYBRIDS A splendid new class, growing only about 3 feet high, and producing a beautiful variety of handsome spikes of bloom ..	1	0
582	CHOICEST MIXED SINGLE. In beautiful variety. From our fine collection of named flowers .. 3d. and	0	6
583	DOUBLE-FLOWERED CHOICEST MIXED. Fine new varieties 6d. &	1	0

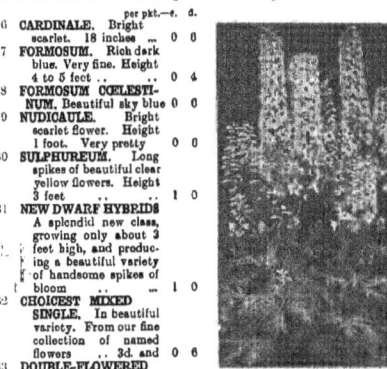

DELPHINIUM—SINGLE-FLOWERED.

DODECATHEON MEADIA.
(American Cowslip.)

per pkt.—s. d.

		s.	d.
584	Beautiful hardy perennial, about 9 inches high, with elegant cyclamen-like flowers of a bright purplish rose colour	1	0

ECCREMOCARPUS SCABER.

per pkt.—s. d.

585 Very useful half-hardy perennial climber of quick growth.
The flowers are of a bright orange scarlet colour. Height
about 10 feet 0 6

ERAGROSTIS ELEGANS.

586 An elegant variety of hardy annual ornamental grass, growing
about 18 inches high. Very pretty to cut for vases, &c. .. 0 3

ERIGERON AURANTIACUS.

587 THE ORANGE DAISY. Beautiful hardy perennial, about
9 inches high, with bright orange-yellow, daisy-like flowers 0 6

ERINUS ALPINUS.

588 A beautiful little hardy perennial Alpine plant, growing about
9 inches high, with bright rosy purple flowers. Excellent
for rockwork or borders 1 0

ERYNGIUM.

Beautiful hardy perennial, growing about 3½ feet in height, with
handsome thistle-like flowers and foliage, very useful for cutting.

589 AMETHYSTINUM. Beautiful blue 0 6

ERYSIMUM.

E. peroffskianum, with its bright rich orange coloured flowers, is very
effective when sown in good clumps or patches on the mixed border.
Whilst the dwarf E. pulchellum, sown in June and planted out in Autumn,
makes one of the best of Spring flowering plants.

590 PEROFFSKIANUM. Showy hardy annual. Height 18 inches.
Flowers bright orange 0 2
591 PULCHELLUM. A hardy perennial, 6 inches high, with pale
yellow flowers. Excellent for Spring gardening 0 4

ESCHSCHOLTZIA.

A brilliant class of showy hardy biennials growing about 1 foot high
and blooming freely the first year from seed. They may be sown and
treated as hardy annuals and will give a beautiful display within a few
weeks of the seeds being sown. " Carmine King," " Mandarin," and " Rose
Cardinal " are highly recommended.

592 CANICULATA ROSEA. Bright rose 0 6
593 CARMINE KING. Brilliant carmine 1 0
594 CROCEA ALBA. Large white 0 3
595   ,,   FL. PL. Orange, double 0 3
596 MANDARIN. Orange, scarlet 0 4
597 ROSE CARDINAL. Beautiful rose 0 4
598 CALIFORNICA. Pale yellow 0 2
599 CHOICE MIXED. In beautiful variety 0 3

EUCALYPTUS.

600 GLOBULUS (Australian Blue Gum). Glaucous green foliage,
fine for sub-tropical garden 0 6
601 CITRIODORA. Lemon-scented foliage, makes a capital pot
plant for the greenhouse. Deliciously fragrant 1 0

EUTOCA VISCIDA.

602 Free-flowering hardy annual, 1 foot high, with pretty sky blue
flowers. Excellent for bees 0 3

FUCHSIAS.

Sow in February or March on a gentle heat, and treat as recommended
for tender annuals. These beautiful free-flowering plants will bloom well
the first year from seed, and plants raised from a first-class strain will
produce the most satisfactory results.

603 CHOICEST MIXED. Single 1 6
604   ,,   ,,   Double 1 6
605 BOLIVIANA. A fine species, with long racemes of splendid
scarlet flowers 1 0

From S. ASHWORTH, Esq., Hendon.

March 3rd.
" I have been so pleased with everything I have had from you that I have every
confidence in your judgment."

GAILLARDIA.

GAILLARDIA, LARGE-FLOWERED SINGLE.

A splendid class of showy hardy perennials. If sown under glass in
March, will bloom freely the first year from seed, and continue quite into
late Autumn. First-class for cut flowers.

per pkt.—s. d.

606 LARGE-FLOWERED SINGLE. Saved from our splendid
strain of choice named flowers. 2 to 3 feet .. 6d. and 1 0
607 LORENZIANA. Double mixed. Very fine for cutting .. 0 6
608 LORENZIANA SULPHUREA. Pale yellow, very showy .. 0 6
609 AMBLYODON. Half-hardy annual, flowers dark red. Height
2 feet .. .. ,0 3

GENTIANA ACAULIS.

610 A splendid hardy dwarf-growing perennial, first-rate for
rockeries or edgings, beautiful deep blue flowers in Spring.
Height 6 inches 0 6

GEUM COCCINEUM FL. PL.

611 A very useful hardy perennial, growing about 2 feet high, with
brilliant scarlet ranunculus-like flowers. Excellent for
cutting 0 3

GILIA.

Very pretty free-flowering hardy annuals, useful for patches on mixed
beds or borders. Excellent for bees.

612 ALBA. White. 18 inches 0 3
613 MAJOR. Pale blue. 18 inches 0 3
614 DICHOTOMA. Pure white, beautiful. 9 inches .. 0 6
615 TRICOLOR. Lavender white and black. 1 foot .. 0 3
616 NIVALIS. Lovely pure white, sweet-scented 0 3

GLAUCIUM LUTEUM.

(The Horned Poppy.)

617 A showy hardy biennial. Succeeds well treated as a hardy
annual. Bright yellow flowers with glaucous green foliage.
Height 2 feet 0 3

GLOXINIA.

GLOXINIA—SPOTTED HYBRID.

These, the most exquisitely beautiful of all greenhouse plants, bloom freely the first year from seed, and should be grown largely by every one having accommodation for them. Sow in February or March on a good moist heat, in the way recommended for Calceolarias. Pot off singly into small pots as soon as the young plants can be handled, and shift into larger as required, keeping the plants going with a good liberal warmth, and finally shift into pots of about six inches diameter, using a light and rich soil, and continuing with a moderate heat and giving air on warm days. Treated in this way, a charming display of bloom may be had during July and August, and some really grand flowers will be the result.

		per pkt.—s.	d.
618	**DANIELS' PRIZE MIXED.** A splendid strain of large, beautifully coloured flowers, including the newest colours ..	2	6
619	,, smaller pkt.	1	6
620	**GIANT-FLOWERED, MIXED.** Very large flowers, more than four inches across and of the most splendid colours ..	2	6
621	**SPOTTED HYBRIDS.** Flowers beautifully spotted ..	1	6

GERBERA.
(The Transvaal Daisy.)

622	**JAMESONI.** A beautiful plant for pots in the greenhouse or a warm dry position out of doors. The plants grow about 15 inches high, and the Marguerite-like flowers are orange or yellow	1	6
623	**JAMESONI, New Hybrids.** A very fine strain of beautiful varieties producing some remarkable and delightful colours. Splendid for pot culture	2	6

GREVILLEA ROBUSTA.

624	Beautiful greenhouse shrub with handsome fern-like foliage	0	6

GYPSOPHILA.

625	**PANICULATA.** A hardy perennial with elegantly branched panicles of small white flowers. Fine for bouquets. Height 2 ft.	0	4
626	**ELEGANS GRANDIFLORA ALBA.** An exceedingly pretty hardy annual, with finely branched elegant stems of white flowers. Splendid for bouquets, 18 inches	0	6

GODETIA.

A magnificent class of brilliant, large-flowered, showy hardy annuals that should be grown freely in every garden where a bold display is desired. They are very effective for mixed beds or borders, and when grown in masses are very charming. For a general display sow thinly in the open ground from early in March to the end of April. If sown in Autumn and transplanted in Spring they will bloom much earlier and finer. Excepting where mentioned the plants grow about 1 foot high.

		per pkt.—s.	d.
627	**CRIMSON GLOW** (new). Intense dark crimson, splendid ..	0	6
628	**CARMINEA AUREA.** Crimson and yellow	0	4
629	**DUKE OF FIFE.** Brilliant crimson	0	4
630	**DUCHESS OF FIFE.** White and carmine	0	4
631	**DUCHESS OF ALBANY.** Pure white	0	4
632	**DUKE OF YORK.** Vivid carmine	0	4
633	**BRIDESMAID.** Rose and white	0	4
634	**GLORIOSA.** Dark crimson	0	3
635	**DWARF CARMINE.** Brilliant carmine, splendid. Height 6".	0	4
636	**DWARF WHITE.** Beautiful pure white satiny flowers. Height 6 inches	0	6
637	**DANIELS' LARGE-FLOWERED.** Mixed, in beautiful variety	0	4
638	**ROSEA GRANDIFLORA FL. PL.** Beautiful double rose-coloured flowers. 2 feet .. .. —	0	4
639	**THE BRIDE.** White petals with crimson base. 2 feet —	0	3
640	**COLLECTION OF 6 SUPERB VARIETIES** —	1	6

LARGE-FLOWERED GODETIAS.

All Flower Seeds quoted in 3d. packets may be had at 2/6 per dozen.

HELICHRYSUM.

HELICHRYSUM.

A brilliant and splendid class of showy hardy annual everlasting flowers, that remain in bloom for a long period. The handsome globular flowers vary in colour from dark crimson or purple, orange scarlet and yellow, to delicate rose and pure white. In association with ornamental grasses these are excellent for the decoration of vases in Winter. The plants grow about 3 feet in height.

		per pkt.—s.	d.
641	FIREBALL. Deep crimson red, fine	0	3
642	PURE YELLOW. Clear golden yellow	0	3
643	PURPLE. Purplish crimson	0	3
644	ROSE. Beautiful clear rose	0	3
645	WHITE. Silvery white, beautiful	0	3
646	LARGE-FLOWERED. 6 separate varieties	1	3
647	" " Choicest mixed, all colours .. 3d. and	0	6
648	DWARF VARIETIES. Choice mixed	0	3

HELIOTROPE.

Although classed as half-hardy perennials, these deliciously scented and highly popular flowers bloom freely the first year from seed, and sown in February or early March in a gentle heat and planted out in May will furnish some nice plants for pot or garden culture. These will commence blooming in July and continue to flower till late in Autumn. The plants grow about 18 inches high.

649	QUEEN MARGUERITE. Rich dark blue, deliciously scented, very large heads of bloom	1	0
650	VERY CHOICE VARIETIES. Mixed .. .. 6d. and	1	0

HEUCHERA SANGUINEA.

651	A charming hardy perennial, growing about 18 inches high, with long slender panicles of brilliant coral red flowers. A first-rate plant for rockeries and borders, and exceedingly useful for cut flowers	1	0

HIBISCUS.

652	AFRICANUS MAJOR. Showy hardy annual. Height 2 feet. The flowers are of a lemon yellow with a dark crimson eye.	0	3

HOLLYHOCK, DOUBLE.

These magnificent hardy perennials form grandly conspicuous objects in the flower garden during Summer and Autumn, and should always be grown where convenient. They are easily raised from seed sown in January or February in a gentle heat, and will bloom finely the same year. When grown in this way, a light rich soil should be used, and the plants should be potted singly into small pots soon as large enough to handle, gradually harden off and plant out in May where intended to bloom; or the seeds may be sown in May or June out of doors, and will provide some strong plants for planting out in Autumn for blooming the following year.

		per pkt.—s.	d.
653	YELLOW. Bright clear yellow	1	0
654	ROSY CARMINE. Splendid colour	1	0
655	PURE WHITE. Beautiful variety, comes quite true from seed	1	0
656	DANIELS' PRIZE MIXED. A superb strain of beautifully coloured, large double flowers	2	6
657	" " smaller pkt. 6d. and	1	0
658	SINGLE-FLOWERED. An attractive and beautiful class, producing some rare and charming colours .. 6d. and	1	0

SEEDLING HOLLYHOCK.

HONESTY.

Very useful early flowering hardy biennial. Fine for shrubbery borders, and valued for its dried silvery seed pods.

		per pkt.—s. d.
659	**CRIMSON.** Bright red, very fine	0 6
660	**PURPLE.** Bright purplish lilac ..	0 3
661	**WHITE.** Pure white, pretty ...	0 3

HUMULUS.

The Japanese Hop. Half-hardy annuals of rapid growth and first class for covering trellises.

662	**JAPONICUS VARIEGATUS.** Handsomely variegated leaves with silvery white markings. Height 8 to 10 feet..	0 6
663	**JAPONICUS.** Large green foliage, a rapid grower. Height 10 feet	0 4

HUNNEMANNIA FUMARIÆFOLIA.

664 A beautiful hardy perennial, growing about 2 feet high, and bearing bright yellow poppy-like flowers. Sown out of doors in March or April, and treated as a hardy annual, will bloom freely in August and September 0 6

IBERIS.

Beautiful dwarf-growing hardy perennials, very useful for Rockeries or Spring gardening. The plants attain a height of about 6 inches.

665	**GIBRALTARICA.** Lilac, shading to white ..	0 6
666	**FRUITI.** White, very early, charming ..	0 6
667	**SEMPERVIRENS.** White, very fine ..	0 3

ICE PLANT.

(Mesembryanthemum crystallinum.)

668 A trailing half-hardy annual of singular appearance. The stem and foliage being covered with icy-looking points. Useful for garnishing.. .. .. 0 3

INCARVILLEA DELAVAYI.

669 Splendid hardy perennial, with large gloxinia-like rosy carmine flowers. The plants grow about 18 inches high, and bloom in June and July. Is easily raised from seeds. Sown out of doors in May or June 0 6

IONOPSIDIUM ACAULE.

670 A charming miniature plant, hardy annual, growing only about 3 inches high and covered with a profusion of small starry white flowers. Excellent for rockwork or edging for small beds 0 3

IPOMŒA.

Beautiful varieties of half-hardy climbing convolvulus, very useful for trellises in the greenhouse or out of doors. May be sown outside in May and treated as hardy annuals.

671	**GRANDIFLORA ALBA.** White, splendid	0 4
672	**COCCINEA.** Scarlet, very fine ..	0 4
673	**HEDERACEA SUPERBA.** Choice mixed. Ivy-leaved, beautiful varieties ..	0 4
674	**RUBRO-CÆRULEA.** Sky blue ..	0 4

JACOBEA.

Free-flowering hardy annuals, growing about 9 inches high, with numerous handsome double flowers. Very useful for bouquets.

675	**DWARF, PURPLE.** Fine colour	0 4
676	**DWARF, WHITE.** Very fine ..	0 4
677	**DWARF, CRIMSON.** Very showy	0 4
678	**DWARF, CHOICE MIXED.** All colours ..	0 3

KAULFUSSIA AMELLOIDES.

679 A pretty little hardy annual only 6 inches high, and throwing up quite a profusion of miniature aster-like blooms .. 0 3

KOCHIA TRICHOPHYLLA.

(Summer Cypress, The True Variety.)

This is undoubtedly one of the most interesting and beautiful plants of recent introduction. The plant which is of an elegant upright habit of growth, with pale green fern-like foliage, attains a height of about eighteen inches, and forms a charming plant for the centres of small beds, or as a " dot " plant on borders amongst dwarfer growing subjects. In the Autumn, the foliage changes to a deep bright crimson colour, when it has a very novel and striking effect. It is easily raised and grown as a half-hardy annual and may be sown in the open ground in April, and thinned out or transplanted, whilst potted up into six or eight inch pots, it forms a charming plant for the greenhouse.

680 Per Packet .. .. 6d. and 1s.

LARKSPUR.

A very fine class of beautiful showy hardy annuals that are of great value for garden decoration. The tall-growing varieties are especially handsome, and the flowers being produced on long, graceful spikes, are very useful for cut flowers.

STOCK FLOWERED LARKSPUR, CARMINE.

			per pkt.—s. d.
681	**STOCK-FLOWERED, CARMINE.** Splendid colour. Height 3 feet		0 6
682	,, **PALE BLUE** (new). Beautiful colour. Height 3 feet		0 6
683	,, **CHOICEST MIXED.** Fine, tall varieties. Height 3 feet		0 3
684	**TALL VARIETIES.** Choice mixed		0 3
685	**EMPEROR, CHOICE MIXED.** Free-flowering branching varieties. Height 2 feet		0 4
686	**BLUE BUTTERFLY.** Very pretty. Height 1 foot ..		0 6
687	**DWARF ROCKET, CHOICE MIXED.** Beautiful early-flowering varieties. Height 1 foot ..		0 3

LOBELIA.

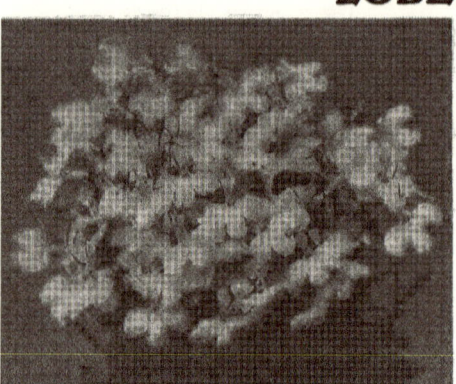

LOBELIA—DANIELS' WHITE BEDDING.

LOBELIA TENUIOR.

To secure fine plants for bedding out the following May, some prefer to sow the seed in Autumn, but February or March is good time for sowing if the plants have careful attention and are grown on freely. Sow the seeds thinly in pans or pots of sandy loam, cover very lightly, and place in a heat of about sixty degrees, keep moist, and soon as the young plants can be handled, pot off singly into small pots of light rich soil, keep near the glass in a gentle heat, and give plenty of air on fine days. Carefully picking off all the flower-buds will greatly assist their growth, and they should on no account be allowed to suffer from want of moisture. Other excellent methods are to prick the young plants five or six in a five-inch pot, or, better still, to plant them thinly in shallow trays of rich soil, keeping in gentle heat, giving air, &c., as recommended. These will generally form compactly grown, sturdy plants, that will quickly produce a beautiful effect when planted out. Lobelias intended for pots or window-boxes succeed best when planted out thinly in good soil in an open situation, and carefully lifted when they have formed nice tufty plants; these will at once commence blooming, and produce an effect that could not be otherwise obtained. For bedding out, we strongly recommend Daniel's Dark Blue and Daniels' White Bedding as most compact in growth and reliable in colour. Royal Purple, and Barnard's Perpetual are also very fine, whilst for pot culture, hanging baskets, and greenhouse decoration, the beautiful Tenuior and the varieties of Ramosa are by far the best.

		per pkt.—s.	d.
688	**DANIELS' DARK BLUE.** A very fine dark blue, compact-growing variety; splendid for edgings and carpet bedding. For a really good dark blue bedder, we recommend this as the best variety for garden decoration.	1	0
689	**DANIELS' WHITE BEDDING.** Pure white dwarf; a beautiful variety for bedding	1	0
690	**ROYAL PURPLE.** Deep rich blue with distinct white eye, splendid; dwarf	0	6
691	**BARNARD'S PERPETUAL.** Bright ultramarine blue, white, at base of lower petals; splendid dwarf variety	0	6
692	**SPECIOSA (true).** Fine dark blue, excellent bedder	0	6
693	**COBALT BLUE.** Fine and distinct colour	0	3
694	**ERINUS ALBA.** White, very useful	0	3
695	**PAXTONI.** Blue and white, dwarf	0	3
696	**TENUIOR.** A charming variety, growing about one foot high, with very large flowers, cobalt blue, with white centre; very graceful in habit and makes a beautiful pot plant, and is excellent for vases and hanging baskets	0	6
697	**RAMOSA BLUE** ⎱ A beautiful upright growing class 9 in. to 1 ft.	0	4
698	" **WHITE** ⎰ high, very useful for pot culture in	0	4
699	" **ROSE** the greenhouse.	0	4

LOBELIA CARDINALIS VICTORIA.

This beautiful perennial, growing about two feet high, with its rich dark metallic foliage and brilliant scarlet flowers, comes quite true from seed, and sown in February or March on a gentle heat will make nice plants for bedding out in May or June for blooming the following Autumn. The roots of these should be protected in severe weather by a covering of cocoa-nut refuse, ashes, or any light similar material, or they may be lifted after flowering, and stored in a cool pit or frame for the Winter, and planted out again the following April or May.

700	Per packet		1s.

LANTANA.

A half-hardy shrubby perennial, with heads of brilliantly coloured flowers. Excellent for bedding out, or as a pot plant for the greenhouse.

		per pkt.—s.	d.
701	**NEW DWARF HYBRIDS, MIXED.** Beautiful varieties, of compact habit. Height 9 inches	0	6

LAVATERA.

Exceedingly beautiful and showy plants. Excellent for cut flowers and of fine effect in the garden.

702	**ROSEA SPLENDENS.** A very beautiful tall growing hardy annual, with large bright rosy-pink flowers that continue in bloom for a long time. Very showy and effective in large beds or borders. 3 feet	0	4
703	**ALBA SPLENDENS.** Large glossy pure white flowers. This and the preceding are excellent as cut flowers. Height 3 feet	0	4
704	**ARBOREA VARIEGATA.** Very fine half-hardy perennial, with large green leaves blotched and marked with white. Height 4 to 6 feet	0	6

LAYIA ELEGANS.

705	A pretty hardy annual from California, about 1 foot high, with large round yellow flowers edged with white	0	3

LEPTOSIPHON.

Free-flowering and exceedingly pretty hardy annuals. L. densiflorus and albus are very useful for beds or borders. The dwarf-growing sorts are well-suited for edgings or rockwork.

			s.	d.
706	**DENSIFLORUS.** Lilac. 1 foot		0	3
707	" **ALBUS.** Pure white, sweet-scented. 1 foot		0	3
708	**AUREUS.** Golden yellow. 3 inches		0	4
709	**CARMINEUS.** Brilliant carmine. 3 inches		0	4
710	**ROSEUS.** Bright rose. 3 inches		0	4
711	**FRENCH HYBRIDS, MIXED.** 3 inches		0	4

LEPTOSYNE STILLMANNI.

712	A beautiful hardy annual growing about 15 inches high with bright golden yellow flowers. This is one of the quickest annuals to bloom from seed and may be had in perfection within five weeks of sowing	0	4

LIMNANTHES DOUGLASI.

713	A free-flowering and useful hardy annual, about six inches high, of a spreading habit, with white and yellow flowers	0	3

From Mr. G. E. BESLEY, Fetbury.
Aug. 11th.
"I was very pleased with the Sweet Peas I had of you this year. You will be pleased to hear that I took First Prize at our Show in the amateur class, and Second in the open class. In this class I was competing for a Silver Cup and against gentlemen who employ gardeners.

LINARIA MAROCCANA.

A charming class of beautiful hardy annuals growing about 18 inches high and throwing up elegant spikes of small Antirrhinum-like flowers. The colours vary from crimson, rose, yellow and pink to the purest white. These are splendid as cut flowers for table decoration.

per pkt.—s. d.

714 CHOICE HYBRIDS, MIXED 0 6

LINUM.

715 GRANDIFLORUM RUBRUM. Very showy hardy annual, producing a profusion of brilliant crimson-scarlet flowers. Height 1 foot 0 3

LOVE-LIES-BLEEDING.

716 AMARANTHUS CAUDATUS. A fine showy hardy annual with long drooping stems of crimson-scarlet flowers. 2 to 3 feet 0 3

LUPINUS.

Handsome and easily-grown showy hardy annuals that well deserve their high popularity. All the varieties are free-flowering and have a very pretty effect on mixed beds or borders.

717 HYBRIDUS ATROCOCCINEUS. Scarlet and white, very showy. 2½ feet 0 3
718 HARTWEGI. Blue and white. 2 feet .. .. — 0 3
719 CRUIKSHANKI. Fine dark blue. Height 3 feet .. — 0 3
720 SULPHUREUS SUPERBUS. Bright yellow. fine. 2 feet .. 0 3
721 SUBCARNOSUS. Dark blue and white, very pretty. 1 foot 0 3
722 LUTEUS ROMULUS. Rich bright yellow, very distinct. 2 ft. 0 4
723 NANUS. Blue. 1 foot .. .. .. — 0 3
724 ,, ALBUS. White. 1 foot .. .. — 0 3
725 ,, ALBO-COCCINEUS. Bright carmine tipped with white, charming variety. 1 foot 0 4

HARDY PERENNIAL LUPINS.

726 ARBOREUS (The Tree Lupin). Handsome shrubby variety, flowers yellow. Height 4 feet 0 4
727 ,, SNOW QUEEN. Long spikes of beautiful pure white flowers, splendid variety. Height 4 feet — 0 4
728 POLYPHYLLUS. Blue. Height 4 feet .. .. — 0 3
729 ,, White. Height 4 feet .. .. — 0 3
730 ,, Choice Hybrids. Fine varieties. Mixed 0 6

LYCHNIS HAAGEANA.

731 ATROSANGUINEA. Showy dwarf-growing hardy herbaceous perennial. 1 foot high. With brilliant crimson-scarlet flowers. Excellent for borders 0 4
732 CHOICEST MIXED. In beautiful variety of brilliant colours 0 3

MAIZE.

733 VARIEGATED JAPANESE. A beautiful variety for pots in the greenhouse or for garden decoration. The plants grow about 4 feet high, and the broad green leaves are elegantly striped with white. Half-hardy annual.. .. .. 0 3
734 NEW GIANT VARIEGATED. A fine variety growing about 6 feet high, with foliage handsomely striped with white, pink and yellow. Fine for sub-tropical garden — — 0 6

MALOPE.

Showy hardy annuals growing about 2 feet high. Very useful for large borders or beds.

736 GRANDIFLORA ROSEA. Bright rose — — — 0 3
736 ,, ALBA. Pure white — — — 0 3
737 ,, PURPUREA. Red — — — 0 3
738 ,, MIXED. Various — — — 0 3

MALVA.

739 MOSCHATA ROSEA. A fine hardy perennial. 18 inches high, and blooming the first year from seed. With bright rose sweet-scented flowers .. .. .. — 0 3
740 MOSCHATA ALBA. A pure white-flowered variety of the preceding. Very free flowering ... ... — 0 3

MATRICARIA.

741 GOLDEN BALL. Hardy perennial. Height 1 foot. Beautiful double yellow flowers. Excellent for beds or borders .. 0 6

MATHIOLA BICORNIS.

(Night-Scented Stock.)

742 One of the most deliciously-scented of all annuals, especially in the evening. Should be grown freely in every garden. Although classed as half-hardy it is best sown in April and treated as a hardy annual.. .. .. 0 3

MARIGOLD.

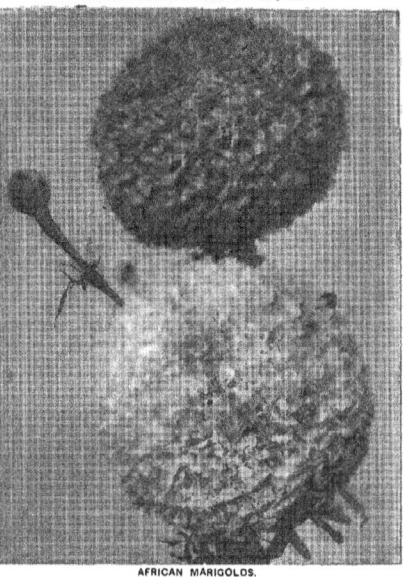

AFRICAN MARIGOLDS.

Seeds of these fine half-hardy annuals should be sown under glass, not earlier than the beginning of April, or the plants are apt to get too forward before planting out, which can only be done with safety when all danger from Spring frosts is over. The African varieties grow about two feet high, and their large showy flowers are very effective in late Summer and Autumn. The French striped are very handsome for garden decoration, whilst the new dwarf varieties are splendid little plants for edgings of beds or borders.

per pkt.—s. d.

743 ORANGE AFRICAN. A magnificent selection from a prize strain, bearing immense, brilliant orange-coloured, perfectly double flowers 0 6
744 ,, ,, smaller pkt. 0 3
745 LEMON AFRICAN. The same as preceding in size and form of flower and habit of plant, but varying slightly in colour 0 6
746 ,, ,, smaller pkt. 0 3
747 DANIELS' STRIPED FRENCH (Scotch Prize). A fine strain of beautifully striped flowers of the most perfect form and double-ness. Grown expressly for our retail trade. Height 1 foot 1 0
748 NEW DWARF, Golden Yellow) 0 6
749 ,, ,, Sulphur Yellow } Very dwarf and double. 0 6
750 ,, ,, Brown and Yellow) Splendid for edgings. 0 6
The above three varieties grow only four inches in height.
751 TALL FRENCH. A very showy strain .. .. 3d. and 0 6
752 DWARF FRENCH. Striped and blotched .. 3d. and 0 6
753 DWARF BROWN FRENCH. Dwarf and double 0 3
754 SIGNATA PUMILA. Single, golden yellow flowers .. 0 3
755 SILVER KING. Single, pale yellow flowers, prettily marked with maroon. Height 9 inches 0 4
756 LEGION OF HONOUR. Single, golden yellow with crimson blotch, very pretty, splendid bedder. Height 9 inches — 0 3

MAURANDYA.

Beautiful climbers for the greenhouse or conservatory.
757 PURPUREA GRANDIFLORA. Purplish blue — — 0 6
758 ALBIFLORA (true). White, fine — — 1 0

We beg to intimate that we cannot "break" packets quoted in this list.

MIGNONETTE.

MIGNONETTE—DANIELS' GIANT RED.

These well-known, deliciously scented, hardy annuals are extremely easy of cultivation. Sow the seeds in the open border where intended to flower any time from the middle of March to the end of June, and thin out the plants to four or six inches apart as soon as they are large enough to handle. For Winter blooming sow any time in August, in pots of five or six inches diameter, and thin out the plants to three or five in a pot, keeping them as hardy as convenient before placing under glass for the Winter. The following list includes the finest varieties of recent introduction for garden or pot culture.

per pkt.—s. d.

759 AUREA MAGNIFICA. A splendid variety far in advance of any other yellow-flowered Mignonette yet sent out. The plants, which attain a height of about one foot, throw up numerous fine spikes of beautiful bright yellow deliciously scented flowers   ..   .. Gd. and   1 0

760 DANIELS' CRIMSON KING. About one foot high, with rich green foliage, and gigantic spikes of the darkest bright red blooms. It is of the most delicious fragrance, and will prove a decided acquisition ..   ..   Gd. and   1 0

761 DANIELS' GIANT RED. Grand variety, growing two feet high, and throwing up very large spikes of red, highly-scented flowers   ..   ..   ..   Gd. and   1 0

762 DANIELS' GIANT WHITE. A superb variety of robust habit, growing about 18 inches high, and bearing very large spikes of almost pure white deliciously fragrant flowers. Undoubtedly by far the finest of all white Mignonettes Gd. &   1 0

763 DANIELS' GOLDEN QUEEN. A beautiful compact-growing variety, with numerous sweet-scented spikes of yellow flowers   ..   .. Gd. and   1 0

764 MACHET. A fine, sturdy, compact-growing variety; one of the best for pots 0 6

765 GIANT MACHET, SALMON-RED. Splendid variety, a great improvement   ..   ..   ..   Gd. and   1 0

766 A COLLECTION OF SIX CHOICE VARIETIES   ..   2 0

767 LARGE-FLOWERED   ..   per lb, 6s. ; per oz. Gd.   0 2

MESEMBRYANTHEMUM.

per pkt.—s. d.

768 CORDIFOLIUM VARIEGATUM. Dwarf-growing variety of spreading habit, foliage yellowish with small purplish-crimson flowers. Excellent for carpet bedding. Half-hardy perennial 0 6

769 TRICOLOR. A capital dwarf-growing, half-hardy annual. Flowers crimson, white and purple. Height 3 inches. Excellent for dry sunny rockeries 0 3

MIMULUS.

A splendid and profuse-flowering class of brilliant half-hardy perennials, blooming the first year from seed, and thriving in damp or shady positions,

770 DANIELS' LARGE-FLOWERED. A grand strain of large beautiful flowers of the richest colours. Height 1 foot   Gd. and   1 0

771 NANUS ROSEUS. A charming variety growing only 4 inches high, with bright salmony-rose coloured flowers ..   0 6

772 HOSE-IN-HOSE VARIETIES. Choice mixed 0 6

773 CHOICE MIXED. In good variety 0 3

MINA LOBATA.

774 A splendid half-hardy annual climber for trellises, &c. It is very free-flowering, the blooms varying from an orange scarlet when first open to white when fully expanded   ..   1 0

MUSK PLANT.
(Mimulus moschatus.)

775 NEW DWARF. A fine compact growing variety. A great improvement on the old variety for pot culture. Very free-flowering and powerfully fragrant. Half-hardy perennial, 4 inches high 0 6

MYOSOTIS.
(Forget-me-not.)

A free-flowering and beautiful class of easily grown hardy perennials, which are in great request for Spring gardening. They will thrive in almost any soil, but prefer a partially-shaded and rather damp position. By sowing in June or July and potting-up, some charming flowers may be had in the greenhouse during the Winter and early Spring.

776 DANIELS' SKY BLUE. A charming dwarf-growing variety, 6 inches high, with a profusion of lovely sky blue flowers. A gem for pots   ..   1 0

777 DANIELS' INDIGO BLUE.' A very fine upright-growing variety, with long sprays of deep indigo blue flowers. First rate for cutting. Height 1 foot   ..   1 0

778 STAR OF LOVE. A beautiful compact-growing variety, only 5 inches high, covered with large bright blue flowers. A gem for pots   ..   1 0

MYOSOTIS—DANIELS' SKY BLUE.

779 DISSITIFLORA, Large-flowered. Sky blue. Height 9 inches. The best variety for Spring gardening 0 6

780 DISSITIFLORA ALBA. White, very fine   ..   1 0

781 PALUSTRIS SEMPERFLORENS. The true marsh Forget-me-not. Height 9 inches. A continuous bloomer from Spring to Autumn 0 4

782 RUPICOLA. Deep sky blue, very dwarf. Exceedingly pretty and charming for pots 1 0

NEMOPHILA.

Extremely pretty early-flowering hardy annuals. Very useful for Spring gardening, beds or borders, or for pots in the greenhouse. The beautiful sky blue " Insignis " is very fine.

783 INSIGNIS. Lovely sky blue with conspicuous white eye. Charming. Height 6 inches 0 3

784 INSIGNIS ALBA. Pure white 0 3

785 MACULATA GRANDIFLORA. White, spotted with violet blue. Height 6 inches 0 3

NASTURTIUMS.
TOM THUMB VARIETIES.

An exceedingly brilliant and indispensable class of easily grown half-hardy annuals. To obtain the best results the seeds should be sown in Spring on rather poor soil in the open ground, and in an exposed sunny position where they will continue in bloom for a long time. Grown in long lines as edgings or in beds or patches they are very showy. The following varieties grow about 1 foot high, and are best treated as hardy annuals.

per pkt.—s. d.
786 EMPRESS OF INDIA. Intense crimson scarlet, with dark leaves. Splendid variety of dwarf habit .. 0 4
787 SNOW QUEEN (new). Very compact and free-flowering variety. The blooms opening creamy and changing to pure white .. 0 6
788 QUEEN OF TOM THUMBS. Dark crimson flowers, with silver variegated foliage. Very pretty .. 1 0
789 CARMINE KING. Bright carmine .. 0 4
790 CÆRULEA ROSEA. Bluish rose .. 0 3
791 CRYSTAL PALACE GEM. Primrose, spotted maroon .. 0 3
792 GOLDEN KING. Rich yellow with dark foliage .. 0 4
793 KING OF TOM THUMBS. Brilliant scarlet .. 0 3
794 KING THEODORE. Dark crimson .. 0 3
795 LADY-BIRD. Golden yellow with scarlet spots .. 0 3
796 RUBY KING. Rosy carmine with dark foliage, fine .. 0 4
797 TERRA COTTA. Terra cotta tinted salmon .. 0 3
798 VESUVIUS. Rich apricot with dark foliage .. 0 3
799 YELLOW. Bright golden yellow .. 0 3
800 CHOICE MIXED. In splendid variety of colours .. 0 3

CLIMBING VARIETIES.

Brilliant and rapid growing annual climbers of splendid effect. First class for walls or trellises or for covering rough fences or banks. All the varieties may be sown in April and treated as hardy annuals.

per pkt.—s. d.
801 BUTTERFLY. Golden yellow with scarlet spots, fine .. 0 4
802 DEFIANCE. Brilliant scarlet .. 0 4
803 MIDNIGHT. Crimson maroon with dark foliage, splendid .. 0 4
804 MOONLIGHT. Pale yellow, beautiful .. 0 4
805 SUNLIGHT. Bright golden yellow .. 0 4
806 VESUVIUS. Deep apricot with dark foliage, very pretty .. 0 4
807 IVY-LEAVED. Scarlet flowers .. 0 4
808 SCARLET. Bright scarlet .. 0 3
809 GOLDEN YELLOW. Very fine .. 0 3
810 CHOICEST MIXED. In beautiful variety of colours .. 0 3

CANARY-BIRD NASTURTIUM.
(Tropæolum canariense.)

811 Well-known useful annual climber of elegant growth with singularly formed yellow flowers .. 0 3

NICOTIANA.

Beautiful half-hardy annuals for pots in the greenhouse, large beds or borders or for sub-tropical gardening. The Sanderæ and Affinis hybrids are very fine.

per pkt.—s. d.
812 AFFINIS. Large, white tubular flowers, deliciously fragrant in the evening. Height 3 feet.. 0 4
813 AFFINIS. New hybrids, mixed. Beautiful shades of pink, violet, mauve, &c. Very sweet scented. Height 3 feet .. 0 6
814 MACROPHYLLA GIGANTEA. The Giant Tobacco. Flowers pink. Height 6 feet .. 0 3
815 SANDERÆ HYBRIDS, Mixed. A splendid race of fine varieties. The flowers vary in colour from white, rose and lilac to dark crimson. Height 3 feet .. 0 6
816 SYLVESTRIS. A very fine variety growing 6 feet high, and bearing a profusion of pure white tubular flowers throughout the Summer .. 0 6

NIGHT-SCENTED STOCK.
See Mathiola Bicornis, page 93.

NIGELLA.

817 DAMASCENA FL. PL. Light blue double flowers surrounded with finely divided foliage. Hardy annual. Height 9 inches 0 3
818 HISPANICA ALBA. White flowers. Hardy annual. Height 18 inches .. 0 3
819 MISS JEKYLL. Very pretty variety, growing 18 inches high, with clear blue flowers on slender stems. Hardy annual .. 0 6

NEMESIAS.

A magnificent class of beautiful half-hardy annuals, producing flowers of the most rare and brilliant colours. They are easily raised by sowing the seeds in boxes or pans of light soil, in March, and placing in a gentle heat or in a cool frame. Plant out in May 5 or 6 inches apart in an open sunny position.

NEMESIA STRUMOSA GRANDIFLORA.

per pkt.—s. d.
820 STRUMOSA GRANDIFLORA, Mixed. Beautiful shades of crimson, yellow, orange and rose to pure white. Height 15 inches .. 1 0
821 STRUMOSA GRANDIFLORA COMPACTA. A fine class of brilliant varieties. Height 9 inches .. 1 0

ŒNOTHERA.
(Evening Primrose.)

822 BISTORTA VEITCHII. Small, yellow flowers, spotted with crimson. Hardy annual. Height 1 foot .. 0 3
823 MACROCARPA. A fine hardy perennial with large pale yellow flowers. Height 6 inches .. 0 4
824 ROSEA. Beautiful dwarf hardy annual, with bright rose-coloured flowers. Height 6 inches .. 0 4
825 LAMARCKIANA. Splendid hardy perennial, with large primrose-yellow flowers. Height 4 feet.. 0 3
826 TARAXACIFOLIA ALBA. A fine variety of dwarf growth, with large pure white flowers. Height 6 inches .. 0 4

OXALIS.

827 ROSEA. Very pretty half-hardy perennial. Excellent for rockwork or pot culture. Flowers bright rose. Height 6 inches .. 0 3
828 TROPÆOLOIDES. Capital hardy perennial for rockwork or pots. The flowers are dark yellow, with brown leaves. Height 4 inches .. 0 3

DANIELS' EXHIBITION GIANT PANSIES.

From Mr. THOS. WILLIAMS, Merry-Corner.

August 7th.
"I have taken second Prize in Open Show, and First in Local with the produce of your **Pansy Seed**."

From Mr. E. CLARIDGE, Rushden, Northants.

July 22nd.
"I am pleased to tell you the **Pansy Seed** I had from you last year produced a remarkable amount of bloom; they made a wonderful show."

From Mr. F. GOLDING, Chislehurst.

July 2nd.
"I have a large bed of your **Exhibition Giant Pansy** that is admired by every one."

From Mr. W. WRAIGHT, Faversham.

July 7th.
"The **Pansy Seed** I had from you last year gave great satisfaction, they were admired by all my friends."

From Mr. D. SAUNDERS, South Nutfield.

July 8th.
"Am pleased to say that the Packet of **Prize Blotched Pansies** I had from you brought forth a splendid lot; the best I ever saw, they were admired by all who saw them."

From Mr. O. BENDON, Stockineh.

June 18th.
"Am pleased to tell you the **Pansy Seed** I had of you last year has proved most satisfactory. I have some splendid bloom."

From Mr. A. J. LONG, Andover.

June 4th.
"Your **Pansies** are very much admired."

From Mr. R. KING, Brentwood.

June 6th.
"The **Pansies** produced from your Seed are so good that everybody wants some of them, and wants me to get them some Seed."

DANIELS' SHOW & BEDDING PANSIES.

These beautiful, free-flowering, hardy plants are easily raised from seed, and will richly repay the small cost and trouble required to grow them to perfection. For blooming in Summer and Autumn, sow in February, March, and April, in pans or boxes of light rich soil placed in a gentle heat, and as soon as the young plants are large enough, prick out about two inches apart on rich soil to strengthen, and finally plant out six or eight inches apart, in ground into which a good quantity of well-decayed manure has been worked. Pansies delight in a somewhat shady position, and plenty of moisture in dry weather. The finest blooms are produced the second year, and grand flowers may be had by sowing in July or August in the open ground, and planting out in the following Spring into good rich soil.

		per pkt.—s. d.
820	**DANIELS' EXHIBITION GIANT.** A superb strain of extra large and beautifully coloured flowers of the highest type, and including the most charming and richly coloured stained and blotched flowers. Many of the blooms from this strain will be found equal to the finest named varieties. Very choice mixed seed	5 0
830	„ „ „ „ „	2 6
831	„ „ „ „ smaller pkt.	1 6
832	**DANIELS' PRIZE BLOTCHED.** A splendid strain of brilliantly coloured flowers of the most exquisite shades of colour, the petals being handsomely stained or blotched, very choice	1 0
833	„ „ „ smaller pkt.	0 6
834	**DANIELS' GIANT WHITE.** Very large flowers, pure white, with dark purple eye; splendid	1 0
835	**DANIELS' GIANT YELLOW.** Very large, pure yellow, a very fine variety	1 0
836	**DANIELS' GIANT PURPLE.** Dark purple, very fine	1 0
837	**DANIELS' GIANT STRIPED.** Beautifully formed flowers, handsomely striped. The perfection of all striped varieties	1 0
838	**PARISIAN.** Large stained. A beautiful class, mostly white ground, with five conspicuous blotches	6d. and 1 0
839	**ORCHID-FLOWERED.** Large beautiful flowers, including some rare and attractive shades	6d. and 1 0
840	**BUGNOT'S CHOICE MIXED.** Fine blotched varieties	1 0

		per pkt.—s. d.
841	**CARDINAL.** Bright red with darker blotch, the brightest red of all the Pansies, very fine	0 6
842	**GOLDEN YELLOW.** Fine spotted; a beautiful and distinct variety	0 6
843	**LORD BEACONSFIELD.** Purple violet, the top petals shading off to white; splendid	0 6
844	**PEACOCK.** A strikingly handsome and very distinct variety. The upper petals are a beautiful peacock blue, the flower shading off to velvety maroon and crimson, edged with white	0 6
845	**PSYCHE.** Beautiful variety with handsome undulating petals, colour a rich velvety violet, the petals broadly margined with white	0 6
846	**TRIMADEAU.** Giant Pansies. A magnificent strain of large-flowered beautiful varieties, choice mixed	1 0
847	**MADAME PERRET, "The Wine Pansy."** A very fine and quite distinct class of large beautiful flowers that continue in bloom throughout the Summer. The colours may be described as a series of wine shades varying from deep port to claret. Many of the flowers are edged with white, the deep coloured velvety blooms are exceedingly handsome, whilst the blooms generally are not only of great size but are delightfully fragrant	6d. and 1 0
848	**MIXED GERMAN.** Ordinary varieties	0 3

BEDDING PANSIES.

The following varieties will be found exceedingly useful for making showy beds in Spring, where distinct colours are desirable, all the sorts being of compact habit and very free-flowering.

		per pkt.—s. d.
849	**CLIVEDEN YELLOW.** Bright yellow	0 6
850	„ **PURPLE.** Purplish maroon	0 6
851	„ **WHITE.** Fine	0 6
852	**EMPEROR WILLIAM.** Ultramarine blue	0 6
853	**SNOW QUEEN.** Pure satiny white; beautiful	0 6
854	**LIGHT BLUE.** Beautiful	0 6

		per pkt.—s. d.
855	**YELLOW GEM.** Golden yellow	0 6
856	**RICH PURPLE.** Fine dark	0 6
857	**GOLD-MARGINED.** Splendid	0 6
858	**KING OF THE BLACKS.** Jet black	0 6
859	**PURPLE AND GOLD.** Golden yellow, the upper petals purple; very showy	0 6

860   Six choice varieties 1s. 6d.

BEDDING VIOLAS OR TUFTED PANSIES.

A PROFUSE-FLOWERING and invaluable class of hardy perennial bedding plants, continuing in bloom from early Spring till late in the Autumn months. Highly desirable for Spring gardening, and afford some charming effects in association with Spring-flowering Bulbs, &c. The following list includes the finest varieties in cultivation, and which we highly recommend. For blooming the same year, sow the seeds in early Spring in a gentle heat, prick out to strengthen, harden off, and plant out in April or May where intended to flower. For spring flowering the following year, sow the seeds in May or June, prick out on Nursery beds and plant out in Autumn or early Spring where intended to flower.

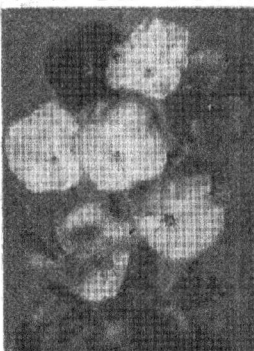

		per pkt.—s. d.
861	**AN ASSORTMENT OF 6 SPLENDID VARIETIES**	2 6
862	**ADMIRATION.** Splendid dark violet, yellow eye	0 6
863	**ARDWELL GEM.** Large rayless primrose-coloured flowers. A fine bedder	1 0
864	**BLUE PERFECTION.** Bluish purple	0 6
865	**GOLDEN GEM.** Rich golden yellow	0 6
866	**MAGNIFICENT.** Deep rich purple	0 6
867	**MARCHIONESS.** Pure white, very fine	1 0
868	**SNOWFLAKE.** Splendid pure white	0 6
869	**CHOICEST MIXED**	1 0
870	„ „ smaller pkt.	0 6

From Mr. L. C. SMYTH, Tullyherim.
June 16th.
"I must say how splendidly all your Seeds did last year. The Pansies, Poppies, and Asters were beautiful."

From Mrs. G. GOOD, Oregon, U.S.A.
Feb. 15th.
"The Exhibition Pansy Seed I had last year was highly satisfactory, I had some fine blooms."

From Mr. E. MOTT, Methwold, Brandon.
May 30th.
"I never had such Pansies as those I raised from your Seed last year."

From W. H. EVANS, Esq., Brecon.
May 23rd.
"The Seedling Pansies I had from you recently are exceptionally good."

From Mrs. JOHN SABERTON, Sawston, Cambs.
April 15th.
"The Pansy Seed sent two years ago flowered most splendidly last year, they were the admiration of all."

From Mr. J. SCUTCHINGS, Aylesbury, Bucks.
July 23rd.
"From the packet of Exhibition Giant Pansies I had from you last year, I have the grandest lot seen in this district."

☞ DANIELS' SUPERB PETUNIAS.

PETUNIA, HYBRIDA GRANDIFLORA.

Petunias in their many beautiful varieties form a highly interesting and desirable class of free-flowering plants for pot or garden culture; those of the Grandiflora section, both single and double-flowered, being especially valuable. The blooms of these are of immense size, beautifully formed, and of the most charming and delicate colours; some of the flowers are exquisitely veined or pencilled, others blotched or striped. The new "Fringed" varieties, both double and single, produce some charming flowers, the edges of the petals being elegantly cut or fringed, whilst the colours are most varied and beautiful. The seed we offer has been carefully saved from fecundated flowers of the finest varieties; but as Petunias raised from seed have a tendency to "sport," we cannot guarantee more than sixty or seventy per cent. of flowers true to description. All will, however, be found well worth growing, and occasionally some fine novelties may be secured. Petunias for indoor cultivation may be sown in January or early in February, but those intended for bedding out do not require to be sown before March. A soil composed of two parts leaf-mould and one part loam, with the addition of a little sharp sand, forms an excellent compost for these, but the seeds being very small require special care in sowing. Fill your pots or seed-pans to near the rim and press the soil down firmly and evenly, sow thinly, and cover the seeds very slightly with fine soil, sprinkle gently with a fine rose water-pot, and place in a gentle heat of sixty or sixty-five degrees, not higher, and keep nicely moist. As soon as the young plants can be handled, prick them out about one inch apart in pots to strengthen, and when sufficiently advanced in growth pot off singly into small pots, gradually harden off when established, and plant out about the middle of May, or shift into large pots as required. In planting Petunias out of doors, ground should be selected that has not been freshly manured, otherwise a superabundant foliage will retard the flowering.

PETUNIA HYBRIDA GRANDIFLORA.

A fine and distinct class of beautiful, large-flowering varieties producing blooms of immense size, and of the most charming colours; much superior to the old varieties of Petunia hybrida. The plants are robust in habit of growth, and admirably suited as pot-plants for the greenhouse or conservatory or for garden decoration.

	per pkt.—s. d.
886 AN ASSORTMENT OF 6 BEAUTIFUL VARIETIES ..	2 6
887 ALBA GRANDIFLORA. Immense pure white flowers; beautiful	1 0
888 BRILLIANT ROSE. With white eye; superb variety	1 0
889 PURPUREA. Immense flowers of the deepest blood crimson colour; magnificent	1 0
890 MACULATA. Very large flowers handsomely blotched or striped	1 0
891 VIOLACEA. Rich velvety violet blue; fine	1 0
892 VERY CHOICE MIXED, IN BEAUTIFUL VARIETY	2 6
893 " " " " smaller pkt.	1 0
894 " " " "	0 6

DWARF BEDDING PETUNIAS.

A very pretty free-flowering class of dwarf compact-growing varieties, exceedingly useful for massing in beds, or as an edging to shrubbery borders, &c. The plants grow only about 6 or 8 inches high.

	per pkt.—s. d.
895 DWARF, PURE WHITE. Beautiful variety, with pure satiny-white flowers ..	1 0
896 DWARF, ROSY CARMINE. Brilliant rosy-carmine, with white throat..	1 0
897 DWARF, STRIPED. Beautiful bright rosy-purple, striped with white	1 0
898 DWARF, MIXED	6d. and 1 0

PETUNIAS—Ordinary Class.

899 CHOICEST MIXED. Beautiful showy varieties for beds or borders		0 6
900 " " smaller pkt.		0 3

PETUNIAS—Daniels' Superb Fringed.

☞ A beautiful class, producing large and strikingly handsome flowers, the edges of the petals being elegantly laciniated or fringed.

	per pkt.—s. d.
871 SINGLE, PURE WHITE. Beautiful	1 6
872 " BRILLIANT ROSE AND WHITE. Splendid variety	1 6
873 " VERY CHOICE MIXED	2 6
874 " " smaller pkt.	1 6
875 DOUBLE, AN ASSORTMENT OF 6 SUPERB VARIETIES	2 0
876 " BRILLIANT ROSE. Beautiful bright rose; most charming variety	1 6
877 " LADY OF THE LAKE. Beautiful large fringed, pure white, double flowers, superb	1 6
878 " CHOICEST MIXED	2 0
879 " " smaller pkt.	1 6

DOUBLE-FLOWERED PETUNIAS.

Saved from carefully hybridised flowers, will produce a good percentage of large, handsome, double flowers.

	per pkt.—s. d.
880 VERY CHOICE MIXED	2 6
881 " smaller pkt.	1 6
882 AN ASSORTMENT OF 6 CHOICE SORTS	2 6
883 PURE WHITE. Beautiful	1 6
884 BRILLIANT ROSE. Splendid	1 6
885 MINIATURE. Small, double flowers, charming variety	1 0

PINKS—Garden.

901 MRS. SINKINS. A fine double-flowered pure white, deliciously scented; quite hardy .. .. .. per pkt. 1s. 0d.

902 HOMER. A fine double dark rose with a crimson centre. A fine variety .. .. per pkt. 1s. 0d.

All Flower Seeds quoted in 3d. packets may be had at 2/6 per dozen.

PHLOX DRUMMONDI.

All the varieties of this beautiful class of annuals are worthy of extensive cultivation, especially those of the grandiflora class, which produce such a profusion and diversity of their large beautifully formed and brilliantly coloured flowers. Those of the compacta section growing only about four to six inches in height are also highly desirable for massing or beds, or for edgings, producing an effect that can probably be obtained by no other plant.

Cultivation.—Sow the seeds in February, March, or early in April, in pans or boxes of light rich soil; sow thinly, press down firmly, cover lightly, water, and place in a gentle heat. The young plants will be up in a few days, and soon as they can be fairly handled they should be pricked out about two inches apart in pans or boxes to strengthen, or potted singly into small pots: keep close for a few days, and when they are established give abundance of air, placing close to the glass to induce a sturdy growth. May is soon enough for planting out, and a rather dry and sunny position is to be preferred. The dwarf kinds should be planted about eight inches apart; the others, which grow from nine inches to one foot in height, with a spreading habit, may be planted one foot or more apart. Towards the end of April and during May, the seeds may be sown where intended to bloom in the open ground, and in an ordinary season a fine display may be had quite into the Autumn.

PHLOX DRUMMONDI GRANDIFLORA.

PHLOX DRUMMONDI, Intermediate.

An exceedingly free-flowering and beautiful class of great value for showy beds or borders. The plants, which are of a compact habit of growth, attain a height of about 8 inches.

			per pkt.—s. d.
003	BRILLIANT SCARLET. Splendid	..	.. 0 6
004	ROSE. Beautiful colour	..	.. 0 6
005	PURE WHITE. Very fine	..	.. 0 6
006	DARK PURPLE. Rich violet purple	..	.. 0 6
007	VERY CHOICE MIXED. All colours	..	.. 0 6

PHLOX DRUMMONDI GRANDIFLORA.

The grandiflora varieties form a magnificent class ; the plants are robust in habit, and the flowers, which are of various rich and beautiful colours, have in many of the varieties large, conspicuous white eyes ; the individual blooms are of fine substance and scarcely inferior in size to the perennial sorts. A decided improvement on the old varieties of P. Drummondi. The plants grow about one foot high.

		per pkt.—s. d.
008	AN ASSORTMENT OF 12 SPLENDID VARIETIES	.. 3 6
009	,, 8 ,, ,,	.. 2 6
910	ALBA. Pure white	.. 0 6
911	ATROPURPUREA. Dark purple	.. 0 6
912	CARMINEA. Beautiful carmine, white eye ..	.. 0 6
913	COCCINEA. Brilliant scarlet	.. 0 6
914	ROSEA. Delicate rose, white eye ..	.. 0 6
915	VIOLACEA. Violet blue, white eye ..	.. 0 6
916	SPLENDENS. Fine vivid crimson ..	.. 0 6
917	CHOICEST MIXED. In beautiful variety ..	1 0
918	,, ,, .. smaller pkt.	0 6

PHLOX DRUMMONDI.
Dwarf Compact Varieties.

A charming class of beautiful dwarf-growing varieties. The plants grow 4 to 6 inches in height and 6 or 8 inches across, and are almost covered with bloom. Splendid for edgings or beds.

		per pkt.—s. d.
919	FIREBALL. An exceedingly fine dwarf-growing and profuse-flowering variety, height six inches, brilliant scarlet ; fine for pots or edging	0 6
920	SNOWBALL. Same height and habit as the preceding, but bearing quite a profusion of large, pure white flowers ..	0 6
921	ROSY GEM. Bright rose, with white eye. Charming variety	0 6
922	CARMINEA. Beautiful carmine..	0 6
923	ATROPURPUREA. Dark purple	0 6
924	DELICATA. Blush, very charming	0 6
925	SPLENDENS. Vivid crimson, with white eye ..	0 6
926	EXTRA CHOICE MIXED. In beautiful variety ..	1 0
927	,, ,, ,, smaller pkt.	0 6
928	SIX BRILLIANT VARIETIES	2 6

PHLOX DRUMMONDI CUSPIDATA.
The New Star Phloxes.

A very pretty class, with neat, stellate flowers of the most beautiful colours ; very useful as cut flowers.

		per pkt.—s. d.
929	CHOICEST MIXED. In beautiful variety	.. 1 0
930	,, ,, smaller pkt.	0 6

PHLOX DRUMMONDI—Original Class.

VERY SHOWY AND FREE-FLOWERING.

		per pkt.—s. d.
931	CHOICEST MIXED. In beautiful variety	.. 0 6
932	,, ,, smaller pkt.	0 3

PERENNIAL PHLOX.

Splendid hardy perennials for large beds or borders. The seed we offer has been saved from a fine collection of beautifully coloured named flowers.

	per pkt.—s. d.			per pkt.—s. d.
933	TALL VARIETIES. Very choice mixed Height 3 feet .. 1 0	934	DWARF VARIETIES. Choice varieties. Height 2 feet .. 1 0

DANIELS' SUPERB FRINGED PRIMULAS

☞ It is with very much pleasure that we offer the grand strains of Primulas named below, all of which have been specially grown for our retail trade, and will give the highest satisfaction. The flowers will be found of great size and perfect form, combined with the most brilliant and charming colours, and a habit of plant which leaves nothing to be desired.

The beautiful varieties of Primula sinensis may be sown in March, April, May, and June. The earlier sown are, however, to be preferred for making fine strong plants with an abundance of bloom. Great care must be taken to have a well-drained pot or seed-pan filled to within half an inch of the top with sifted leaf-mould; leave the surface rather rough, and sprinkle the seeds thinly upon it. The most successful raisers do not cover with soil, but after sowing the seed press down the surface tolerably firm, and place a square of glass over the pot. Place in a good strong heat, shaded from strong light, and water very gently when the soil becomes dry. The seeds will germinate in two or three weeks, after which remove the glass and keep in a shady position. Pot off into small pots when the young plants are about half an inch above ground, and place near the glass in the frame or greenhouse. In their after culture Primulas should be kept as near as convenient to the glass, have plenty of fresh air, and never be kept for a long period in a high temperature or in a dry heated atmosphere.

DANIELS' WHITE PERFECTION.

		per pkt.—s. d.
939	**ALBA MAGNIFICA.** Beautifully fringed, pure white flowers, with citron-yellow eye	1 6
940	**CHISWICK RED.** Brilliant, crimson-scarlet	1 6
941	**MAGENTA QUEEN.** New, brilliant, and charming ..	1 6
942	**ORANGE KING** (new). A superb variety of quite a new colour in Primulas. The beautiful orange colour in the bud ☞ and the orange salmon shade around the edge of the terra-cotta coloured petals give the flower a most pleasing and distinct appearance .. .. 1s. 6d. and	2 6
943	**NEW GIANT PINK.** The finest of the Giant Primulas, blooms ☞ nearly 3 inches across, of a lovely bright rosy pink colour with petals of great substance. Magnificent 1s. 6d. and	2 6
944	**NEW GIANT SALMON.** Beautiful salmon pink or salmon flowers .. .. 1s. 6d. and	2 6
945	**THE DUCHESS** (new). Beautiful white, with rosy-carmine zone surrounding a yellow eye; splendid 1s. 6d. and	2 6
946	**CRIMSON KING** (new). The darkest coloured and richest of ☞ all Crimson Primulas, splendid flowers, with a black ring round the centres; most superb variety 1s. 6d. and	2 6
947	**DANIELS' CHOICEST RED VARIETIES, MIXED**	1 0
948	**DANIELS' CHOICEST WHITE VARIETIES, MIXED** ..	1 0
949	**DANIELS' CHOICEST MIXED.** In beautiful variety, including some of the finest .. .. 1s. 6d. and	2 6
950	**DANIELS' QUEEN OF ROSES.** Beautiful soft rosy pink, a flower of great size and substance .. 1s. 6d. and	2 6
951	**DANIELS' WHITE PERFECTION.** A beautiful pure white of the fern-leaved type, of splendid habit 1s. 6d. and	2 6
952	**DANIELS' SUPERB BLUE.** Carefully saved from beautifully fringed flowers of perfect form and of the deepest shade of blue; splendid colour .. .. 1s. 6d. and	2 6
953	**DANIELS' EMPRESS, GIANT WHITE.** Immense white flowers, borne on strong stems, with very robust foliage; a grand variety	2 6

PRIMULA STELLATA (Star Primula).

An improved form of the Star Primula, differing only in the formation of its flowers, which are nearly equal in substance and size to some of the best of the Chinese varieties. The snow-white flowers are beautifully fringed, and stand well above the dark foliage and purple stems, which make it even more attractive than those of the older type.

		per pkt.—s. d.
935	**KING OF THE STARS.** Magnificent variety, immense heads of deep crimson-carmine flowers	1 6
936	**BLUE STAR.** Beautiful porcelain blue	1 6
937	**CHOICEST MIXED STAR.** A charming mixture ..	1 6
938	**GIANT WHITE STAR.** The grandest White Star Primula yet raised. The pure white massive flowers are produced in great abundance, and contrast admirably with the rich dark foliage; splendid for cutting	1 6

DOUBLE-FLOWERED FRINGED VARIETIES.

Exceedingly useful for flowering in the greenhouse during Winter.

		per pkt.—s. d.
954	**DOUBLE PURE WHITE,** Fringed. Very useful for cutting ..	2 6
955	,, **BLUE** (new). Bright blue, fringed	2 6
956	,, **BRIGHT CRIMSON.** Splendid	1 6
957	,, **BLUSHING BEAUTY.** A grand new variety, with large double flowers of a lovely shade of blush pink ..	2 6
958	**DOUBLE. CARNATION-FLAKED,** Fringed	2 6
959	,, **MARGINATA.** Lilac, edged with white	2 6
960	,, **PRINCE OF WALES,** Fern-leaved. Rich glowing scarlet, splendid	2 6
961	,, **CHOICEST MIXED** .. .. 1s. 6d. and	2 6

HARDY AND HALF-HARDY PRIMULAS.

PRIMULA OBCONICA.

A beautiful class of free-flowering half-hardy perennials growing about eight inches high, admirably suited for pot culture in the cool greenhouse. The blooms are very useful for cutting.

		per pkt.—s. d.
962	**ALBA GRANDIFLORA.** Pure white, with small yellow eye	1 0
963	**ROSEA** ,, Large, finely-formed, bright rosy lilac flowers	1 0
964	**VERY CHOICE MIXED.** In beautiful variety ..	1 0

PRIMULA JAPONICA.

		per pkt.—s. d.
965	A very fine hardy plant, growing about 18 inches high, with whorls of various coloured flowers. Choice mixed seed	0 6
966	**PRIMULA KEWENSIS.** Beautiful half-hardy Autumn and Winter bloomer for the greenhouse. Flowers bright yellow, 1 ft.	2 6

PRIMULA ROSEA GRANDIFLORA.

		per pkt.—s. d.
967	A charming dwarf hardy species, with very pretty bright rose coloured flowers. The plant grows only about six inches high, and is an excellent subject for dry rockeries ..	1 0

PASSIFLORA CÆRULEA.
(The Passion Flower.)

per pkt.—s. d.

903 **GRANDIFLORA.** Splendid hardy climber, with large pale blue flowers. Much superior to the old variety — .. 0 6

PEA, EVERLASTING.
(Lathyrus latifolius.)

Splendid hardy perennial climbers for walls, trellises, &c.

969 **RED or SCARLET** 0 4
970 **WHITE.** Pure white 0 4
971 **ROSE.** Pale rose, charming 0 4

PELARGONIUMS—GERANIUMS.

Sow in February or March in pots or pans of light rich soil, covering the seeds to the depth of about a quarter of an inch, and place in a heat of about sixty-five or seventy degrees. Pot off the young plants singly into small pots, and shift into larger as these fill with roots. With liberal treatment these will bloom the first year, and, although many will not be up to the standard of first-class florists' flowers, some really beautiful varieties may be expected from a good strain of seed.

972 **FRENCH BLOTCHED or REGAL.** Beautiful large-flowered varieties, with handsomely blotched petals .. 2 6
973 " smaller pkt. 1 6
974 **FANCY VARIETIES.** Very choice mixed.. .. 1 6
975 **ZONAL.** Single-flowered, from finest named sorts.. 1 0
976 **IVY-LEAVED.** Single and double-flowered varieties. Choice mixed 1 6

PENTSTEMONS.

Those beautiful free-flowering plants succeed admirably when treated as half-hardy annuals, and sown in February or March on a gentle heat and planted out in May they commence blooming in July and continue to throw up their lovely spikes of flowers till late Autumn. The new large-flowered hybrids produce some charming flowers, many of them being equal to the finest named sorts. The plants grow about 18 inches high.

977 **NEW LARGE-FLOWERED HYBRIDS.** Choicest mixed, from a magnificent strain 1 0
978 Smaller packet 0 6

POLYANTHUS.

LARGE-FLOWERED POLYANTHUS.

A beautiful free-flowering class of hardy perennials which has been highly improved of late years. The plants are about six inches high, and bloom about the same time as primroses. The large-flowered varieties in their many beautiful colours are very charming and should be used extensively for Spring gardening.

per pkt.—s. d.

979 **LARGE-FLOWERED, CHOICEST MIXED.** A very fine strain of beautiful varieties, very free-flowering .. 1 0
980 " smaller pkt. 0 6
981 **POLYANTHUS-PRIMROSE** (bunch-flowered). Choicest mixed hybrids, special selection 1 6
982 **NEW GIANT, Crimson** ⎫ Fine showy varieties for 1 0
983 " " **White** ⎬ bedding out, &c. 1 0
984 " " **Yellow** ⎭ 1 0
985 **GOLD-LACED.** Fine varieties, from a choice collection of beautifully laced flowers .. .. 6d. and 1 0
986 **HOSE-IN-HOSE VARIETIES.** Choice mixed 1 0

HARDY PRIMROSES.

Profuse flowering and very charming hardy perennials, growing six inches high, invaluable for Spring gardening. The hybrid varieties vary in colour from the palest and most delicate sulphur yellow, through all the soft shades of rose and purple to the most intense and brilliant crimson. In a mild season many of the varieties will commence blooming in the Autumn and continue through the Winter, but from the beginning of April to the middle of May they are generally in full bloom, and present a most lovely appearance. A partially shaded border, with a westerly aspect, will grow them to perfection in almost any moderately rich soil, and they will thrive on almost any shady bank amongst grass, but water should be given in very dry weather during summer.

987 **LARGE-FLOWERED HYBRIDS.** Grand strain of beautiful high-coloured flowers, all of the true Primrose type, with the flowers large and brilliant; very fine .. 1 6
988 **VERY CHOICE, MIXED.** From a good collection.. 1 0
989 **WHITE QUEEN.** Pure white, beautiful 1 0
990 **BLUE-FLOWERED** (G. F. Wilson's). Rich purple blue, very fine and quite distinct 1 6
991 **COMMON YELLOW** 0 6

DANIELS' SELECTED POPPIES.

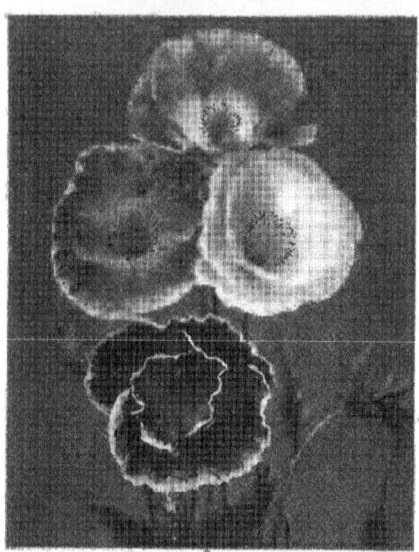

SHIRLEY POPPIES.

ANNUAL POPPIES.

A brilliant and charmingly effective group of hardy annuals of great value for garden or shrubbery decoration. The single-flowered varieties are especially valuable as cut flowers, and if cut when the blooms are just beginning to expand, will retain their beauty for a long period. The beautiful Shirley Poppy, sown at intervals from early Spring to the end of June, will give a charming display quite into the Autumn.

per pkt.—s. d.

992 **DANIELS' SELECTED SHIRLEY.** The fine strain we offer has been carefully selected and includes all the most brilliant and exquisite shades of colour. Highly recommended for cut flowers. Height 2 feet. Choicest mixed .. 3d. and 0 6

993 **COMMUTATUM** (Papaver). A splendid showy variety, growing about 18 inches high and bearing quite a profusion of brilliant scarlet flowers with a black blotch at base of petals. Very effective 0 6

994 **THE TULIP POPPY** (Papaver glaucum). Vivid scarlet, very effective. Height 15 inches 0 4

995 **CARDINAL.** Large double flowers, beautifully fringed, of an intense scarlet colour. Height 18 inches 0 4

996 **WHITE SWAN.** Large, double, pure white flowers, beautifully fringed. Height 2 feet 0 4

997 **CARNATION-FLOWERED,** Double. Fine double flowers in many brilliant colours. 2 feet.. .. .. .. 0 3

998 **FRENCH RANUNCULUS.** A very fine class of handsome, brilliantly-coloured double flowers. Height 18 inches .. 0 3

999 **PÆONY-FLOWERED,** Double. A fine race of large handsome double flowers in beautiful variety of colour. Height 3 feet. Choice mixed 0 3

PERENNIAL POPPIES.

The seeds of the beautiful Nudicaule varieties, for blooming the same year from seed, should be sown in February or March in a gentle heat, and planted out in May. The large-flowered Orientale varieties are best sown thinly in the open ground in May or June, and transplanted in Autumn or early Spring where intended to bloom. The same treatment will apply to the dwarf Alpinum and other perennial sorts.

NUDICAULE (The Iceland Poppy)—

Charming dwarf-growing hardy perennial, with beautifully coloured single flowers on long slender stems. Will bloom the first year from seed. Height 1 foot

per pkt. s. d.

1000   "   **MINIATUM.** Brilliant orange scarlet .. 0 6
1001   "   **ALBUM.** Pure white 0 6
1002   "   **CROCEUM.** Bright yellow 0 6
1003   "   **VERY CHOICE MIXED** 0 6
1004   "   **NEW EXCELSIOR STRAIN.** Many exquisite shades of colour 1 0

1005 **ALPINUM.** Beautiful little hardy perennial, growing only 6 inches high. Flowers of various pretty colours. Excellent for rockwork 0 6

1006 **ORIENTALE HYBRIDS,** Choice Mixed. Magnificent hardy perennials, with large single flowers, including beautiful shades of red, rose, lilac, mauve, &c. Height 3 feet .. 1 0

1007 **ORIENTALE.** Immense, brilliant scarlet flowers, very hardy. Height 3 feet 0 6

PORTULACA.

A brilliant class of half-hardy annuals. The plants are of a dwarf spreading habit and are first rate for dry rockeries or an edging on warm borders. The seeds may be sown out of doors in April where intended to bloom. Height 6 inches.

per pkt. s. d.

1008 **GRANDIFLORA ALBA FL. PL.** White, double flowers .. 0 6
1009   "   **AUREA FL. PL.** Golden yellow .. 0 6
1010   "   **SPLENDENS FL. PL.** Brilliant crimson .. 0 6
1011   "   **DOUBLE,** Choice Mixed .. 6d. and 1 0
1012   "   **SINGLE,** Choice Mixed 0 6

PERILLA.

Valuable plants for bedding with richly coloured dark foliage.

1013 **ATROPURPUREA LACINIATA.** Handsome laciniated foliage, deeper in colour than P. nankinensis. 2 feet .. 0 6
1014 **NANKINENSIS.** Fine dark leaves. 2 feet 0 3

PHACELIA CAMPANULARIA.

1015 A showy hardy annual from California, growing about 1 foot high, with bell-shaped flowers of a bright blue colour, which continue for a long time 0 4

PYRETHRUM—GOLDEN FEATHER.

(Pyrethrum parthenifolium aureum.)

Exceedingly useful for bedding. Sow the seeds under glass in February or March and plant out in May for the best results. The plant is a hardy perennial, but plants that have withstood the Winter are not satisfactory.

1016 **GOLDEN FEATHER,** Selected. Bright yellow foliage. Fine for bedding. Height 6 inches 0 4

1017 **LACINIATUM PERFECTION.** Bright yellow, finely cut bright yellow leaves ; very pretty. Height 6 inches .. 0 6

1018 **SELAGINOIDES.** A beautiful fern-leaved variety with bright golden foliage. A splendid bedder. Height 6 inches .. 0 6

PYRETHRUM HYBRIDUM.

Very fine hardy herbaceous perennials. Excellent for mixed borders, and useful for cut flowers.

1019 **DOUBLE-FLOWERED,** Choicest Mixed. Double and semi-double flowers. Height 2 feet.. .. .. 1 6

1020 **SINGLE-FLOWERED.** Splendid mixed, saved from a fine collection. Height 2 feet 0 6

Oct. 11th.   From Mr. C. PIPER, Instore.

"I am really pleased with the Seeds you sent me last year, they gave me every satisfaction. I can highly recommend your Flower Seeds to any of my friends."

Jan. 20th.   From Mrs. RAMSAY, Torquay.

"The Poppy Seed you kindly sent me made a lovely display."

We beg to intimate that we cannot "break" packets quoted in this list.

SALPIGLOSSIS.

LARGE-FLOWERED SALPIGLOSSIS.

A charming class of half-hardy annuals of great value for large beds or borders, and exceedingly useful for cut flowers. The large blooms are beautifully veined, and vary in colour from dark purple and crimson to orange, golden yellow and scarlet. Sow in the open ground in March to April, and thin out. Height 3 feet.

LARGE-FLOWERED VARIETIES—

		per pkt.—s.	d.
1021 **CRIMSON.** Veined with gold	..	..	0 6
1022 **GOLDEN YELLOW.** Very fine	..	..	0 6
1023 **RICH PURPLE.** Fine colour	..	..	0 6
1024 **BLUE.** Veined with gold, beautiful	..	..	0 6
1025 **SIX BEAUTIFUL VARIETIES,** Separate	..	..	1 6
1026 **VERY CHOICE MIXED**	..	6d. and	1 0

REHMANNIA ANGULATA.

1027 **PINK PERFECTION.** A charming half-hardy herbaceous perennial of fine effect for conservatory decoration 1 0

RHODANTHE.

Beautiful half-hardy annual Everlasting. Very useful for pot culture, and much valued for Winter decorations. Height 1 foot. To preserve for Winter decoration, the blooms should be gathered before fully expanded.

1028 **MACULATA.** Bright rose	..	..	..	0 4
1029 „ **ALBA.** Silvery white	..	..	..	0 4
1030 **SINGLE,** Choice mixed	..	..	..	0 4

RICINUS.
(Castor Oil Plant.)

Stately plants with large handsome foliage. Splendid for sub-tropical garden or conservatory decoration. Half-hardy Annual.

1031 **SANGUINEUS.** Large green leaves, red stems. Height 6 feet	0 4
1032 **COMMUNIS MAJOR.** Very fine. Height 6 feet	..	0 4
1033 **GIBSONI.** Bold dark foliage. Very attractive. 4 feet	..	0 4

RIVINA HUMILIS.

1034 A handsome plant for the greenhouse. Long racemes of white flowers, followed by scarlet currant-like fruit. Greenhouse perennial. Height 2 feet 0 6

ROCKET, SWEET.
(Hesperis matronalis.)

Deliciously fragrant Spring-flowering hardy herbaceous perennial.

	per pkt.—s.	d.
1035 **EARLY DWARF WHITE** Very free-flowering and sweet-scented. Height 1 foot	0 6
1036 **PURPLE.** Bright purple. Height 2 feet	..	0 3
1037 **WHITE.** Very sweet-scented. Height 2 feet	..	0 3

RUDBECKIA NEUMANNI.

1038 A splendid hardy perennial growing about 2 feet high, with bright golden yellow flowers and black disc. An almost continuous bloomer, and excellent for cut flowers.. .. 0 6

SCABIOUS—SWEET.

Beautiful hardy biennials with large fragrant flowers of many rich and beautiful shades of colour, blooming the first year from seed. Sow in March under glass and transplant or sow in April in the open ground and treat as hardy annuals.

1039 **THE BRIDE** (new). Large double pure white flowers, very sweet. Height 3 feet	..	..	0 3
1040 **FIRE KING** (new). Deep crimson, large double flowers. A splendid variety	..	..	0 6
1041 **ROSE PINK.** Beautiful variety. Height 3 feet	..	0 6
1042 **BLACK PRINCE.** Large double flowers of the richest dark purple colour. Height 3 feet	..	..	0 6
1043 **MAUVE QUEEN.** Fine double flowers of a beautiful lilac-mauve colour. Height 3 feet	..	..	0 6
1044 **6 LARGE-FLOWERED VARIETIES,** Separate. Our selection	1 6
1045 **LARGE-FLOWERED,** Splendid double mixed. Height 3 feet. 3d. and	0 6

LARGE-FLOWERED SWEET SCABIOUS.

From Mrs. L. C. SMYTH, Tullyherim.

May 26th.
" I must say how splendid all your Seeds did last year. The Pansies, Poppies and Asters were beautiful."

SALVIA.

Beautiful free-flowering half-hardy perennials, splendidly effective for beds or borders in Summer and Autumn.

per pkt.—s. d.

1046 **MINIATURE, New Dwarf.** A splendid variety, with large, pure scarlet flowers. First class for pot culture or for bedding. Height 1 foot   ..   1 0
1047 **SPLENDENS.** Brilliant scarlet. Height 2 feet   ..   0 6
1048 **ARGENTEA.** Silvery white foliage, very fine. Height 6 inches   0 4
1049 **PATENS.** Intense pure blue. A fine variety for beds. Height 2 feet   ..   1 0

SALVIA—BLUE BEARD.

1050 A showy hardy annual growing about 18 inches high, with spikes of bright bluish purple bracts, very showy ..   0 3

SCHIZANTHUS.

A beautiful class of half-hardy annuals of elegant growth and of great value for pots in the greenhouse where they are charmingly effective. They also succeed well grown out of doors. The flowers vary in colour from delicate pink and rose to carmine-yellow, apricot, mauve, crimson and other lovely shades, the long sprays of bloom being very useful when cut, and last a long time.

1051 **WISETONENSIS.** Daniels' Selected strain, charming shades of beautiful colours, very fine. Height 18 inches   ..   1 0
1052 **HYBRIDUS GRANDIFLORUS.** Very fine large-flowered varieties. Height 18 inches 0 6
1053 **PINNATUS.** Lilac spotted. Height 18 inches   ..   0 3
1054   „   Dwarf rose, very pretty. Height 1 foot   ..   0 6
1055 **RETUSUS ALBUS.** Flowers large pure white, blotched with yellow. Height 18 inches   ..   0 4
1056 **CHOICE MIXED.** Showy varieties   ..   0 3

SCHIZANTHUS WISETONENSIS.

From J. PYATT, Esq., Nottingham.

March 20th.

"I should like to take this opportunity of saying how very suitable I was with the Seeds I had from you last year, the Stocks were specially fine and greatly admired. I gathered the last lot in November."

SAPONARIA.

per pkt.—s. d.

1057 **SCARLET QUEEN.** A compact-growing hardy annual, with numerous bright rosy scarlet flowers. Excellent for beds or edgings. Height 6 inches   ..   0 4
1058 **CALABRICA.** Produces a profusion of small pink flowers. A good hardy annual for edgings. Height 6 inches   0 3
1059   „   **ALBA.** Pure white. Height 6 inches   ..   0 3
1060 **OCYMOIDES.** Hardy perennial of elegant trailing habit. Flowers rose 0 3

SCABIOSA CAUCASICA.

1061 Splendid hardy perennial producing large bluish mauve flowers. Sown early under glass and planted out will bloom the first year from seed. Height 2 feet   ..   1 0

SENSITIVE PLANT.
(Mimosa pudica.)

1062 A beautiful greenhouse shrub with handsome acacia-like foliage 0 6

SILENE.

Brilliant, profuse-flowering hardy annuals of dwarf compact growth, splendidly effective when grown in broad lines or beds, and much prized for Spring gardening.

1063 **BONETTI.** Deep rose flowers, with dark foliage. 1 foot ..   0 3
1064 **PENDULA.** Double rose, rosy-carmine double flowers, very compact. Height 1 foot   ..   0 3
1065   „   **Double White dwarf.** Rosy-white double flowers, beautiful variety. Height 4 inches   ..   0 4
1066   „   **Dwarf rose.** Bright rose, very compact, one of the best for Spring bedding. Height 4 inches   ..   0 4
1067 **SNOW KING.** White. Very dwarf, an abundant bloomer. Height 4 inches   ..   0 4

SOLANUM HYBRIDUM.

1068 Half-hardy compact-growing shrub, bearing pretty orange-scarlet fruit. Very useful for table decoration or the greenhouse. Height 1 foot   ..   0 6

STATICE.

1069 **SINUATA HYBRIDA.** Flowers, various shades of mauve, yellow and white. Excellent as a pot plant for the greenhouse. The dried blooms are very useful for Winter decoration. Half-hardy annual. Height 18 inches   0 6
1070 **SPICATA.** A dwarf-growing hardy annual with long spikes of bluish pink flowers. Useful as an Everlasting. Height 1 foot 0 3
1071 **SUWOROWI.** Very useful hardy annual Everlasting, with flowers of a bright rose colour. Height 18 inches   0 3

STREPTOCARPUS.

1072 **LARGE-FLOWERING HYBRIDS.** A very fine strain of large beautiful flowers, varying in colour through all the shades of pink, lavender-blue, purple, &c., to pure white. Greenhouse perennials. Height 9 inches 1 6

SUNFLOWER.
(Helianthus.)

1073 **GIANT YELLOW, Double.** Enormous flowers, very double. Colour a rich yellow. Height 6 to 8 feet   ..   0 4
1074 **GIANT YELLOW, Single.** Immense flowers, yellow with black disc. Height 6 to 8 feet   ..   0 3
1075 **PRIMROSE DAME.** Large flowers. Primrose-yellow with black disc. Height 5 to 6 feet   ..   0 4
1076 **DWARF, Double.** Deep yellow double flowers. Height 4 feet 0 4
1077 **MINIATURE, Single.** Small bright yellow flowers, very useful for cutting. Height 4 feet   ..   0 4
1078 **ORION, Single.** Bright yellow, fine for cutting. Height 4 feet 0 4
1079 **STARLIGHT, Single.** Pale primrose with pointed petals. Height 3 feet. Charming for cut flowers   ..   0 6
1080 **STELLA, Single.** Long bright yellow petals, with small black centre. First rate for cutting. Height 4 feet ..   0 4

SWEET SULTAN.
(Centaurea.)

SWEET SULTAN—GIANT WHITE.

Very fine hardy annuals, deliciously scented, and very useful for cut flowers, remaining fresh for a long time in water.

per pkt.—s. d.

1081 GIANT WHITE. A superb variety, with large pure white, sweet-scented flowers, quite double the size of the old sort.
Height 2 feet 0 6

1082 GIANT BLUE. Large bluish mauve flowers. Very fine.
Height 2 feet 0 6

1083 NEW GIANT HYBRIDS (Centaurea Imperialis). A superb strain of giant flowered Sweet Sultans, growing about 2½ feet high, producing very large, sweet-scented flowers of the most beautiful and novel shades of colour .. .. 6d. and 1 0

1084 YELLOW. Bright yellow. 18 inches .. .. — 0 3

1085 PURPLE. Height 2 feet .. .. .. — 0 3

1086 WHITE. Useful for cutting. 2 feet .. .. — 0 3

1087 MIXED. Sweet-scented varieties .. — — 0 3

SWEET PEAS.
See pp. 65 to 68.

TACSONIA VAN VOLXEMI.
(The Scarlet Passion Flower.)

1088 A superb evergreen climber for the greenhouse, with brilliant crimson-scarlet flowers .. .. — — 1 0

THUNBERGIA.

Beautiful annual climbers for pots in the greenhouse. The plants grow about 4 feet high, with pretty flowers of yellow shades and white with black centres.

1089 VERY CHOICE MIXED SEED 0 4

TORENIA FOURNIERI.

1090 Free-flowering greenhouse annual. Flowers purple and white. Makes an excellent pot plant — — — 1 0

From Mr. A. G. WRIGHT, Purley.

July 20th.

"I have the pleasure to inform you that I took First Prize at our Rose Show for three bunches of White Sweet Peas raised from your seed."

SWEET WILLIAM.

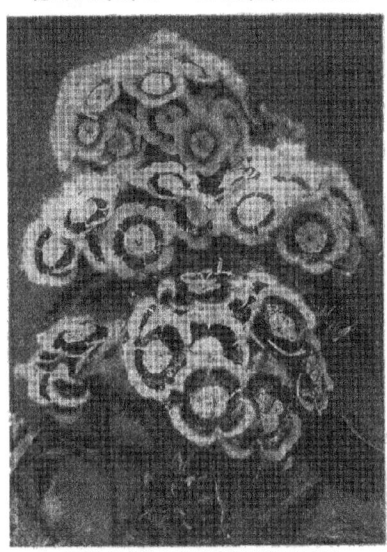

SWEET WILLIAM—DANIELS' PRIZE AURICULA EYED

We have given great attention for several years past to our splendid strain of these, which we have much pleasure in offering. The sorts embrace a great variety of the choicest Auricula-eyed, margined, selfs, &c., of the most brilliant types. The flowers are beautifully formed, of good substance, and are almost invariably awarded First Prize wherever exhibited. Sow the seeds thinly, in any sheltered place out of doors, in May or early in June, and plant out one foot apart in August or September where intended to bloom.

per pkt.—s. d.

1091 DANIELS' PRIZE AURICULA-EYED. A magnificent strain of the choicest large-flowered Auricula-eyed varieties.
The flowers perfectly formed and of the most brilliant and beautiful colours. Highly recommended ; mixed seed 1 0
and beautiful colours. Highly recommended ; smaller pkt. 0 6

1092 „ „ „ „ smaller pkt. 0 6

1093 DARK CRIMSON. Splendid colour 0 3

1094 PINK BEAUTY. Large heads of lovely salmony-rose coloured flowers 0 6

1095 SCARLET BEAUTY (new). Intense scarlet very showy .. 0 6

1096 PURE WHITE, DOUBLE. Fine 0 3

1097 MIXED. Beautiful varieties, including Auricula-eyed and self-coloured flowers .. .. 3d. and 0 6

The "HORTICULTURAL ADVERTISER" for July 6th, referring to our Strain of Sweet Williams, says:—

"The Auricula-Eyed forms are delightful, and represent one of the best strains we have seen for years past. The trusses are good, and most of the pips 1¼ inches in diameter ; the rich crimson and purple markings leave no opening for criticism by the most exacting florist, being perfectly even, and showing no tendency to run into the pure white of the ground colour. It is pleasing to find these old-fashioned favourites still receive in some quarters the attention they richly merit."

From Mr. S. GAPPER, Axminster.

May 5th.

" The Sweet Williams were splendid and much admired by every one, who admitted they had never seen better flowers."

All Flower Seeds quoted in 3d. packets may be had at 2/6 per dozen.

DANIELS' SELECTED WALLFLOWERS.

DANIELS' CHOICE SINGLE WALLFLOWERS.

SINGLE WALLFLOWERS.

The single-flowered varieties of this beautiful class of hardy flowers should be freely grown wherever there is room for them. No plant is easier of cultivation, and their charming colours and delicious perfume, added to their profusion of bloom render them highly desirable for Spring gardening. The splendid varieties—Eastern Queen, Vulcan, Cloth of Gold, Selected blood-red, and the New White Queen are particularly worthy of notice, as are also the New Tom Thumb varieties which make a fine edging for large beds or borders. May and June are the best months for sowing the seeds. Excepting where mentioned, the plants grow about 18 inches high.

per pkt.—s. d.

1098	**WHITE QUEEN.** The plants grow only about one foot high, and are very free-flowering. The sweet-scented blooms, when first open, are of a delicate pale primrose colour, changing in a day or two to almost pure white ..		0 6
1099	**GOLDEN MONARCH** (new). Magnificent variety. Large, rich, golden yellow flowers .. .. .. 6d. and		1 0
1100	**DANIELS' EARLY QUEEN.** Beautiful golden yellow flowers tinged with brown; remarkably early, sown in March will bloom the first year from seed		0 6
1101	**EASTERN QUEEN.** A peculiar shade of chamois, changing to salmon rose, giving a most pleasing and striking effect ..		0 6
1102	**VULCAN.** Splendid variety, with large velvety-crimson flowers		0 6
1103	**PRIMROSE DAME.** Clear primrose		— 6
1104	**RUBY GEM.** Rich satiny ruby violet		0 6
1105	**HARBINGER.** Rich dark brown, early		0 3
1106	**BLOOD RED.** Selected; splendid colour..		0 6
1107		smaller pkt.	0 3
1108	**CLOTH OF GOLD.** Dwarf, large-flowered		0 3
1109	**BLUE or VIOLET.** Beautiful colour		0 6
1110	**DANIELS' CHOICEST MIXED.** Including the most beautiful varieties		1 0
1111		smaller pkts. 3d. and	0 6
1112	TOM THUMB, **Golden Yellow**		0 6
1113	" " **Dark Brown**		0 6
1114	" " **Purple or Violet**		0 6
1115	" " **Choicest Mixed** .. .. 6d. and		1 0

The Tom Thumb varieties constitute quite a new class. The plants are only about nine inches high, and produce a profusion of bloom. Very showy for beds or edgings.

DOUBLE GERMAN WALLFLOWERS.

The double German Wallflowers produce grand spikes of handsome double blooms in April and May, but being less hardy than the single varieties, require to be planted in a more sheltered position.

per pkt.—s. d.

1116	**AN ASSORTMENT OF 6 CHOICE VARIETIES.** Separate ..	2 0
1117	**TALL VARIETIES,** Splendid mixed. Large double sweet-scented flowers. Height 2 feet	1 0
1118	" " smaller pkt.	0 6
1119	**DWARF VARIETIES,** Choicest mixed. Stout spikes of large double sweet-scented flowers. Height 1 foot ..	1 0
1120	" " smaller pkt.	0 6

VENUS' LOOKING-GLASS.

Useful free-flowering hardy annuals, growing about 9 inches high, with pretty bell-shaped flowers.

1121	**BLUE.** Bluish purple with white throat	0 3
1122	**WHITE.** Pure white, very pretty	0 3

VENUS' NAVEL-WORT.

1123	A pretty hardy annual with silvery leaves and white flowers. Height 1 foot	0 3

VERBENA.

Beautiful free-flowering half-hardy perennials, producing an abundance of bloom during the Summer and Autumn. Exceedingly useful for beds or borders. The plants grow about one foot high. Sow in February or March in pans or trays of light rich mould, and place in a gentle heat. As soon as the young plants have made three or four leaves pot them off singly into small pots, keep close till established, when they should be placed near the glass and have plenty of air, gradually harden off and plant out in May where intended to flower. Seedling Verbenas are almost invariably vigorous in growth, and if raised from a good strain of seed will produce some charming flowers.

1124	**LARGE-FLOWERED,** Pure White. Beautiful trusses of pure white flowers		0 6
1125	" " Rose and Carmine. Lovely shades of colour		0 6
1126	" " Scarlet and Crimson. Very rich colours		0 6
1127	" " Purple shades. Very fine ..		0 6
1128	**EXTRA CHOICE MIXED,** including all the most brilliant and beautiful varieties		1 0
1129	" " smaller pkt.		0 6
1130	**DWARF COMPACT.** Brilliant scarlet, very compact, splendid bedder		1 0
1131	**AURICULA-FLOWERED.** Beautiful large-flowered varieties, with conspicuous white eyes, very showy. Choice mixed..		1 0

VERBENA VENOSA.

1132	A handsome hardy perennial about one foot high. Blooms first year from seed if sown under glass in March and bears numerous trusses of bright purple flowers till late in Autumn	0 6

VERONICA SPICATA.

1133	Hardy herbaceous perennial of an elegant pyramidal habit of growth. Flowers bright blue. Height 18 inches.. ..	0 3

VIOLET.

1134	**PRINCESS OF WALES.** Large deep-blue flowers with long stems, deliciously fragrant. Height 9 inches ..	1 0
1135	**THE CZAR.** Deep purple flowers, fine scented ..	0 6
1136	**WHITE.** Large-flowered, very sweet-scented ..	0 6

VIRGINIAN STOCK.

Early flowering hardy annuals, much grown for their pretty effect in beds, &c. Excellent for Autumn sowing.

1137	**CRIMSON KING.** Bright rosy-crimson. Height 6 inches ..	0 4
1138	**WHITE.** Large-flowered. Height 9 inches ..	0 3
1139	**RED.** Bright, rosy-red. Height 9 inches ..	0 3
1140	**MIXED.** Various colours	0 3

VISCARIA.

Brilliant, free-flowering hardy annuals of easy cultivation. Very showy when grown in masses. Height 1 foot.

1141	**CARDINALIS.** Brilliant crimson-scarlet, very showy ..	0 3
1142	**ELEGANS PICTA.** Pale rose with crimson eye ..	0 3
1143	**OCULATA CÆRULEA.** Bright, deep lavender-blue, fine ..	0 3
1144	**OCULATA, Dwarf Carmine.** Bright carmine red flowers, very pretty. Height 6 inches	0 6

ZINNIA.

These splendid half-hardy annuals are of great value as bedding and border plants, and should always be grown for their brilliant and beautiful colours. The middle of March is quite soon enough to sow the first batch of Zinnias under glass. Successive sowings may be made till the latter part of April. Sow the seeds in pans or pots of light, rich, finely made soil, and place in a moderate heat. Soon as the young plants are large enough to handle, they should be potted off singly into small pots or pricked out into larger pots or pans to strengthen. To prevent the plants drawing up too much, keep as close as convenient to the glass, give plenty of air on fine warm days, and if the leading flower buds are pinched out as they make their appearance, a more bushy and vigorous growth will follow. Planting out should not take place till all danger from May frosts is over. An open sunny position with fairly rich soil should be chosen and the plants should not be less than a foot apart. Weak liquid manure given once or twice a week before the plants come into flower, will assist in the development of some fine blooms. The flowers of Zinnias have a tendency to sport, and although the seeds of these have been carefully saved we cannot guarantee that the flowers will be absolutely true to the colours mentioned.

DANIELS' LARGE-FLOWERED. A splendid strain of beautiful varieties, growing about two feet high, with large, handsome double flowers of the most splendid colours.

	per pkt.—s. d.
1150 AN ASSORTMENT OF 6 SPLENDID VARIETIES	1 6
1151 BRILLIANT SCARLET. Splendid colour	0 4
1152 WHITE. Creamy white	0 4
1153 ROSE. Delicate rose	0 4
1154 YELLOW. Clear yellow	0 4
1155 PURPLE. Rich colour	0 4
1156 STRIPED VARIETIES. Large double blooms, handsomely striped	0 6
1157 DANIELS' CHOICEST MIXED. A splendid strain, including the most beautiful varieties	1 0
1158 „ „ „ smaller pkts. 3d. and	0 6

DANIELS' GIANT-FLOWERED. A superb class of a robust habit of growth, producing beautiful double flowers of an immense size and of the most charming colour. Height 2 to 2½ feet.

1159 PURE WHITE. Very large double flowers. Splendid variety	0 6
1160 VERY CHOICE MIXED, including the most beautiful colours	1 0
1161 „ „ „ smaller pkt.	0 6
1162 FIRE KING (new). A magnificent variety, growing about 18 inches high; very free-blooming, with splendid double flowers of a deep rich scarlet colour	1 0
1163 DWARF, DOUBLE. Compact-growing varieties, about 15 inches high, with handsome double flowers in many beautiful colours. Choicest mixed	0 6
1164 MINIATURE or POMPONE. A pretty class of very dwarf compact growing varieties, only nine inches high with brilliantly-coloured double flowers. Very choice mixed	0 6

ZINNIA HAAGEANA, FL. PL.

1165 A quite distinct and pretty variety, growing about one foot high, and of a trailing habit of growth, with small double bright orange-coloured flowers	0 4
1166 GIPSY GIRL. A beautiful dwarf growing variety producing for a long period a profusion of double and semi-double flowers, bright crimson-brown with golden yellow edged petals. Very pretty	0 6

From Mr. H. HARPHAM, Juns., Alford.

Jan. 13th.
"I won First Prize with your Asters, Stocks, and Zinnias at four Shows last year."

From Mr. A. BRITTEN, Barking.

Jan. 3rd.
"I had some splendid Asters, Zinnias, Stocks, etc., from your seed last year."

From Mr. J. WILSON, King's Lynn.

Nov. 22nd.
"I took First Prize for cut flowers with your Asters Zinnias and Stocks."

DANIELS' LARGE-FLOWERED ZINNIAS.

WHITLAVIA GRANDIFLORA.

per pkt.—s. d.
1145 Pretty hardy annual for borders, with dark blue Campanulato flowers. Height 1 foot 0 3

WINTER CHERRY.

1146 GIANT SCARLET (Physalis Franchetti). A splendid hardy perennial, growing about 2 feet high, producing very large globular pods of a bright orange-scarlet colour 0 6

XERANTHEMUM.

Very handsome free-flowering hardy annual Everlastings. Excellent for garden decoration, Winter bouquets, &c.

1147 ALBUM FL. PL. Double white flowers. Height 2 feet ..		0 3
1148 SUPERBISSIMUM FL. PL. Double purple flowers, very fine. 2 feet		0 4
1149 CHOICE MIXED. Several pretty shades of colour		0 3

All Flower Seeds quoted in 3d. packets may be had at 2/6 per dozen.

FLOWER SEEDS IN PENNY PACKETS.

For the convenience of those having but small gardens, or requiring but small quantities, we have much pleasure in offering the following popular varieties of Flower Seeds in Penny Packets, all being of the same good quality as those quoted at higher rates for larger packets.

In ordering from the following list the numbers only will be sufficient.

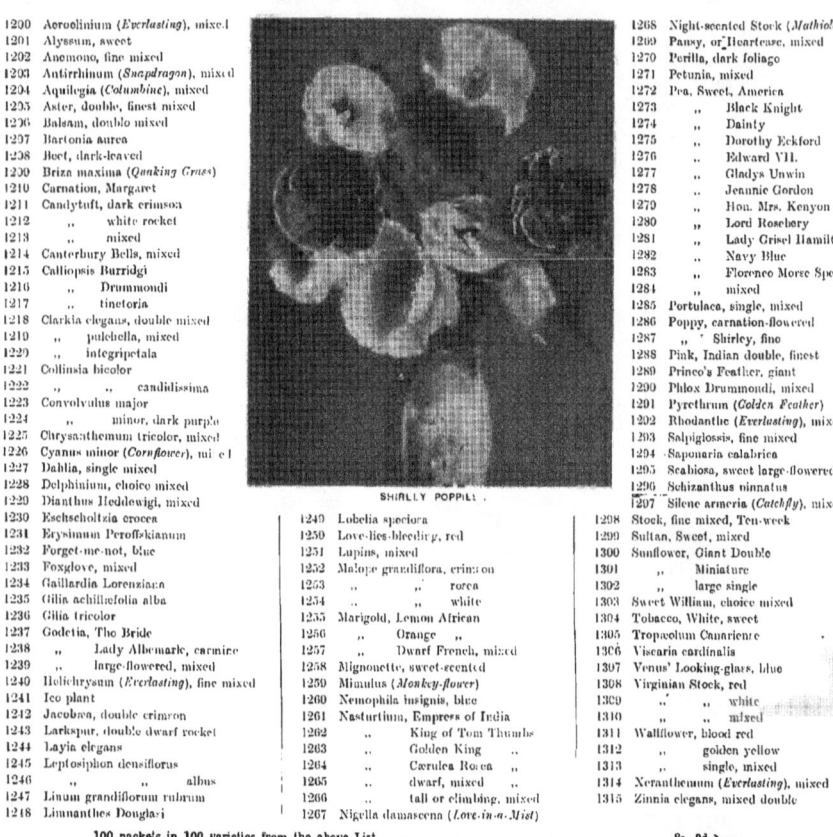

SHIRLEY POPPIES.

1200 Acroclinium (*Everlasting*), mixed
1201 Alyssum, sweet
1202 Anemone, fine mixed
1203 Antirrhinum (*Snapdragon*), mixed
1204 Aquilegia (*Columbine*), mixed
1205 Aster, double, finest mixed
1206 Balsam, double mixed
1207 Bartonia aurea
1208 Beet, dark-leaved
1209 Briza maxima (*Quaking Grass*)
1210 Carnation, Margaret
1211 Candytuft, dark crimson
1212   ,,   white rocket
1213   ,,   mixed
1214 Canterbury Bells, mixed
1215 Calliopsis Burridgi
1216   ,,   Drummondi
1217   ,,   tinctoria
1218 Clarkia elegans, double mixed
1219   ,,   pulchella, mixed
1220   ,,   integripetala
1221 Collinsia bicolor
1222   ,,   ,,   candidissima
1223 Convolvulus major
1224   ,,   minor, dark purple
1225 Chrysanthemum tricolor, mixed
1226 Cyanus minor (*Cornflower*), mixed
1227 Dahlia, single mixed
1228 Delphinium, choice mixed
1229 Dianthus Heddewigi, mixed
1230 Eschscholtzia crocea
1231 Erysimum Peroffskianum
1232 Forget-me-not, blue
1233 Foxglove, mixed
1234 Gaillardia Lorenziana
1235 Gilia achillefolia alba
1236 Gilia tricolor
1237 Godetia, The Bride
1238   ,,   Lady Albemarle, carmine
1239   ,,   large-flowered, mixed
1240 Helichrysum (*Everlasting*), fine mixed
1241 Ice plant
1242 Jacobæa, double crimson
1243 Larkspur, double dwarf rocket
1244 Layia elegans
1245 Leptosiphon densiflorus
1246   ,,   ,,   albus
1247 Linum grandiflorum rubrum
1248 Limnanthes Douglasi

1249 Lobelia speciosa
1250 Love-lies-bleeding, red
1251 Lupins, mixed
1252 Malope grandiflora, crimson
1253   ,,   ,,   rosea
1254   ,,   ,,   white
1255 Marigold, Lemon African
1256   ,,   Orange   ,,
1257   ,,   Dwarf French, mixed
1258 Mignonette, sweet-scented
1259 Mimulus (*Monkey-flower*)
1260 Nemophila insignis, blue
1261 Nasturtium, Empress of India
1262   ,,   King of Tom Thumbs
1263   ,,   Golden King   ,,
1264   ,,   Cærulea Rosea   ,,
1265   ,,   dwarf, mixed   ,,
1266   ,,   tall or climbing, mixed
1267 Nigella damascena (*Love-in-a-Mist*)

1268 Night-scented Stock (*Mathiola*)
1269 Pansy, or Heartsease, mixed
1270 Perilla, dark foliage
1271 Petunia, mixed
1272 Pea, Sweet, America
1273   ,,   Black Knight
1274   ,,   Dainty
1275   ,,   Dorothy Eckford
1276   ,,   Edward VII.
1277   ,,   Gladys Unwin
1278   ,,   Jeannie Gordon
1279   ,,   Hon. Mrs. Kenyon
1280   ,,   Lord Rosebery
1281   ,,   Lady Grisel Hamilton
1282   ,,   Navy Blue
1283   ,,   Florence Morse Spencer
1284   ,,   mixed
1285 Portulaca, single, mixed
1286 Poppy, carnation-flowered
1287   ,,   Shirley, fine
1288 Pink, Indian double, finest
1289 Prince's Feather, giant
1290 Phlox Drummondi, mixed
1291 Pyrethrum (*Golden Feather*)
1292 Rhodanthe (*Everlasting*), mixed
1293 Salpiglossis, fine mixed
1294 Saponaria calabrica
1295 Scabiosa, sweet large-flowered
1296 Schizanthus pinnatus
1297 Silene armeria (*Catchfly*), mixed
1298 Stock, fine mixed, Ten-week
1299 Sultan, Sweet, mixed
1300 Sunflower, Giant Double
1301   ,,   Miniature
1302   ,,   large single
1303 Sweet William, choice mixed
1304 Tobacco, White, sweet
1305 Tropæolum Canariense
1306 Viscaria cardinalis
1307 Venus' Looking-glass, blue
1308 Virginian Stock, red
1309   ,,   ,,   white
1310   ,,   ,,   mixed
1311 Wallflower, blood red
1312   ,,   golden yellow
1313   ,,   single, mixed
1314 Xeranthemum (*Everlasting*), mixed
1315 Zinnia elegans, mixed double

100 packets in 100 varieties from the above List   ..   ..   8s. 0d. ⎫
  50   ,,   50   ,,   ,,   ,, ...   4s. 0d. ⎬ **POST FREE.**
  25   ,,   25   ,,   ,,   ,, ...   2s. 0d. ⎭

THE COTTAGER'S PACKET OF CHOICE FLOWER SEEDS.

(REGISTERED.)

Containing Twelve selected varieties, including Aster, Stock, Sweet Peas, Mignonette, Scarlet Linum, &c.

Post Free, One Shilling; Twelve Packets, 10s. 6d.

FLOWER SEEDS BY WEIGHT.

The following popular annuals, &c., which are often required in larger quantities, we shall be pleased to supply by weight at the following moderate rates, all of the same high class excellence as sold in packet.

	per oz.—s.	d.
ALYSSUM, SWEET ..	1	0
" LITTLE GEM ..	1	0
ANTIRRHINUM. Tall mixed ..	1	6
" TOM THUMB. Dwarf mixed	2	0
ASTER. Daniels' Improved Victoria, mixed	10	6
" Giant Comet, pure white	10	0
" mixed	10	0
" Ostrich Plume, pure white	10	0
" mixed	10	0
" Dwarf Chrysanthemum, mixed	8	6
BARTONIA AUREA	0	9
CALLIOPSIS TINCTORIA	0	9
" TOM THUMB, Mixed	0	9
" DRUMMONDI	0	6
" Tall varieties. Choice mixed	0	6
CANDYTUFT. Empress, pure white	1	0
" Creamy white	1	0
" Large-flowered, dwarf mixed	1	6
" Rose cardinal, carmine	1	6
" Extra dark crimson	1	0
" Mixed, all colours per lb. 5s.	0	9
CANTERBURY BELLS. Single, choice mixed	1	0
" Double, choice mixed	5	0
" Calycanthema varieties, mixed	4	6
CENTAUREA MARGARITA. Giant white	2	0
" Giant blue	2	0
CHRYSANTHEMUM BURRIDGEANUM	1	0
" DUNNETTI. Double white	0	9
" CARINATUM CHAMELEON	1	0
" ANNUAL. Daniels' splendid mixed	1	0
CLARKIA INTEGRIPETALA. Rose	1	0
" White	1	0
COLLINSIA BICOLOR	0	9
" CANDIDISSIMA	0	9
CONVOLVULUS MAJOR. Mixed	0	6
" MINOR. Dark blue	0	6
CYANUS MINOR (Cornflower). Dark blue	0	9
" Choice mixed	0	6
DELPHINIUM. Hybrid Perennial, choice mixed	1	0
DIANTHUS HEDDEWIGI. Choice mixed, single	1	6
" CHINENSIS (Indian Pink). Finest double, mixed	1	6
DIGITALIS (Foxglove). Finest spotted, mixed	0	9
ESCHSCHOLTZIA CROCEA. Yellow	0	9
" Extra choice, mixed	1	0
" MANDARIN. Orange scarlet	1	0
" Rose cardinal, bright rose	1	0
GAILLARDIA HYBRIDA GRANDIFLORA. Mixed	0	9
GILIA TRICOLOR	0	6
GODETIA. Bridesmaid	1	0
" Duchess of Fife	1	0
" Duke of York } Splendid large-flowered varieties	1	0
" Duchess of Albany } for beds or borders	1	0
" Choicest mixed, large-flowered	1	0
" Lady Satin Rose. Dwarf	1	0
HELICHRYSUM. Choice mixed	0	6
Larkspur. Dwarf Rocket	0	6
" Tall, branching	0	6
LAVATERA ROSEA SPLENDENS	1	0
" ALBA	1	0
LEPTOSIPHON DENSIFLORUS	0	9
" ALBUS	0	9
LIMNANTHES DOUGLASI	0	6
LINUM GRANDIFLORUM RUBRUM	0	6
LOVE-LIES-BLEEDING. Red	0	6
LUPINUS NANUS. Blue	0	6

	per oz.—s.	d.
LUPINS. Tall, mixed	0	4
MAIZE. Variegated, Japanese	0	6
MALOPE GRANDIFLORA. Rose	0	6
" Scarlet	0	6
" White	0	6
" Mixed	0	6
MATHIOLA BICORNIS. Night-scented Stock per lb. 6s.	0	6
MIGNONETTE. Machet, selected Giant Crimson	2	0
" Crimson Pyramidal	1	0
" Golden Queen	2	0
" Large-flowered per lb. 6s.	0	6
NASTURTIUM. Tom Thumb, Carmine King	0	9
" " Crystal Palace Gem	0	9
" " Empress of India	0	9
" " Golden King	0	9
" " King	0	9
" " Vesuvius	0	9
" " Mixed, all sorts per lb. 6s.	0	6
" CLIMBING. Finest mixed 6s.	0	6
" " Dark crimson	0	9
" " Bright yellow	0	9
NEMOPHILA INSIGNIS. Blue	0	6
" MACULATA	0	6
NICOTIANA AFFINIS. Tobacco, sweet-scented	1	0
NIGELLA DAMASCENA (Love-in-a-Mist)	0	6
PERILLA NANKINENSIS	0	6
PHLOX DRUMMONDI GRANDIFLORA. Mixed	2	6
PANSY. Daniels' Prize Blotched	12	6
" German Mixed	2	6
POPPY. Shirley, selected, very fine strain per lb. 10s. 6d.	1	0
RICINUS GIBSONI (Castor Oil Plant)	0	6
RHODANTHE MACULATA. Mixed, charming everlasting	2	0
SALPIGLOSSIS. Large-flowered, mixed	2	6
SAPONARIA CALABRICA. Pink	0	9
SCABIOUS. Large-flowered	1	0
SCHIZANTHUS. Choice mixed	1	0
SILENE PENDULA COMPACTA	0	9
STOCK. Daniels' Large-flowered Ten-week, choice mixed	10	6
" Perpetual Perfection, choice mixed	10	6
" Dwarf German, finest mixed	7	6
" Brompton. Choicest mixed	12	6
SUNFLOWER. Miniature	0	6
" Large double	0	6
" Single, Primrose Dame	0	6
" Giant Yellow	0	6
SWEET PEAS. Large-flowered, Daniels' special mixed per pint 4s. 6d.	0	9
" Good mixture 2s. 0d.	0	6
SWEET SULTAN. Purple, white, and yellow each	0	9
" Fine mixed	0	9
SWEET WILLIAM. Auricula eyed, very fine strain	1	6
TROPAEOLUM CANARIENSE	1	0
VENUS' LOOKING-GLASS. Blue	1	0
VERBENA HYBRIDA. Choice mixed	2	6
VIRGINIAN STOCK. Red or white each	0	6
" Mixed per lb. 5s.	0	6
VISCARIA CARDINALIS. Scarlet	1	0
WALLFLOWER, SINGLE. Blood Red	1	0
" Golden Yellow	1	0
" Primrose Dame	1	0
" Extra choice mixed per lb. 12s.	1	0
" Eastern Queen	1	0
" Ruby Gem	1	0
" DOUBLE GERMAN. Splendid mixed	12	6
ZINNIA ELEGANS. Choicest double mixed	1	6

Choice Flower Seeds in Mixture.

FOR SOWING ON BANKS, ROCKERIES, WASTE PLACES, &c.

We offer a splendid mixture of the choicest dwarf-growing Hardy Annuals, suitable for the above purposes, and which will make a very pretty display for a long period. The mixture includes:—Godetias, Clarkias, Candytufts, Mignonette, Poppies, Gilias, Viscarias, and other free-flowering subjects, and will give the highest satisfaction.

MIXED FLOWER SEEDS, Choicest Dwarf Varieties, per lb. 5s. ; per oz. 6d.

TUBEROUS-ROOTED BEGONIAS.

We have much pleasure in offering tubers of our grand strains of Tuberous-rooted Begonias. These have been grown and selected at our Nurseries during the past season, and for form, size, substance of flower, and beauty and variety of colouring are second to none.

DANIELS' DOUBLE-FLOWERED BEGONIAS.

The Double-flowered Begonias are especially recommended for pot culture. The colours of the flowers vary from the darkest crimson and scarlet, through all the most beautiful shades of salmon, rose, and yellow, to the purest white. They are easily grown, and with their large massive blooms form strikingly handsome objects for the greenhouse or conservatory.

per doz.—s. d.

FOR POT CULTURE. A superb collection of choice sorts, equal to named varieties, the flowers being of the most perfect form, and of the most varied and beautiful colours. Highly desirable for conservatory or greenhouse decoration .. .. 9s. and 12 0

MIXED DOUBLES FOR BEDDING. A capital variety of large, full, double flowers, in beautiful variety of colour .. .. per 100, 30s. 4 6

DOUBLE BEGONIAS IN DISTINCT COLOURS FOR POTS OR BEDDING OUT.

Fine double flowers carefully selected when in bloom, and first class for pot culture or the garden.

per doz.—s. d.

DARK REDS AND SCARLETS   PURE WHITE   YELLOW SHADES }
ROSE SHADES   ORANGE AND SALMON SHADES   RED SHADES }   .. .. per 100, 40s. 6 0

DANIELS' SINGLE BEGONIAS FOR BEDDING.
IN DISTINCT COLOURS.

Distinct and beautiful colours, specially selected for effective bedding, all of the large-flowered erect growing class, and good strong tubers. Highly recommended.

per doz.—s. d.

DANIELS' BRILLIANT SCARLET   DANIELS' PURE WHITE   DANIELS' DARK RED AND CRIMSON }
DANIELS' SALMON ROSE SHADES   DANIELS' ORANGE SHADES   DANIELS' YELLOW SHADES }   per 100, 28s. 4 0

CHOICE MIXED, SEEDLINGS. In beautiful variety, all approved flowers from our fine collection   per 1000, £10 ; per 100, 25s. ; per doz. 3s. 6d

SINGLE-FLOWERED BEGONIAS FOR POT CULTURE.

per doz.—s. d.

FOR GREENHOUSE AND CONSERVATORY. A very fine mixture of choice selected flowers, mostly equal to the named sorts, perfect in form, and of the most beautiful colours .. .. 9s. and 12 0

FOR POT CULTURE. A capital mixture of beautiful colours, the varieties all being carefully selected and really good. Considering the high-class quality, we consider these remarkably cheap .. .. per 100, 40s. 6 0

☞ The prices quoted above are for dormant tubers, and these can only be supplied to the end of April.

In May and June we supply strong plants from single pots at the following rates :—

SINGLE-FLOWERED, choice mixed, per doz. 4s. 6d. ; 100, 30s.   DOUBLE-FLOWERED, choice mixed, per doz. 6s. ; 100, 42s.

BEGONIAS—NEW FRINGED SINGLE.

A remarkably fine new strain of handsomely fringed flowers. The large finely-formed blooms, which are elegantly frilled and crested, are borne on stiff, erect stems, carried well above the foliage, and are possessed of the most beautiful variety of colouring known amongst Begonias. This splendid class will be found first-class for pot culture.

PURE WHITE, beautiful .. .. .. each 1s. ; per doz. 10s. 6d.
VERY CHOICE MIXED, in fine variety .. .. per doz. 9s.

BEGONIA ERECTA CRISTATA.

A remarkable strain of great beauty. The plants are of a dwarf, sturdy, upright growth, and first-class for pot culture. The petals are of great substance, and the flowers of the most charming colours each petal carrying on its upper surface a handsome crest resembling a Cockscomb. Singularly beautiful, and quite unique.

VERY CHOICE MIXED, in beautiful variety

per doz. 7s. 6d. ; each 9d.

LILIES (Lilium) for Spring Planting.

For growing Lilies in pots a compost of about equal parts of sandy loam, leaf mould, and peat, is, perhaps, the best. Fine Lilies may, however, be grown in almost any good light and rich soil, especially those of the Auratum type. For single specimens use pots of about six inches diameter. These will be found very useful for house decoration; but pots of eight or ten inches diameter, with five or six bulbs in each, form grand objects for the conservatory when in bloom. Pot firmly, any time during Spring, with the bulbs about two inches below the surface, and plunge the pots with their rims about six inches deep in some light material, such as ashes or cocoa-nut fibre, in some sheltered position out of doors. When the stems have pushed their way well through the plunging material, they may be lifted and removed to a cool pit or frame till the flower-buds are developed, when they may be removed to the greenhouse or conservatory.

All the sorts mentioned in the following list are suitable for Spring planting out of doors. For pot culture, however, we strongly recommend the beautiful varieties of Auratum and Speciosum, with the addition of the fine longiflorum giganteum as the most suitable.

LILIUM AURATUM.

	each—s.	d.
AURATUM (The Golden-rayed Lily of Japan). Large white flowers with yellow stripes and brownish-red spots; deliciously fragrant, extremely hardy; a very free bloomer, and first rate for pot culture.		
„ Strong flowering bulbs per 100, 31s.; per doz. 5s. 0d.; 6 for 2s. 9d.	0	6
„ Very fine bulbs, nine to eleven inches circumference, per doz. 7s. 6d.	0	9
„ Extra fine, grand roots, ten to twelve inches circumference, per doz. 15s. 0d.	1	6
„ rubro-vittatum. Magnificent variety, immense flowers, petals pure white, with a distinct broad band of deep crimson down the centre 1s. 6d. and	2	6
„ virginale. Very large flowers, white, with pale yellow bands; most beautiful variety 1s. 0d. and	2	6
„ platyphyllum (macranthum). Gigantic flowers of great substance, very broad petals, white with yellow bands, slightly spotted; very fine —	1	6
SPECIOSUM. A fine hardy class; excellent for pot culture; deliciously scented.		
„ Kraetzeri. Pure white; finest variety for pot culture, per doz. 7s. 6d.	0	9
„ melpomene. Most beautiful variety; flowers large; splendid form, and of a lovely purplish crimson colour; heavily spotted, makes a splendid pot plant per doz. 7s. 6d.	0	9
„ punctatum. White, rose-spotted per doz. 5s. 0d.	0	6
„ rubrum. White, spotted and shaded crimson „ 5s. 0d.	0	6
„ roseum. White, crimson-spotted — „ 5s. 0d.	0	6
LONGIFLORUM GIGANTEUM. A fine early flowering dwarf growing species bearing large beautiful pure white trumpet flowers, deliciously scented. Fine for pot culture. [Strong bulbs, per 100, 31s. 6d.; per doz. 4s. 6d.	0	6
„ **HARRISII** (Bermuda Lily). Beautiful pure white deliciously scented flowers. Splendid for pot culture in the greenhouse and for forcing Good flowering roots per doz. 7s. 6d.	0	9
„ Extra strong roots „ 10s. 6d.	1	0
HENRYI (The Orange-yellow Speciosum). Too much cannot be said in praise of this fine Lily. It is very hardy and of robust constitution. It produces stems six feet high, bearing fifteen or twenty flowers, which are of a deep orange-yellow colour, and set off by the deep green foliage. One of the most remarkable Lilies ever introduced, and one which we can confidently recommend — 3s. 6d. and	5	0

	each—s.	d.
BROWNI. Large, creamy white trumpet-shaped flowers, the outside of the petals being of a rich purplish brown colour	2	6
CHALCEDONICUM (Scarlet Turk's Cap). Splendid old variety, flowers medium sized, reflexed, and of a deep rich scarlet colour; finely effective per doz. 21s.	2	0
COLCHICUM (Szovitzianum). Pale yellow, spotted with black; finely scented per doz. 10s. 6d.	1	0
CROCEUM. Light orange, spotted black per doz. 5s.	0	6
DAVURICUM FULGIDUM. Deep orange red flushed with yellow, very showy per doz. 5s. 0d.	0	6
GIGANTEUM (the noble Himalayan Lily). White, with broad bands of crimson violet 3s. 6d., 5s. and	7	6
HUMBOLDTI. A fine species, growing about five feet high, with large golden-yellow flowers, spotted purple	2	0
KRAMERI. Similar to Auratum, but of a beautiful pink colour; deliciously scented per doz. 7s. 6d.	0	9
PARDALINUM. Bright scarlet shading to orange, spotted maroon; large flowers per doz. 5s.	0	6
MARTAGON (Turk's Cap). Purple per doz. 4s. 6d.	0	6
„ **ALBUM.** Pure white-flowered form of the preceding; extremely scarce	2	6
„ **DALMATICUM.** A magnificent variety, with deep velvety crimson purple flowers	3	6
POMPONIUM VERUM. An elegant species, with bright scarlet flowers per doz. 7s. 6d.	0	9
PYRENAICUM (the Yellow Martagon). Deliciously scented flowers, yellow, spotted black per doz. 7s. 6d.	0	9
SUPERBUM. A fine yellow Lily with purple spots. Flowers often fifteen to twenty on a stem per doz. 7s. 6d.	0	9
TESTACEUM (Excelsum). Nankeen-coloured flowers, delightfully fragrant; four feet high per doz. 15s.	1	6
THUNBERGIANUM ATROSANGUINEUM. Scarlet, spotted black per doz. 5s.	0	6
TIGRINUM SPLENDENS. The finest of the Tiger Lilies. Orange scarlet, black spots per doz. 4s. 6d.	0	6
„ **FL. PL.** Scarlet, spotted brown, very double	0	6

We have many other species and varieties of choice Lilies in stock, which from want of space we are unable to enumerate here.

Lilies in Collections—our own selection.

Carefully arranged Collections of Lilies, 6s., 9s., 12s., 18s., and 24s. per dozen. Carriage Free.

From Mr. H. ENNOR, Wadebridge.

Feb. 1st.
"Last year you supplied me with three Lilium Auratum, and they were perfect. Kindly send me two more."

From Mr. Thos. WARD, Handsworth.

April 20th.
"The White Lily Bulbs I had early in the season are very fine plants now."

MISCELLANEOUS BULBS, ROOTS, &c.

MONTBRETIAS GERMANIA.

LILY OF THE VALLEY.

For early forcing, single crowns of these should be planted about twelve in a five-inch pot, with the buds well above the surface. Cover the crowns with a little moss or an inverted flower-pot and place them in a good heat of say 85 to 90 degrees; water frequently with tepid water, and if judiciously looked after they will bloom in four or five weeks from time of potting. Good single crowns are much the best for this purpose.

SELECTED SINGLE CROWNS FOR FORCING

per 1000, 50s.; per 100, 6s.; per doz. 1s.

LILY OF THE VALLEY.
Fortin's Giant-flowered.

A very fine variety with remarkably large handsome bells on long sturdy stalks. It is not so early and does not force so well as the ordinary variety, but will bloom splendidly out of doors in a sheltered position. Quite hardy.

STRONG FLOWERING CROWNS ..   per 100, 12s. 0d.; per doz. 2s. 0d.
GOOD PLANTING CROWNS ..   .. „   7s. 6d. „   1s. 6d.

MONTBRETIAS.

Beautiful showy plants, producing graceful spikes of brilliantly coloured flowers which are exceedingly useful for cutting. Planted in Spring they will bloom freely during August and September, and form permanent clumps that will increase in beauty from year to year. The plants grow 18 inches to 2 feet high and will thrive anywhere.

	per 100.		per doz.	
	s.	d.	s.	d.
GEORGE DAVISON. Pale orange yellow, a very fine variety ..	12	6	2	0
GERMANIA. Orange-scarlet, large flowers, beautiful ..	15	0	2	6
KOH-I-NOOR. Rich pure orange, on apricot base, extra fine ..	15	0	2	6
NORVIC (new). Large pure yellow, stained red outside each 1s.	—		10	6
PROMETHUS (new). Deep orange, with carmine central ring each 2s.	—		21	0
STAR OF FIRE. Bright vermilion, centre yellow, outside blood red ..	6	0	1 0 1 0	
CHOICE MIXED SEEDLINGS, containing many beautiful colours	5	0	0	9

LARGE-FLOWERED CANNAS.

These magnificent plants with their beautiful spikes of brilliantly coloured Gladiolus-like flowers and handsome foliage, have become highly popular for bedding out on lawns, &c., and for greenhouse and conservatory decoration. They are as easily grown as most bedding plants, and are greatly effective in groups or centres of beds. Break up the ground and manure as for Dahlias, and plant out in May as soon as danger from frost is over. They will soon start into growth and bloom, and if mulched with short well-rotted manure and well watered should the weather be dry, they will give a splendid show of beautiful flowers till killed by the frost in Autumn. In October or November they may be taken up, and after a short period of rest, divided and potted, when they will again start into growth and bloom in the greenhouse; or the roots may be kept dormant till Spring, when they should be divided and potted up for turning out again in May. If grown for their beautiful foliage alone they are well worth growing, and with additional charm of their gorgeous spikes of beautiful flowers they cannot be too highly recommended.

We have a very fine collection of these, including the most brilliant and beautiful colours.

CHOICE NAMED VARIETIES, our selection ..   per 100, 75s.; per doz. 12s.
CROZY'S DWARF VARIETIES, CHOICE MIXED IN BEAUTIFUL VARIETY. Splendid for massing in large beds, &c.

per 100, 40s.; per doz. 5s. 6d.

DAHLIAS, POT ROOTS (Dry Tubers).

We offer as below, dry tubers from our splendid collection of choice named Dahlias, which includes the finest varieties in commerce. Considering the low prices at which these are quoted, it must be distinctly understood that the selection of varieties must, in all instances, be left to ourselves.

CACTUS-FLOWERED. Choice named sorts, carefully selected, beautiful varieties ..   per 100, 30s.; per doz. 4s. 6d.
SHOW AND FANCY. Finest named exhibition varieties ..   per doz. 3s. 6d.
POMPONE. From our choice collection ..   per doz. 2s. 6d.

TUBEROSES.

These deliciously fragrant and exceedingly useful flowers are much more easily grown than is generally supposed, and will well repay the little trouble that is necessary to have them in perfection. For early forcing pot singly into five or six-inch pots, as early in the season as the bulbs can be obtained, and plunge in a good moist heat, withholding water till the foliage makes its appearance, when water may be given abundantly till the flower-buds are formed, when they may be removed to the greenhouse or conservatory and less water given. For Autumn blooming, pot singly into five or six-inch pots in March or April, using a light rich compost, and plunge the pots about six inches above their rims in cocoa-nut fibre, coal ashes, or any light material, under the stage of a greenhouse or in a cool pit or frame; when the foliage of these makes its appearance they should be removed and plunged under a south wall, removing them to the greenhouse or indoors as the flower buds are formed. Dry roots may also be planted in sheltered places in the open ground, from the middle of April to the latter part of May, and will produce beautiful flowers in Autumn if taken up and potted when coming into flower, and will furnish a supply of beautiful bloom in the greenhouse almost up to Christmas.

DOUBLE, "AMERICAN PEARL," Fine new dwarf variety from the United States; deliciously fragrant, with large double flowers, pure white.

Selected roots, per 100, 12s. 6d.; per doz. 2s. 0d.; each 3d.

ANEMONES—Single and Double-flowered.

ANEMONE, ST. BRIGID.

ANEMONE, St. Brigid.

A brilliant and very beautiful class of large semi-double flowers of the most striking and charming shades of colour, ranging from crimson and scarlet to rose, lilac, dark blue, &c., to the purest white. Nearly all the blooms have conspicuous white centres, which add greatly to their beauty. They are first-class for cut flowers, and if cut when the bloom is beginning to open and the stems placed in water, they will retain their beauty for a long time.
Very Choice Mixed. In beautiful variety

per 1000, 45s. ; per 100, 5s. ; per doz. 9d.

NEW PINK SPIRÆAS.

These grand varieties are suitable alike for forcing or planting in the open ground, when planted outside the colours will be much deeper.

QUEEN ALEXANDRA. Bright pink   per doz. 15s. ; each 1s. 6d.
PEACH BLOSSOM. Pale pink ..   per doz. 15s. ; each 1s. 6d.
These made quite a sensation when exhibited at Holland House, and were awarded the Gold Medal of the Royal Horticultural Society.

ANEMONES.
SUPERB DOUBLE-FLOWERED.

Producing large, handsome, double flowers of various beautiful colours; some of the varieties are strikingly brilliant.

	per 100.	per doz.
	s. d.	s. d.
CHOICE NAMED SORTS, our selection	7 6	1 0
CHOICEST MIXED, from named sorts	6 0	1 0

GIANT FRENCH SINGLE.
(Poppy Anemones.)

A magnificent class, producing immense double and semi-double flowers of the most beautiful colours; splendid for garden decoration.

	per 100.	per doz.
	s. d.	s. d.
Very Choice Mixed. Single ..	5 0	0 9

ANEMONES IN MIXTURE.

	per 100.	per doz.
	s. d.	s. d.
DUTCH, finest mixed, double, fine roots .. per 1000, 30s.	3 6	0 6
„ „ single, fine roots .. „ 21s.	2 6	0 6
SCARLET, FINEST DOUBLE. Fine roots	5 0	0 9
„ „ SINGLE. Strong roots	2 6	0 6
PURE WHITE, SINGLE, "THE BRIDE." Splendid ..	2 6	0 6

ANEMONE FULGENS.

Beautiful large-flowered varieties with dazzling vermilion scarlet blooms. Particularly valuable for cut flowers. Planted in September may be bad in bloom in February. Quite hardy.

	per 100.	per doz.
	s. d.	s. d.
FULGENS. Single scarlet ; very fine	7 6	1 0
FULGENS FL. PL. A fine new double scarlet ..	6 0	0 9

RANUNCULI.

The Ranunculi are very free-flowering and beautiful. They will succeed in almost any soil or position, and planted any time up to the middle of April will bloom abundantly during the Summer ; very useful for cutting.

	per 100.	per doz.
	s. d.	s. d.
TURBAN, DANIELS' GIANT. A splendid and robust-growing class, very superior to the common Turban varieties ; grows to the height of eighteen inches ; each plant producing from forty to fifty splendid double flowers .. per 1000, 35s.	4 6	0 9
„ SCARLET. Admirably adapted for filling beds, ribbon borders, or massing .. .. per 1000, 21s.	2 6	0 4
„ MIXED. All colours ; a beautiful variety ..	2 6	0 4
FRENCH GIANT. Very fine .. .. per 1000, 35s.	4 6	0 9
PERSIAN, CHOICEST MIXED. In beautiful variety „ 1000, 25s.	3 0	0 6

TIGRIDIAS—TIGER FLOWERS.

Beautiful showy plants growing about one foot high ; quite hardy.

	per doz.	each.
	s. d.	s. d.
CANARIENSIS. Yellow, spotted with scarlet ..	1 6	0 3
CONCHIFLORA. Brilliant yellow, spotted with scarlet ..	2 6	0 4
PAVONIA. Scarlet and orange	1 6	0 3
GRANDIFLORA ALBA. Creamy white, spotted with red, and having a violet centre ; a fine and beautiful form ..	1 6	0 3

EREMURUS HIMALAICUS.

A magnificent hardy plant, throwing up stately spikes of white campanulate flowers 6 or 8 feet high. Splendidly effective when planted in groups amongst shrubs, &c. .. .. .. each 3s. 6d., 5s., and 7s. 6d.

HYACINTHUS CANDICANS.

A splendid hardy bulbous-rooted plant blooming in August and throwing up fine spikes of white bell-shaped flowers three to four feet high. It makes a capital plant for pots in the greenhouse, and is finely effective when planted out of doors in association with Gladiolus Brenchleyensis, which blooms at the same time. Fine Bulbs, per 100 5s. 6d. : per doz. 10d.

GLADIOLI.

These beautiful flowers succeed well in almost any soil or situation, and planted in association with Dwarf or Standard Roses, with hardy herbaceous plants, or on the shrubbery border, they have a very fine appearance. They also do well as pot plants, and are capitally suited for growing in outside window boxes.

The hybrids of G. Gandavensis are perhaps the best known and most popular. We would, however, strongly recommend all who have not yet grown them to procure the new Childsi, Giant-flowered hybrid, the varieties of Nanceianus and Lemoinei, and Groff's new hybrids, all of which can be highly recommended for making a display of rare beauty in the garden.

Plant the corms or roots firmly, three or four inches deep and eight or nine inches apart, in clumps of three, five, or more as required, and put a neat stake to each when the flower buds make their appearance. March is the best month to plant for blooming in July and August, and by a few successive plantings in April and the early part of May, a succession of handsome flowers may be had to the end of September.

Gladioli are of especial value as cut flowers for decorative purposes. If the flower spikes are cut and placed in water just as the blooms are beginning to expand, they will all open in succession to the topmost bud, and will retain their beauty for a longer time than if remaining on the plant.

GLADIOLUS GANDAVENSIS HYBRIDS.

A very fine free-flowering class, growing about three feet high and producing long, handsome spikes of lovely flowers, ranging in colour through all the shades of scarlet and crimson, mauve, rose, pink and yellow to pure white. Highly recommended for garden decoration or for cut flowers.

CHOICE NAMED VARIETIES IN COLLECTIONS.   Our own selection.

24 in 12 fine varieties	..	..	..	8s. 6d.
18 in 18 choice sorts	..	..	..	6s. 6d.

12 in 12 choice sorts	..	..	..	4s. 6d.
12 in 12 good varieties	..	..	..	3s. 6d.

Gladiolus Gandavensis—In Mixtures from Finest Named and Seedling Sorts.

☞ We highly recommend our mixture of these, which includes a splendid variety of the most beautiful colours, varying from the most intense scarlet and crimson through all the shades of rose, salmon, pink, yellow, and carmine to the purest white. First class for cut flowers.

Choicest Mixed, per 100, 15s. ; per doz. 2s.

GLADIOLUS BRENCHLEYENSIS.

A well-known and splendid variety of fine effect for massing; the flowers are of a rich bright scarlet colour, and being produced in handsome spikes, are first-class to cut for church and other decorations.

Good flowering roots, per doz. 1s. ; per 100, 7s. 6d.
Extra fine roots, per doz. 1s. 6d. ; per 100, 10s. 6d.

GLADIOLUS CHILDSI.
New Giant-flowered Hybrids.

An important and valuable floral introduction. The flowers of this splendid class are of great substance and gigantic size. The form of both the flower and spike is perfection itself, and they last a long time in bloom before fading, owing to their great substance and vigour.

☞ "AMERICA" (new). A superb variety, producing fine spikes of enormous flowers, colour a soft flesh pink, slightly tinged with lavender giving it the colouring of the most beautiful Loelias.

Each 8d. ; per doz. 7s. 6d.

ATTRACTION. Deep crimson with large conspicuous white throat, very beautiful.

Each 9d. ; per doz. 7s. 0d.

BLANCHE. Large pure white, faintly marked.

Each 9d. ; per doz. 7s. 6d.

CARDINAL. Large flower and spike, colour intense scarlet.

Each 9d. ; per doz. 7s. 6d.

One of each 12 superb varieties, 6s. ; 6 varieties, 3s. 6d.
Finest mixture of Hybridised Seedlings, per doz. 3s. ; per 100, 20s.

GLADIOLUS LEMOINEI.
Hardy Hybrid Gladioli.

This fine new race of Hybrid Gladioli blooms somewhat earlier than those of the Gandavensis section, and are much more hardy, so hardy in fact, that their bulbs do not need to be lifted in Winter. The flowers are very striking and handsome in appearance, all having conspicuous blotches on the lower petals, whilst the colours are very diversified and beautiful. These will be found splendid alike for garden decoration or for cut flowers.

☞ BARON HULOT. A quite novel and very beautiful variety of the hardy Lemoinei class of Gladioli. The large flowers, which are produced on handsome spikes, are of a lovely rich dark violet blue. A colour quite unique amongst Gladioli and of striking effect.

Each 1s. 0d. ; per doz. 10s. 6d.

GELRIA STRAIN. A beautiful strain, containing mostly pale blue, yellow, and heliotrope shades.

Per doz. 1s. 6d.

LEMOINEI VARIETIES. Choice mixed, in beautiful variety.

Per 100, 10s. 6d. ; per doz. 1s. 6d.

GLADIOLUS, WHITE LADY.

A beautiful pure white flowered variety of the Gandavensis type, throwing up long, handsome spikes of bloom that last for quite a long time. A charming flower for cutting.

Per doz. 7s. 6d. ; each 9d.

GLADIOLUS NANCEIANUS.

A magnificent class of beautiful flowers, producing large, brilliantly coloured blooms.

☞ PRINCEPS. A magnificent variety of the Nanceianus class, bearing enormous flowers, often six inches across, of a dazzling scarlet colour, with a small white band on each of the lower petals. This is a superb novelty that will be much admired wherever grown.

Each 1s. 0d. ; per doz. 10s. 6d.
Very Choice Mixed, per doz. 7s. 6d.

GLADIOLI—Groff's New Hybrids.

A splendid new class of large-flowered brilliantly coloured varieties including some rare and exquisite shades. These are splendid for garden decoration, and are highly recommended.

Very Choice Mixed, per 100, 17s. 6d. ; per doz. 2s. 6d.

EARLY FLOWERING GLADIOLI.

Beautiful showy varieties, blooming in June and July. Splendid for cut flowers.

	per 100. s. d.	per doz. s. d.
ACKERMANNI. Salmon, flaked carmine, with violet eye ; a splendid variety	5 0	0 9
BLUSHING BRIDE. Lovely white, with pink and carmine flakes on lower petals, beautiful	5 0	0 9
CARDINALIS ELEGANS. Bright scarlet, flaked white	7 6	1 0
COLVILLEI ALBA, " THE BRIDE " Pure white ; a gem for cutting and forces well	4 0	0 8
NON PLUS ULTRA. Beautiful large rosy-red, flaked with white, shaded magenta	7 6	1 0
PEACH BLOSSOM. Delicate peach-pink, extra fine	5 0	0 9
QUEEN VICTORIA. Vermilion scarlet, flaked with white	7 6	1 0
„ WILHELMINA. Pure white, blotched with rosy red ; very pretty	7 6	1 0
ROSY GEM. Delicate rosy pink ; splendid for cutting	5 0	0 9
SALMON QUEEN. Beautiful salmon-red, with white and crimson flakes	7 6	1 0
VERY CHOICE MIXED	5 0	0 9

Assortment of 18 in 6 beautiful varieties to name, 1s. 6d.

GLADIOLI--Hybrids of Gandavensis.

(Reduced from a Photograph).

·NURSERY· DEPARTMENT

APPLES.

Our fine stock of Apples are principally worked on the Crab Stock, but we have a large collection of the most suitable kinds worked on the broad leaved Paradise Stock, the varieties we can supply of these being marked with an asterisk (*). The best time for planting is as early as convenient in October or November, after the young trees have shed their leaves, but planting may be done with safety any time to the end of March if the weather is fairly open.

Dwarf Apples on the Paradise Stock are of especial value both for large or small gardens, and have come very much into favour of late years. They are much dwarfer in growth, come into bearing and profit much sooner, are easier to thin and spray, and they produce almost continuously abundant crops of much finer fruit. For small holdings, or where the tenure is uncertain, they are specially recommended.

PRICES OF APPLES.

In all cases where customers leave the selection of varieties to us, they may rely on only good trees of the best kinds being supplied. It is most important, however, that the style or shape of trees required should be clearly stated when ordering. Orders entrusted to us in this way are invariably filled to the entire satisfaction of our clients.

ON ORDINARY CRAB STOCK.

		each. s. d.	per doz. s. d.
MAIDENS	.. .. ..	1 0	10 0
DWARFS OR BUSHES	.. ..	1 6	15 0
PYRAMIDS, Good ..	.. ..	2 0	20 0
„ Selected ..	.. ..	2 6	25 0
„ Extra Strong Fruiting	..	3 0	30 0
DWARF TRAINED ESPALIERS	.. 3s. 6d. to 5 0		—
STANDARDS. Good	.. ..	1 6	15 0
„ Selected ..	.. ..	2 0	20 0
„ Extra Strong Fruiting	..	2 6	25 0
CORDONS, SINGLE	.. ..	1 6	15 0

Special Quotations for Larger Quantities.

ON PARADISE STOCK.

Highly recommended.

		each. s. d.	per doz. s. d.
MAIDENS ..	.. ..	1 0	10 0
DWARF FRUITING BUSHES	..	2 0	20 0
PYRAMIDS. Strong	.. ..	2 6	25 0
„ Extra Strong	.. ..	3 6	35 0
CORDONS, SINGLE	.. ..	1 6	15 0

Special Quotations for Larger Quantities.

When it is proposed to form new Orchards or to plant a quantity of Fruit Trees, for market purposes, we shall be most happy to quote special prices on our customers naming the varieties and styles they desire to have.

NEW AND VERY CHOICE APPLES.

*BARON WOLSELEY (K.). An enormous fruit of the Warner King type, but larger and with more colour, being flushed with bronzy red. A good grower and free bearer. A splendid Exhibition Apple. One Year Trees on Paradise, 1s. 6d. each; Two Year Trees on Paradise, 2s. each; Cordons, 2s. 6d. each; Standards, 3s. 6d. each.

*BEN'S RED (D.). It is similar in shape to Devonshire Quarrenden, and the colour is a brilliant bronzy red. The flavour is first class, and is a very free bearer. Award of Merit, R.H.S. One Year Trees on Paradise, 1s. 6d. each; Two Year Trees on Paradise, 2s. each; Cordons, 2s. 6d. each.

CORONATION. The fruit is round and of good form, with a skin of yellow-ground colour, streaked and blotched with red. The fruit has soft flesh and rich mellow flavour. It appears to be in season at about the middle of September, and is best eaten at that time, when moist and refreshing. Maidens, 1s. 6d. ; Pyramids, 3s. 6d. ; Standards, 3s. 6d.

*CRIMSON BRAMLEY (K.). Similar in every respect except colour to the well-known Bramley's Seedling, equally hardy, robust grower, and heavy bearer. The entire surface of the fruit develops a brilliant crimson colour with a deeper shade on the exposed side. A handsome Apple and one that should be in great demand. It promises to be one of the best varieties in the country. One Year Trees on Paradise, 2s. 6d. each; Standards, 3s. 6d. each.

EDWARD THE VII. Similar to "Golden Noble," but very much larger, flushed on exposed side, good cropper. Maidens, 1s. 6d. ; Bush, 2s. 6d.

*ENCORE (K.). A very large and handsome cooking variety, raised from Warner's King and Old Northern Greening, and with the size of the former it combines the splendid late keeping qualities of the latter, as Encore has been kept in good condition until June. In colour it is yellow streaked and flushed with red, flesh crisp and juicy, strong grower and free bearer. One Year Trees only on Paradise, 2s. each.

*FELTHAM BEAUTY (new). A splendid new highly coloured early dessert variety, raised from "Cox's Orange Pippin" and "Mr. Gladstone." The fruit is of fair size, flesh crisp, sweet, and of rich aromatic flavour ; a first-class and profitable market variety. One Year old Trees, 3s. each.

*LORD STRADBROKE. A large and handsome late cooking variety ; the fruit are of very large size, slightly ribbed, greenish yellow in colour, suffused with rich crimson on the exposed side ; a first-rate show variety, and will become a great favourite when known. One Year old Trees, each ; Two Year old Bushes, 3s. each.

RED VICTORIA. This is not a red form of the popular "Early Victoria," but a very highly coloured early culinary variety ; flesh white and juicy, a good cropper and free grower. We can very highly recommend this variety to our customers. Maidens, 2s. 6d. ; Bush, 3s. 6d.

STAR OF DEVON. This is a valuable late apple. The fruits are of moderate size, richly coloured with red on the sunny side, and streaked with red over the yellow on the other side ; flesh soft and sweet, and a good flavour. Maidens, 1s. 6d. ; Bush, 2s. 6d.

If desired we can supply permanent "Acme" Labels for all Fruit Trees. For prices see page 60.

APPLES—General List of Select Varieties.

D denotes dessert.   K Kitchen.   Those marked (*) can be supplied on Paradise Stock.

*ALFRISTON (K). A large and useful variety. Nov. to April.

ALLINGTON PIPPIN. A splendid medium-sized Apple introduced a few years ago, and which has taken a position in the front rank as a first-rate dessert variety and a reliable bearer. In form it resembles "Cox's Orange," but is much handsomer, and the flavour, whilst as rich, is more brisk than in that variety. Has been awarded a First Class Certificate by the Royal Horticultural Society. Maidens, each 1s.; Dwarfs on Paradise Stock, 2s.; Pyramids, 3s. 6d.; Standards, 2s.

*ANNIE ELIZABETH (K). A very fine late Apple of excellent keeping qualities. Dec. to May.

*BEAUTY OF BATH (D). A very handsome early variety, has a brisk sub-acid flavour. July and Aug.

*BEAUTY OF KENT (K). A handsome, large, and first-rate culinary Apple; excellent bearer. Oct. to Feb.

*BISMARCK (K). One of the best varieties in cultivation for market or the private garden. Oct. to Dec.

*BLENHEIM ORANGE (D.K). Well-known and splendid variety; large handsome fruit. Dec. to Feb.

*BRAMLEY'S SEEDLING (K). A large handsome fruit, resembling Blenheim Pippin. Sept. to Jan.

CELLINI (D.K). A fine, showy, and handsome Apple of the first quality. Oct. and Nov.

CHARLES ROSS (new). A cross between Cox's Orange Pippin and Peasgood's Nonsuch. One of the finest dessert Apples yet raised. Nov. to Jan.

*CHELMSFORD WONDER (K). Fruit large, skin smooth, deep yellow shaded with brilliant crimson. Nov. to Jan.

CHRISTMAS PEARMAIN (D). Medium, of excellent flavour, rich scarlet cheek and russet markings, an enormous cropper. The tree is a good grower, free from canker. We consider it will take the place of the King of Pippins for dessert or market, as the latter is subject to canker and can only be grown well in few localities. Nov. to Dec.

*CLAYGATE PEARMAIN. A valuable variety. Nov. to March.

*COX'S ORANGE PIPPIN (D). A highly popular and first-rate dessert Apple; fruit medium-sized, finely coloured, rich, crisp and juicy, and of delicious flavour. Oct. to Mar.

DEVONSHIRE QUARRENDEN (D). A fine hardy, free-bearing variety of excellent quality; fruit small. Aug. and Sept.

*DUMELOW'S SEEDLING (K). A large and excellent variety; one of the most useful of culinary Apples; a strong grower, and an excellent bearer. Nov. to May.

EARLY VICTORIA (K). A pale lemon-coloured, very early variety of the Codlin type; very free bearer. July and Aug.

*ECKLINVILLE SEEDLING (K). A large and useful sort; flesh white and tender; a great bearer. Oct. to Dec.

*EMPEROR ALEXANDER (K.D). Very large, handsome; free cropper. Oct.

*GASCOIGNE'S SCARLET (K). A remarkably handsome Apple of very fine quality; very large. Nov. to Jan.

GOLDEN NOBLE (K). Large, handsome, yellow, tender, juicy; a valuable culinary Apple. Nov. to Jan.

*HAMBLING'S SEEDLING (K.D). A very large and most remarkably late-keeping variety. First-rate in every way. Dec. to March.

*IRISH PEACH (D). One of the best early dessert Apples. July and Oct.

*JAMES GRIEVE (D). Medium-sized fruit; flavour of "Orange Pippin." Oct. to Dec.

JOANETING (RED) (D). A very popular early variety. July and Aug.

*KERRY PIPPIN (D). Small fruit, sweet, crisp, juicy, and richly flavoured; one of the best dessert Apples. Sept. and Oct.

KESWICK CODLIN (K). One of the earliest and most useful of kitchen Apples; very prolific. Aug. and Sept.

*KING OF PIPPINS (D). Fruit medium-sized; a richly flavoured and excellent dessert variety; in season during Aug. and Sept.

*LADY HENNIKER (K). Large, handsome fruit; a free bearer, and good keeper. Oct. to Feb.

*LADY SUDELEY (D). Large, yellow with crimson streaks; very fine Summer Apple. Sept.

*LANE'S PRINCE ALBERT (K). Large, handsome fruit; a great bearer, and one of the very best kitchen Apples. Oct. to March.

*LORD DERBY (K). Large, handsome, heavy cropper; one of the best. Nov. and Dec.

LORD GROSVENOR (K). A large and handsome culinary Apple. Sept. to Nov.

LORD SUFFIELD (K). A fine variety of the Keswick Codlin type. It is an early and prolific bearer, and one of the very best of early cooking Apples. Aug. and Sept.

MOTHER (D). Medium, a most delicious conical fruit, rich and aromatic; does admirably as a pyramid, and is good even in the North. One of the best flavoured kinds with soft flesh.

*MR. GLADSTONE (D). Medium, mottled red, yellow streaks; the earliest dessert, free-bearer; fine flavour. July and Aug.

NEWTON WONDER (K). Large; a valuable new kind, between "Wellington" and "Blenheim"; a handsome fruit, keeping soundly, free grower and bearer; one of the best among recent sorts. In growth and sturdiness this surpasses all others, and the fruit we have grown and exhibited has attracted great attention. A sterling kind for orchard or garden. F.C.R.H.S. Nov. to May.

*NORFOLK BEAUTY (now K). A cross between "Warner's King" and "Dr. Harvey." Fruit large, pale green changing to yellow. In appearance, intermediate between the two parents. Maidens, each 1s. Pyramids, 2s. 6d. and 3s. 6d.; Standards, each 2s.

NORTHERN GREENING (K). Medium, heavy cropper; first-class keeper. Jan. and March.

*NORWICH PIPPIN (D). A splendid variety resembling Cox's Orange but brighter in colour. It is a splendid keeper and may be had in good condition up to April or May, whilst the flavour is excellent. Maidens, each 1s.; Pyramids, 2s. 6d. and 3s. 6d.; Standards, 2s.

*OLD NONPAREIL (D). A richly flavoured and first-rate dessert Apple of excellent keeping qualities. Jan. to May.

*PEASGOOD'S NONSUCH (D.K). A large, handsome Apple of the Blenheim Orange type; excellent for dessert or kitchen. Sept. to Jan.

POTT'S SEEDLING (K). Large, angular, yellow; very heavy cropper. Aug. and Sept.

RED ASTRACHAN (K.D). Large, brilliantly coloured; handsome. Aug. and Sept.

*REINETTE DU CANADA (D.K). A large and excellent Apple, suitable for dessert or culinary purposes. Nov. to April.

*RIBSTON PIPPIN (D). Well-known splendid old sort, but tree rather subject to canker. Nov. to March.

*RIVERS' CODLIN (K) (*syn. Thomas Rivers*). A cooking variety of rich flavour, very large, and of brilliant colour; flesh very firm in texture. Sept. to Dec.

*SCARLET NONPAREIL (D). A capital dessert Apple of first rate quality; in season from Jan. to March.

STONE'S APPLE (K) (*syn. Loddington*). A large and handsome kitchen Apple; an immense bearer. Sept. to Dec.

STIRLING CASTLE (K). An early and free-bearing Apple; a great bearer, and well suited for dwarf culture. Aug. and Sept.

THE HOUBELON (D). Similar to Cox's Orange Pippin, but higher colour, and will keep much longer. Dec. to Feb.

*THE SANDRINGHAM (K). A fine, large, and very handsome Apple of excellent quality. Feb. to May.

*VICAR OF BEIGHTON (K). One of the handsomest, most prolific, and best keeping Apples in cultivation. The fruit is large and roundish, and of a deep bright crimson colour, mottled and striped with yellow and green. Nov. to May.

*WARNER'S KING (K). A very large and splendid Apple of first-rate quality; the tree is a free and vigorous grower, a great bearer, and not subject to disease. Nov. to March.

*WHITE ASTRACHAN (Transparent) (D). Medium-sized, handsome fruit of pleasant flavour. Aug. and Sept.

WORCESTER PEARMAIN (K.D). Handsome early variety, suitable for kitchen or dessert; a great favourite in the market. Aug. and Sept.

*WEALTHY (D.K). Fruit medium sized; very handsome; a free-bearer of great excellence. Oct. and Nov.

YORKSHIRE BEAUTY (K). Large; fine kitchen Apple. Aug. to Oct.

CRABS (Pyrus baccata).

The following varieties, which we consider by far the best and most useful, are excellent for making preserves. They are also very pretty as ornamental trees, the bright-coloured fruits hanging in abundance, as they generally do, for a long time in Autumn, being very handsome and effective amongst other ornamental trees, shrubs, &c.

DARTMOUTH. Very handsome dark crimson fruit; an abundant bearer	..	..	—	Standards, each 2s.;	Maidens, each 1s.
JOHN DOWNIE. Bright crimson, conical fruit of good size and quality; very handsome ..	"	"	"	2s.;	"	1s.
PAUL'S IMPERIAL. A very fine variety. Very scarce ..	..	"	"	2s. 6d.		
RED SIBERIAN. Bright scarlet fruit, round and resembling those of the Cherry ..	—	"	"	2s.	"	1s.

SELECT PEARS.

Pears should be much more freely grown than they are. The young trees come into bearing much earlier than is generally supposed, especially when worked on the Quince stock. Many of the varieties are exceedingly prolific, whilst the fruit are more valuable than Apples, choice sorts always finding a ready sale at good prices.

PRICES OF PEARS.

ON ORDINARY PEAR STOCK.

	each. s. d.	per doz. s. d.			each. s. d.	per doz. s. d.
MAIDENS, One Year old	1 0	10 0	STANDARDS,	Good	1 6	15 0
DWARFS OR BUSHES	1 6	15 0	"	Selected	2 0	20 0
PYRAMIDS, Good	2 0	20 0	"	Extra Strong	2 6	25 0
" Selected	2 6	25 0	DWARF TRAINED ESPALIERS			
STANDARDS, TRAINED	5 0	—		3s. 6d. and	5 0	

ON QUINCE STOCK.

(Marked*). Highly recommended for early bearing.

	each. s. d.	per doz. s. d.
MAIDENS, One year old	1 3	12 6
DWARF FRUITING BUSHES	2 0	20 0
PYRAMIDS. Selected	2 6	25 0
CORDONS. Single	1 6	15 0

SPECIAL QUOTATIONS FOR LARGER QUANTITIES.

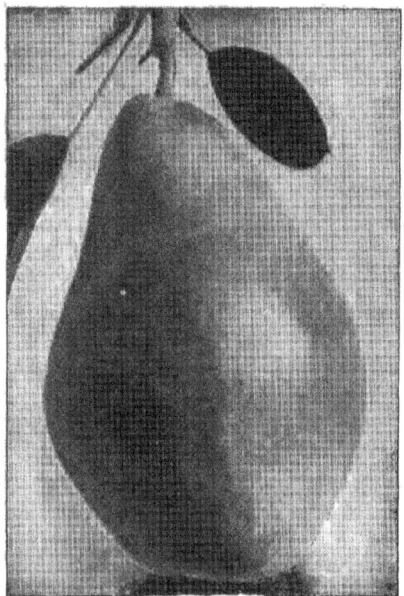

PITMASTON DUCHESS.

Our Pears are mostly worked on the ordinary pear stock. Those marked with an asterisk (*) we can, however, supply in dwarfs and pyramids on the quince. These come into bearing and profit much earlier than those worked on the ordinary stock, and are specially recommended to the notice of allotment holders or where the tenure is uncertain.

SELECT PEARS—General List.

*BERGAMOTTE ESPEREN. A most delicious late pear; melting, juicy, and sugary; medium-sized fruit. Feb. to April.

*BEURRE D'AMANLIS. Fruit large, one of the best early pears. Sept.

BEURRE CAPIAUMONT. A good hardy variety, succeeds well as a standard, and is a great bearer Oct.

*BEURRE D'AREMBERG. A highly-flavoured rich juicy pear, of medium size. Dec. and Jan.

BEURRE BOSC. A large, delicious half-melting dessert pear. It does best in a warm soil and situation, when it is a very free bearer. Nov.

*BEURRE DIEL. Fruit very large, does well on a wall. A hardy and vigorous variety of first-rate quality. Oct. and Nov.

*BEURRE HARDY. A fine, large dessert pear of most excellent quality. As a pyramid it is a very great bearer. Oct.

BEURRE RANCE. A valuable late dessert pear; an excellent bearer. Feb. to May.

BEURRE SUPERFIN. One of the best pears in cultivation; fruit large, very handsome, and of splendid quality. Sept. and Oct.

*CATILLAC. Fruit large; one of the best stewing pears. Does not succeed well as a Pyramid or Standard unless well sheltered. Dec. to April.

CLAPP'S FAVORITE. A medium-sized dessert early pear. Aug.

*CONFERENCE. Fruit large; very prolific, a valuable market sort. Nov.

CONSEILLER DE LA COUR. Fruit large, one of the finest pears in cultivation. Oct. and Nov.

DOYENNE DU COMICE. Fruit large and of first-rate quality; a healthy grower and a good bearer. Oct. and Nov.

*DOYENNE BOUSSOCH. A very large lemon-coloured pear of good quality, juicy, and melting; good bearer. Oct.

*DUCHESSE D'ANGOULEME. A delicious dessert pear of great excellence. An abundant bearer. Oct. and Nov.

*EMILE D'HEYST. A very useful and good pear. Fruit large, juicy, and finely flavoured. Tree hardy and a prolific bearer. Nov. and Dec.

GENERAL WAUCHOPE (new). Fruit of medium size, pale green changing to yellow, with small brown dots and russet blotches, flesh soft and f of delicious flavour. Award of Merit, R.H.S. Dec. Two-year Bush Trees on Pear Stock, 2s. 6d. Large Fruiting, 2s. 6d. each.

*GLOU MORCEAU. A very fine dessert pear. Dec. and Jan.

HESSLE. Well-known good market sort; abundant bearer. Oct.

*JARGONELLE. A large handsome pear of excellent quality; first-class for wall culture in the Northern Counties. Aug.

*JOSEPHINE DE MALINES. A fine pear of most delicious flavour; the tree is hardy and an excellent bearer. Jan. to May.

*LOUISE BONNE OF JERSEY. Fruit medium-sized and of most delicious quality; very free bearing. Oct.

LE LECTIER. Very large, flesh fine, melting and very juicy. A new variety. Dec. to Feb.

MARIE LOUISE. A large-fruited and exceedingly fine sort, of the highest merit as a dessert pear. Oct. and Nov.

*MARIE LOUISE D'UCCLE. A large useful pear of first-rate quality; a great cropper. Oct.

*MARGUERITE MARILLAT. Very large and showy, with aromatic flavour; handsome in colour and shape; the finest in its season. Sept.

*PITMASTON DUCHESS. A very fine pear indeed, the fruit are very large and handsome, and of first-rate quality. Oct. to Dec.

*PRINCESS. A handsome pear; large, melting, flavour very good; the fruit will keep good until Christmas.

*ROOSEVELT. A new pear of immense size, sometimes measuring 16 inches in circumference, skin smooth, yellow-tinted with salmon pink, and of delicious flavour; highly recommended. One-year Trees on Quince 2s. 6d. each; Two-year Trees on Quince 3s. 6d. each; Fruiting Cordons 2s. 6d. each; Stout Standards 3s. 6d. each.

*SANTA CLAUS (new). Ripe at Christmas, and certainly the finest pear fit for use at that season. Two-year Trees on Quince 3s. each; Maidens 2s. each; Stout Standards 3s. 6d. each.

*SOUVENIR DU CONGRES. A splendid pear of first size and handsome appearance, capital bearer. Aug. and Sept.

*UVEDALE'S ST. GERMAIN. A very large pear, first-class for stewing. Jan. to April.

*VICAR OF WINKFIELD. A very handsome and excellent pear, of large size, but requires a wall to ripen it well. Nov. to Jan.

WILLIAMS' BON CHRETIEN. Well-known splendid old dessert pear; very hardy and a good bearer. Aug. and Sept.

WINTER ORANGE. A large stewing pear of first-class quality, yellow covered with russet brown; a good grower and bearer. Feb.-Mar.

*WINTER NELIS. Fruit small but of most delicious flavour; quite hardy and an excellent bearer. Nov. to Feb.

SELECT PLUMS.

Although as a rule, Plums attain the greatest perfection when grown as wall fruit, most of the varieties will succeed admirably when grown as Pyramids or Standards. Dwarf trees should be lifted and root-pruned from time to time, if making too strong a growth, and the branches should be thinned out to admit air and induce the formation of fruit buds. For growing on walls the following are highly recommended:—Green Gage, Golden Gage, Coe's Golden Drop. For general purposes the following are amongst the very best:—Cox's Emperor, Early Prolific, Diamond, Jefferson's, Magnum Bonum, Victoria, Sultan, Pond's Seedling, The Czar, Grand Duke.

DWARFS OR MAIDENS	.. ..	each 1s. 0d. ; per doz. 10s. 0d.
DWARF TRAINED	.. ..	„ 3s. 6d. ; „ 35s. 0d.
STANDARDS	.. ..	each 1s. 9d. ; per doz. 17s. 6d.
„ TRAINED (list of sorts on application)	..	each 5s. 0d.
PYRAMIDS	each 2s., 2s. 6d. and 3s. 6d. ; per doz. 20s., 25s. and 35s.	

PLUM—THE CZAR.

General List.

D denotes dessert, K kitchen.

BELLE DE LOUVAIN (K). Very large handsome fruit, red, of rich flavour. A good strong-growing orchard or garden variety.

COE'S GOLDEN DROP (D). Large oval fruit, pale yellow spotted with red ; one of the very best for dessert or preserving. End of Sept.

COX'S EMPEROR (K). Large dark reddish-purple fruit, firm flesh, sweet, rich, and juicy. A very fine bearer. Sept.

DAMSON PRUNE (K). Small oval fruit, a great bearer. Sept.

DENNISTON'S SUPERB (D). Large oval fruit, greenish-yellow blotched purple ; a delicious dessert plum, and an abundant bearer. Aug.

DIAMOND (K). Large oval, dark purple fruit ; an excellent variety for cooking or preserving. Sept.

EARLY PROLIFIC (D). A certain bearer ; very valuable market sort ; ripens middle of July on a wall, and when fully ripe is good for dessert, and one of the best flavoured when cooked. July.

EARLY YELLOW. Medium to small fruit of deep yellow colour with good bloom, ripening a week before Early Prolific, flesh yellow, parting freely from the stone ; a good bearer. F.C.C., R.H.S.

GIANT PRUNE (new) (Burbanks). A very large, long oval fruit of dark red colour, with yellow flesh of excellent flavour. The tree is a splendid grower, hardy and a good bearer. Fruit firm and does not split. A valuable plum for market purposes.
    One-year trees, 1s. each ; two-year trees, 2s. each.

GOLDEN GAGE (D). Large fruit, of very rich and delicious flavour ; a most excellent and prolific sort. Sept.

GREENGAGE (D). Well known to be the very best and richest of all. In common with all the Gages, this race requires vigorous root pruning, and then bears freely ; as Pot trees they succeed in an Orchard House, but as Standards they are not satisfactory, the birds taking the best buds in Winter. Aug.

JEFFERSON'S (D). A large and delicious plum, hardy, and a good bearer. Sept.

KIRKE'S (D). One of the very best of the blue plums, the fruit is medium-sized and richly flavoured ; a first-class dessert variety. Sept.

MAGNUM BONUM, WHITE (K). Large yellow fruit ; an excellent kitchen variety. Sept.

MONARCH (K). One of the best late plums, of large size and splendid flavour, dark purplish blue ; it is a heavy bearer and fruit does not crack with rain. A valuable late market plum. Sept.

ORLEANS (K). A good cooking or preserving plum ; a great bearer. Aug.

POND'S SEEDLING (K). Very large, good bearer and a sturdy grower. Forms a spreading tree ; fruit is enormous from a wall ; valuable for late market or garden culture. Early in Sept.

PRIMATE (new) (Rivers). A splendid new late plum, purplish red in colour, dotted with good bloom ; very large and late variety. A valuable addition.

REINE CLAUDE DE BAVAY (D). Large, round, greenish-yellow fruit of the "gage" type, rich and delicious flavour ; the tree is hardy and a great bearer. Beginning of October.

SULTAN (K). Fruit above medium size, skin dark purple ; covered with a thick blue bloom. A culinary plum of great excellence. Middle of August.

THE CZAR (D.K.). Very large, purple fruit of rich flavour ; it is an abundant bearer, and will prove most valuable to market growers on account of its earliness, fine appearance, and excellent quality. End of July.

VICTORIA (K). A well-known and very fine variety ; the tree is hardy and an almost constant bearer. The most useful kind of the season. Early in Sept.

CHERRIES.

DWARFS OR MAIDENS	.. .. ..	each 1s. ; per doz. 10s.
DWARF TRAINED ..	..	each 3s. 6d. and 5s. ; per doz. 35s.
STANDARDS	..	each 2s. and 2s. 6d. ; per doz. 20s. and 25s.
STANDARDS, TRAINED (list of names on application)	..	each 5s.
PYRAMIDS	each 2s., 2s. 6d., and 3s. 6d. ; per doz. 20s., 25s., and 35s.	

BIGARREAU. Large and of first-rate quality ; a capital bearer. July.

BIGARREAU NAPOLEON. Good bearer, hardy and excellent, follows the Bigarreau ; valuable as extending the season ; first rate for market, handsome, and indispensable for garden culture.

BLACK BIGARREAU. Fruit large and good ; an excellent variety.

BLACK EAGLE. Fruit of good size and flavour ; excellent. July.

BLACK HEART. A capital early black cherry of good quality, free bearer.

EARLY RIVERS. Large, shining black, very handsome, rich flavour ; one of the best for forcing or cherry house, and valuable for wall. As an orchard tree it requires close pruning for three or four years, and then forms a grand tree. The fruit makes a very high price in the market.

DOWNTON. Fruit above medium size, flesh pale amber, mottled with deep red, very rich and high flavour.

ELTON. Large, rich and excellent. July.

FROGMORE EARLY PROLIFIC. A capital early sort, very prolific.

GOVERNOR WOOD. Large, yellow, mottled with red, sweet and rich ; a good bearer ; excellent. July.

KNIGHT'S EARLY BLACK. Flesh deep purple, tender, rich, and juicy ; a delicious early cherry. End of June.

MAY DUKE. Large, juicy, rich, and excellent ; an abundant bearer as a standard or a bush. July.

MORELLO. Valuable for preserving and bottling. Pyramid trees produce fruit equal to that from a wall. Succeeds on north walls, and is occasionally planted as a Standard.

THE NOBLE. Very large, flesh firm, of rich flavour. This new variety is a great addition both for Garden or Market culture. It is a profuse bearer, and the fruit keeps well after gathering. It proves quite distinct from others in our collection.

WHITE HEART. Flesh firm, sweet and pleasant.

SELECT PEACHES.

MAIDENS, 2s. each. DWARF TRAINED, 5s. and 7s. 6d. each. STANDARD TRAINED, marked (*), 8s. 6d. 10s. 6d., and 15s. each.

PEACH—ROYAL GEORGE.

'*ALEXANDRA NOBLESSE. Very large fruit, flesh tender, juicy, and richly flavoured. Middle of Aug.

'*BARRINGTON. Large fruit of rich vinous flavour, and first-rate quality. The tree is hardy and a good bearer. Sept.

***ALEXANDER.** A very early Peach. Brilliant colour. July.

BELLEGARDE. Fruit round, deep red all over; flesh pale yellow. Middle of Sept.

CONDOR. Large bright crimson fruit, handsome and of rich flavour; a capital variety for forcing. Early in Aug.

CRAWFORD'S EARLY. Very large fruit, of splendid colour; very tender and melting, remarkably succulent and delicious. Aug. and Sept.

CRIMSON GALANDE. Large; deep crimson; flesh tender, melting, rich, and deliciously flavoured. Aug.

***DR. HOGG.** Large, fruit remarkable for its high colour; it is firm yet melting, and of rich sugary flavour; a fine, hardy, and prolific variety. Middle of Aug.

DUKE OF YORK. Large free stone, fruit well coloured and of excellent flavour; ripe about the same time as Alexandra. Maidens 2s. 6d. Dwarf trained 7s. 6d.

DYMOND. Fruit large, skin greenish yellow; flesh white, rich, melting, juicy. Middle of Sept.

***EARLY RIVERS.** Large, pale straw-coloured fruit, very rich and fine flavour; first-rate for forcing. End of July.

EARLY LOUISE. Medium size, bright red; melting, very juicy. July.

EARLY GROSSE MIGNONNE. Medium size, melting; one of the finest early Peaches. Aug.

GOSHAWK. Large fruit of exquisite flavour, good bearer; colour pale with red flesh, very hardy. Sept.

***GROSSE MIGNONNE.** Large, melting, excellent fruit; one of the finest in cultivation. Early in Sept.

***HALE'S EARLY.** Large size; melting and very good. July.

LADY PALMERSTON. Large, melting, and very good skin, greenish yellow marbled with crimson; very handsome, flesh pale yellow. End of Sept.

LATE ADMIRABLE. Fruit very large; skin yellowish green, flesh greenish white. End of Sept.

LORD PALMERSTON. The largest of Peaches, skin creamy white with pink cheek, flesh firm, melting, and juicy. Sept.

***NOBLESSE.** Large, melting, and excellent; one of the best either for forcing or the open wall. Sept.

PEREGRINE. Distinct Mid-season variety of fine constitution, fruit large and handsome with brilliant crimson skin, flesh rich and highly flavoured, and parting readily from the stone. Maidens 2s. 6d. Dwarf trained 7s. 6d.

PRINCE OF WALES. Large, rich melting fruit; an excellent late variety.

PRINCESS OF WALES. One of the largest Peaches and best; and one of the most beautiful; skin cream with a rosy cheek, melting and rich. End of Sept.

***ROYAL GEORGE.** Large, melting, and excellent; a good variety for the open wall Sept.

***SEA EAGLE.** A very large Peach of good flavour; remarkable for its brilliant colour and size. End of Sept.

***STIRLING CASTLE.** A fine hardy Peach of the *Royal George* type, large, skin deep red on sunny side, rich and highly flavoured; excellent for early forcing. Aug.

***WATERLOO.** A superior first early variety; bears freely in pots and is hardy when grown outside. Six weeks earlier than *Royal George.*

SELECT APRICOTS.

MAIDENS, 2s. 0d. each. DWARF TRAINED, 5s. 0d. and 7s. 6d each. STANDARD TRAINED, 10s. 6d., 15s., and 21s. each.

BREDA. Small, rich, vinous, and agreeably flavoured. Aug.

HEMSKERK. Flesh tender, juicy, and richly flavoured. July and Aug.

KAISHA. Middle size, flesh deep orange, juicy and rich. Aug.

LARGE EARLY. Very rich and juicy. July and Aug.

MOORPARK. One of the best. Aug. and Sept.

PEACH. Very large, rich, and juicy; one of the finest of all. Aug. and Sept.

ROYAL. Large, rich and juicy. July and Aug.

SELECT NECTARINES.

MAIDENS, 2s. 0d. each. DWARF TRAINED, 5s. and 7s. 6d. each. STANDARD TRAINED, marked (*) 10s. 6d., 15s., and 21s. each.

'*EARLY RIVERS. A seedling Nectarine, raised by Mr. T. F. Rivers. ripening twenty-one days before *Lord Napier*. It is a certain and heavy cropper, and promises to be one of the most valuable Nectarines yet introduced.

***DOWNTON.** Fruit large, oval, skin greenish in the shade, dark red on sunny side; melting, juicy, rich, and highly flavoured; an excellent variety. End of Aug.

***ELRUGE.** Medium-sized fruit, melting, rich and juicy; one of the best. Aug. and Sept.

HUMBOLDT. A very large Nectarine of splendid flavour. Sept.

***LORD NAPIER.** Medium size; pale cream with red cheek, flesh melting, very early, one of the best.

NEWINGTON. Fruit large, rich, sweet, and finely flavoured. Early in Sept.

***PINEAPPLE.** Large, bright red on the sunny side, very rich and sweet. Sept.

***PITMASTON ORANGE.** Large bright orange, dark brownish-red on the sunny side; melting, juicy, and rich; an excellent Nectarine, a good bearer. Aug. and Sept.

RIVERS' ORANGE. Similar to *Pitmaston Orange*, but earlier.

ROMAN. Large, deep red; juicy, rich, highly flavoured. Sept.

VICTORIA. Very rich, large, and sugary; a fine fruit when grown under glass.

VIOLETTE HATIVE. Medium-sized, melting, rich, and excellent. Aug.

CURRANTS.

CURRANT, BOSKOOP GIANT BLACK.

Generally speaking, the Black Currant thrives best on a damp soil and the Reds and Whites on a light soil, but with good cultivation they will succeed in almost any soil. Trained on a north wall or fence the Reds and Whites are exceedingly prolific and splendid fruit may be had well into September. Liquid manure is very beneficial where extra fine fruit are desired.

BOSKOOP GIANT BLACK. The finest Black Currant yet introduced. It is of extraordinarily vigorous growth, with long bunches of enormous fruit. Flavour, sweet and rich. A first-rate variety for exposed situations, and although it flowers late it ripens early. F.C.C.
per 100, 30s.; per doz. 4s.; each 6d.

FAY'S PROLIFIC. One of the best Red Currants we have. The bush is a strong grower, wonderfully prolific and comes into bearing early. The fruit is large, bright red, and of excellent flavour.
per doz. 4s. 0d.; each 6d.

RABY CASTLE. A strong and good grower, very large berries of rich crimson colour; hangs late on the bushes; a great bearer. per doz. 4s.

VICTORIA BLACK. This is one of the finest and largest Black Currants in cultivation. The fruit is of great size, splendid quality and flavour; and the plant is a most abundant bearer. A first-rate market sort. Strong young bushes, per doz. 4s.; each 5d.

OTHER VARIETIES—
Strong Bushes .. per 100, 21s. and 30s.; per doz. 3s. and 4s.

BLACK—	RED—	WHITE—
Baldwin's Black	Cherry	Transparent
Black Grape	Red Dutch	White
Lee's Prolific	Victoria	White
Naples		Dutch

We have a fine lot of Fan-trained Currant Bushes. Our selection from the above named varieties 1s. 9d. each, 18s. per doz.

From Mr. R. G. RANDALL, Brumblejean.
Aug. 11th.
"You will be glad to hear that all the trees I had from you have done well. I had a fine crop of Gooseberries from the lot before you sent."

From Mr. E. TANNER, Moss Side, Manchester.
Feb. 23rd.
"The Currant Trees I had last year were very fine, and we are very pleased with them."

GOOSEBERRIES.

LANCASHIRE PRIZE VARIETIES.

A very fine class, much esteemed for the splendid size of their fruit and their value for exhibition or dessert. When well ripened they are of delicious flavour and equal to many forced fruits.

LANCASHIRE PRIZE GOOSEBERRIES.

RED—	WHITE—	YELLOW—
Clayton	Alma	Broom Girl
Lancashire Lad	Freedom	Criterion
London	Mitre	Gold Purse
Roaring Lion	Snowdrop	Leader
Rifleman	White Eagle	Pilot
Speedwell	White Swan	Ringer

GREEN—General—Queen Victoria—Turnout.

And many other first-class varieties.

Our own Selection in choice variety in strong 2 and 3-year old bushes,
per doz. 6s.; per 100, 40s.

Other Varieties.

KEEPSAKE. A very large straw-coloured variety of excellent flavour and one of the best and earliest for gathering green.
Strong bushes, per 100, 25s.; per doz. 3s. 6d.; each 6d.

NORWICH LATE RED (new). Fruit very large, the bushes are of free growth and good habit, very heavy bearer, and a great improvement on Whinham's "Industry," being three weeks later.
Two-year Bushes, 1s. each; per doz. 10s. 6d.

MAY DUKE. One of the earliest Gooseberries in cultivation. It is a heavy cropper, and the fruit is large and handsome; colour deep red, thin skin .. .. per doz. 4s.; each 6d.

WHINHAM'S "INDUSTRY." A superb variety, bearing a wonderful profusion of large handsome fruit, which are of a dull red colour when ripe. Strong bushes, per 100, 25s.; per doz. 3s. 6d.

OTHER VARIETIES. Strong Bushes—
Our Selection, per 100, 21s. to 30s.; per doz. 3s., 4s. 6d.

We can supply Fan-trained Gooseberries from the above varieties 1s. 9d. each, 18s. doz.

GOOSEBERRY, WHINHAM'S "INDUSTRY."

RASPBERRY, SUPERLATIVE.

RASPBERRIES.

This splendid fruit is well deserving and will pay well for good cultivation.

Ground intended for these should be deeply trenched and heavily manured. The canes should be planted (not too deeply) about 2 feet apart and the rows should be 5 or 6 feet apart, and after planting a mulching of well-decayed manure should be placed on the surface. Newly planted canes should be cut back to 2 feet to encourage the formation of suckers for the following season.

RED ANTWERP. WHITE ANTWERP. Per 100, 12s. ; per doz. 2s.

BAUMFORTH'S SEEDLING. A fine variety ; fruit very large, of the most beautiful crimson colour ; an abundant bearer of good habit,
per 100, 12s. ; per doz. 2s.

HORNET (Rivers). A very fine Raspberry, fruit deliciously flavoured, and the most juicy of any variety. A splendid cropper, and will be largely grown when better known. First Class Certificate, Royal Horticultural Society .. .. per 100, 15s. ; per doz. 2s. 3d.

NOVEMBER ABUNDANCE. A splendid Autumn bearing variety. The fruit, which is borne in large clusters, is of a deep red colour and of excellent flavour, whilst the canes are strong and vigorous.
per 100, 17s. 6d. ; per doz. 2s. 6d.

PERFECTION. This is an absolutely new and distinct variety, being distinguishable from any other by the brilliant red of the cane. It is an exceptionally strong grower and makes a better plant the first year than any other variety ; the growth here attains a height of 6 to 8 feet. It is a good cropper, producing fruit from base to top of cane of a bold size, firm, fine, acidulous flavour, and brilliant scarlet colour, the high colour being retained even when the fruit is fully ripe.
per 100, 15s. ; per doz. 2s. 3d.

SUPERLATIVE. Fruit very large, mostly freely produced ; an excellent variety .. .. .. per 100, 12s. ; per doz. 2s.

BLACKBERRIES.

PARSLEY-LEAVED. Very ornamental cut-leaved variety which bears large fruit, good, and productive .. .. per doz. 5s. ; each 6d.

WILSON JUNIOR. One of the finest and most prolific in cultivation, producing very large, glossy black fruit of delicious flavour.
per doz. 5s. ; each 6d.

STRAWBERRY PLANTS—Prepared Runners.
KING GEORGE V.

This fine new early forcing and outdoor Strawberry was raised by crossing Louis Gauthier × Royal Sovereign. It is a really magnificent fruit, quite as large, if not larger than Sovereign, but ripens quite a week earlier grown side by side. The colour is of the brightest scarlet, but the flesh right throughout is orange-red. The flavour is delicious, quite excelling Royal Sovereign. It is even a heavier cropper than Sovereign ; forms splendid crowns, and sets and swells particularly freely, and we have no hesitation in saying it will make the forcing Strawberry of the future. Stock very limited.
Strong young Plants in small pots, per 100, 100s. ; per doz. 15s.

"PROFIT."

This is a main crop fruit which we have confidence in recommending for size, firmness, flavour, cropping qualities and vigour of plant combined. The colour is a dark vermilion scarlet, conically wedge-shaped. The best mid-season variety of recent introduction.
Strong open ground Plants, per 100, 15s. ; per doz. 2s. 6d.

OTHER VARIETIES.

"THE CROPPER." An exceedingly prolific main crop variety of a rich crimson colour, bluntly conical in shape, the flesh is white and solid with a good firm exterior skin, very rich and luscious in flavour, medium to large in size, with a fine constitution, succeeding well on almost any soil, and forces well as a second early.
Strong Plants, per 100, 6s. ; per doz. 1s.

PROGRESS. The flavour of this variety is very rich. The fruit, which is large, is of a flattish wedge shape, and in colour and appearance partakes very much of the "Queen" type, is produced in large clusters with bold vigorous foliage. It is a wonderful grower, and does exceedingly well on almost any soil, thus indicating a good constitution ; it is really late.
Strong Plants, per 100, 6s. ; per doz. 1s.

The following Sorts all at 9d. per dozen, 5s. per 001. Not less than 50 supplied at the rate per 100.

REWARD (Laxton's). The result of crossing "Royal Sovereign" and "British Queen," the result being a really grand acquisition. The fruit is very large, wedge-shaped, and the quality excellent, being of the richest Queen-like flavour ; flesh red throughout, the external skin being of a most brilliant glowing crimson colour ; the fruit is also very firm and will bear handling ; a really handsome fruit.
Per 100, 5s.

BEDFORD CHAMPION. Without doubt the largest Strawberry placed in commerce. The fruit is often 2½ to 3 ozs. in weight, with a circumference of 6 ins. ; the colour of the skin is a bright scarlet, the flesh of the fruit being white ; fruit is broadly conical, sweet and luscious in flavour ; borne on enormous trusses of great size and vigour.
Per 100, 5s.

KENTISH FAVOURITE. The heaviest cropping Strawberry yet sent out. The fruit, when ripe, are of a beautiful bright scarlet colour ; of a flat three-cornered shape, and often measures 3½ inches diameter ; the flavour is much superior to Royal Sovereign.
Per 100, 5s.

LAXON'S LATEST. A fine flavoured, very late variety. The fruit is very large. The colour is a deep rich crimson.
Per 100, 5s.

	per 100–s. d.			per 100–s. d.
FILLBASKET. The colour is a good bright scarlet similar to *Royal Sovereign*, the flesh is white and firm. The flavouring is excellent, beautifully juicy, yet sweet and luscious ..	5 0		**BRITISH QUEEN.** Well-known superb variety ; the finest flavoured Strawberry in existence ; requires good cultivation	5 0
GIVON'S LATE PROLIFIC. A fine new variety raised from *Waterloo* and *Latest of All*. Large, wedge-shaped fruit of rich colour ..	5 0		**SIR JOSEPH PAXTON.** Hardy early variety	5 0
WATERLOO. Fruit large and of a fine dark crimson colour, almost black when ripe ; a good grower	5 0		**"ST. ANTOINE DE PADOUE."** Said to be by far the finest perpetual bearer yet raised. Superior to *St. Joseph*	5 0
ROYAL SOVEREIGN. This fine early Strawberry is the best variety for pot culture	5 0		**SENSATION.** An enormous second early or mid-season variety of good flavour. The fruit and flesh of a rich crimson colour..	5 0
			THE LAXTON. A cross between *Royal Sovereign* and *Sir Joseph Paxton*. One of the finest and best early	5 0

100 in 10 choice varieties, our own selection .. .. .. 5s. 6d.

GRAPE VINES.

The best time for the Spring planting of these, either on inside or outside borders, is in March or April, when the sap is beginning to flow and the buds show signs of bursting into leaf. Ground intended for growing Grapes should be carefully drained, if the soil is wet, and should be well broken up to a depth of two feet, and well mixed with some old well-rotted manure and rough loam, with the addition of some old lime rubbish, if procurable.

Our stock of Grape Vines for the present season is very fine. The canes have all been grown from eyes and are well-ripened, strong and healthy. The buds are thoroughly matured and plump.

The fruiting canes we offer are extra strong and stout, from eight to ten feet in length; and if cultivated in pots should bear from eight to twelve bunches each next season.

H denotes those varieties that require a heated vinery.   *C denotes those suitable for growing in a cool vinery.*

BLACK ALICANTE (H). One of the largest and handsomest grapes in cultivation. The fruit is of oval form and carries a fine bloom.. It is of excellent flavour and very prolific. Its flavour is at the best when allowed to hang till Christmas.

BLACK HAMBURGH (C). Berries large, round, sweet and juicy. Large broadly shouldered bunches. A well-known most excellent variety and probably the most popular in cultivation. The best for general use.

BUCKLAND'S SWEET WATER (C). Large bunches and berries of amber colour. An excellent variety for a cool vinery.

FOSTER'S SEEDLING (C). Pale amber, an excellent variety.

GROS COLMAR (H). Bunches and berries very large. Dark purple with beautiful bloom. A very handsome and deservedly popular variety.

GROS MAROC (H). An exceedingly handsome large-fruited grape of delicious flavour and one that ripens early.

LADY DOWNE'S SEEDLING (H). Large black berries of good flavour. This is a splendid keeper and will hang till March.

MADRESFIELD COURT MUSCAT (H). Long bunches and large black berries of delicious Muscat flavour, will hang for a long time without shrivelling.

MUSCAT OF ALEXANDRIA (H). Long and large bunches of large red amber-coloured berries of the most delicious Muscat flavour. The most popular of all the "Muscats."

ROYAL MUSCADINE. A fine hardy white grape that will succeed well on a south wall   ..   ..   each 3s. 6d., 5s., and 7s. 6d.

Prices for the above varieties, with the exception of Royal Muscadine.

    STRONG PLANTING CANES, in pots   ..   ..   each 3s. 6d. and 5s.

    FRUITING CANES, in pots, very fine   ..   ..   each 7s. 6d. and 10s. 6d.

FIGS.

BROWN TURKEY. Most abundant bearer; the finest for out-door culture, and very free setter in pots for forcing.

NEGRO LARGO. Very luscious, free bearer, strong grower; large rich chocolate purple fruit; splendid for second crop under glass, but not fertile outside. F.C.

WHITE ISCHIA. Small, sweet and delicious; produces three crops a year in heat; forces well; great bearer; for indoor culture only.

    STRONG PLANTS, in pots, Trained, flat   ..   each 2s. 6d.

    FRUITING ,,   ,,   ..   each 3s. 6d., 5s., and 7s. 6d.

ALMONDS.

STANDARDS   -   each 1s. 6d. and 2s. 6d.

MEDLARS.

STANDARDS   ..   each 2s. 6d.

NUTS AND FILBERTS.

We have a very fine stock of these in good strong plants.

DREADNOUGHT (new). A very large and excellent cob nut of excellent flavour. Very prolific.

    STRONG FRUITING BUSHES   ..   3 for 2s. 6d.; each 1s.

NORWICH PROLIFIC. An excellent variety and a great bearer.

    per doz. 10s. 6d.; each 1s.

Also the following sorts:—Cosford, Kentish Cob, White Filbert, Red Filbert, Purple Leaved Filbert, &c.

STRONG FRUITING DWARFS or **BUSHES** in first-class condition for removal ..   ..   ..   per doz. 9s.

MULBERRIES.

STANDARDS   ..   ..   each 5s. to 7s. 6d.

WALNUTS.

FINE STANDARDS ..   ..   each 2s. 6d., 3s. 6d., and 5s.

QUINCE.

STANDARDS   ..   ..   each 2s. 6d.

PHENOMENAL BERRY.
(Novelty.)

A further cross between the Logan Berry and the Raspberry, the shape and colour of the Logan Berry, with the flavour of a Raspberry. Without the hard core of the Logan Berry, and will be a most suitable fruit of the future for dessert or preserving, which will ripen before the "Lowberry." This is a very strong grower and should be planted in the same way as the Logan Berry.

    PLANTS FROM GROUND   ..   ..   each 1s. 6d.; in pots, 2s. each.

LOGAN BERRY.

This fine American fruit has proved a decided acquisition and is now being extensively grown for market purposes. Grown in the same way as Raspberries it fruits freely and will often succeed where these fail. It is of very strong growth and makes a capital plant for poles or pillars; it also makes an excellent fence, and is very useful for pergolas. Plant 6 or 8 feet apart.

    STRONG PLANTS from layers, the true variety   each 9d.; per doz. 6s.

THE LOWBERRY.

A very fine new variety of the Logan Berry, producing an abundance of handsome black fruit without core, and of delicious flavour.

    each 2s. 6d.

For plants of Asparagus, Herbs, Rhubarb, & Sea Kale. *See page 51.*

From Mr. H. MARSH, Sherwood.

"I must say that the Guinea Collection of Fruit Trees you sent me is very fine, and I am highly satisfied with them."

From Mr. R. MEECH, Poole.

"The four Grape Vines that you supplied a little while since, I am pleased to say, are doing remarkably well, and I are making very satisfactory progress."

OUR GUINEA COLLECTION OF CHOICE FRUITS.

We have much pleasure in offering the following liberal Collection of Fruits which will be found admirably suited to the requirements of a small garden, or where the space for fruit growing is limited. The Fruit Trees will in all instances be Dwarfs, but of these and other fruits included, only good varieties will be sent. The selection of sorts must be left to ourselves. We make no charge for package, but in consequence of the extreme cheapness of this Collection we cannot pay carriage of same and must ask that all orders be accompanied by a remittance of Cheque or P.O.O.

OUR GUINEA COLLECTION OF FRUITS CONTAINS

6 APPLES. Best sorts for succession.	2 CHERRIES. Two varieties.	2 LOGAN BERRIES.
4 PEARS. In good variety.	12 GOOSEBERRIES. In variety.	12 RASPBERRIES. Best sorts.
4 PLUMS. Most useful sorts.	18 CURRANTS. Red, Black, and White.	50 STRAWBERRIES. In four sorts.

No charge for Package.

DANIELS' GRAPE VINES

BLACK HAMBRO'

MUSCAT OF ALEXANDRIA

DANIELS BROS Ltd.
NORWICH.

1. Lady Ashtown
   2. Hugh Dickson
3. Richmond
   4. Lyon-Rose

HYBRID PERPETUAL & H. T. ROSES.

These magnificent and beautiful Roses are better adapted than any others for exhibition and pot culture. They continue in flower from the early part of June to the end of October, and are by far the most desirable for general cultivation.

The "NORWICH" Collection
of 12 Champion Bush Roses, 10/6 Carr. Paid.

CAROLINE TESTOUT	FRAU KARL DRUSCHKI	LADY HILLINGTON	MRS. J. LAING
CAPTAIN HAYWARD	HUGH DICKSON	LYON ROSE	MARGARET DICKSON
COUNTESS OF GOSFORD	KAISERIN AUGUSTA VICTORIA	MADAME ABEL CHATENAY	PHARISAER

The "TOWN CLOSE" Collection
of 18 Very Choice Bush Roses for Exhibition, 15/- Carr. Paid.

ALFRED COLOMB	EDU MEYER	KILLARNEY	MARQUIS DE LITTA
BESSIE BROWN	FRAU KARL DRUSCHKI	LA FRANCE	MRS. JOHN LAING
CAPT. HAYWARD	GENL. JACQUIMINOT	LYON ROSE	MRS. S. CRAWFORD
CAROLINE TESTOUT	GUSTAVE REGIS	MADAME RAVARY	PRINCE CAM DE ROHAN
DEAN HOLE	JOSEPH LOWE		

The "NORFOLK" Collection
of 24 Choice and Well-known Bush and Climbing Roses for 20/- Carr. Paid.

ABEL CARRIERE	FRAU KARL DRUSCHKI	LYON ROSE	MRS. J. LAING
ALFRED COLOMB	FRAU LILA RAUTENSTRAUGH	MADAME RAVARY	PRINCE CAM DE ROHAN
BARONESS ROTHSCHILD	GENERAL McARTHUR	MADAME VICTOR VERDIER	PRINCE DE BULGARIE
CRIMSON RAMBLER, climbing	HIAWATHA, climbing	MARIE BAUMANN	ULRICH BRUNNER
DOROTHY PERKINS, climbing	J. B. CLARKE	MRS. SHARMAN CRAWFORD	WHITE DOROTHY PERKINS
DUKE OF EDINBURGH	LADY GAY, climbing	MRS. W. M. KIRKER	WM. SHEAN (climbing

The "POPULAR" Collection
of 12 Dwarf Roses, in 12 Varieties (our selection) 7/6 Carr. Paid.

The "CLIMBING" Collection
for Pergolas or Arches, 12 of the best for 10/6 Carr. Paid.

BLUSH RAMBLER	DOROTHY PERKINS	LADY GAY	TAUSENDSCHON
CARMINE PILLAR	DELIGHT	MADAME ALFRED CARRIERE	THALIA
CRIMSON RAMBLER	HIAWATHA	MRS. T. W. FLIGET	WHITE DOROTHY PERKINS

The "WALL" Collection
for Walls and Pillars, 12 of the best for 10/6 Carr. Paid.

AIMEE VIBERT	CHESHUNT HYBRID	GLOIRE DE DIJON	REINE M. HENRIETTE
BOUQUET D'OR	CLIMBING LA FRANCE	GRUSS AN TEPLITZ	TRIER
CELINE FORESTIER	,, CAROLINE TESTOUT	J. B. CLARKE	WM. ALLAN RICHARDSON

HYBRID PERPETUAL AND OTHER ROSES.
Choice New Roses.

CHATEAU DE CLOS VOUGEOT (H.T.). Red velvety scarlet shaded fiery red, passing to dark velvety crimson, which is said to keep its colour under a hot sun. Flowers large, full and globular; a grand variety, strongly recommended .. .. each 1s. 6d.

CLAUDIUS (H.T.). Colour bright glowing rose, of uniform shade throughout, strong and sturdy growth, flowers carried erect on stout stems; sweetly scented .. .. each 3s. 6d.

COUNTESS OF SHAFTESBURY (H.T.). Bright silvery carmine, one of the most perfect type of Hybrid Teas in habit and growth; an ideal exhibition Rose. Gold Medal N.R.S. .. .. .. each 7s. 6d.

DUCHESS OF WELLINGTON (H.T.). A very fine new variety. The colour of the flower is quite novel, and of marvellous beauty. In the young stage it is an intense saffron yellow, stained with rich crimson, which as the flower develops becomes a deep coppery saffron yellow—a shade hitherto unknown among roses. The blooms possess a delightful fragrance, and the plant is of good constitution and free flowering. per doz. 24s.; each 2s. 6d.

EDWARD MAWLEY (H.T.). A superb Rose of a rich velvety crimson colour (with huge petals of the type of Melaine Soupert), in fact, in form it resembles that grand rose only much larger. It is a splendid grower and as free as any of the Hybrid Teas. It is a gorgeous variety for the garden and the exhibitor. Gold Medal N.R.S., 1910 .. .. each 7s. 6d.

ETHEL MALCOLM (H.T.). This is one of the finest roses grown, the colour is ivory white, passing to pure white as the flower expands, with a delicate peach shading in centre of bloom, delicately sweet scented. Gold Medal N.R.S. .. .. each 3s.

JAMES COEY (H.T.). The colour is deep golden yellow, edges of petals white; the flowers are medium size, fairly full, and are carried on stiff stems. In the bud state the form is perfection, and colour a delightful shade of orange yellow. A truly lovely and most charming rose .. .. each 2s.

JULIET. Outside petals old gold, interior rich rosy red, base of petals deep yellow; large flowers distinct and attractive .. each 3s. 6d.

If desired we can supply permanent "Acme" Labels for all Roses. See page 60 for prices.

Choice New Roses, H. P. and H. T. *(continued).*

JONKHEER J. L. MOCK (H.T.). Colour carmine, changing to imperial pink, full and of fine form, may be called a much improved La France, vigorous grower and most promising new rose .. each 2s. 6d.

LADY ALICE STANLEY (H.T.). Deep coral red, inside pale flesh (Gold Medal) .. .. each 2s. 6d.

LADY HILLINGDON (T.). Fine golden yellow novelty, a cross between Papa Gontier and Lady Roberts, with long pointed buds producing a glorious effect.. .. .. .. per doz, 21s., each 2s, 0d.

LADY PIRRIE (H.T.). A most delightful rose of distinct colouring, the outside of petals deep coppery reddish salmon, inside of petals apricot, a vigorous grower. Gold Medal N.R.S., 1910 each 2s. 6d.

LESLIE HOLLAND (H.T.). Deep scarlet crimson, heavily shaded deep velvety crimson, it is a flower of immense size and great substance, sweetly scented. Gold Medal N.R.S. .. .. each 7s. 6d.

MARY COUNTESS OF ILCHESTER (H.T.). This rose is remarkably free flowering, the colour is crimson carmine, of immense size each 2s.

MISS CYNTHIA FORDE (H.T.). This fine new rose is possessed of all the ideal requirements of a first-class garden or exhibition variety. In colour it is a deep brilliant rose pink, shading at the back of the petals to light rosy pink. The flower is very large, perfectly formed. The petals being abundant and evenly formed. The plant is of upright, vigorous growth, and blooms quite throughout the season. It is very sweetly perfumed, and the blooms last a long time in good condition when cut .. .. each 2s.

MOLLY SHARMAN CRAWFORD (T.). A splendid rose of sturdy growth and branching habit, flowering most profusely and continuously. The colour is a delicate eau-de-Nil white, which, as the flower expands, becomes a dazzling pure white. It is delicately perfumed, and will be a great acquisition .. .. .. each 2s.

MRS. ARTHUR MUNT (new) (H.T.). Deep cream suffused peach which becomes creamy ivory; good for exhibition .. each 2s.

MRS. AMY HAMMOND (H.T.). This is perhaps best described as a highly improved Madame A. Chatenay which has hitherto been considered as the best of its class of colour. Mrs. Amy Hammond is a better grower, a freer bloomer, its flowers are longer and more pointed, the colour a blend of amber and apricot. Very fine .. .. each 7s. 6d.

MRS. HERBERT STEVENS (T.). A hardy variety said to withstand our winters in this climate. The bloom is as long and even more pointed than that of the Maman Cochet family, faultless in shape and form, colour white, with a distinct fawn and peach shading towards centre. The petals are of great depth and substance, retaining their beautiful pointed form to the last .. .. each 2s. 6d.

MRS. FOLEY HOBBS (T.). Tea scented variety of sterling quality. Grand flower of delicate ivory white tinged pink on edges of petals each 3s, 6d.

MRS. JOSEPH H. WELSH (H.T.). Rose pink colour, this is a monster Rose, one bloom was quite five inches deep; said to be a vigorous grower. A distinct and good Rose for all purposes, especially valuable for exhibition and for pot culture. Gold Medal N.R.S., 1910. each 5s.

MRS. MAYNARD SINTON (H.T.). A grand variety, the colour is silvery white with porcelain shading, suffused pink towards the edges, the most distinct amongst roses, of enormous size with high pointed centre. A model exhibition flower. Gold Medal N.R.S., 1909 each 3s, 6d.

MRS. W. CHRISTIE-MILLER (H.T.). Colour inside of petal soft pearly blush shaded salmon, outside of petal clear vermilion rose, delightful scheme of colouring which makes it a most remarkable variety, enormous size .. .. each 2s. 6d.

PINK LIBERTY. A sport from the well-known popular variety, with the exact habit of its parent, and need only to be announced to be appreciated. "Pink Liberty" blends the shades of "Old Rose" and "Rose du Barri" colours, which will appeal to all. Plants in pots, 5s.

RAYON D'OR (new). A pure yellow Rose resembling in colour Persian Yellow, the buds are orange yellow with crimson flush, the open flower is clear yellow. Splendid bedder. Faintly Tea scented. each 3s. 0d.

H. P. & H. T. ROSES—General Select List.

In ordering from the following list, please give a few supplementary names of varieties to be sent in case of our being sold out of those first named. The prices quoted in this list are for dwarf or bush plants from open ground.

STANDARD ROSES We can only supply our own selection of varieties H. P. and H. T. at 21s. and 24s. per dozen. HALF-STANDARDS, 18s. and 21s. per dozen.

In all cases where one dozen or more Roses of any one variety are ordered, we will supply them as follows :—Those priced at 9d. each, at 8s. 0d. per doz. ; at 1s. each, at 10s. 6d. per doz. ; at 1s. 6d. each, at 10s. 0d. per doz., &c., pro rata.

	Dwarfs	s.	d.
ABEL CARRIERE. Deep velvety crimson	–	0	9
ALFRED COLOMB. Brilliant fiery red	–	0	9
ALFRED K. WILLIAMS. Fine carmine red	–	1	0
ALICE GRAHAME (H.T.). Flower of large size, enormous substance, and perfect form ; colour ivory white tinted salmon		1	0
BARONESS ROTHSCHILD. Delicate rose, beautiful form ; splendid		0	9
BEAUTY OF WALTHAM. Bright red, large ; splendid form		0	9
BEN CANT (H.P.). Deep clear crimson with dark shading		0	9
BESSIE BROWN (H.T.). Creamy white; the blooms are perfectly formed and of large size ; highly perfumed		1	0
CAPTAIN CHRISTY (H.P.). Flesh-coloured rose		1	0
CAROLINE TESTOUT (H.T.). Bright satiny-rose, with brighter centre, large, full, and globular, very free and sweet		1	0
CHARLES LEFEBVRE. Velvety crimson		0	9
CLIO. Flesh colour, shaded in the centre with rosy pink		0	9
COUNTESS OF DERBY (H.T.) (1905). Colour salmon centre, outer petals rose ; flowers large, full, and of perfect shape..		1	0
COUNTESS OF GOSPORT (H.T.). Clear salmon pink, the base of petals suffused with yellow ; large, full and free		1	0
DEAN HOLE (H.T.). This is a most distinct and magnificent Rose; colour silvery carmine, shaded salmon ..		1	0
DOROTHY (H.T.). Clear bright flesh colour, shading to delicate blush at the edges of petals ; large and splendidly formed		1	0
DOROTHY PAGE ROBERTS (H.T.). Coppery yellow with apricot yellow at base of petals ..		1	0
DR. HOGG (H.P.). Deep violet, nearest the blue colour desired in roses; vigorous and good shape ..		0	9
DUCHESS OF PORTLAND. Colour a pale, sulphury yellow. The blooms are very large and full. A most charming rose ..		1	0
DUKE OF EDINBURGH. Rich vermilion ..	–	1	0
DUKE OF TECK. Vivid bright crimson scarlet	–	0	9
DUKE OF WELLINGTON. Bright red, shaded crimson, very lovely ..		0	9
EARL OF DUFFERIN. Flowers of large size ; colour rich brilliant velvety crimson, shaded with dark maroon ..		1	0
EARL OF WARWICK (H.T.). Colour soft salmon pink, with deeper centre ; large, perfectly formed flowers		1	0
ELIZABETH BARNES (H.T.) (new). Large full flowers with pointed centre, most perfectly formed and delightfully fragrant. The colour is a satiny salmon rose, with a fawn centre ..		1	0
ETOILE DE FRANCE (H.T.). The flowers are very large ; colour brilliant velvety crimson. Very sweet scented ..		1	0

GENERAL McARTHUR.

Hybrid Perpetual and H. T. Roses—General List *(continued).*

LYON ROSE.

Dwarfs—s. d.

FLORENCE PEMBERTON (H.T.). The colour is creamy white, with "suspicion" of pink, the edges of the petals occasionally flushed peach 1 0
☞ FRAU KARL DRUSCHKI. Flowers large, perfectly formed with shell-shaped petals, and of the purest white, opening well; splendid 1 0
FRAU LILA RAUTENSTRAUCH (H.T.). Apricot orange, suffused yellow, tinted rose; flowers large and very full .. 1 0
GENERAL JACQUIMINOT. Brilliant crimson scarlet .. 0 9
GENERAL McARTHUR (H.T.). Dark velvety scarlet, very sweet scented 1 0
GEORGE C. WAUD (H.T.) (new). A remarkably distinct and beautiful variety. The flowers are large, full, perfectly formed, with high-pointed centre, and of a brilliant orange-vermilion colour that does not fade. It is highly perfumed, and one of the very finest of the new sorts 1 6
GERTRUDE (H.T.). A very beautiful sport from "Countess of Caledon" 1 0
GRACE MOLYNEAUX (H.T.). Creamy apricot flesh in the centre; the outer petals, when fully developed, are creamy white inside. A splendid rose for garden decoration, button-holes, or exhibition 1 6
GUSTAVE REGIS (H.T.). Nankeen yellow, very long pointed buds of perfect shape; a continuous bloomer and first-rate for button holes 1 0
HARRY KIRK (H.T.). Deep sulphur yellow. A splendid rose, much the best of its colour 1 0
HEINRICH SCHULTHEIS. Delicate purplish-rose with a white shading, bold form; a distinct Rose 0 9
☞ HUGH DICKSON (H.P.). One of the finest additions to its class that has been sent out for several years past. In colour it is an intense brilliant crimson shaded scarlet. It is deliciously fragrant 0 9
☞ HUGH WATSON (H.P.). The blooms are very large, full, and most perfect shape, quite exhibition form. Very sweetly perfumed. Colour crimson, shaded carmine .. 0 9
JACQUES VINCENT (H.T.). Coral red with a yellowish shade, flowers very large, and perfectly formed 2 0

Dwarfs—s. d.

JEANNIE DICKSON. Colour, rosy pink edged with silvery pink, perfectly formed large flowers 0 9
JOHANNA SEBUS (H.T.). Rosy-cerise, very large and well formed 1 0
J. B. CLARKE (H.T.). Bright deep scarlet; flowers extra large, with perfect pointed centre, (Gold Medal. N.R.S.) .. 1 0
JOSEPH LOWE (H.T.). A sport from Mrs. W. J. Grant, with rather more substance in the flowers. Colour salmon pink in the way of Madame A. Chatenay 1 0
☞ KAISERIN AUGUSTA VICTORIA (H.T.). Lemon delicately shaded with cream; very large, of most perfect form .. 1 0
KILLARNEY. Flesh colour, shaded white, and suffused pale pink; blooms large, buds long and pointed 1 0
☞ LADY BATTERSEA (H.T.). Bright rosy crimson tinged with orange, and changing to soft pure rose; long oval buds, vigorous growth 1 0
LA FRANCE. Bright lilac rose; beautiful 1 0
LADY ASHTOWN (H.T.) (1905). Colour very pale rose, shading to yellow at base of petals, reflex of petals, silvery pink.. 1 0
LADY HELEN VINCENT (H.T.). Pink shaded yellow at base... 1 0
LIBERTY (H.T.). Brilliant crimson, large, elongated, beautifully formed buds; a splendid Rose for forcing 1 0
LYON ROSE (H.T.). Edges of petals shrimp pink, centre coral red or salmon pink shaded with chrome yellow; growth vigorous, distinct and quite first rate .. .. Standards 3s. 1 6
MADAME ABEL CHATENAY (H.T.). Bright carmine rose shaded to deep salmon; long pointed full-sized flowers .. 1 0
MADAME CHARLES MEURICE. Deep velvety purple .. 0 9
MADAME LEONE PAIN (H.P.). Similar in every way to Madame Abel Chatenay, but do not fade in the hot sun .. 1 6
MADAME MELAINE SOUPERT (H.T.). Colour pale saffron yellow, suffused with pink and carmine; flowers large, full and of perfect form 1 6
MADAME RAVARY (H.T.). Golden yellow, shaded orange; a continuous bloomer and splendid bedder 1 0
MARCHIONESS OF LONDONDERRY. Ivory-white petals of great substance, shell-shaped and reflexed; very large .. 0 9
MARGARET DICKSON (H.P.). White, with pale flesh centre, very large, stout shell-shaped petals 0 9
☞ MILDRED GRANT (H.T.) (new). The blooms are of immense size and substance, with high-pointed centres, the petals unusually long. Ivory white, flushed with pale peach .. 1 0
MME. SEGOND WEBER (H.T.). Clear bright salmon rose, extra large fine stiff petals, lasting well 1 0
MONS. JOSEPH HILL (H.T.). Salmon pink, shaded yellow. The buds are long, and the flowers large and of perfect shape 1 0
MONS. PAUL LEDE (H.T.). Deep rose shaded yellow, large full, perfect shape 1 0
MRS. E. G. HILL (H.T.). Colour alabaster white inside the pink, the reverse coral red, long pointed buds, borne on long stalks; very fine 1 0
MRS. A. M. KIRKER (H.P.). A Rose of great beauty, flowers large and full. Colour bright cerise; it possesses great fragrance .. 0 9
MRS. PETER BLAIR (H.T.). Lemon yellow with golden yellow centre; full perfectly-shaped flowers 1 6
MRS. J. LAING (H.P.). A seedling from François Michelon; flowers large and finely shaped; colour a beautiful soft pink .. 0 9
MRS. R. G. SHARMAN CRAWFORD. Deep rosy pink, the outer petals shaded with pale flesh; the flowers are large, perfectly formed, and abundant 0 9
MRS. W. J. GRANT (H.T.). Imperial pink, of very good form, large flowers borne on good stout stems, retaining perfect form 1 0
MRS. AARON WARD (H.T.). Colour Indian yellow, similar to Catherine Mermet in form, one of the best yellow Roses .. 1 0
PHARISAER (H.T.). Rosy white shaded salmon, bud long, opening into a large, full, and well-formed flower, growth vigorous 1 0
PRINCE CAMILLE DE ROHAN. Dark crimson maroon, fine form 0 9
QUEEN OF SPAIN (H.T.). Large, full perfectly-formed flowers of great substance and fine finish. Colour pale flesh .. 1 6
REYNOLDS HOLE. Dark maroon 0 9
SIR ROWLAND HILL. Rich deep port wine colour, with violet shading, changes to claret 0 9
SOUVENIR DE PIERRE NOTTING (H.T.). Blooms very large; surpassing in form and beauty those of Maman Cochet. Colour, deep apricot yellow shaded with orange. Splendid .. 1 0
ULRICH BRUNNER. Cherry crimson; fine 0 9
WHITE KILLARNEY (H.T.) (new). A pure white sport from the well-known old pink favourite, with the same splendid size and beautiful form of flower. A valuable acquisition .. 1 6
WILLIAM ASKEW (H.T.). Bright pink, shaded delicate pink at tips of petals; large, full, and good form 1 0
XAVIER OLIBO (H.P.). Velvety black 0 9

ROSES—TEA-SCENTED AND NOISETTE.

ROSE, LADY HILLINGDON.

	E. Dwarfs—s.	d.
HOMER. Rose, centre salmon	1	0
INNOCENTE PIROLA. Pure white, slightly rosy	1	0
ISABELLA SPRUNT. Sulphur yellow	1	0
JEAN DUCHER. Salmon yellow, shaded with rose	1	0
LADY HILLINGDON. Fine golden yellow novelty, a cross between "Papa Gontier" and "Lady Roberts," with long pointed buds, producing a glorious effect .. doz. 21s.	2	0
LADY ROBERTS. Rich apricot, shaded pale orange, buds long pointed, blooms large and of perfect form	1	0
MADAME CONSTANCE SOUPERT (T). Colour yellow with pretty peach shading, large full pointed flowers, freely produced	1	0
MADAME CUSIN. Rosy purple, with pale yellow at base of petals, exquisitely formed	1	0
MADAME FALCOT. Apricot yellow, very distinct	1	0
MADAME JULES GRAVEREAUX. Lemon yellow with rosy peach centre; buds large, long, and beautifully formed	1	0
MADAME LAMBARD. Salmon shaded rose, variable	1	0
MADAME DE WATTEVILLE. Salmony white edged with bright rose and pink; beautiful and distinct variety	1	0
MAMAN COCHET. Clear flesh mingled with salmon rose, outer petals splashed with bright rose; flowers very large and well formed	1	6
MARIE VAN HOUTTE. Lemon yellow edged with lively rose, medium size, good form, beautiful	1	6
MOLLY SHARMAN CRAWFORD (T). A splendid rose of sturdy growth and branching habit, flowering most profusely and continuously. The colour is a delicate eau-de-Nil white, which, as the flower expands, becomes a dazzling pure white. It is delicately perfumed, and will be a great acquisition	2	0
MRS. E. MAWLEY. Bright carmine, shaded salmon. Large blooms of great substance and beautiful form. A variety of marvellous beauty	1	0
MRS. FOLEY HOBBS (T). See page 128	3	6
MRS. HERBERT STEVENS (T). A hardy variety said to withstand our winters in this climate. The bloom is as long and even more pointed than that of the Maman Cochet family, faultless in shape and form, a flower of exquisite grace and refinement, unsurpassed by any in its class: colour white, with a distinct fawn and peach shading towards centre. The petals are of great depth and substance, retaining their beautiful pointed form to the last	2	0
NIPHETOS. Pale lemon, changing to white .. 1s. 6d. and	2	0
PAPA GONTIER. Rosy crimson buds, excellent to force for cutting	1	0
PERLE DES JARDINS. Straw colour	1	6
RAINBOW. A sport from "Papa Gontier." Flowers pink striped with crimson	1	6
REVE D'OR (Noisette). Deep yellow	1	6
SAFRANO. Bright apricot; beautiful	1	6
SOUVENIR DE S. A. PRINCE. The finest white	1	6
SOUVENIR DE STELLA GRAY (T). Very novel shade, orange splashed yellow and salmon; medium flowers	2	0
SUNRISE. The outer petals are of a lovely salmony-carmine shading to a delicate fawn and apricot	1	6
THE BRIDE. A pure white sport from "Catherine Mermet"	1	0
VICOMTESSE FOLKESTONE. Creamy pink	1	0
WHITE MAMAN COCHET. A white sport from the well-known "Maman Cochet." This is a fine addition	1	6

	Dwarfs—s.	d.
AMAZON. Deep lemon yellow; very useful for cutting..	1	0
ANNA OLIVIER. Flesh-coloured rose	1	0
BEAUTE INCONSTANTE (T). Coppery red, shaded with carmine and yellow	1	0
BELLE LYONNAISE. Deep canary yellow	1	0
BOUQUET D'OR (Noisette). Deep yellow, coppery centre	1	0
CATHERINE MERMET. Flesh-coloured rose	1	0
CELINE FORESTIER (Noisette). Pale yellow	1	6
CLEOPATRA. Creamy flesh shaded rose; a superb variety	1	6
COMTESSE DE NADAILLAC. Bright rose, with yellow	1	6
CORALLINA. Deep rosy crimson, large petals, very beautiful	1	6
DEVONIENSIS. White, tinted yellow, beautiful	1	6
ENCHANTRESS. Flowers large creamy white, tinted with buff in the centre; a splendid Tea Rose	1	6
FRANCISCA KRUGER. Copper yellow, shaded peach	1	6
GEORGE SCHWARTZ (T). Deep golden yellow, well formed flowers	1	6

Our own selection, in choice variety, plants mostly established in 5 in, per doz. 15s., 18s. and 21s.

DWARF POLYANTHUS ROSES.

	s.	d.
CECIL BRUNNER. Blush, shaded pale pink, small pointed buds..	0	9
JESSIE. Bright orange red, in clusters	2	0
MRS. W. CUTBUSH. Bright pink, distinct, a most valuable bedding rose	1	0

	s.	d.
LEONIE LAMESCH. Bright copper red with golden centre	0	9
PERLE D'OR. Nankeen yellow, pointed bud, best of this class	0	9
PHYLLIS. Clear soft pink flowers in large clusters	1	6
WHITE PET. Creamy white, a profuse bloomer	0	9

We have some Short Standard Polyanthus Roses, our selection, 2 to 2½ ft. stems, 1s. 0d. each, 18s. per doz.

ROSES IN POTS.

In April, May, and June, we supply the following Roses in pots for flowering under glass, or late planting in the garden, at prices as below. The pots vary in size from six to seven inches.

ALFRED COLOMB	GENERAL JACQUIMINOT	PRINCE CAMILLE DE ROHAN	CECILE BRUNNER
CAROLINE TESTOUT	HUGH DICKSON	RICHMOND	WHITE PET
CAPTAIN HAYWARD	LA FRANCE	ULRICH BRUNNER	and other varieties in 6 and
DUKE OF EDINBURGH	MRS. J. LAING	FRAU LILA RAUTENSTRAUGH	7 inch pots.
FRAU KARL DRUSCHKI	MRS. SHARMAN CRAWFORD	BLUSH CHINA	

HYBRID PERPETUAL AND HYBRID TEA.	TEA-SCENTED AND NOISETTE.	STRONG CLIMBING VARIETIES, RAMBLERS AND OTHER SORTS.
Our selection .. .. per doz. 21s. to 24s.	Our selection .. .. per doz. 21s. to 24s.	Our selection .. each 2s. 6d., 3s. 6d., and 5s.

CLIMBING, PILLAR AND WEEPING ROSES.

The following list of Climbing Roses includes the most beautiful and useful sorts in cultivation.

NOTE:—Climbing Roses priced at 2/6, 3/6 and 5/- are large plants in pots with shoots 6 to 12 feet in length; those quoted at 1/- being plants from the open ground.

AGLAIA (Yellow Rambler). Large trusses of canary-yellow flowers 1s., 2s. 6d., and **3 6**

AIMEE VIBERT (Noisette). Pure white flowers in clusters .. **1 0**

ALLISTER STELLA GRAY. Pale yellow with orange centre .. **1 0**

AMERICAN PILLAR. Very strong climbing Rose; a lovely rosy pink colour .. .. 1s., 2s. 6d., and **3 0**

BANKSIA ALBA. Pure white, in pots **1 6**

    ,,   LUTEA. Fine yellow, in pots **1 6**

BLUE RAMBLER. Steel blue, very distinct and pleasing. Strong **1 0**

BLUSH RAMBLER (Polyantha). Beautiful soft blush 1s., 2s.6d., & **3 6**

CAROLINE TESTOUT. A very strong growing, climbing sport from Caroline Testout, making strong shoots 1s., 2s. 6d., and **3 6**

CHESHUNT HYBRID. Bright cherry carmine, large open flowers; a very hardy and strong grower .. .. 1s., 2s. 6d., and **3 6**

CHRISTIAN CURLE (Wichuriana). (New). A very fine and delightful sport from "Dorothy Perkins," having the same robust habit of growth and profusion of bloom. The colour, however, is a pale flesh pink, of the colour of a "Duchess of Fife Carnation" **1 0**

CLIMBING DEVONIENSIS (T). Flowers creamy white with blush centre; deliciously scented 1s., 2s. 6d., 3s. 6d., and **5 0**

CLIMBING KAISERIN AUGUSTA VICTORIA. Cream shaded lemon, good climber .. .. 1s. and **3 6**

CLIMBING NIPHETOS. Pure white 1s. 6d., 2s. 6d., 3s. 6d., and **5 0**

CRIMSON RAMBLER. A splendid free-growing variety, with bright glossy-green foliage, and large pyramidal trusses of bright crimson flowers .. .. 1s., 2s. 6d., and **3 6**

DELIGHT (P). Climber. Bright carmine, shading to carmine at base, bright yellow stamens. Very free-flowering 1s., 2s. 6d., and **3 0**

DOROTHY PERKINS (Hybrid Wichurians). Clear soft pink flowers in large clusters, very fragrant and lasting 1s., 2s. 6d., and **3 0**

STANDARD WEEPING ROSE, DOROTHY PERKINS,
in a customer's garden, three years after planting.

EXCELSA. The Red Dorothy Perkins. This is without doubt the prince of Ramblers, it is equally as brilliant as Hiawatha 1s., 2s. 6d. and **3 6**

FLOWER OF FAIRFIELD. The perpetual flowering crimson Rambler. Very fine **1 0**

FRAU KARL DRUSCHKI. Flowers similar to the dwarf-growing variety, but a stronger grower .. .. 1s., 2s. 6d., and **3 6**

GARDENIA (W). Colour bright yellow, paler as flowers expand **1 0**

GLOIRE DE DIJON (T). Buff, with orange centre, well-known 1s., 2s. 6d., 3s. 6d., and **5 0**

GOLDFINCH. Strong growing Rambler, producing large clusters of yellow flowers .. .. .. 1s., 2s. 6d., and **3 0**

HIAWATHA (POLYANTHA). A seedling from Crimson Rambler. The flowers are single, deep crimson, shading to white at the base of the petals. The growth is very vigorous, and the very pretty flowers last a long time when cut 1s., 2s. 6d., and **3 0**

LA FRANCE. A climbing form of the well-known La France 1s., 2s. 6d., and **3 0**

LADY GAY (Wichurians). A brilliant and lovely shade of rose-pink .. .. 1s., 2s. 6d., and **3 0**

L'IDEAL (Noisette). Yellow and metallic red, streaked and tinted golden yellow .. .. 1s., 2s. 6d., 3s. 6d., and **5 0**

LONGWORTH RAMBLER. A fast growing continuous bloomer, producing wreaths of brilliant crimson flowers 1s., 2s. 6d., and **3 0**

JERSEY BEAUTY. Single flowers, pale yellow, with bright yellow stamens, produced in great profusion .. **1 0**

LADY GODIVA (Wichuriana). Soft pale flesh pink like a carnation; a sport from "Dorothy Perkins," of same habit of growth .. **1 0**

MINNEHAHA (Wichuriana). Deep rose, very double flowers produced in small panicles **1 0**

MARECHAL NIEL (Noisette). Beautiful golden yellow of the most lovely form and delicious fragrance; well-known superb variety 1s. 6d., 2s. 6d., 3s. 6d., and **5 0**

MONSIEUR DESIR. Velvety crimson, shaded with violet, large and double; a good dark climber **1 0**

MRS. F. W. FLIGHT. Pink with white centre, semi-double, and of fair size, produced in enormous trusses .. .. .. 1s., 2s. 6d., and **3 6**

MRS. W. J. GRANT. A vigorous growing free-flowering sport from Mrs. W. J. Grant. A great acquisition to the Climbers .. 1s., 2s. 6d., and **3 6**

PAUL'S CARMINE PILLAR. Bright rosy carmine single flowers, produced very freely, charming **1 0**

PERLE DES JARDINS. Colour same as the dwarf growing variety, but a good climber .. .. 1s. 6d., 2s. 6d., and **3 6**

PHILADELPHIA RAMBLER. A fuller, larger, and brighter form of Crimson Rambler, earlier, and retains its colour better **1 0**

QUEEN ALEXANDRA. Large corymbs of bloom in the way of Crimson Rambler, but paler **1 0**

REINE MARIE HENRIETTE. Bright cherry carmine, long pointed flowers; fine for cutting .. .. .. 1s., 2s. 6d., and **3 6**

STARLIGHT. White, suffused rose-violet, a single variety recommended for pillars or pergolas **2 0**

TAUSENDSCHON. Bright satin-pink flowers, two inches in diameter, produced singly and in trusses of three to five on long stems, standing well out from the plant .. .. 1s., 2s. 6d., and **3 6**

THALIA (White Rambler). A multiflora Rose, double-white flowers **3 0**

TRIER (Multiflora). Large pyramidal trusses of white flowers 1s., 2s. 6d., and **3 6**

WALTHAM BRIDE (new). Snow-white sprays or clusters, very fragrant. F.C.C. of Merit .. .. .. 1s. 6d., 2s. 6d., and **3 6**

WHITE DOROTHY PERKINS. A splendid white sport from the well-known Dorothy Perkins, the same style of flower but pure white; a great acquisition .. .. 1s. 6d. and **3 6**

WILLIAM ALLEN RICHARDSON (Noisette). Fine deep orange yellow, very showy .. .. 1s. 6d., 2s. 6d., 3s. 6d., and **5 0**

STANDARD WEEPING ROSES.

The varieties named below can be supplied on tall Standards. These are the very best and most suitable varieties for this purpose. All who have seen these charming subjects will at once acclaim their worth.

AMERICAN PILLAR	GARDENIA	MINNEHAHA
BLUSH RAMBLER	GOLDFINCH	MRS. F. W. FLIGHT
CRIMSON RAMBLER	HIAWATHA	TAUSENDSCHON
DELIGHT	LADY GAY	TRIER
EXCELSA. 5s. each.	LONGWORTH RAMBLER	WH. DOROTHY PERKINS

4 to 5 feet stems, 3s. 6d. each.   5 to 6 feet stems, 5s. 6d. each.

A few sorts can be supplied on 8 to 10 foot stems. Prices and varieties on application.

Wire Frames for Weeping Roses, 2 feet in diameter, 3s. 6d. each.

CLEMATISES.

These magnificent hardy climbers are highly popular amongst amateur growers, and, considering their great beauty, freedom of blooming, and the facility with which they may be trained on any kind of wall, trellis, verandah, or pillar, and in almost any aspect, it is surprising that Clematises are not found in abundance in every garden. The plants we offer are established in pots, and can be removed at any time of the year. The sorts blooming after June are the best for bedding purposes; they flower on the young wood, and therefore require, before growth commences in Spring, to be cut down to within six or twelve inches of the ground, as likewise do all the late-flowering kinds; and early sorts, flowering from May to July on the old wood, should be pruned similarly to Roses. When the selection of sorts is left to ourselves customers may rely on our sending a really good variety.

A richly manured soil is indispensable if the best result is aimed at. Manure ought to be well mixed with the soil when planting, and used annually as a mulch for Winter protection, forking it in very lightly in the Spring. The addition of chalk or lime to the soil when planting is also beneficial.

CLEMATISES. *From a Photograph. One-third in size.*

	Months of each. Flowering s. d.	
ALBA MAGNA. Large white broad sepalled flowers, sometimes very faintly tinted lavender ..	—	1 6
BEAUTY OF WORCESTER. Large and handsome, producing double and single flowers on same plant, lovely bluish violet	Ju Oc	2 0
BELLE OF WOKING. Silvery grey, double ..	Ju	1 6
BLUE GEM. Pale cærulean blue	Jy Oc	1 6
COCCINEA. Very elegant bell-shaped flowers, cream inside and crimson outside	—	1 6

	Months of each. Flowering s. d.	
COUNTESS OF LOVELACE. Bluish lilac, double ..	Ju Jy	1 6
DUKE OF EDINBURGH. Rich violet purple	My Jy	1 6
DUCHESS OF EDINBURGH. The best of all the double whites, deliciously scented	Ju Jy	1 6
EARL OF BEACONSFIELD. Rich royal purple ..	Jy Oc	1 6
FAIRY QUEEN. Pale flesh, pink bar	Jy Oc	1 6
FLAMMULA. Sweet scented, white	—	1 0
GIPSY QUEEN. Dark velvety purple.. ..	Jy Oc	1 6
HENRYI. Beautiful large creamy white ..	Jy Oc	1 6
JACKMANII. Intense violet purple	Jy Oc	1 6
JACKMANII, RED. A fine new red variety of true Jackmanii type	Jy Oc	1 6
JACKMANII SUPERBA. Similar to "Jackmanii," but the colour more intense	Jy Oc	1 6
KING EDWARD VII. (new). Beautiful pucy violet with crimson bar down the centre of each petal, large flowers..	Jy Oc	2 0
LA FRANCE. Deep violet purple, dark anthers ..	Jy Oc	1 6
LA LORRAINE. Colour, a soft clear rose tinted with blush. A great acquisition	Jy Oc	1 6
LADY NORTHCLIFF (new). Beautiful deep lavender, tinted bright blue, with purple bars and white stamens	Jy Oc	2 0
LORD NEVILLE. Very bright heliotrope blue, with white filaments and chocolate anthers	—	1 6
LANUGINOSA. Pale lavender	Jy Oc	1 6
LUCIE LEMOINE. Double, white	Ju Jy	1 6
MADAME EDOUARD ANDRE. Beautiful bright velvety red; very distinct and free-flowering ..	Jy Oc	1 6
MISS BATEMAN. White, red anthers	My Jy	1 6
MRS. CHOLMONDELEY. Lavender	My Ju	1 6
MRS. HOPE. Satiny mauve	Ju Au	1 6
MRS. GEO. JACKMAN. Satiny white, beautiful ..	Ju Oc	1 6
MRS. QUILTER. Pure white, very fine ..	Jy Oc	1 6
NELLY MOSER. Light mauve, with bright red bars ..	Jy Oc	1 6
PAPA CHRISTEN. Large flowers, colour, a delicate mauve with broad band of deep carmine down the centre of each petal	Jy Oc	1 6
PRESIDENT. Purple, suffused with claret, good ..	Jy Oc	1 6
PRINCESS OF WALES. Deep bluish mauve ..	Jy Oc	1 6
PURPUREA ELEGANS. Deep violet purple ..	Jy Oc	1 6
QUEEN ALEXANDRA. Beautiful pale lavender lilac, purple base, silvery white down centre of each sepal. Very pretty	Jy Oc	1 6
SENSATION. Rich satin mauve of large size ..	—	1 6
SNOW WHITE JACKMANII. The flowers are pure white, about the same size as those of the old purple Jackmanii but produced in greater profusion. Superb variety ..	—	1 6
VENUS VICTRIX. A fine double-flowered variety, delicate lavender blue, beautiful form	Jy Oc	1 6
VILLE DE LYON. Bright carmine, red ..	Jy Oc	1 6
VILLE DE PARIS. Pale flesh, pink bar, of great merit..	Jy Oc	1 6
WILLIAM KENNETT. Deep lavender, fine ..	Jy	1 6

Choice named varieties from the above list, our own selection, per doz. 12s. and 15s.

Clematis montana Rubens.

A very charming new variety, very hardy. The flowers, which are produced in great abundance, are of a soft bright rosy lilac with white.

Each 2s. 6d.

Clematis montana grandiflora.

A beautiful early free-flowering variety, blooming in May and June, and producing a profusion of large, pure white starry flowers. Splendid for covering trellises, porches, &c.   Each 1s. 6d.

CLEMATIS MONTANA .. .. .. Each 1s.

HARDY CLIMBING & OTHER PLANTS.

SUITABLE FOR TRAINING ON WALLS, &c.

These are mostly grown in pots, and can be supplied and planted at any time of the year with perfect safety.

ea h—s. d.

AKEBIA QUINNATA. Purplish brown flowers 1 6
AMPELOPSIS (Virginian Creepers). Well-known beautiful climbers, the leaves changing to a deep crimson in Autumn.
   ,, **HENRYANA** A strikingly handsome variety, each leaflet is marked by a silvery band which greatly adds to the effectiveness of the plant .. 1 6
   ,, **LOWII** (new). A beautiful new Ampelopsis with small Palmata leaves and a delightful graceful habit. The foliage going red as Autumn advances. 1 6
   ,, **VEITCHII.** Small-leaved, very beautiful variety. Clings to walls with great tenacity .. 1s. and 1 6
   ,, **PURPUREA.** A beautiful dark-leaved variety .. 1 6
   ,, **Hederacea.** Common Virginian Creeper 1 0
   ,, **Sempervirens.** Evergreen 1 6
ARISTOLOCHIA SIPHO. Deciduous .. 1 6
AZARA MICROPHYLLA. Beautiful plant for walls .. 1 6
BIGNONIA RADICANS (Trumpet Flower) .. 1 6
BUDDLEIA GLOBOSA. Orange globose flowers 1 6
CEANOTHUS, GLOIRE DE VERSAILLES. Large panicles of sky blue flowers, fine 2 0
   ,, **Azureus.** Pale blue .. 2 0
   ,, **Divaricatus.** Very pale blue .. 1 6
   ,, **VEITCHII** blue, very fine. In pots 1 6
CHIMONANTHUS FRAGRANS. Very sweet-scented .. 1 6
COTONEASTER MICROPHYLLA. Very handsome with scarlet berries in Autumn .. 1 6
CRATÆGUS LÆLANDII. Red-berried and splendidly effective in the Autumn and Winter .. 1s. 6d. and 2 6
ERCILLA SPICATA (Bridgesia) 1s. 6d. and 2 6
ESCALLONIA MACRANTHA. Evergreen, with bright rosy crimson flowers, very pretty .. 1s. 6d. and 2 6
EMBOTHRIUM COCCINEUM (The Fire Tree.) One of the most beautiful flowering shrubs ever introduced. The flowers are brilliant crimson, and are borne in great profusion. Quick grower.. 5 0
GARRYA ELLIPTICA. A beautiful plant for the wall .. 1s. 6d. and 2 6
IVY (Hedera)—Cavendishii. Silver-margined 1 6
   ,, **Clouded Gold.** Fine .. 1 6
   ,, **Crippsi.** One of the most beautiful silvery-leaved Ivies .. 1 6
   ,, **CHRYSOPHYLLA.** Medium sized leaf, bright sulphur yellow, not affected by smoke .. 1 6
   ,, **Palmata.** Handsome variety .. 1 0
   ,, **PURPUREA.** Hardy and smoke resisting. Leaves purplish bronze 1 0
   ,, **DENTATA.** Very large dark-green foliage, strong growing variety .. 1 0
   ,,   ,, **VARIEGATA** (new). The finest and most striking golden variegated Ivy in commerce .. 2 6
   ,, **Emerald Green.** Beautiful glossy bright leaves; very distinct .. 1 0
   ,, **MADEIRENSIS VARIEGATA.** Fine robust-growing variety, beautiful silver edged foliage .. 1s. 6d. and 2 6
   ,, **IRISH.** A fine quick-growing variety, very useful for covering large trellises, walls, &c.
Strong plants from open ground per 100 21s.; per doz. 3s. 0d.
Fine plants in pots, 4 to 6 ft. doz. 10s. 6d. 1 0

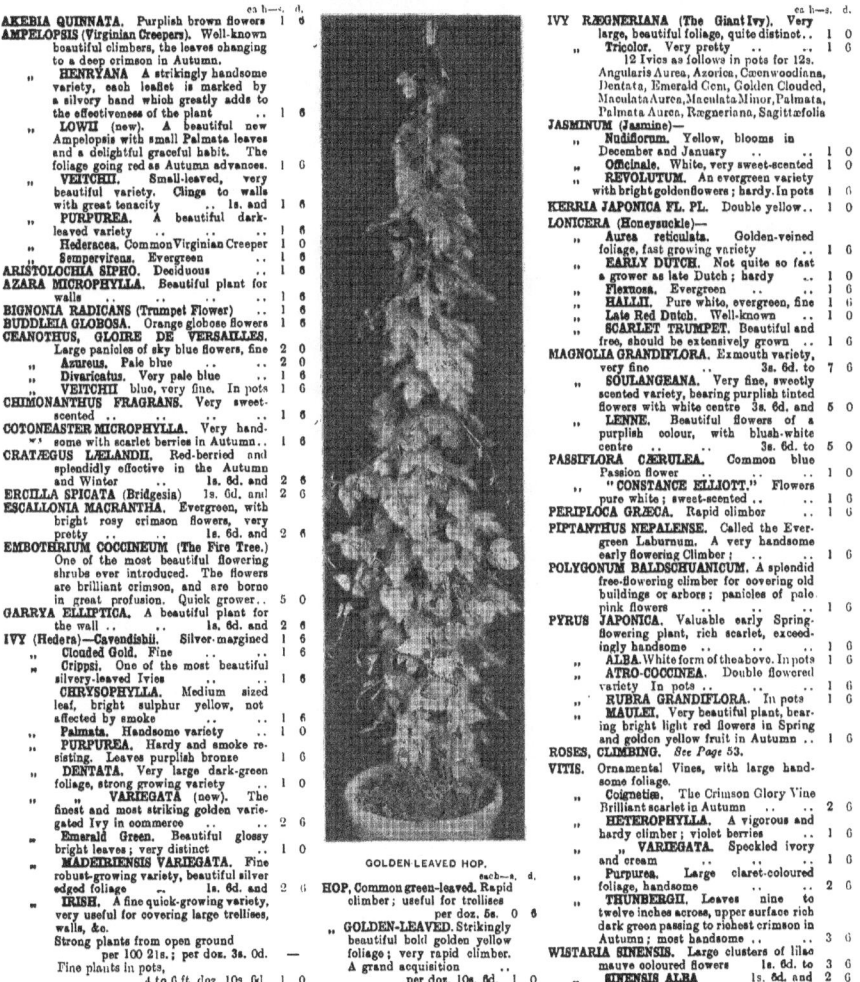

GOLDEN-LEAVED HOP.

each—s. d.
HOP, Common green-leaved. Rapid climber; useful for trellises per doz. 5s. 0 6
   ,, **GOLDEN-LEAVED.** Strikingly beautiful bold golden yellow foliage; very rapid climber. A grand acquisition .. per doz. 10s. 6d. 1 0

ea h—s. d.

IVY RÆGNERIANA (The Giant Ivy). Very large, beautiful foliage, quite distinct.. 1 0
   ,, **Tricolor.** Very pretty .. 1 6
12 Ivies as follows in pots for 12s.
Angularis Aurea, Azorica, Cæenwoodiana, Dentata, Emerald Gem, Golden Clouded, Maculata Aurea, Maculata Minor, Palmata, Palmata Aurea, Rægneriana, Sagittæfolia
JASMINUM (Jasmine)—
   ,, **Nudiflorum.** Yellow, blooms in December and January .. 1 0
   ,, **Officinale.** White, very sweet-scented 1 0
   ,, **REVOLUTUM.** An evergreen variety with bright golden flowers; hardy. In pots 1 0
KERRIA JAPONICA FL. PL. Double yellow.. 1 0
LONICERA (Honeysuckle)—
   ,, **Aurea reticulata.** Golden-veined foliage, fast growing variety .. 1 6
   ,, **EARLY DUTCH.** Not quite so fast a grower as late Dutch; hardy .. 1 0
   ,, **Flexuosa.** Evergreen .. 1 6
   ,, **HALLII.** Pure white, evergreen, fine 1 6
   ,, **Late Red Dutch.** Well-known .. 1 0
   ,, **SCARLET TRUMPET.** Beautiful and free, should be extensively grown .. 1 6
MAGNOLIA GRANDIFLORA. Exmouth variety, very fine .. 3s. 6d. to 7 6
   ,, **SOULANGEANA.** Very fine, sweetly scented variety, bearing purplish tinted flowers with white centre 3s. 6d. and 5 0
   ,, **LENNE.** Beautiful flowers of a purplish colour, with blush-white centre .. 3s. 6d. to 5 0
PASSIFLORA CÆRULEA. Common blue Passion flower .. 1 0
   ,, **"CONSTANCE ELLIOTT."** Flowers pure white; sweet-scented .. 1 6
PERIPLOCA GRÆCA. Rapid climber .. 1 0
PIPTANTHUS NEPALENSE. Called the Ever-green Laburnum. A very handsome early flowering Climber; .. 1 6
POLYGONUM BALDSCHUANICUM. A splendid free-flowering climber for covering old buildings or arbors; panicles of pale pink flowers .. 1 6
PYRUS JAPONICA. Valuable early Spring-flowering plant, rich scarlet, exceedingly handsome .. 1 0
   ,, **ALBA.** White form of the above. In pots 1 6
   ,, **ATRO-COCCINEA.** Double flowered variety In pots .. 1 6
   ,, **RUBRA GRANDIFLORA.** In pots .. 1 6
   ,, **MAULEI.** Very beautiful plant, bearing bright light red flowers in Spring and golden yellow fruit in Autumn .. 1 6
ROSES, CLIMBING. *See Page 53.*
VITIS. Ornamental Vines, with large handsome foliage.
   ,, **Coignetiæ.** The Crimson Glory Vine Brilliant scarlet in Autumn .. 2 6
   ,, **HETEROPHYLLA.** A vigorous and hardy climber; violet berries .. 1 6
   ,,   ,, **VARIEGATA.** Speckled ivory and cream .. 1 6
   ,, **Purpurea.** Large claret-coloured foliage, handsome .. 2 6
   ,, **THUNBERGII.** Leaves nine to twelve inches across, upper surface rich dark green passing to richest crimson in Autumn; most handsome .. 3 6
WISTARIA SINENSIS. Large clusters of lilac mauve coloured flowers 1s. 6d. to 3 6
   ,, **SINENSIS ALBA** 1s. 6d. and 2 6

Choice Hardy Climbers, our own selection, including Roses and Clematises, per doz. 12s. 6d. and 15s. ; per 100, 80s. and 100s.

HARDY ORNAMENTAL TREES AND SHRUBS.

This class includes the loveliest and most charming trees for the garden, pleasure grounds, shrubberies and park. Many of them are remarkable for their graceful form and flowers, and for the highly ornamental effect produced by their delightful tints. We take great pains to ensure the trees being of the best possible quality. Careful attention is also given to pruning and staking, and our stock is regularly transplanted to ensure their safe removal. There is scarcely any spot, even under the greatest natural disadvantages, which cannot be made to look bright by the judicious planting of Ornamental Trees.

SPECIMEN ROW OF MOP-HEADED ACACIA GROWING IN OUR NURSERIES.

ACACIA (Robinia).
" **HISPIDIA** (Rose Acacia). Dwarfs, height 3—4 ft. 1/6 each. Standards, 3/6 each.
" **INERMIS** (Mop-headed Acacia). Standards, 3/6 each.
ACER (Maple). **NEGUNDO CALIFORNICUM AUREUM.** This is a specially good variety, with large, broad golden foliage. Standards, with 3—4 ft. stem, 2/- each, 21/- per doz.
ÆSCULUS. See *Horse Chestnuts.*
ALMOND. Purple-Leaved. Dwarfs, 1/- each, Standards, 2/- each.
" **Common.** Dwarfs, 9d. each, Standards, 1/6 each.
ALTHÆAS. In choice variety, 1/6 each.
ANDROMEDA FLORIBUNDA. Dwarf-compact growing shrub, pure white bell-shaped flowers. Height 9—12 in. 1/6 each, 12—18 in. 2/- each.
ASH (*Fraxinus*). **ELCELSIOR PENDULA** (Weeping). This is a splendid weeping tree. Standards, 5/- and 7/6 each.
" **MARGINATA PENDULA.** Gold leaved, Weeping, 3/6 each.
AUCUBA JAPONICA VARIEGATA. 1½—2 ft. 10/6 per doz, 70/- per 100. Larger specimens 1/6 and 2/6 each.
BAY (Sweet) (*Laurus Nobilis*). 1½—2 ft, 1/6 each; 2—3 ft., 2/- each. We also have a supply of strong plants in Tubs, grown as Pyramids and Standards from 10/6 each.
BEECH (*Fagus*) **ATROPUREA.** Height 7—8 ft. 2/6 each, 10—12 ft. 3/6, 5/- each.
" **FERN LEAVED.** 2/- and 3/6 each.
" **PURPUREA PENDULA.** Purple leaved, Weeping, 5/- and 7/6 each.
BERBERIS STENOPHYLLA. One of the best very graceful, small evergreen leaf, and covered with bright yellow flowers. Height 1—1½ ft. 5/- per doz., 2—3 ft. 7/6 per doz.

BERBERIS THUNBERGII. Pretty early blooming species. White flowers; leaves in Autumn are tinted crimson. Height 1—1½ ft. 6/- per doz., 2—2½ ft. 8/- per doz.
" **VULGARIS** (Common Barberry). All are very hardy shrubs with pretty foliage. Height 2—3 ft., 8/- per doz.
BIRCH (Betula). See also page 140.
" **PENDULA** (Weeping Birch). Standards, 2/- each.
" **YOUNGII.** Beautiful fern-leaved form, very distinct. Height 7—8 ft. Standards, 3/6 each.
BOX (*Buxus*). **HANDSWORTHII.** This is the best of the green varieties of Box, close growing and of erect habit. Height 12—18 in. 6/- per doz. 40/- per 100, 18—24 in. 7/- per doz. 45/- per 100, 2—3 ft. 15/- per doz. 80/- per 100. Larger Specimens, 1/6 and 2/- each.
BOX EDGING. One Nursery yard plants 3 yards. 6d. per Nursery yard.
BROOM (Cytisus).
" **ANDREANUS.** Most distinct and beautiful, maroon-crimson and yellow flowers. In pots, 1/- and 1/6 each, Dwarf Standards, 3/6 each.
" **PRÆCOX.** Free flowering early. In pots, 1/6 each, Dwarf Standard Variety, 2/6 and 3/6 each.
" **WHITE PORTUGAL.** Free flowering, most effective. 6d. each, 5/- per doz.
" **COMMON YELLOW.** 6d. each, 4/- per doz.
BUDDLEIA GLOBOSA. Orange globose flowers. 1/6 each.
" **VARIABILIS MAGNIFICA.** A deep shade of rosy purple, 2/- each.
" **VARIABILIS VEITCHI.** In pots, 1/6 each.

CALYCANTHUS (Allspice). Maroon coloured flowers, very fragrant. Height 2 ft. 1/- each.
Height 12—18 in. 9d. each.
CARYOPTERIS MASTACANTHUS (Blue Spiræa). Height 12—18 in. 9d. each.
CATALPA AUREA. Very handsome, Golden foliage. Height 4 ft. 2/6 each.
CHERRY (Cerasus).
" **RHEXII FLORE PLENA.** Double white cherry. Dwarf Bush 1/- each, Standards 2/- each.
" **ROSEA PLENA,** Double Rose. Beautiful rose, 2/6 and 3/6 each.
" **JAMES H. VEITCH.** The finest variety yet introduced. Height 4—5 ft. 1/3 each, Standards 2/6 each.
" **SINENSIS ROSEA** (Weeping). Beautiful weeping tree of graceful habit. Standards 2/6 each.
CERCIS SILIQUASTRUM (Judas Tree). Flowers early in Spring. Height 2—3 ft. 9d. each.
CHOISYA TERNATA. Lovely white, sweet-scented. In pots 1/6 each.
CISTUS LADANIFERUS (The Gum Cistus). A handsome shrub. In pots 1/- each.
CORNUS AUREA TRICOLOR. Most beautiful variegated trees. Dwarfs 1/6 each.
" **SPATHII AUREA.** Dwarfs 1/- each.
COTONEASTER, HORIZONTALIS. Fan shaped for rockeries. In pots, 1/6 each. Open ground, 9d. each.
" **MICROPHYLLA.** Fine for rockeries or walls, one of the best. Height 12—18 in. 9/- per doz.
" **SIMONSII.** Tall growing scarlet berries. Height 2—3 ft. 6/- per doz.
CRATÆGUS. See *Thorns.*
CYDONIA (Pyrus). **JAPONICA.** Japanese Quince, bright scarlet, splendid for walls, 1/- and 1/6 each.
" " **ALBA.** White form of the above. In pots 1/6 each.

STANDARD SWEET BAY.

Hardy Ornamental Trees and Shrubs (continued).

WEEPING ELM. True Camperdown variety.

DAPHNE CNEORUM (The Garland Flower). Very sweet evergreen, trailing. 1/6 each.
„ **MEZEREUM.** Of fragrant purple flowers, early. 1/- and 1/6 each.
„ „ **ALBUM.** Pure white, fragrant. 1/- and 1/6 each.

DEUTZIA, CRENATA. Single white, June and July. 6d. each, 5/- per doz.
„ „ **FL. PL.** Double rose-coloured flowers. 6d. each, 5/- per doz.
„ **GRACILIS.** Pure white. 6d. each, 4/- per doz.
„ **LEMOINEI.** Beautiful white variety. 6d. each, 5/- per doz.

ELÆAGNUS PUNGENS AUREA PICTA. In pots, 2/- each.

ELDER (Sambucus).
„ **SERRATIFOLIA FOLIUS AUREUS.** Magnificent fern-like leaf, bright golden in colour. Height 2 ft. 1/- each. Other varieties. See page 141.

ELM, ENGLISH. (Ulmus Campestris.) Height 6—7 ft. 9d. each 7/6 per doz., 7—8 ft. 1/- each 10/6 per doz.
„ „ **WEEPING.** The true Umbrella Elm. 5/- and 7/6 each.
„ „ **DAMPIERI AUREA.** This is a splendid Golden Elm in habit and growth and colour. Height 5—6 ft. 2/6 each.
„ „ **LOUIS VAN HOUTTE.** Golden. Height 5—6 ft. 1/6 each.
„ **WHEATLEYII.** Height 6—8 ft. 1/6 each 16/- per doz.
„ **GLABRA** (Cornish or Guernsey). Height 6—8 ft. 1/6 each 16/- per doz.
„ **HUNTINGDON or CHICHESTER.** Height 6—8 ft. 1/6 each 15/- per doz.

ERICA CARNEA (Heath), Red and white. 7/6 per doz. See also page 137.

EUONYMUS EUROPÆUS (Spindle Tree). Very pretty in Autumn. Height 4—5 ft. 9/- per doz.
„ **JAPONICUS.** Green-leafed varietyi 6/- doz. Various gold and silver variegated varieties. 9/- per doz.
„ „ **RADICANS.** 4/- per doz.
„ „ **VARIEGATUS.** Hardy dwarf variety, for edgings. per doz. 5/-

FAGUS. See Beech.

FORSYTHIA SUSPENSA. Suitable for wall or rockwork. 9d. each.
„ **FORTUNEI.** 9d. each.

FORSYTHIA VIRIDISSIMA. 9d each.

FRAXINUS. See Ash.

GORSE (Ulex) **EUROPÆUS.** Double, in pots, 1/- each 10/6 per doz.

HAZEL, Purple Leaved. Fine broad leaved variety. 1/- each 10/6 per doz. See also p. 141.

HEATH (See Erica).

HOLLY (Ilex) **ARGENTEA MARGINATA.** Broad-leaved, silver, free grower and hardy. Height 2—2½ ft. 2/6 each, 2½—3 ft. 3/6 each.
„ „ „ **REGINA (Silver Queen).** Height 2½—3 ft. 3/6 each.
„ „ **AUREA PENDULA.** Waterer's Gold Weeping. 7/6 and 10/6 each.
„ „ **GOLDEN QUEEN.** Height 2½—3 ft. 3/6 each, 3—4 ft. 5/- each.
„ „ **FEROX FRUCTO LUTEA.** Golden-fruited Holly. Height 2 ft. 3/6 each.

HORSE CHESTNUT (Æsculus).
„ **SCARLET.** Splendid subject for avenues, or for planting as park specimens. Height 4—5 ft. 1/6 each. Specimen Standards 2/6 each.
„ **BRIOTII.** Bright red. Early-blooming variety of the well-known scarlet chestnut. Height 7—8 ft. 2/6 each.
„ **DOUBLE WHITE.** Height 7—8 ft. 2/6 each. For Common Chestnuts. See page 140.

HYDRANGEA. In pots.
„ **PANICULATA GRANDIFLORA.** Quite hardy, producing drooping panicles of white flowers. Height 2—3 ft. 9d. each 7/6 per doz.

GREEN HOLLY. See page 136.

HYPERICUM (St. John's Wort).
„ **MOSERIANUM.** Handsome evergreen shrub. 5/- per doz.
„ „ **TRICOLOR,** in pots. Height 12—15 in. 1/3 each 12/- per doz.

ILEX. See Holly.

KALMIA GLAUCA. Very free flowering lilac flowers. Height 1½—2 ft. 2/- each.
„ **LATIFOLIA.** Rose coloured flowers. Height 1½—2 ft. 2/- each.

KERRIA JAPONICA. Yellow shrub, free-flowering. 9d. each.
„ „ **FLORA PLENA.** A double variety of above. 1/- each.

LABURNUM ADAMI (Purple). Height 6—8 ft. 2/- each.
„ **ALPINUM (Scotch).** Standards. 2/- each.
„ **VOSSI.** Distinct yellow flowers, the best of this class. Standards, 2/6 each.

LAUREL, CAUCASICA. Rich green foliage, very compact habit. Height 1½—2 ft. 4/- per doz. 25/- per 100, 2—3 ft. 6/- per doz. 40/- per 100.
„ **LAUREL, COLCHICA.** This is one of the best varieties for seaside. 1—1½ ft. 4/- per doz. 25/- per 100, 1½—2 ft. 5/- per doz. 30/- per 100.
„ **LATIFOLIA.** Fine broad-leaved variety. Height 1½—2 ft. 4/- per doz. 25/- per 100, 2—3 ft. 6/- per doz. 40/- per 100.
„ **ROTUNDIFOLIA.** Height 1½—2 ft. 4/- per doz. 30/- per 100, 2—2½ ft. 6/- per doz. 40/- per 100, 4—5 ft. 1/6 each.
„ **PORTUGAL (Lusitanica).** Height 2—2½ ft. 1/6 each 15/- per doz., 3—4 ft. 2/6 each Standard Laurels, with nice clear stems and good heads. 3/6 and 5/- each.

LAURUSTINUS. Height 2—3 ft. 1/6 each.

LAURUS NOBILIS. See Bay (Sweet)

LAVENDER, COMMON (Lavendula). 4/- per doz. 30/- per 100.
„ **NANA (Dwarf Lavender).** 4/- per doz. 30/- per 100.

LEYCESTERIA FORMOSA. Beautiful Spring flowering Shrub with a profusion of golden-yellow blooms, very handsome. Height 2—3 ft. 9d. each 7/6 per doz.

LILAC ALBA. The common single white lilac. Height 3—4 ft. 1/- each 10/6 per doz.
„ **CHARLES X.** Single deep purplish Lilac. 1/3 each 12/- per doz.
„ **LEMOINEI.** Double rose, changing to bluish lilac, with white centre. Height 2—3 ft. 1/6 each.
„ **MADAME CASIMIR PERIER.** Double creamy white, extra good flower. Height 2—3 ft. 1/6 each.
„ **MADAME LEMOINE.** Double, compact, spike of the purest white. Height 2—3 ft. 1/6 each.
„ **MARIE LEGRAYE.** Height 2—3 ft. 1/6 each, 3—4 ft. 2/- each.
„ **PRESIDENT GREVY.** Double blue, shaded rose, large. Height 2—3 ft. 1/6 each.
„ **VULGARIS.** The common single purple lilac. Height 2—3 ft. 1/- each, 3—4 ft. 1/6 each.
„ **SOUVENIR DE LOUIS SPATH.** Height 2—4 ft. 2/6 each.

LIMES. Red Twigged from Layers. Standards, 1/-, 1/6, 2/6 each. Smaller sizes. See page 140.

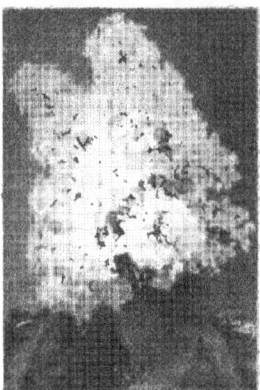

LILAC, MARIE LEGRAYE.

Hardy Ornamental Trees and Shrubs *(continued).*

LIQUIDAMBAR STYRACIFLUA (Sweet Gum).
Leaves very fragrant and thrives well on
damp situations. Height 3—4 ft. 1/6 each.

MAGNOLIA GRANDIFLORA. Large white
flowers and very fragrant, requires a south aspect. In pots, height 2—3 ft. 3/6 and 5/- each.

" **LENNE.** Beautiful flowers of a purplish
colour with white blush centre. In pots,
height 2—3 ft. 2/6 and 3/6 each.

" **SOULANGEANA.** Very fine sweetly scented
variety, purplish tinted flowers. In pots,
height 2—3 ft. 3/6 each.

MAPLES, JAPANESE (Acer). In pots.

" **ACER JAPONICA AUREA.**
" " **PURPUREA.**
" **PALMATA.**
" " **ATRO-PURPUREA.**
" " **DISSECTUM.**
" " " **RUBRUM.**
" " **ROSEA MARGINATA.**
" " **SANGUINEUM.**
" " **SEPTEMLOBEN.**

Extremely handsome, may be grown in
pots for conservatory, or planted out of
doors ; colours ranging from yellow to rich
dark crimson and purple, broadly palmate
and delicately cut leaves. Purchaser's
selection, 2/6 and 3/6 each. Our selection,
2/- each 21/- per doz. All in pots.

GOLDEN LEAVED PRIVET.

MAPLES, NORWAY.

" " **FOLIUS ARGENTEUS.** Silver. Leaf
beautifully variegated, a most effective tree.
Pyramids, 3—4 ft. 1/6 each, 15/- per doz.,
Standards, 2/- each, 21/- per doz.

" **PLATANOIDES.** This is also a beautiful
form, very effective. Standards, 1/6 each.

MOCK ORANGE (Philadelphus).

" **CORONARIUS.** Useful for shrubberies;
flowers freely Height 2—4 ft. 7/6 and
10/6 per doz.

" **GRANDIFLORUS.** Very large-flowered
variety. Height 2—4 ft. 7/6 and 10/6 per doz.

" **LEMOINEI.** Height 2—4 ft. 7/6 and 10/6
per doz.

" " **BOULE D'ARGENT.** Dwarf habit,
flowers very large. Height 2—4 ft. 7/6 and
10/6 per doz.

" " **GERBE DE NEIGE.** Large white
flowers, sweet. Height 2—4 ft. 7/6 and
10/6 per doz.

OAK (Quercus). **COCCINEA** (Scarlet Oak).
The Scarlet Oak is one of the finest of our
ornamental trees. 6—8 ft. 1/6 each 15/- doz.

" **CONCORDIA** (Golden Oak). Fine trees.
Height 5—6 ft. 2/6 each.

" **ILEX** (Holm, or Evergreen Oak). Grown
specially in pots. Height 1—1¼ ft. 1/- each
10/6 per doz., 3—4 ft. 3/6 each.

OLEARIA HAASTII. Height 12—18 in. 1/-
each 10/6 per doz.

" **GUNNIANA.** Numerous heads of white
flowers in great profusion. In pots, 1/6
and 2/- each.

OSMANTHUS ILICIFOLIUS. Height 1½—2
ft. 1/6 each 15/- per doz.

PLANE, LONDON (Platanus Acerifolia).
7—8 ft. 2/- each, 8—10 ft. 2/6 each. Larger
specimens, extra good heads, 3/6 & 5/- each.

PRIVET (Ligustrum).

" **JAPONICUM.** Large, broad, shining green
foliage. 1/6 each.

" **OVALIFOLIUM FOLIUS AUREUS** (Golden-
Leaved Privet). A most showy hardy
plant, foliage broadly margined with bright
gold ; useful alike for hedges, or for planting
singly in borders. Height 1½—2 ft. 1/- each
7/6 per doz., 2—3 ft. 1/6 each 12/- per doz.
Selected Standards, 1/6 and 2/6 each. Selected Half-stds., 1/6 each. *See also page* 130.

PRUNUS PISSARDII (Purple Leaf Plum). A
handsome foliage tree with white flowers,
quite hardy. Standards, 3—4 ft. stems and
good heads, 1/6 and 2/- each. Pyds. 3—5
ft. 1/3 each 12/- per doz.

" **TRILOBA.** Double pink, useful for forcing.
Bush, 2—3 ft. 1/6 each. Stds., 2/6 each.,

PYRUS (Apple).

" **FLORIBUNDA.** Dwarfs, 4—5 ft. 1/6 each
15/- per doz., Stds., 6—7 ft. 2/- each 21/- doz.

" **MALUS.** Dartmouth Crab. Very fine.
Standards, 1/6 each.

" " **JOHN DOWNIE.** A beautiful variety.
Standards, 1/6 each

QUERCUS. *See Oak.*

RIBES AUREUM SANGUINEUM (Flowering
Currant). 2—3 ft. 6d. each 5/- per doz.

RIBES FLORA PLENA. Flowers double red.
Height 2—3 ft. 9d. each 7/6 per doz.
Standards, height 3—4 ft. stems 2/- each.

KINIIIA JAPONICA. Female variety. Height
12—15 in. 1/6 each.

NOWDROP TREE (Halesia Tetraptera).
Height 1½—2 ft. 1/- each.

NOWY MESPILUS (Amelanchier).

" **CANADENSIS.** Standards 1/6 and 2/- each.

PIREA AUREA. The golden-leaved variety.
6d. each 5/- per doz.

" **ARGUTA.** 9d. each 7/6 per doz.

" **CALLOSA.** Free flowering, red flowers.
6d. each 5/- per doz.

" " **ALBA.** 9d. each 5/- per doz.

" **CONFUSA.** 9d. each 7/6 per doz.

" **DOUGLASII.** Rose-coloured flowers, free-
flowering. 6d. each 5/- per doz.

" **ANTHONY WATERER.** Dwarf-growing.
Crimson flowers 9d. each 7/6 per doz.

STAPHYLEA COLCHICA. Pretty creamy white
flowers. 9d. each 7/6 per doz.

SUMACH, VENETIAN (Rhus Cotinus). Lovely
foliage which deepens in Autumn. Height
2 ft. 9d. each 7/6 per doz.

" **ATROPURPUREA.** Very ornamental with
purple flowers. 2 ft. 9d. each 7/6 per doz.

" **GLABRA LACINIATA.** Pretty fern-like
foliage. 1½—2 ft. 1/- each 10/6 per doz.

SYCAMORE (Acer).

" **ALBA VARIEGATA.** These are very beautiful trees. Height 4—5 ft. 1/- each, 5—6 ft.
1/6 each, 6—8 ft. 2/- each ; Larger specimens
3/6 and 5/- each.

" **LEOPOLDII.** Beautiful purple, flesh
coloured. Standards, 7—8 ft. 2/6 each.

THORNS (Cratægus).

" **OXYACANTHA PLENA.** Handsome free-
flowering trees. Double Crimson, Paul's.
Pyramids, 1/3 each. Standards, 1/6 each
2/- each.

" **Single** Scarlet, Pyramids, 1/6 each.
Standards, 1/6 and 2/- each.

" **Double White** (Paul's), Standards, 2/- each.

TULIP-TREE (Liriodendron Tulipitera).
A deciduous tree allied to the Magnolia.
Standards. Height 6—8 ft. 2/- each.

VERONICA TRAVERSII. 9d. each 5/- per doz.

VIBURNUM OPULUS (Guelder Rose). Height
2—3 ft. 9d. each 7/6 per doz.

" " **STERILE** (Snowball Tree). Beautiful
flowering Shrub with large globular white
flowers. Height 2—3 ft. 9d. each 7/6 per doz.

" **PLICATUM.** One of the best. Height 2—3
ft. 1/6 each 15/- per doz.

VINCA (Periwinkle). **MAJOR.** Blue, 5/- per doz.

" **ELEGANTISSIMA.** With beautiful
variegated foliage. 7/6 per doz.

VIBURNUM PLICATUM.

WEIGELIA. A very handsome and desirable
class of beautiful flowering Shrubs, blooming
in June ; highly recommended.

" **AMABILIS.** Bright pink. 9d. each 7/6 per doz.

" **ABEL CARRIERE.** Rosy carmine, very
free. 9d. each 7/6 per doz.

" **ALBA.** Pure white, 9d. each 7/6 per doz.

" **EVA RATHKE.** A very beautiful variety,
flowers dark red and carried in great quantities. 1/- each 10/6 per doz.

" **LOOYMANSII AUREA.** A splendid form
with golden foliage and rose coloured flowers.
1s. 6d. each.

" **ROSEA.** Rose coloured, 9d. each 7/6 per doz.

WISTERIA. *See page* 133.

WILLOW (Salix). *See also page* 141.

" **ALBA** (White Willow). 6—8 ft. 9d. each.

" " **CŒRULEA** (Bat Willow) *See page* 141.

" **BABYLONICA** (Weeping Willow). Standards. Height 6—8 ft. 1/- each.

" **NIGRA.** Black barked. Height 6—8 ft.
9d. each.

" **HUNTINGDON WILLOW.** Height 6—8 ft.
9d. each.

" **KILMARNOCK.** This is a splendid Weeping
variety. Height 6—8 ft. 2/- each.

WYCH HAZEL (Hamamelis). Flowers in mid-
Winter, 3/6 each.

YUCCA FILAMENTOSA. Most useful plant,
flowers freely. 9d. each 6/- per doz.

RHODODENDRONS.

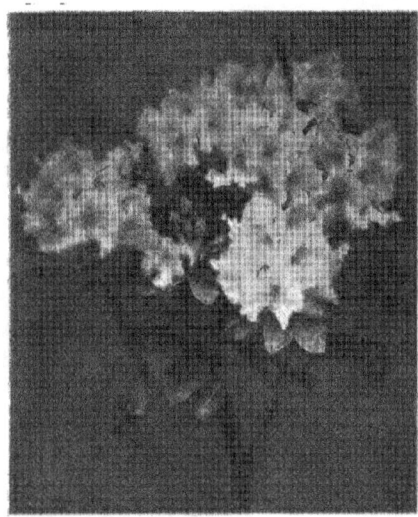

RHODODENDRON, PINK PEARL.

The cultivation of these beautiful hardy evergreen flowering shrubs has been greatly on the increase since the discovery that peat soil is not absolutely necessary for their successful growth. Sandy peat suits them best, but they do well in sandy loam or even clayey loam, if free from calcareous matter, whilst we have seen beautiful specimens growing in ordinary light garden soil. The colours of flowers range from most intense crimson to the most delicate shades of rose and pure white.

CHOICE HYBRIDS.

	each—s.	d.
ALARM. Crimson, white centre	2	6
ATROSANGUINEUM. Deep blood-red, very hardy	2	6
BARCLAYANUM. Deep rosy crimson, fine truss	2	6
BOULE-DE-NEIGE. Pure white	2	6
BRAYANUM. Deep rosy scarlet	2	6
BROUGHTONII. Rosy red, very large truss, early	2	6
CHARLES BAGLEY. Cherry red	2	6
CHARLES NOBLE. Deep scarlet	2	6
CYNTHIA. Rosy crimson	2	6
DONCASTER. Intense scarlet, fine trusses, superb variety	2	6
DR. HOGG. Bright crimson. This variety was the leading feature in the Royal bed at the Royal Agricultural Show, Norwich, June 26th, 1911		
FATUOSA FLORA PLENA. Mauve, large and double flowers	2	6
GRAND ARAB. Brilliant crimson scarlet	2	6
JAMES MASON. Bright scarlet	2	6
JOHN WATERER. A fine dark crimson variety	2	6
KATE WATERER. Rosy crimson, large yellow centre	2	6
LADY ARMSTRONG. Pale rose	2	6
MRS. JOHN CLUTTON. The best hardy white Rhododendron	2	6
MRS. JOHN WATERER. Bright rose, spotted	2	6
MRS. TOM AGNEW. Blush white with lemon blotch	2	6
PINK PEARL. F.C.C., R.H.S. The most remarkable and finest variety of Rhododendron that has ever been introduced. The colour is a beautiful flesh tinted pink, a shade that makes it absolutely unique.		
Fine Plants, set with buds .. 5s., 7s. 6d. and	10	6
PRINCESS ALICE. Blush white, large truss	2	6
ROSABELLE. Pale rose, fine foliage and habit	2	6
VANDYKE. Bright crimson, fine truss	2	6

In Choice Varieties, our selection, 25s. per doz.

RHODODENDRONS.

Choice Hybrid Seedlings.

These are from seed gathered from the best named varieties, and include all the most beautiful shades to be found amongst the best named sorts, being extra selected plants.

For general effect in the borders they are most excellent, and being of very hardy and robust constitution are in very great demand. We strongly recommend them to our customers.
Height 12—18 in. 12/- per doz. 85/- per 100, 18—24 in. 16/- per doz. 105/- per 100.

CUNNINGHAMII. The best white for forcing. Height 12—15 in. 12/- per doz. 75/- per 100, 18—24 in. 18/- per doz. 125/- per 100.

JACKSONII. Good strong stuff, extra bushy. Height 1½—2 ft. 2/- each.

PRÆCOX. Rosy lilac, dwarf and very early, often seen in bloom in February in sheltered borders. Height 12—15 in. 1/6 each 15/- per doz., 15—18 in. each 21/- per doz.

PONTICUM. All good, bushy stuff, well rooted. Height 12 to 15 in. 6/- per doz. 40/- per 100, 15—18 in. 8/- per doz. 60/- per 100. 24—30 in. 12/- per doz. 70/- per 100.

STANDARDS.

These are very beautiful for lawns. We can supply a few of the best sorts with good heads, 10/6 and 15/- each.

These are excellent for forcing, or for out-door planting.

AZALEAS.

GHENT VARIETIES. In fine shades of orange, flesh pink, rose and salmon, all well set with buds. 2s. 6d. each, 24s. per doz.

MOLLIS. In choice colours. Our selection of colours. All well set with buds and nice bushy plants. Height 12—15 in. 1/6 each 15/- per doz., 15—18 in. 2/- each 18/- per doz.
We can also supply above as Standards, 5/- and 7/6 each.

MOLLIS-ANTHONY KOSTER. Bright golden yellow, the largest flowers and the finest variety yet raised. Strong plants, well set with buds, 2/6 and 3/6 each.
Standards, 5s. each.

RUSTICA (Flora Plena). A most lovely section, colours from pure white to dark red, and sweetly scented; very easy to force. Nice plants, set with buds, 2/6 each 24/- per doz.

PONTICA. Orange yellow, sweetly scented, very free. 12—15 in. 9/- per doz. 60/- per 100, 15—18 in. 12/- per doz. 75/- per 100.

TREES ESTABLISHED IN POTS AND TUBS.

We have usually on hand several specimens of Oaks, Sycamores, Limes, Beech, Birch, and a nice collection of Shrubs (both Evergreen, Coniferous, and Flowering), of various sizes, ranging from 2s. upwards, according to size.
Prices and sizes on application.

HARDY HEATHS.
(ERICAS.)

These beautiful plants are most useful for edging beds of Azaleas and Rhododendrons.

ALPORTI. The best crimson. 7/6 per doz. 60/- per 100.

AUREA. Golden foliage. 7/6 per doz. 60/- per 100.

CARNEA. Abundance of reddish flesh-coloured flowers in March and April. 9/- per doz.

" **ALBA.** White variety of above. 9/- per doz.

HAMMONDII. The lucky White Heath. 7/6 per doz. 60/- per 100.

SEARLEII. White, very distinct. 7/6 per doz. 60/- per 100.

HARDY BAMBOOS.

ARUNDINARIA FORTUNEII, variegata. Beautiful bright green leaves, striated white. 1/6 and 2/- each.

" **JAPONICA (Bambusa Metake).** Stems 15 ft. long with dark green sharply pointed leaves. 1/6 and 2/- each.

" **SIMONII.** Tall, straight, slender stems, runs very freely at the root. 2/6 and 3/6 each.

BAMBUSA TESSELLATA. The largest leaved of all the hardy Bamboos. 2/- each.

PHYLLOSTACHYS AUREA. Stems yellow, very straight, erect growing close round the base. 2/6 and 3/6 each.

" **NIGRA.** Stems glossy black after the first year. 3/6 and 5/- each.

CONIFERÆ.

In the following list we have aimed at offering only the most popular and useful kinds. They are most striking objects either planted singly, or in groups, and if rightly placed amongst deciduous and ornamental trees the effect is very pleasing.

All have been recently transplanted so as to ensure as far as possible safety in removal, abundance of room and attention have been given so that each tree may be a perfect specimen. Our trees are all hand pruned with a knife, which is a most important point.

We offer well shaped plants, suitable for potting or window boxes, in good variety, our selection.
12 to 18 inches, 6s. per doz., 45s. per 100. 18 to 24 inches, 9s. per doz., 60s. per 100.

CEDRUS DEODARA.

ABIES CANADENSIS (Hemlock Spruce). Very graceful tree, grows well, and well worthy of a prominent sheltered place in the pleasure grounds. Height 2—3 ft. 1/3 each, 12/- per doz., 4—5 ft. 2/- each, 21/- per doz.

" **NOBILIS.** Very fast-growing Fir; hardy. Height 1½—2 ft. 2/- each, 2—3 ft. 3/0 each.

" **NORDMANNIANA.** Very handsome tree, and should be more extensively planted. Height 1—1½ ft. 1/6 each, 1½—2 ft. 2/6 each, 2—3 ft. 3/6 each.

" **PINSAPO.** Very thick-growing, and most distinct. Height 2—3 ft. 2/6 each, 3—4 ft. 5/- each.

ARAUCARIA IMBRICATA. This is a most distinct tree, and specimens should be planted more extensively. Height 2—3 ft. 5/- each, 3—4 ft. 7/6 each.

CEDRUS ATLANTICA. This is a very fast-growing and ornamental tree with silvery foliage, and of more upright habit than Libani. Height 2—3 ft. 2/6 each, 3—4 ft. 3/6 each, 5—6 ft. 7/6 each.

" " **GLAUCA.** Glaucous-leaved, very pretty variety, appearing in the distance as if covered with hoar frost; most graceful tree, silvery foliage and splendid for planting singly on lawns. Height 2—3 ft. 3/6 each, 3—4 ft. 5/- each.

" **DEODARA.** Height 2—3 ft. 2/- each, 21/- per doz., 3—4 ft. 3/6 each, 5—6 ft. 7/6 each.

" **LIBANI (Cedar of Lebanon).** A handsome bold tree. 1½—2 ft. 2/- each, 2—3 ft. 3/6 each, 3—4 ft. 5/- and 7/6 each.

CRYPTOMERIA JAPONICA (Japanese Cedar). Bright green foliage, and very rapid growth. 1½—2 ft. 2/- each, 2—3 ft. 3/6 each.

" **ELEGANS.** Plumose habit, very ornamental, with bronzy crimson foliage in Winter. Height 1½—2ft. 1/6 each, 2—3 ft. 2/6 each.

CUPRESSUS LAWSONIANA. *See page* 139.

CUPRESSUS LAWSONIANA ALBA-SPICA. The young, beautiful foliage tipped with white. Height 1½—2 ft. 1/6 each, 2—3 ft. 2/6 each.

" **ALLUMII.** Very hardy, compact, upright habit, foliage rich silver blue. 1½—2 ft. 1/3 each 12/- per doz., 2½—3 ft. 2/- each, 3—4 ft. 3/6 each.

" **ERECTA VIRIDIS.** Good Cupressus of erect habit. Height 1½—2 ft. 1/- each 10/6 per doz., 2—3 ft. 1/6 each 16/- per doz., 3—4 ft. 2/6 and 3/6 each.

" **GRACILIS.** Very graceful, drooping habit. Height 2—3 ft. 2/6 each.

" **LUTEA.** A beautiful, golden form of the Lawson's Cypress. Height 2—2½ ft. 3/6 each, 2½—3 ft. 5/- each.

" **SILVER QUEEN.** One of the most beautiful and fairly hardy. Height 2—3 ft. 2/- each, 3—4 ft. 3/6 each.

" **MACROCARPA** (In pots). A very handsome variety, of rapid growth. Height 1½—2 ft. 1/6 each, 2—3 ft. 2/6 each.

PICEA PUNGENS GLAUCA KOSTERIANA.

CUPRESSUS MACROCARPA LUTEA (In pots). A very good golden Cupressus. Height 1½—2 ft. 1/6 to 2/6 each 25/- per doz.

" **NOOTKATENSIS.** Very pretty, and one of the best Conifers grown. Height 1½—2 ft. 1/6 each 15/- per doz., 2—3 ft. 2/- each 21/- per doz.

GINKGO (Maiden Hair Tree) (Salisburia adiantifolia). Height 1½—2 ft. 6d. each 4/6 per doz., 2—3 ft. 9d. each 6/- per doz., 3—4 ft. 1/- each 9/- per doz.

JUNIPERUS (Juniper).

" **CHINENSIS AUREA.** Bright golden foliage, very attractive. Height 1—1½ ft. 3/6 each.

" **COMMUNIS FASTIGIATA (Irish Juniper).** A beautiful and effective Conifer for landscape planting, of close, upright growth. Height 1—1½ ft. 1/3 each 12/- per doz., 1½—2 ft. 1/9 each 18/- per doz., 2—2½ ft. 2/6 each 24/- per doz.

JUNIPERUS, VIRGINIANA (Red Cedar). Good hardy variety of upright growth. Height 2½—3 ft. 1/6 each.

PICEA EXCELSA (Spruce Fir). *See page* 140.

" " **ALBA (White Spruce).** Height 2—2½ ft. 1/6 each.

" **PUNGENS.** Height 2—2½ ft. 1/6 each.

" " **GLAUCA (Blue Spruce).** A lovely Spruce, with glaucous leaves. Height 1½—2 ft. 3/- each, 2—3 ft. 5/- each.

" " " **KOSTERIANA.** This is the finest of all, a most magnificent tree, glaucous leaves, very hardy, splendid specimen for planting singly on lawns. Height 2—3 ft. 5/- each.

PRUMNOPITYS ELEGANS (Plum-fruited Yew). Height 2—3 ft. 2/6 each.

PINUS CEMBRA. Very distinct species of conical growth. Height 1½—2 ft. 1/- each 10/6 per doz., 2—3 ft. 1/6 each 15/- per doz., 3—4 ft. 2/6 each.

" **AUSTRIACA.** *See Austrian Pine, page* 140.

" **EXCELSA.** Pale glaucous-green foliage. Height 1¼—1½ ft. 9d. each 6/- per doz., 1½—2 ft. 1/- each 9/- per doz.

" **PINASTER.** Valuable tree for seaside planting, stands breeze well and good shelter tree. Height 2—2½ ft. 1/- each.

RETINOSPORA OBTUSA. Light green foliage, forms a good specimen for single planting. Height 2—3 ft. 1/6 each 16/- per doz., 3—4 ft. 2/- each 21/- per doz.

" **PISIFERA.** Height 1½—2 ft. 1/6 each, 2—3 ft. 2/6 each, 3—4 ft. 3/6 each.

" " **AUREA.** Very beautiful. Height 1—1½ ft. 1/9 each 18/- per doz., 1½—2 ft. 2/6 each 24/- per doz., 3—4 ft. 5/- each.

" **PLUMOSA AUREA.** Soft, dense habit, should be regularly clipped. Height 2—2½ ft. 1/- each, 2½—3 ft. 1/6 each.

RETINOSPORA PISIFERA AUREA.

Coniferæ (continued).

TAXODIUM DISTICHUM. Very ornamental, light feathery foliage, should be closely pruned when transplanting, changing to rich brown in Autumn. Height 2—3 ft. 1/- each 10/6 per doz., 4—5 ft. 2/- each 21/- per doz.

TAXUS AUREA (Golden Yew). Height 1—1½ ft. 1/9 each 18/- per doz., 1½—2 ft. 2/6 each 25/- per doz., 2—3 ft. 3/- each 35/- per doz., 3—4 ft. 5/- and 7/6 each.

„ **FASTIGIATA (The Irish Yew).** Very dark foliage, with upright habit. Height 1½—2 ft. 1/6 each 15/- per doz., 2—3 ft. 2/- each 21/- per doz., 3—4 ft. 3/6 each 30/- per doz.

TAXUS AUREA (Golden Irish Yew). Resembling the above in shape and habit, but golden colour. Height 1—1½ ft. 1/6 each, 2—3 ft. 3/6 each, 3—4 ft. 7/6 each.

„ **BACCATA (Common Yew).** *See below.*
THUJOPSIS DOLABRATA. This is a beautiful Conifer, compact habit, most pleasing appearance, massive bright glossy green foliage. Height 1—1½ ft. 9d. each 7/6 per doz., 2—3 ft. 2/- each 21/- per doz., 3—4 ft. 3/6 each.

„ **VARIEGATA.** Variegated form of Dolabrata. Height 1½—2 ft. 1/6 each 15/- per doz., 2—3 ft. 2/6 each 24/- per doz.

THUJA LOBBII. A very hardy, ornamental shrub, suitable for any position. Height 2½—3 ft. 1/- each 10/6 per doz., 3—4 ft. 1/6 each 15/- per doz., 4—5 ft. 2/- each 21/- per doz., 5—6 ft. 3/6 each.

„ **OCCIDENTALIS.** *(Arbor-Vitæ.)* See below.

„ „ **LUTEA (Golden Arbor-Vitæ).** Nice golden coloured. These are among the best of our beautiful Conifers. Height 2—3 ft. 2/- each 18/- per doz., 3—4 ft. 3/6 each.

„ **VERVAENEANA.** Beautiful golden tinted variety. Height 2—3 ft. 1/6 each 15/- per doz., 3—4 ft. 2/- each 21/- per doz., 4—5 ft. 3/6 each.

HEDGING PLANTS.

For Ornamental Hedges the Arbor-Vitæ, Tree Box, Beech, Holly and Common Yew are admirably adapted. Of these the Holly makes the most durable, impenetrable and at the same time elegant fence, and may be planted in any soil not too damp.

Myrobella for rapidity of growth has no equal, and even on poor soil a capital fence may be formed in three or four years.

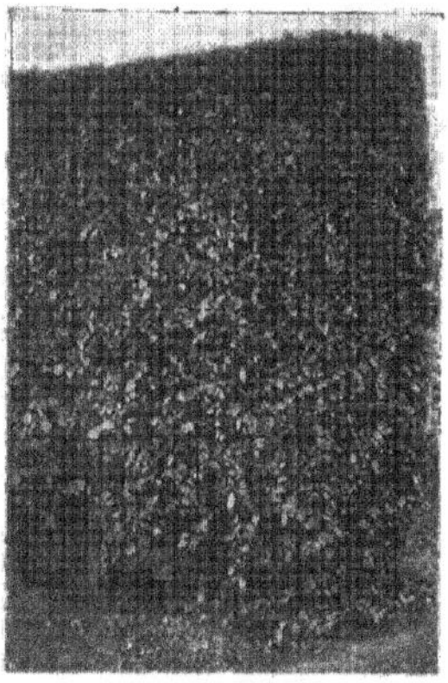

PORTION OF BEECH HEDGE IN OUR NURSERIES.

ARBOR-VITÆ (Thuya Occidentalis). Very compact and hardy. Height 1—1½ ft. 15/- per 100, 1½—2 ft. 25/- per 100, 2—3 ft. 35/- per 100, 3—4 ft. 9/- per doz. 60/- per 100. Larger specimens, 1/-, 1/6, 2/- each.
BEECH, Common. Makes a splendid hedge. Height 1½—2 ft. 7/- per 100, 60/- per 1000, 2—3 ft. 10/- per 100, 80/- per 1000.
BOX TREE. This forms a handsome hedge. Height 1½—2 ft. 25/- per 100, 2—3 ft. 35/- per 100, 3—4 ft. 6/- per doz. 45/- per 100, 4—5 ft. 12/- per doz. 80/- per 100.
COTONEASTER SIMMONDII. Very rapid growing. Height 1½—2 ft. 4/- per doz. 30/- per 100, 2—3 ft. 6/- per doz. 40/- per 100.
CUPRESSUS LAWSONIANA. The most popular of all the Cupressus. Height 1—1½ ft. 4/- per doz. 30/- per 100, 1½—2 ft. 5/- per doz. 35/- per 100, 2—2½ ft. 6/- per doz. 50/- per 100, 3—4 ft. 12/- per doz. 80/- per 100, 4—5 ft. 18/- per doz.
HOLLY, Green. Forms a beautiful hedge if planted in double rows, leaving 12 ins. between each row, also well adapted for mixing with thorn. Height 1½—2 ft. 6/- per doz. 50/- per 100, 2—2½ ft. 12/- per doz. 80/- per 100, 2½—3½ ft. 18/- per doz.
For other kinds see page 135.

HORNBEAM. Grows very close and rapidly, much used for hedges. Height 1½—2 ft. 4/6 per 100 40/- per 1000, 2—3 ft. 6/- per 100 50/- per 1000.

MYROBELLA
or CHERRY PLUM.

This is the quickest [growing] hedge plant and largely used in England. Extra fine, well rooted, 4/6 per 100, 40/- per 1000. Second size, 3/6 per 100, 30/- per 1000.

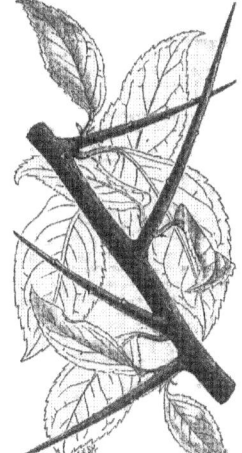

MYROBELLA BRANCH WITH SPINES.

The best time for planting is in November or early Spring, or it may be done in open weather at any time during the Winter months, but in fairly moist weather successful plantings may be made as late as the middle or end of April. In planting plant firmly, placing the sets from six to nine inches apart, according to size. When growth commences, they should be cut down to eight or ten inches in height. It should be cut at least twice a year—about the end of July and in Spring whilst in a dormant state,

PRIVET, EVERGREEN. Ornamental when cut well back. Height 1½—2 ft. 4/6 per 100 40/- per 1000, 2—3 ft. 6/- per 100 50/- per 1000.

„ **OVAL-LEAVED.** Invaluable for planting in towns, no plant stands smoke better and makes a beautiful ornamental hedge. Height 1½—2 ft. 6/6 per 100 50/- per 1000, 2—3 ft. 10/- per 100 90/- per 1000, 3—4 ft. 12/- per 100 100/- per 1000.

„ **GOLDEN.** Height 1—1½ ft. 9d. each 6/- per doz. 40/- per 100, 1½—2 ft. 1/- each 7/6 per doz. 50/- per 100, 2—3 ft. 1/6 each 12/- per doz. 80/- per 100.

THORNS or QUICKS. This is the best of all plants for an efficient hedge. Height 1—1½ ft. 3/- per 100 25/- per 1000, 1½—2 ft. 4/- per 100 30/- per 1000, 2—2½ ft. 6/- per 100, extra strong.

YEW, Common. This is the most Ornamental of all evergreen hedges, it should not be planted in any situation accessible to animals that might eat it. It is hardy and a compact grower. Height 1—1½ ft. 5/- per doz. 30/- per 100, 1½—2 ft. 7/6 per doz. 50/- per 100, 2—2½ ft. 10/6 per doz. 80/- per 100, 3—3½ ft. 24/- per doz. Specimens, 2/6, 3/6, 5/- each.
For other kinds see Taxus, above.

ENGLISH YEW.

TRANSPLANTED FOREST TREES.

SPECIMEN ROW OF LIME TREES IN OUR NURSERIES.

To meet the demand for Forest Trees we have considerably increased our Stock in this direction, and it will be found to comprise all the best varieties for Forest and Estate planting ; further, we make it a practice to grow our trees thinly in wide rows, which ensures their being thoroughly hardened when moved to exposed situations. We shall be pleased to give estimates, free of cost, for all kinds of planting, Forest or otherwise, and will carry out the entire work if desired.

Our prices, taking quality into consideration, are exceeding moderate, and we are prepared to compete with any respectable firms in the trade. Extra Selected Plants, and smaller quantities than quoted, will be charged proportionately higher.

We shall be pleased to submit samples of any Forest Trees, Carriage Free.

ACACIA, Common. *See also page* 134.
Very ornamental tree, growing freely on poor sandy soil. Height 1½—2 ft. 4/- per 100, 35/- per 1000, 2—2½ ft. 5/- per 100, 45/- per 1000. Specimen Trees, 1/- 1/6 and 2/- each.

ALDER, Common. Grows well on wet, undrained soils. Height 2—3 ft. 4/- per 100 35/- per 1000, 3—4 ft. 5/- per 100 40/- per 1000. Specimen Trees, 1/-, 1/6, and 2/6 each.

ASH, Common. *See also page* 134.
Requires good land ; timber very valuable when well grown. Height 2—3 ft. 4/- per 100 35/- per 1000, 3—4 ft. 5/- per 100 45/- per 1000, 4—6 ft. 6/- per 100 55/- per 1000.

,, MOUNTAIN. Very ornamental tree, most valuable for exposed situations ; fruit valued by many for making preserves for eating with game. Height 4—5 ft. 10/- per 100 90/- per 1000, 6—8 ft. 12/- per doz. Specimen Trees, 1/6 and 2/6 each.

BEECH, Common. *See also page* 134.
Grows well on any good light soil, also makes a splendid hedge, retaining its foliage during Winter. Height 2—3 ft. 4/- per 100 60/- per 1000, 3—3 ft. 10/- per 100 80/- per 1000. Selected Specimen Trees, 1/-, 1/6, 2/6 each.

BIRCH, Common. *See also Betula, page* 134.
Timber fine-grained and valuable. Makes the best charcoal for gunpowder. Height 2—3 ft. 4/- per 100 40/- per 1000, 3—4 ft. 5/- per 100 45/- per 1000, 6—10 ft. 9/-, 12/- 15/- per doz.

,, SILVER. One of the most beautiful of our forest trees. Succeeds in moist situations. Height 3—4 ft. 6/- per 100 55/- per 1000, 9—12 ft. 1/6, 2/6, 3/6 each.

CERASUS, or WILD CHERRY. *See also page* 134.
Attains a good size ; trees free-flowering, richly coloured foliage in Autumn. Standard Trees, 1/6 and 2/6 each.

CHESTNUT, HORSE. *See also page* 135.
Very handsome flowering tree. Splendid for avenues or parks, requires good land. Height 3—4 ft. 12/6 per 100 100/- per 1000, 5—6 ft. 15/- per 100. Specimen Trees, 9/- per doz., 1/-, 1/6, 2/6 each.

CHESTNUT, SPANISH. Highly ornamental and rapid grower. Requires a sheltered situation. Height 2—3 ft. 6/- per 100, 50/- per 1000. Specimen Trees, 1/- and 1/6 each.

ELM, WYCH. Most valuable timber tree, very hardy and grows freely. Height 2—3 ft. 5/- per 100 45/- per 1000. Specimen Trees, 1/-, 1/6, and 2/6 each.

,, ENGLISH. This is a tall and elegant tree of rapid and erect growth. Height 2—3 ft. 4/6 per 100 40/- per 1000, 3—4 ft. 6/- per 100.

FIR, DOUGLAS (Abies Douglasii). This is a fast-growing, magnificent timber tree, its foliage is a rich green. Height 1½—2 ft. 18/- per 100.

,, DOUGLAS (Colorado Variety). This is undoubtedly the finest type of the Douglas Fir. Compact habit, foliage rich glaucous green, much slower growth than the above. Specimens, 1/- and 1/6 each.

,, SCOTCH. The true Highland Pine is now much planted, grows freely on all exposed late districts. Height 12—15 in. 3/6 per 100 30/- per 1000, 15—18 in. 4/6 per 100 40/- per 1000, 1½—2 ft. 6/- per 100 50/- per 1000. Strong quartered Trees, 4/- per doz. 30/- per 100.

,, SILVER. A beautiful tree of very rapid growth, and valuable for timber. Height 12—15 in. 20/- per 100.

,, SPRUCE (Pinus excelsa). Height 12—18 in. 6/- per 100 50/- per 1000, 18—24 in. 10/- per 100 70/- per 1000. Xmas trees in various sizes, from 3—8 ft. Prices on application.

HAZEL. *See page* 135 and 141.

HORNBEAM. Handsome trees when grown singly ; also is an excellent hedge plant for exposed situations. Height 2—3 ft. 6/- per 100 50/- per 1000.

LABURNUM, Common. *See also page* 135.
Very handsome early-flowering tree, covered with yellow blossom. Height 2½—3 ft. 10/- per 100. Specimens, 1/-, 1/6 and 2/6 each.

LARCH, Native. The above are all grown from Seed had from the North of Scotland, and are splendidly rooted. Height 1—1½ ft. 3/- per 100 25/- per 1000, 1½—2 ft. 4/- per 100 35/- per 1000, 2—2½ ft. 5/- per 100.

,, JAPANESE. This variety is coming more and more into demand, owing to its rapid growth and being late in showing leaf is not so apt to be cut down with late Spring frosts. Height 1—1½ ft. 8/- per 100, 2—2½ ft. 10/6 per 100.

LIMES, Red Twigged from Layers. Very ornamental tree when grown singly, most useful for Parks or Avenue planting, very hardy and large specimens, transplants safely. Height 2—3 ft. 3/- per doz. 15/- per 100, 5—6 ft. 4/- per doz. 25/- per 100, 6—7 ft. 6/- per doz. 30/- per 100. Specimen Standards, 1/-, 1/6, 2/6, 3/6 each.

MAPLE, NORWAY. *See also Acers, page* 136.
Height 3—4 ft. 7/6 per 100, 70/- per 1000, 8—10 ft. 9/- per doz. 70/- per 100. Large specimens, 1/-, 1/6 and 2/6 each.

OAK, ENGLISH. Height 2—3 ft. 7/- per 100 65/- per 1000. Specimen Trees, 1/- and 2/6 each.

,, SCARLET. One of the most beautiful trees, scarlet foliage with rich Autumn shade. Height 3—4 ft. 15/- per 100. Specimen Trees, 1/-, 1/6, and 2/- each.

PINE, AUSTRIAN. Succeeds on high, dry, exposed situations, and on sea-shore. All well transplanted trees. Height 1—1½ ft. 12/6 per 100 95/- per 1000, 3—4 ft. 2/6 each 24/- per doz.

,, CORSICAN (Laricio). The Corsican Pine makes rapid growth, and comes early to maturity. One of the best trees for shelter. Height 1—1½ ft. 7/6 per 100 65/- per 1000.

,, WEYMOUTH (Pinus Strobus). The White Canadian Pine of soft and delicate appearance, with silky foliage. Height 1½—2 ft. 6/- per doz. 30/- per 100, 3—4 ft. 1/- each 15/- per doz.

Forest Trees (continued).

POPLAR ABELE, Silver. Very valuable quick-growing tree, useful for exposed situations, with silvery leaf; grows freely on the coast. Height 4—6 ft. 2/- per 100, 6—8 ft. 22/6 per 100. Specimen Trees, 1/- and 1/6 each.

" **BLACK ITALIAN.** The most rapid growing of all our forest trees, grows fully in most soils and is invaluable for shelter. Height 4—6 ft. 10/- per 100, 80/- per 1000, 8—9 ft. 5/- per doz., 35/- per 100. Specimen Trees, 9d., 1/6, and 2/6 each.

" **DELTOIDEA (Canadensis).** This is undoubtedly the coming Poplar for street, park, or avenue planting. It does splendidly in smoky towns and is of fine pyramidal habit with bold shining foliage. Height 5—6 ft. 12/- per 100, 80/- per 1000. Very large specimens for parks or planting singly, 1/-, 1/6 and 2/6 each.

" **AUREA.** This variety is becoming a favourite, grows very freely, with rich golden foliage. Standards. Height 6—8 ft. 1/6 each, 8—10 ft. 2/- each.

" **LOMBARDY.** Very ornamental upright growing tree, often introduced in Landscape with effect, grows well in almost any soil, and most useful for close planting to act as a block. Height 5—6 ft. 8/- per 100, 70/- per 1000, 6—8 ft. 10/- per 100. Specimens, 1/-, 1/6, 2/- each.

" **BALSAM.** Very early to bud in Spring, with large fragrant foliage. Height 6—8 ft. 10/- per 100 80/- per 1000. Large Specimens, 6/- doz., 1/-, 1/6, 2/- each.

POPLAR ONTARIO. This is a very robust variety, large foliage, very hardy, and grows freely in any soils. Height 4—6 ft. 10/- per 100 80/- per 1000. Large Specimens, 6/- per doz, 1/-, 1/6, 2/- each.

THE TRUE BAT WILLOW,
Growing in our Nurseries.

7th Dec.

From W. LINFOOT, Esq., Docking, Braintree.

"*I am very well pleased with the Bat Willows you have sent me, and have got them all safely planted.*"

SERVICE TREE. A beautiful tree, handsome dark green foliage; splendid avenue tree and should be more grown. Height 3—4 ft. 15/- per 100. Specimen Trees, 10/6 per dozen, 1/- and 1/6 each.

SYCAMORE. Very hardy, and stands the sea winds better than most other trees; grows freely in any soil, very ornamental, and excellent timber. Height 2—3 ft. 4/- per 100 35/- per 1000, 3—4 ft. 5/- per 100 45/- per 1000, 5—6 ft. 7/6 per 100. Specimen Trees, 6/- doz., 1/6 and 2/6 each.

WILLOW BAT (Salix alba cœrulea). This is the true variety grown from cuttings taken by Mr. Shaw, the eminent Bat maker, from a tree which he selected as being of the best variety for making high-class Cricket Bats.

Any one having low lying grass land will find it most remunerative to plant this Willow, which thrives under these conditions, and will be of a size to put on the market for Bat-making at a period of from 15—20 years from the time of planting. Fine selected standards, 8—10 ft. per doz. 9/-, per 100 60/-. Strong two-year old plants, 5—6 ft. per doz. 6/-, per 100 40/-. Strong one-year old, well rooted per 100 20/-.

" **BITTER OSIER.** Splendid for covers, not liable to be destroyed by Rabbits. Height 3—4 ft. 4/6 per 100 40/- per 1000, 4—5 ft. 5/6 per 100 50/- per 1000.

" **HUNTINGDON.** Makes valuable timber, ornamental, and of rapid growth. Height 3—4 ft. 6/6 per 100 60/- per 1000.

" **YELLOW OSIER.** Very ornamental when planted near water. Height 3—4 ft. 4/6 per 100 40/- per 1000.

UNDERWOOD.

The following plants thrive splendidly under trees and afford ample cover for game. The Rhododendron Ponticum for ornamental underwood is now extensively planted, since it has been satisfactorily proved that rabbits and hares will not touch it. Berberis, Spiræa and Hypericum are very suitable for undergrowth, in that they rapidly spread by throwing out side roots and suckers, and so form large clumps.

AUCUBA JAPONICA VARIEGATA. Grows well under shade of trees. Height 1½—2 ft. 10/6 per doz. 70/- per 100.

BLACKTHORN or SLOE. A splendid plant for Fox covers and for hedges. Height 1½—2 ft. 6/- per 100 45/- per 1000.

BERBERIS AQUIFOLIUM. This is one of our finest shrubs for underwood; flowers and seeds freely, excellent for game covers and shrubberies. Height 1½—2 ft. 15/- per 100 125/- per 1000.

" **DULCIS.** Fruit very sweet. Height 1½—2 ft. 7/6 per doz. 50/- per 100.

" **DARWINII.** Large yellow flowers. Height 12—18 in. 6/- per doz. 30/- per 100. Specimens, 9d. and 1/- each.

" **VULGARIS.** Height 2—2½ ft. 6/- per doz. 40/- per 100.

BRAMBLES. 6/- per 100 50/- per 1000.

" **SWEET.** Height 2—3 ft. 6/- per doz. 20/- per 100.

BRIAR, DOG. 6/- per 100 50/- per 1000.

BROOM, Common. Seedlings, 3/6 per 100 30/- per 1000. Transplanted, 7/6 per 100 50/- per 1000.

DOGWOOD, Scarlet. Very effective for massing. Height 2—3 ft. 3/- per doz, 10/6 per 100, 3—4 ft. 4/- per doz. 12/6 per 100.

ELDER, Common. Height 2—3 ft. 3/- per doz 18/- per 100.

" **Golden Leaved.** Height 3—4 ft. 4/- per doz. 25/- per 100.

" **Silver variegated.** Height 2—3 ft. 4/- per doz. 25/- per 100.

HYPERICUM CALYCINUM. An excellent covert plant for growing under the shade of large trees, beautiful when in flower, and not liked by Rabbits. Transplanted, 3/- per doz. 20/- per 100.

HAZEL. Height 3—4 ft. 6/- per 100 50/- per 1000.

IVY, IRISH. Open ground. Transplanted, 3/- per doz. 21/- per 100. Stronger, height 3—4 ft. 6/- per doz. 45/- per 100.

LAUREL ROTUNDIFOLIA. *See also page 135.* Height 1½—2 ft. 4/- per doz. 30/- per 100, 2—2½ ft. 5/- per doz. 40/- per 100.

" **CAUCASICA.** Height 2—3 ft. 6/- per doz. 45/- per 100.

LAURUSTINUS. Height 1½—2 ft. 1/- each, 10/6 per doz.

LEYCESTERIA FORMOSA. Very useful as a covert plant. The fruit is much relished by game. 9d. each 7/6 per dozen.

PERIWINKLE (Vinca). 5/- per doz. 30/- per 100.

PRIVET, Common. Height 2—3 ft. 6/- per 100 50/- per 1000.

RHODODENDRON PONTICUM. *See also p. 137.* Height 15—18 in. 8/- per doz. 60/- per 100, 2—2½ ft. 12/- per doz. 70/- per 100. Special offer for large quantities.

" " **SEEDLING HYBRIDS.** The Ponticum is a most beautiful and useful plant for game covers. Height 1½—2 ft. 15/- per doz. 80/- per 100.

ROSA RUGOSA. One of the finest hardy and ornamental berried shrubs introduced from Japan. Forms a dense bush between 4 and 5 ft. high with handsome foliage; produces annually an abundant crop of large hips. 6/- per doz. 35/- per 100.

SEA BUCKTHORN. Height 1½—2 ft. 6/- per doz. 40/- per 100.

SNOWBERRY. Height 2—3 ft. 4/6 per 100 40/- per 1000.

SPIRÆAS (Shrubby). The Spiræas are all beautiful flowering shrubs. Colours vary from pure white to crimson; well adapted for forming clumps for game coverts, &c. In variety. 9d. each 7/6 per doz.

WHIN, GORSE, or FURZE. Seedlings, 3/- per 100 20/- per 1000. Transplanted, 5/- per 100 30/- per 1000.

From JAS. TEMPLE, Esq., Edgefield.

April 19th.

"Mr. Temple wishes to say the Trees and Shrubs he has had from you have always given him the greatest satisfaction, and the last lot are doing splendidly."

From Mr. J. BUTLER. Clydach.

Nov. 6th.

"I beg to acknowledge the safe delivery of Trees, with which I am very pleased."

From Mrs. GORDON, Lothian.

Mar. 26th.

"My lady has requested me to say she is delighted with the Trees and Shrubs which I selected at your Nurseries, and to thank you very much for the extra trees enclosed."

DAHLIAS—Cactus-flowered.
NEW AND SELECT VARIETIES.

The following varieties, which are all of the true Cactus type, include what we consider the very choicest flowers for exhibition or decorative purposes, and cannot fail to give the highest satisfaction.

Strong Plants from single pots ready in May.

	each—s.	d.

C. E. WILKINS. A magnificent variety. The colour is an exquisite shade of bright clear salmon pink overlaying yellow 0 6

CHARLES H. CURTIS. A noble flower, large, full and strikingly incurved in form. The colour is a rich crimson scarlet .. 0 6

CORAL (1910). Large beautiful flowers. The base of the florets chrome yellow, the upper part light red 1 0

DAINTY. Pale yellow ground, overlaid with light pink, tips of petals golden yellow; very distinct and beautiful .. 0 6

DOROTHY. Deep and well-formed flowers of good size and with full centres. The colour is a lovely bright silvery pink .. 0 6

ELSA ELLRICH. Colour pearly-white, slightly tinted blush in early stages, florets long and narrow, splendid variety 0 6

FLAME. A large and splendid flower of a brilliant orange-scarlet colour of a very rich and telling shade 0 6

HAROLD PEARMAN. A deep pure yellow, one of the most constant and free-flowering yet introduced 0 6

H. H. THOMAS (1910). Beautifully formed incurving flowers of good size; colour a deep rich crimson. Splendid exhibition variety 1 0

H. L. BROUSSON (1911) (new—*see Plate*). A first-class flower of great depth, with long, narrow, slightly incurved florets. The colour is a deep, rich rose, lighter at the tips 2 0

H. SHOESMITH. Brilliant crimson, florets very narrow .. 0 6

INDOMITABLE (1910). Long incurved narrow florets and well-formed large blooms; the colour is a beautiful lilac mauve .. 1 0

IOLANTHE (1910). Deep coral red, every floret distinctly tipped with gold. A charming variety and first-class for exhibition .. 1 0

IVERNIA. The colour is an art shade of bright salmon-fawn with a lighter centre which gives it the most charming appearance 0 6

J. B. RIDING. The blooms are large and splendidly formed, the centre a rich yellow, with apricot red outer petals 0 6

J. H. JACKSON. Brilliant crimson maroon, long narrow pointed and incurving petals; splendid dark variety of good form .. 0 6

JOHANNESBURG (1910). A gigantic flower with splendid centre, borne on long, stout stems. Colour a bright rich golden yellow. A fine exhibition flower 1 0

MARATHON. Very large handsomely quilled flowers, colour yellow in the centre, shading to rosy carmine, and tipped with white. A superb variety 0 9

MRS. A. F. PERKINS. Colour a lovely sulphur yellow tipped with white, true Cactus form 0 6

MRS. ALFRED DYER. A most fascinating flower of splendid form. The colour is a soft lemon yellow in the centre, shading to a deep rose-pink towards the tips 0 9

MRS. H. SHOESMITH. One of the finest pure whites yet sent out 0 6

MRS. DOUGLAS FLEMING (1911) (new—*see Plate*). The finest white Cactus Dahlia yet raised. A splendid exhibition flower, of good constitution, and free blooming 2 0

MRS. F. GRINSTEAD. Deep rich crimson. A fine incurved flower of splendid exhibition qualities 0 6

MRS. J. J. CROWE. Beautiful clear canary yellow; undoubtedly the best yellow Cactus-flowered 0 6

MRS. REGINALD GURNEY. One of the most charming. The colour is a lovely amber with a faint shade of rose .. 0 6

NEW YORK (1911) (new—*see Plate*). A magnificent flower of great size and splendid form, orange yellow in the centre, shading off to deep bronzy salmon. First-class 2 0

RED ADMIRAL (1910). One of the most brilliant Dahlias in existence. The blooms are large, well formed, and of the richest fiery scarlet colour 1 0

REV. ARTHUR BRIDGE. A novel and charming variety. The colour is exceedingly beautiful, being a bright clear yellow, heavily tipped and suffused with bright deep rose pink .. 0 6

REV. T. W. JAMIESON. Magnificent variety with large incurved blooms, yellow, edged with rosy lilac, very striking .. 0 9

RUBY GRINSTEAD. An exquisitely beautiful and delicately coloured variety. The centre of the flower is a soft tinted yellow, which becomes a rich shade of rosy fawn 0 6

SWEET BRIAR (1911) (new—*see Plate*). One of the most beautiful varieties of recent introduction. The flowers are large and borne well above the foliage. The colour is an exquisite, soft bright pink 2 0

THE IMP (1910). Dark maroon crimson, almost black, quite distinct. It is of good Cactus form and quite remarkable with regard to its colour 1 0

SATISFACTION. Most beautiful variety, and one of the very best of the incurved type. The colour is a lovely rose pink, approaching to white in the centre 0 9

SAXONIA. A splendid new deep crimson that will prove of great value as an exhibition flower 0 9

SNOWDON. Very large beautifully formed flowers of the purest white, a splendid variety for exhibition 0 9

SNOWSTORM. A magnificent pure white, dwarf and sturdy in growth, and a continuous bloomer 0 9

THOMAS PARKIN. Pale terra-cotta, long narrow incurved florets; splendid variety 0 6

WHITE SWAN. Well-formed pure white flowers borne on long wiry stems. A distinct and splendid variety 0 6

WILLIAM MARSHALL. Immense flowers of the most perfect form. Rich orange, bright yellow in the centre 0 6

Choice selected sorts, our selection .. ..   per doz. 6s.; 6 for 3s. 6d.; per 100 40s.

Showy and popular varieties, our selection ..   per doz. 4s. 6d.; 6 for 2s. 6d.; per 100 30s.

SPECIAL OFFER

We offer eighteen grand Exhibition Cactus-flowered Dahlias as named below, 11s. 6d., Carriage Free.

*CORAL	†IOLANTHE	MRS. A. DYER	†REV. T. W. JAMIESON
CHARLES H. CURTIS	*†J. H. JACKSON	†MRS. J. J. CROWE	*†SNOWSTORM
ELSA ELLRICH	*†JOHANNESBURG	MRS. SHOESMITH	*†SATISFACTION
*†H. H. THOMAS	J. B. RIDING	†RED ADMIRAL	†THOMAS PARKIN
†INDOMITABLE	†MARATHON		

Twelve Superb Varieties, marked (†) 8s. 6d.   Six Very Choice Sorts, marked (*) 4s. 6d.

From Mr. J. MARTIN, Fletching Mill.
June 20th.
"The Mont Blanc Dahlias I had from you last year did so well."

From R. HUXLEY, Esq., Newsouthgate.
June 8th.
"I am very pleased with the healthy appearance of the Dahlia Plants."

SUPERB NEW
CACTUS DAHLIAS

SWEET BRIAR

NEW YORK

H.L.BROUSSON

MR DOUGLAS FLEMING

POMPONE DAHLIAS.

A brilliant and charming class of a neat compact habit of growth, with beautifully formed perfectly double miniature flowers, which are produced in profusion throughout the Summer and Autumn. The colours vary from deep crimson and brilliant scarlet to the softest primrose, pure white, &c., three colours being sometimes blended in the same flower. Very useful as cut flowers for decorative purposes. Our list given below includes all the most distinct and beautiful varieties.

SELECT VARIETIES.

	each—s. d.		each—s. d.
ADRIENNE. Crimson scarlet, small beautifully shaped flowers ..	0 6	**MERCURY.** Reddish salmon, heavily tipped with white, perfect form ..	0 6
BACCHUS. Bright scarlet. One of the best ..	0 6	**NERISSA.** Soft rose, tinted with silver; good centre and outline;	
CHEERFULNESS. Old gold, tipped scarlet crimson	0 9	quite a new colour, and of splendid habit ...	0 6
CYRIL. Bright crimson, very fine ..	0 6	**QUEEN OF WHITES.** Pure white, good dwarf habit ..	0 6
DAISY. Amber and salmon, a neat and charming flower	0 6	**SOVEREIGN.** Beautiful bright golden yellow — ..	0 6
DARKEST OF ALL. Very dark maroon crimson	0 6	**SUNNY DAYBREAK.** Pale apricot, edged with rosy red	0 6
DOUGLAS. Rich deep maroon, shaded crimson	0 6	**THE DUKE.** The colour is deep velvety crimson; habit very dwarf	0 6
ELEGANT. Primrose, prettily tipped with lake ..	0 6	**TOMMY KEITH.** Cardinal red, tipped with white	0 6
GANNYMEDE. Amber or fawn tinted lilac, novel and distinct.		**WHITE ASTER.** Pure white, quilled flower of the most free-	
Height three feet ..	0 6	flowering habit; an extremely useful variety for cutting —	0 6
LORNA DOONE. Rosy purple, dark purple tip ..	0 6		

Very good varieties, our selection .. **6 for 2s. 6d.; per doz. 4s. 6d.**

Twelve in 12 popular varieties .. .. .. **3s. 6d.**

POMPONE CACTUS DAHLIA, THE BRIDE.

DAHLIAS—Pompone Cactus.

These charming diminutive varieties are the latest development of the Dahlia. In habit of growth they resemble the ordinary Pompones. The small cactus-shaped blooms are very pretty and exceedingly useful for cut flowers.

	each—s. d.
ALWYN (new). Indian yellow, shaded salmon, free	0 9
ARGUS. Rich crimson-lake, shaded scarlet, very free flowering, and of good habit ..	0 6
CORONATION. Crimson scarlet, very fine; splendid variety for cutting ...	0 6
GRACIE. Yellow tipped with pale pink; a lovely little flower. Free bloomer ...	0 6
LITTLE DOLLY. Clear mauve-pink. A true Pompone Cactus; very free ...	0 6
MARTHA (new). Orange red, madder red at tips of florets; very pretty ...	1 0
MARY. Centre of petals pure white, edged with crimson; very striking ...	0 6
MIGNON. Bright pink with lighter base. A profuse bloomer ...	0 6
NAIN. Deep orange, of true cactus form, free flowering and good ...	0 6
PEACE. A free-flowering, erect-growing creamy white Pompone Cactus Dahlia. Excellent for decoration of the garden or for cut flowers ...	0 6
SOVEREIGN. Rich golden yellow, very free ...	0 9
THE BRIDE. Small, perfectly-formed pure white flowers on long wiry stems, exceedingly useful for cut flowers .. 3 for 2s.	0 9

Six Choice Varieties, our selection .. .. **2s. 6d.**

From Mr. W. REA, Birmingham.

July 30th.
"The Dahlias and Chrysanthemums I had from you in May are doing splendidly, and I am very pleased with them."

From Mr. J. MARTIN, Fletching Mill.

June 20th.
"The Mont Blanc Dahlias I had from you last year did well."

DAHLIAS—SHOW AND FANCY.

The following list includes the finest varieties. The prices quoted are for strong plants from single pots in May.

SELECT VARIETIES.

S denotes Show, F Fancy. All in the following list 6d. each.

BUTTERCUP (S). Yellow tinged with red, very fine.
COLONIST (S). Chocolate and fawn, very distinct.
COMEDIAN (F). Orange ground, flaked crimson and tipped with white.
DIADEM (S). Deep crimson, fine and constant.
DR. KEYNES (S). A pretty rich buff, having a reddish tint at the back of the petals; a good flower and quite distinct.
DUKE OF FIFE (S). Fine rich cardinal, large.
FLORENCE TRANTER (S). Blush white, distinctly edged rosy purple; a good flower, very constant; one of the best.
GOLDFINDER (S). Yellow, tipped with red.
HARRY KEITH (S). Rosy purple, very fine and constant.
LOTTIE ECKFORD (F). White, beautifully striped with purple.
MATTHEW CAMPBELL (F). Buff or apricot, beautifully striped with crimson.
MAUD FELLOWES (S). French white, tinted and shaded with purple; a grand show flower.
MONT BLANC (S). Pure white; large full flower, of exceptional beauty; a grand exhibition variety.
MRS. SAUNDERS (F). Yellow tipped with white. Fine.
MRS. GLADSTONE (S). Delicate blush, with white centre; a most charming flower.
MRS. N. HALLS (F). Bright scarlet, tipped with white.
MRS. STANCOMBE (S). Canary yellow, tipped with fawn.
MURIEL (S). Clear yellow, a splendid flower.
WARRIOR (S). Intense scarlet, grand colour; fine form.
WILLIAM POWELL (S). Primrose yellow; splendid form.

PRICES OF SHOW AND FANCY DAHLIAS.
Our own selection of popular and beautiful varieties,
per doz. 4s. 6d.; six for 2s. 6d.

SINGLE-FLOWERED DAHLIAS.

The Single-flowered Dahlias are charming as cut flowers, and splendidly effective when well staged for exhibition. They commence blooming about the end of July, and are resplendent with a profusion of their lovely flowers till killed by the frost in Autumn. The small or medium-sized flowers are the most useful, either for exhibition or decorative purposes, as it is found they retain their beauty for a much longer period when cut than the larger blooms. Customer's selection from those priced at 6d. each. per doz. 4s. 6d., or 6 for 2s. 6d.

SELECT VARIETIES.

	each—s. d.
BRILLIANT. Rich crimson scarlet with golden centre, a variety of splendid effect ..	0 6
BETTY (new). Rosy lilac with a dark crimson ring in centre, a superb exhibition flower	0 9
COLUMBINE. Bright rose with a suggestion of orange in the centre; a perfectly formed flower..	0 6
DEMON. Rich bright blackish maroon; the finest dark Single Dahlia yet sent out; fine for exhibition	0 6
DONNA CASILDA. Copper orange, with dark maroon ring	0 6
DUCHESS OF WESTMINSTER. Pure white, splendid	0 6
FORMOSA. Dazzling crimson with golden centre	0 6

	each—s. d.
HILDA. White, flushed with flesh colour, each petal having a yellow margin; beautiful form and habit ..	0 6
LESLIE SEALE. Silvery-lilac with crimson disc	0 6
MISS ROBERTS. Clear yellow, of perfect shape	0 6
PUCK. Bright orange, with rich crimson ring round disc; the most richly coloured of the dark-eyed section	0 6
PRINCESS OF WALES. Lovely soft pink, shaded mauve	0 6
SUNRISE. Salmony-orange, with dark ring around centre	0 6
WILLIAM PARROTT. Rich orange scarlet, tipped with white; very pretty and distinct. Beautiful smooth petals and splendid outline. First Class Certificate ..	0 6

NEW PÆONY-FLOWERED DAHLIAS.

A remarkably fine and distinct new class, growing four to five feet in height, and producing enormous beautifully coloured semi-double flowers which at a short distance resemble huge Pæonies. Massed in large beds or in groups on the shrubbery border, they are splendidly effective, and are also well suited as a background to herbaceous borders, &c.

	each—s. d.
ADMIRATION (new). Buff ground flushed with rosy carmine. Immense flowers on long wiry stems. Splendid ..	0 9
DR. K. W. VAN GORKOM. White shaded rose; fine ..	0 6
DUKE HENRY. Rosy cerise, large splendidly formed flowers	0 6
GERMANIA. Brilliant crimson scarlet, very showy; four feet ..	0 6
GLORY OF BAARN. Bright pink, enormous flowers; very fine ..	0 6
HOLMAN HUNT (new). Deep scarlet, large, splendidly formed flowers on long wiry stems ..	1 0
KAISERIN A. VICTORIA. Yellow shading to white, very fine ..	0 6

	each—s. d.
KING LEOPOLD. Canary yellow. A fine variety ..	0 6
LIBERTY (new). Bright scarlet, very large flowers ..	0 9
QUEEN ALEXANDRA. White shading to white at tips ..	0 9
SOLFATERRE. Soft rose. Distinct and beautiful ..	0 6
SNOW WHITE. Pure white, the blooms are of moderate size with pointed cactus-like petals. A charming variety for cut flowers	0 9
THE GEISHA. Orange-red and yellow; very fine ..	0 6
SIX BEAUTIFUL VARIETIES, our selection, including Snow White	2 6

CHRYSANTHEMUMS—JAPANESE.

☞ The following list includes the finest of the varieties exhibited at the great London and other shows during the past Autumn. All ready for sending out in March and April, in strong healthy plants from single pots. Carriage Free at prices quoted.

EXHIBITION CHRYSANTHEMUM.

NEW AND SELECT VARIETIES.

each—s. d.

ALGERNON DAVIS. A really grand yellow Japanese, of the richest golden yellow, and of graceful drooping form ; a splendid doer. Award of Merit, Royal Horticultural Society 0 6

BESSIE GODFREY. Large beautiful flowers of superb form, colour a beautiful canary yellow deepening towards the centre, the outer petals shaded carmine 0 6

BEECHAM KEELING. A splendid exhibition flower of enormous size, colour amber shaded cinnamon red 0 6

COUNTESS OF GRANARD. Rich yellow shaded bronzy buff, large flowers. Strikingly handsome 1 0

DECEMBER GOLD. Rich deep yellow of splendid size, borne on long stiff stems. A first-class and beautiful variety for late blooming 0 6

DUCHESS OF SUTHERLAND. Richest golden yellow, with extra long curly florets 0 6

EDITH JAMIESON. Creamy white overlaid with rich pink ; very large flower with long drooping petals 0 6

E. J. BROOKS. Purplish crimson with white reverse. A superb variety for exhibition 0 6

F. S. VALLIS. Pale yellow, immense flowers ; fine for exhibition .. 0 6

FORMALITY. Lovely ivory white, with graceful reflexing florets. A grand variety of good habit 0 6

HELENA WILLIAMS. A very fine pale golden yellow, sport from Madame Oberthur 0 6

HON. MRS. LOPES (new). A flower of immense size and great substance. Colour a rich golden yellow, fine 0 6

Those priced at 6d. each, Customer's Selection, 4s. 6d. per doz. ; 35s. per 100.

each—s. d.

J. H. SILSBURY. Bright light crimson with shiny yellow reverse, long drooping florets ; a very fine variety 0 6

J. W. MOLYNEUX. Velvety crimson, large flowers with drooping pointed florets. Splendid for exhibition 0 6

JOSEPH STONEY. Bright deep rich crimson, long drooping florets, one of the best exhibition crimsons 0 6

LADY TALBOT. Pale primrose with narrow florets. A deep and splendid flower 0 6

MASTER DAVID. Very large flower, without the slightest coarseness. The florets are medium to broad, of splendid substance, drooping and pleasingly reflexed ; the colour is a remarkable tone of bright crimson with gold reverse 0 9

MASTER JAMES. A large beautiful flower of the finest Exhibition quality, long drooping florets of medium width, colour rich glowing chestnut, suffused with a beautiful rosy tint ; very fine 0 6

MISS ANNIE NICOLL. A superb pure white, sport from Walter Jinks. A fine show flower 0 9

MR. H. THORNTON. Immense flower, of a beautiful blush white, with a fine suffusion of mauve at the tips. The flowers are 9 inches across and 10 inches deep, quite a distinct and invaluable Exhibition flower 0 9

MRS. A. HERBERT. Creamy white large flowers with broad reflexing florets. Splendid variety 1 0

MRS. DAVID SYME. Pure white. A fine Exhibition flower, and one of the best late varieties 0 9

MRS. A. T. MILLER (J.L.). An enormous Japanese incurved. The finest pure white yet seen, and a splendid acquisition for the exhibitor. Award of Merit, Royal Horticultural Society 0 6

MRS. NORMAN DAVIS. A pure white flower of the Madame Carnot type, of immense size and splendid form. The finest of its class yet raised, and one that will give every satisfaction 0 6

MAGNIFICENT. A grand crimson, with golden reverse ; large and very distinct. A fine show flower 0 6

MADAME G. RIVOL. Clear yellow shaded old rose, very fine .. 0 6

MADAME PAOLI RADAELLI. Magnificent variety, colour a delicate rosy white, the late flowers a charming rose colour ; one of the very best 0 6

MADAME R. OBERTHUR. Pure white, immense flowers, with long drooping petals 0 6

MARY FARNSWORTH. A magnificent Jap. of huge size and massive appearance. Colour a beautiful golden pink with buff reverse. A superb exhibition flower. A.M., R.H.S. .. 0 9

MRS. G. MILEHAM. Beautiful rosy mauve pink ; one of the best 0 6

MRS. BARKLEY. Beautiful mauve pink, long broad florets .. 0 6

MRS. CHARLES PENFORD. An immense flower. Rich yellow shaded crimson bronze with extra long drooping florets .. 0 6

NORFOLK BLUSH. Beautiful blush pink. Large handsome flowers.. .. .. 0 9

NORMAN DAVIS. Rich chestnut overlaid with bright gold ; long reflexing florets, splendid habit, very fine 0 6

POCKETT'S CRIMSON (new). Deep crimson reflexing florets, large flower, plant dwarf and of good habit 0 6

PURITY. A splendid large white with curly florets of great length, of easy culture and good habit 0 6

REGINALD VALLIS. Light rosy Amaranth, immense flower .. 0 6

ROSE POCKET (new). Old gold shaded salmon. A large and finely formed flower 0 6

SPLENDOUR. Immense flower with very long drooping petals, red incurved at the tips. The colour is a beautiful crimson with old gold reverse ; very fine 0 6

SUPERB (new). Rosy crimson, a massive flower with broad drooping florets. Fine for Exhibition 0 6

THOMAS STEVENSON. Deep golden yellow. An immense flower 0 6

THE DUCHESS. Chrome yellow, with long curling florets. A large and deep flower 0 6

W. BEADLE. Violet Amaranth striped and shaded crimson, long narrow reflexing florets. Distinct and beautiful .. 0 6

From Mr. W. BUSSEY, Lowestoft.

June 28th.
"The Chrysanthemums, etc., arrived last night quite safely. Please accept my best thanks for the same, also for the beautiful way in which they were packed."

From Mr. BARNES, Carrick-on-Suir.

Sept. 21st.
"The Early-flowering Chrysanthemums supplied by you last year were very handsome."

CHRYSANTHEMUMS.

EARLY-FLOWERING LARGE-FLOWERED VARIETIES.

A splendid class for Garden Decoration.

This beautiful class commence to bloom about the end of August or early in September, and continue till killed by the frost. They are easily grown and not only produce a fine display in the garden, but are exceedingly useful for cut flowers. For growing fine plants, plant out in May 18 inches or 2 feet apart on well-dug fairly rich soil, and place a good stick to each plant. Stop the shoots once or twice to induce a bushy growth, but do not stop them after the end of June. Water should be given freely in very dry weather.

CHRYSANTHEMUM –ROI DES BLANCS.

SELECT LIST.

	each—s.	d.
ALMIRANTE (new). Red with scarlet shading, a very taking colour; free bloomer, 3 ft. F.C.C., N.C.S.	1	0
BOULE DE NEIGE. Pure white, large bold flowers	0	6
CHAMP D'OR. Deep canary yellow; fine dwarf habit	0	6
CRIMSON DIANA (new). Brilliant crimson sport from Diana	0	6
CRIMSON MARIE MASSE. Bright crimson; very fine	0	6
CRANFORD WHITE. A very fine white, best disbudded	0	6
DIANA. Deep bronze-orange, shaded gold; very fine	0	6
DOROTHY ASHLEY (new). Pink shaded with bronzy salmon. Dwarf, and free blooming. very distinct. F.C.C., N.C.S.	1	0
EDEN. Bright rose, incurving flowers; splendid variety	0	6
ETHEL BLADES. Chestnut scarlet, very bright flowers	0	6
GOACHER'S CRIMSON. The finest early crimson yet sent out	0	6
GOACHER'S PINK. Bright pink, large flowers	0	6
GOLDEN MADAME DESGRANGE. One of the best	0	6
GUSTAVE GRUNERWALD. Beautiful soft pink. large	0	6
HOLLICOT WHITE (new). Pure, glistening white, reflexed blooms, splendid for cutting. F.C.C., N.C.S.	1	0
HORACE MARTIN. Deep yellow, lovely colour	0	6
LESLIE (new). Rich buttercup yellow. A splendid variety	0	6
LILLIE. Pearly-pink, splendid habit	0	6
MADAME DESGRANGE. White; very useful for out-doors	0	6
MABEL ROBERTS. Deep pink, with fine long sprays	0	6
MIGNON. Delicate rosy mauve, one of the finest varieties	0	6
MRS. A. THOMPSON. Deepest golden yellow, lovely colour	0	6
MRS. BURRELL. Pale primrose; very early	0	6
NINA BLICK. Bright scarlet-red, finishing off with a rich golden bronze ; a splendid variety for bunching	0	6
QUEEN OF THE EARLIES. Pure white ; splendid	0	6
RABBIE BURNS. A sport from Madame Marie Masse; colour a distinct and beautiful shade of salmon-pink	0	6
ROI DES BLANCS. Pure white, large flowers, splendid variety	0	6
ROI DES PRECOCES. Rich dark crimson; dwarf	0	6
RYECROFT SCARLET. Bright red and bronze, forming an immense bush. Fine for massing	0	6
TAPIS DE NEIGE. Purest snow-white, very free and of stiff upright habit. Fine for cutting	0	6
WELLS' SCARLET. Bright scarlet terra-cotta, very bright	0	6
WELLS' CRIMSON. Bright crimson with golden reverse; splendid habit ; one of the best	0	6

**Strong Plants from single pots in April, our selection,
4s. 6d. per doz. ; 6 for 2s. 6d.**

INCURVED EXHIBITION VARIETIES.

Strong plants from single pots in March and April, our selection, 4s. 6d. per doz. ; 6 for 2s. 6d.

	each—s.	d.
BONNIE DUNDEE. Orange, shaded rosy bronze	0	6
BUTTERCUP (new). Clear rich buttercup. yellow without shading; magnificent variety	0	6
CHARLES H. CURTIS. Deep yellow, one of the best	0	6
CLARA WELLS (new). Rich cream colour ; a large true incurved	0	6
DUCHESS OF FIFE. An enormous flower of great depth, white sometimes slightly tinted rose	0	6
EMBLEME POITEVINE. Beautiful canary yellow ; large flowers	0	6
LADY ISABEL. Lovely clear, lavender blush, fine	0	6
MA PERFECTION. Pure white, beautifully incurved	0	6
MRS. J. P. BRYCE. Very large beautifully formed flowers of the purest white	0	6
MRS. JAMES HYGATE (new). Pure white, an immense flower	0	6
THE KING. Largest size and perfect form, colour rich lake with silvery reverse	0	6
TOPAZE ORIENTAL. Very large, pale straw yellow ; splendid	0	6

SINGLE-FLOWERED CHRYSANTHEMUMS.

These beautiful flowers are now growing fast in public favour. Their long, wiry flower-stems and graceful Marguerite-like blooms making them of especial value as cut flowers for Table Decoration, and as pot plants for the greenhouse.

	each—s.	d.
BELLE OF WEYBRIDGE. Bright chestnut crimson, very fine	0	6
CALEDONIA. Beautiful rosy lilac, white ring round the disc	0	6
CALLIOPE. Large pure white, beautifully reflexed	0	6
CROWN JEWEL IMPROVED (new). Rich rosy chestnut	0	6
CAPELLA (new). Rich golden yellow, with fine clear disc	0	6
EDITH PAGRAM. Lovely deep pink, with white ring round disc sometimes slightly tinted rose	0	6
EDWIN NOTTELL (new). Delicate primrose; a beautiful flower	0	6
ELSIE NEVILLE. Terra-cotta red, beautiful dwarf habit	0	6
FRAMFIELD BEAUTY. Deep rich velvety crimson. Very handsome	0	6
J. B. LOWE. Brilliant crimson scarlet	0	6
KITTY BOURNE. Deep yellow, very fine	0	6
MISS TAKEY BIRD. Primrose; a large beautiful flower	0	6
MENSA. Pure white. A fine exhibition flower	0	6
PEGASUS (new). Pure white ; a magnificent variety	0	6
PRINCESS OF WALES. Bright rosy-pink with pure white ring	0	6
SYLVIA SLADE. Beautiful deep rose, white centre	0	9

SINGLE-FLOWERED ZONAL PELARGONIUMS.

NEW AND SELECT VARIETIES.

All Autumn Struck. Strong young plants from single pots.

NEW ZONAL PELARGONIUMS.

	s. d.
BLENHEIM. Brilliant scarlet with white eye, large	0 6
CALEDONIA. Blush pink, very large perfectly formed flowers	0 6
GARMANIA. Soft salmon rose, large flowers, distinct	0 6
COUNTESS OF JERSEY (new). Coral salmon, splendid flower	0 6
DR. ERNEST RAWSON. Deep purple velvety crimson	0 6
DR. NANSEN. Finest pure white	0 6
DUKE OF BEDFORD. Dark crimson with white eye, large flowers	0 6
GERTRUDE PEARSON. Pure rose pink, with conspicuous white blotch on two upper petals	0 6
LADY ROSCOE. Beautiful shade of pink	0 6
LADY WARWICK. Beautiful white with a bright pink edge	0 6
LORD ROSEBERY. A deep rich salmon	0 6
MR. J. A. BELL. White and shrimp pink, very pretty	0 6
MRS. WRIGHT. The nearest to a blue yet raised	0 6
SNOWSTORM. A splendid dwarf growing pure white; first-class	0 6
SAXONIA (new). Brilliant scarlet, very large flowers	0 9
ST. LOUIS (new). Scarlet crimson, immense flowers	0 9
VIRGINIA. Pure snow white; flowers large	0 6
WARLEY (new). Orange and white mottled; a superb flower	0 6

PRICES OF SINGLE ZONAL PELARGONIUMS.

Twelve in 12 superb varieties, our selection .. .. 4s. 6d.

Six in 6 extra fine varieties, our selection .. .. 2s. 6d.

A splendid class of beautiful free blooming plants, admirably suited for greenhouse or conservatory decoration, and may be had in bloom nearly all the year round.

DOUBLE-FLOWERED ZONAL PELARGONIUMS.
(A FINE CLASS FOR POT CULTURE.)

SELECT VARIETIES.

	each—s. d.
PAUL CRAMPEL DOUBLE (new). Magnificent variety, bearing large trusses of deep scarlet double flowers. Splendid for Greenhouse decorations	1 0
CALIFORNIAN GOLD. Brilliant orange scarlet; fine	0 6
DR. DESPRES. Deep crimson, enormous pips and trusses	0 6
JULES LAFORGNE. Fine trusses of very large semi-double purplish crimson flowers with distinct white eye; splendid	1 0
MADAME ROZAIN. A very fine double, pure white; plant dwarf, and free blooming, large flowers	0 6
MISTRAL. Brilliant clear scarlet large semi-double flowers with conspicuous white eye, very fine showy variety	0 9

	each—s. d.
PICOTEE (Fraicheur). Beautiful pure white, the petals delicately edged with deep rosy pink	0 6
RASPAIL IMPROVED. Bright rich scarlet; large flowers	0 6
TRIOMPHE DE FRANCE. Salmon-red, with creamy edges; splendid variety	0 6
VIOLET DANIELS. A fine variety of immense size. The colour is a beautiful transparent salmony-gold	0 6
VESUVIUS. Intense vermilion scarlet	0 6
WHITE KING OF DENMARK (new). A very fine variety bearing large handsome trusses of pure white double flowers	2 0
CHOICE VARIETIES, our selection per doz. 4s. 6d., 6 for 2s. 6d.	

DOUBLE-FLOWERED IVY-LEAVED PELARGONIUMS.

A splendid Class for Pots, Hanging Baskets, Vases, &c. They are also charming when planted out of doors in small beds, and are very useful for Cut Flowers.

SELECT VARIETIES.

	each—s. d.
ACHIEVEMENT. The splendid large double flowers, which are produced in grand trusses, are of a brilliant rosy carmine colour. This is highly recommended as a beautiful variety 3 for 2s.	0 9
COL. BADEN POWELL. Soft blush lilac flowers, produced freely in large trusses; a beautiful variety	0 6
CUVIER. Beautiful rich violet purple, very fine	0 6
HIS MAJESTY THE KING. A lovely shade of dark cerise, large trusses of bloom and very free-flowering	0 9
LEOPARD. Clear lilac-pink, heavily blotched with crimson all over the upper petals; very distinct	0 6
JAMES T. HAMILTON (new). A grand new hybrid, ivy-leaved variety, bearing a profusion of large trusses of semi-double flowers of an intense glowing carmine-crimson colour. A.M., R.H.S.	2 0
JEANNE D'ARC. White, suffused with lavender	0 6
MILLFIELD GEM. A cross between an Ivy-leaf and Zonal, the flower is blush white with blotches of crimson shaded with pink. A very distinct and beautiful variety	0 9

	each—s. d.
MADAME THIBAUT. Brilliant crimson cerise	0 6
PURITY. Splendid pure white, with large full double flowers, by far the best white, and one that will be found exceedingly useful for cut flowers	0 6
QUEEN OF ROSES. The flowers are very large, 2½ to 3 inches across, perfectly double, of splendid form and substance, and of the most beautiful rosy crimson carmine colour	0 6
RED CROUSSE (new). Rosy crimson, splendid for hanging baskets	0 9
RYECROFT SCARLET. Very large bloom, the very best of its colour and a very free grower	0 6
RYECROFT SURPRISE. It has a fine bold vigorous upright habit, it is wonderfully free, blooming at nearly every joint. Colour, a lovely salmon-pink	0 6
SOUVENIR DE CHARLES TURNER. Splendid variety, large, well-formed flowers of a beautiful deep rose colour, and borne in large trusses	0 6
CHOICE VARIETIES, our selection — 6 for 2s. 6d.; per doz. 4s. 6d.	

From Mr. W. REA, B. Lam.

July 30th.

"The Dahlias and Chrysanthemums I had from you in May are doing splendidly and I am very pleased with them."

From Mr. W. GRAY, Lingfield.

April 20th.

"The Chrysanthemum Plants arrived safely and I am quite satisfied with them."

MRS. E. G. HILL.

FUCHSIAS—Select Varieties.

Those marked (*) are double-flowered.

each—s. d.

*ALFRED RAMBAUD. Very large double flowers; sepals of a lovely scarlet; and the petals deep violet 0 6

BEAUTY OF EXETER. Immense bright salmon rose blooms, most abundantly produced on a plant of a vigorous habit; most charming variety 0 6

CADMUS (new). A large beautifully formed flower, sepals scarlet, corolla ivory white; very fine .. .. — 0 9

*DUCHESS OF EDINBURGH. A superb variety bearing large well-formed flowers; tube and sepals are of a rich crimson-scarlet; the corolla a creamy white .. 0 6

EARL OF BEACONSFIELD. A splendid hybrid variety, flowers over three inches long, carmine, with deep carmine corolla 0 6

FASCINATION (new). A most charming variety with long white tube and sepals which are broad and prettily recurved; corolla a lovely shade of rose-pink 0 9

*JUPITER. Large, beautiful double flowers; sepals well reflexed, brilliant scarlet; corolla a deep plum violet 0 6

*LA FRANCE. The sepals a bright rich scarlet, the corolla a bright light violet .. 0 6

*MADAME BRUANT. Immense flowers; tube and sepals a rich scarlet, corolla a beautiful lilac-mauve veined with rosy red. The blooms are very double 0 6

MADAME ROZAIN. A truly grand variety, bearing immense flowers of the most elegant form; the tube and sepals a deep rich scarlet crimson colour, the corolla a charming creamy white 0 6

*MAGNIFICENT. A grand variety, bearing immense double flowers. The sepals are well reflexed, of a bright rich crimson colour, the corolla deep violet blue.. .. 0 6

*MOLESWORTH. Tube and sepals a bright deep carmine-crimson colour; full double white corolla 0 6

*MRS. E. G. HILL. This magnificent Fuchsia is one of the most splendid ever sent out. The plants are short-jointed and sturdy in growth, with beautiful dark green foliage. The flowers are of an immense size, the tube and sepals being of a deep rich scarlet colour, the corolla a beautiful creamy white, veined with pink; grand variety 0 9

MURIEL (new). Very large finely reflexed flowers, sepals a brilliant scarlet, corolla violet red, very distinct and fine 0 6

*P. RADAELLI. Enormous double corolla of a rich bluish-violet colour, striped and stained with lovely carmine. The tube and sepals are of a rich red, the sepals well recurved 0 6

PRINCESS MAY. A most charming variety. The tube and sepals are of a lovely creamy white, the corolla a brilliant carmine-rose colour. The plant is of a dwarf, compact habit of growth, a wonderfully profuse bloomer of beautiful effect .. 0 6

ROYAL PURPLE. Corolla dark velvety purple, sepals clear crimson scarlet; immense massive flowers 0 9

Twelve choice named varieties, our own selection .. .. per doz. 3s. 6d. and 4s. 0d.
Six   „   „   „   „   „   .. .. 2s. 0d. and 2s. 6d.

HARDY FUCHSIAS.

A fine class of beautiful hardy plants of shrubby growth, very effective in Summer and Autumn, with their numerous scarlet and purple flowers; should have a slight protection the first Winter after planting.

CONICA. Scarlet. Height 2 feet.
EXONIENSIS. Globular-shaped scarlet flowers. Height 2 feet.
GRACILIS. Drooping, graceful habit. Height 3 feet.
MADAME CORNELLISEN. Scarlet with white corolla. Height 3 feet.
RICCARTONI. Very free flowering, forms a dense bush during the Summer. Very hardy, and of the best.
THOMPSONI. A dwarf growing variety about 18 inches high. Very free flowering and handsome.

Strong young plants from single pots, customers' selection, per doz. 5s.; each 6d.

HELIOTROPES.

These are delightful subjects for pots in the greenhouse or for planting out of doors in Summer, their delicious perfume being always welcome. When grown outside they should be planted in a partially shaded position and kept well supplied with water in dry weather. These will grow into fine plants and may be taken up and potted in the Autumn for Winter blooming in the greenhouse. Planted out or grown in large pots in a moderately heated greenhouse, the plants will live for several years and will be almost continually in bloom.

per doz.

BOUQUET BLANC. Pure white; very fragrant 3 6
MADAME DE BUSSY. Beautiful blue, with large white eye; deliciously scented .. 4 0
MADAME ARTHUR GUE. Flowers violet with white centre; free flowering and very fragrant .. 4 0
QUEEN OF VIOLETS. Dark violet with white eye, very free flowering and of good habit .. 3 6
WHITE LADY. Deliciously scented 3 6

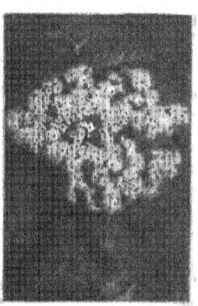

HELIOTROPE.

CAMPANULAS.

each—s. d.

MAYI (new). A lovely trailing variety, beautiful lavender blue flowers; a gem for pots .. .. .. 3 for 2s. 6d. 1 0
ISOPHYLLA, BLUE. Lilac blue .. .. .. 3 for 1s. 3d. 0 6
„ ALBA. White; beautiful .. .. 3 for 1s. 3d. 0 6

Beautiful dwarf trailing species, with large salver-shaped flowers; splendid for suspended pots, &c.

PYRAMIDALIS. Blue } Beautiful upright- } 3 for 1s. 3d. 0 6
„ ALBA. White } growing vars. } 3 for 2s. 0d. 0 9

COLEUS.

NEW LARGE-LEAVED HYBRIDS. We offer seedlings, in May, from our splendid strain of large-leaved, brilliantly coloured varieties. Strong young plants from single pots .. .. per doz. 1s. 6d.

MARGUERITES.

NEW DWARF WHITE. Very compact and free-flowering; a gem for pots or window boxes .. .. .. per doz. 5s.; each 6d.
MRS. F. SANDER (new). Large, beautiful, white double flowers; a splendid pot plant for the greenhouse .. per doz. 7s. 6d.; each 9d.

HARDY PERENNIAL FLOWERING PLANTS.

We have a fine collection of these popular, interesting, and beautiful plants, which are daily coming more and more into favour with the Gardening Public. All the varieties are perennial, extremely hardy, and many of them produce flowers of the most exquisite beauty, which are very valuable for cutting, whilst the dwarfer-growing sorts are admirably suited for rockeries or edgings. No special soil or position is necessary, as with but very few exceptions, they will thrive almost anywhere, and with a good collection, a charming variety and succession of bloom may be had throughout the Spring and Summer. The plants we offer are all grown in pots, and may be removed at any time or season.

SELECT LIST.

ACHILLÆA PTARMICA, THE PEARL. Large double, pure white flowers; fine for cutting. Height 2 feet .. .. per doz. 5s.; each 6d.
ALYSSUM SAXATILE COMPACTA. A charming Spring-flowering Perennial; yellow, dwarf rockery plant per doz. 3s.; each 4d.
" **FL. PL.** Same habit as Compacta, but with double flowers; very showy .. .. per doz. 5s.; each 6d.
ANCHUSA ITALICA, DROPMORE VARIETY. The finest blue-flowered herbaceous plant in existence. Very free blooming. Height about 4 feet per doz. 7s. 6d.; each 9d.
" **OPAL.** A sky-blue variety of the new popular Dropmore Variety. Height 3 feet, 1s., each.
ANEMONE ALPINA SULPHUREA. 2 feet high, with large pale yellow flowers each 1s. 6d.
" **COUP D'ARGENT.** Beautiful white flowers. Height 18 inches
per doz. 5s.; each 6d.
" **JAPONICA ALBA.** One of the very best Autumn-blooming plants. Flowers of a beautiful pure white per doz. 5s.; each 6d.
" " **LADY ARDILAUN.** Fine new, pure white .. .. per doz. 5s.; each 6d.
" " **ROSEA.** Rose " 5s.; " 6d.
" " **RUBRA.** Rosy red .. each 6d.
" " **WHIRLWIND.** Flower white, with more than one row of petals
per doz. 5s.; each 6d.
" **SYLVESTRIS PLENA.** Double, snow-white flowers; a most beautiful variety each 1s.
ANTHEMIS TINCTORIA DANIELSII. Height 3—4 ft., bearing a profusion of large bright golden yellow flowers. Very useful for cutting .. per doz. 4s. 6d.; each 6d.
" **PALLIDA.** Beautiful pale primrose yellow flowers on long stems. First-rate for cutting per doz. 4s. 6d.; each 6d.
ANTHERICUM LILIASTRUM MAJOR. Very fine; pure white per doz. 5s.; each 6d.
" " (St. Bruno's Lily). Fragrant white flowers .. .. per doz. 5s.; each 6d.
AQUILEGIA CŒRULEA (Rocky Mountain Columbine). Large pale blue flowers with white corolla .. per doz. 5s.; each 6d.
" **CHRYSANTHA.** Golden yellow flowers per doz. 5s.; each 6d.
ARABIS ALPINA, FL. PL. A beautiful double-flowering form, produces spikes of pure white flowers resembling miniature stocks per doz. 4s.; each 6d.
" **VARIEGATA.** A capital edging plant. Height six inches. Suitable for rockwork per doz. 5s.; each 6d.
ARMERIA GRANDIFLORA. Grass-like foliage with large heads of bright rose-coloured flowers. Height 1 foot each 6d.
" **PLANTAGINEA ROSEA.** Large heads of rose-coloured flowers
per doz. 5s.; each 6d.
ARENARIA BALEARICA. A minute species covering stones or wood with sheets of dark-green foliage studded with white flowers. Height one inch. Splendid for rockeries .. .. per doz. 5s.; each 6d.
ASPERULA LONGIFLORA. Small white flowers, very pretty. Shade-loving plants, easily grown .. .. each 6d.

A PORTION OF AN HERBACEOUS BORDER AT OUR NURSERIES.

ASTERS

MICHAELMAS DAISIES.

Beautiful Autumn bloomers.
ASTER BEAUTY OF COLWALL (new). The first and only double-flowered Michaelmas Daisy in cultivation. The blooms are perfectly double and of a pleasing shade of lavender. Height 4 feet each 1s. 6d.
" **BESSARABICUS.** Purplish-blue, very large. Height two feet each 6d.
" **CLIMAX** (new). The largest in cultivation, flowers a clear light blue, with bright golden centre .. .. each 1s.
" **CRENATA.** Dark blue, large flowers, about 2½ feet each 6d.
" **CREVIS.** Light blue. Height three feet. Splendid for borders .. .. each 6d.
" **DUMOSUS.** Rosy blush, very compact. Height 1½ feet each 6d.
" **ELSIE PERRY.** Rose pink, very pretty. Height two feet each 6d.
" **ESME.** Large pure white flowers, good habit. Height two feet each 6d.
" **FELTHAM BLUE** (new). Clear dark-blue, large flower with bright yellow centre. Grand variety. Height four feet each 9d.
" **HYBRIDUS NANUS.** Rosy pink. 15 inches each 6d.
" **MADAME SOYNEUCE.** Bright clear rose-colour. Height 1½ ft., per doz. 5s.; each 6d.
" **MARGARET.** Rosy blush. A superb variety. Height 4½ feet each 9d.
" **MULTIFLORUS.** Handsome spikes of miniature pure white flowers; very pretty. Height 4 feet per doz. 5s.; each 6d.
" **NOVÆ ANGLIÆ.** Large bluish-purple. Blooms in October per doz. 5s.; each 6d.

ASTER NOVÆ ANGLIÆ ELEGANS. Lilac. Height four feet .. .. each 6d.
" " **BELGEII DENSUS.** Blue. Height about 2 feet .. .. each 6d.
" **PERRY'S FAVOURITE.** A beautiful red-flowered variety of A. amellus, the only one of the family yet raised each 1s.
" **ST. BRIGID.** Lovely soft rose. Height 4 feet .. .. each 6d.
" **ST. PATRICK.** Soft silvery grey, large, loose and wavy. Height 4 feet each 9d.
" **SENSATION.** White, golden centre, branching habit. Height 2½ to 3ft. each 9d.
" **SNOWDON.** Quite new, most charming, about 4 feet in height, lovely bracts of almost pure white flowers with pale yellowish disc .. .. each 9d.
" **THE PEARL.** Blush white, a superb variety. Height 3 feet each 9d.
" **TOP SAWYER.** Clear blue, large flowers. Height 5 feet per doz. 5s.; each 6d.
" **TRIUMPH.** Very dark pink. Height 5 feet .. .. each 6d.
" **VENUS.** Pale lavender, flushed with pink flowering from top to base. Height 2½ feet .. .. each 9d.
" **VIMINEUS PERFECTUS.** White, pink centre, a charming variety. Height 3 feet each 1s.
Our Selection, 4s. 6d., 6s., 9s. per dozen.
AUBRIETIA HENDERSONII. Deep Violet purple; fine for rockwork .. each 6d.
" **DELTOIDEA.** Pale lavender .. " 6d.
" **VARIEGATA.** Silver variegated foliage; a gem for dry rockeries each 6d.
" **LEICHTLINII.** Rich crimson, profuse flowering plant per doz. 5s.; each 6d.

Hardy Perennial Flowering Plants (continued).

AURICULAS, ALPINE. Choice seedlings, self coloured and laced varieties doz. 3s. 6d.
BUPTHALMUM SALICIFOLIUM. Golden yellow flowers; very showy. each 6d.
CAMPANULA CARPATICA. Dark blue, dwarf. Very showy .. per doz. 5s. ; each 6d.
  „ GRANDIFLORA ALBA. Pure white, very fine for rockeries per doz. 5s. ; each 6d.
  „ MARIESII. Very large beautiful dark blue flowers; splendid dwarf growing varieties .. .. each 6d.
  „ „ MOERHEIMI. Long spikes of semi-double pure white flowers per doz. 5s. ; each 6d.
  „ PERSICIFOLIA ALBA GRANDIFLORA. A fine upright growing variety, with large pure white flowers per doz. 8s. ; each 6d.
  „ „ CORONATA ALBA. A most beautiful variety, growing about 3 feet high, and throwing up lovely panicles of pure white flowers. Charming as a cut flower each 1s.
  „ PUSILLA. SYN. PUMILLA. Pale blue, dwarf habit, very profuse. Height 3 inches .. .. each 6d.
  , PYRAMIDALIS (The Chimney Campanula). Long spikes of blue salver-like flowers per doz. 5s. ; each 6d.
  „ „ ALBA. A white flowering form of the preceding ; a fine pot plant .. each 6d.

ANCHUSA OPAL.

CHRYSANTHEMUM MAXIMUM. Pure white flowers. Fine .. per doz. 5s. ; each 6d.
  „ „ MRS. C. LOWTHIAN BELL. A magnificent early-flowering dwarf variety, producing enormous pure white, finely formed flowers with deep centres. A grand acquisition. Awarded a First Class Certificate, R.H.S.
per doz. 10s. 6d. ; each 1s.
  „ „ KING EDWARD VII. One of the finest varieties, about 3 feet high, with large, beautiful, white flowers ; erect stems. Blooming from July to October
per doz. 5s. ; each 6d.
  „ LATIFOLIUM. Pure white, invaluable for Autumn decoration
per doz. 5s. ; each 6d.
  , FILIFERUM. Of free, vigorous habit, with large flowers, the narrow flat petals being cleft or sub-divided each 6d.
  ■ PERFECTION. Snow-white flowers per doz. 5s. ; each 6d.

CENTAUREA GLASTIFOLIA. Tall, with silvery foliage and yellow heads per doz. 5s. ; each 6d.
  „ MACROCEPHALA. A fine ornamental plant, with massive foliage and large rich golden flowers per doz. 5s. ; each 6d.
CHEIRANTHUS ALPINUS. Dwarf species ; flowers lemon-yellow, borne in great profusion in Spring per doz. 4s. 6d. ; each 6d.
COREOPSIS GRANDIFLORA. Flowers 2½ to 3 inches across, bright golden yellow per doz. 5s. ; each 6d.

DELPHINIUMS.

Single and Double-flowered. These fine hardy plants are deserving a place in every garden ; they continue in bloom for a long time in summer, many of the varieties producing spikes of bloom one foot to two feet in length, and of the most intense and delicate colours.
DELPHINIUM MOERHEIMI (new). Has large flowers of the purest white ; it is doubtless the best hardy perennial introduced in the last ten years .. .. .. each 5s.
  „ BELLADONNA. Lovely sky-blue, one of the finest in cultivation
per doz. 10s. 6d. ; each 1s.
  „ „ GRANDIFLORUM. Stronger stems and larger flowers than the above ; a striking acquisition per doz. 21s. ; each 2s.
  „ BLACK and WHITE. Grand new and distinct flower, large circular white blossoms with black eye which is most conspicuous, flowers measuring 2 inches across
each 3s. 6d.
  „ CAPRI. The best sky-blue single Delphinium in commerce. each 5s.
  „ FRANCIS F. FOX. One of the very best Delphiniums, with large flowers of a fine dark blue ; brilliant colour each 1s. 6d.
  „ K. TH. CARON. Bright gentian blue, with white centre ; quite distinct each 1s. 6d.
  „ LIZE VAN VEEN. Remarkable for the immense size of the single flowers, which are a blue colour .. .. each 2s.
  „ MR. J. S. BRUNTON. Flowers are of the finest sky-blue, in the style of Belladonna ; produces an immense quantity of long, graceful spikes {.. each 1s. 6d.
  „ PLEIAS. Fine azure blue, inner petals shaded rose, white eye .. .. each 1s.
  „ QUEEN OF THE LILACS. Lovely rich lilac, white eye, which gives it a striking appearance .. .. .. each 2s.
  „ THOS. TILROOK. Rich French blue, base of petals rosy mauve, large flower
each 1s.
  „ USTANE. Light blue, inner petals rosy mauve, dark eye, splendid .. each 1s.
OUR OWN SELECTION OF SORTS,
each 9d., 1s., and 1s. 6d.
per doz. 7s. 6d., 10s. 6d., and 15s.
DIANTHUS GRANITICUS (new). Tufts of dark spring foliage and myriads of rosy flowers on wiry stems, lasting in bloom for several months. Height 9 inches .. each 1s. 6d.
DIELYTRA SPECTABILIS. Lovely bending sprays of deep rose-coloured flowers, handsome divided foliage .. .. each 6d.
DICTAMNUS FRAXINELLA (Burning Bush). This remarkable plant is one of the most singularly interesting herbaceous perennials in existence .. .. .. each 6d.
  „ ALBA. A fac-simile of the preceding, but with pure white flowers ; very showy .. .. each 6d.
DODECATHEON JEFFREYANUM. Large umbels of Cyclamen-like blossoms, rose coloured, with a yellow ring at the orifice of the corolla per doz. 7s. 6d. ; each 9d.
  „ MEADIA (The American Cowslip). Very pretty heads of lilac and crimson Cyclamen-like flowers ; capital for rockeries each 6d.

DORONICUM, HARPUR CREWE (Plantagineum excelsum). A magnificent variety, bearing bold golden yellow flowers
per doz. 5s. ; each 6d.
DRACOCEPHALUM VIRGINICUM. Erect stems, 2½ feet high, with numerous bright pink flowers .. per doz. 5s. ; each 6d.
  „ „ ALBUM. Fac-simile of preceding, with white flowers per doz. 5s. ; each 6d.
EPILOBIUM OBCORDATUM. Rosy crimson, fine for rockwork. Ht. 6 inches each 4s.
EREMURUS HIMALAICUS. A magnificent hardy plant throwing up grand spikes of white flowers six or eight feet in height ; splendidly effective when planted in groups each 3s. 6d., 5s. and 7s. 6d.
  „ BUNGEII. Beautiful variety, growing only about 3 feet high, with handsome spikes of bright yellow flowers
each 5s. and 7s. 6d.
  „ ROBUSTUS. Huge spikes of bright peach-coloured flowers, eight to ten feet high, with three to four feet of bloom, sweetly scented. Beautifully striking
each 2s. 6d., 3s. 6d., and 5s.
ERIGERON SPECIOSUM SUPERBUM. Large lavender-blue flowers, with yellow centre. Height three feet per doz. 5s. ; each 6d.

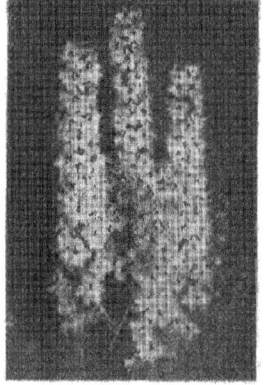

DELPHINIUM.

ERYNGIUM OLIVERIANUM. A plant of handsome appearance, flowers of a lovely amethystine blue
per doz. 5s. 6d. ; each 6d.
  „ PLANUM. Numerous small blue heads. Height three feet. July to September 6d.
FUCHSIAS. Perfectly hardy Fuchsias are very interesting. They delight in well drained land in sunny positions. We offer a set of six different species named for 3s.
FUNKIAS. A beautiful genus of handsome foliage plants, exceedingly attractive either for pot culture or for planting in the open per doz. 5s. ; each 6d.
GAILLARDIAS, CHOICE MIXED SEEDLINGS
per doz. 4s. 6d. ; 6 for 2s. 6d.
GALEGA OFFICINALIS. Numerous blue flowers on branching stems. Height four feet
per doz. 5s. ; each 6d.
  „ „ ALBA. Similar to preceding, with white flowers per doz. 5s. ; each 6d.
GENTIANA ACAULIS. Intense blue
per doz. 5s. ; each 6d.

Hardy Perennial Flowering Plants (continued).

ASTER, BEAUTY OF COLWALL.

GERBERA JAMESONI. Brilliant orange-scarlet flowers, three to four inches across. A beautiful plant for the cool greenhouse, or will succeed if planted on a sheltered border and slightly protected in Winter   each 1s. 6d.

GEUM HELDREICHII. Rich orange-coloured flowers   per doz. 7s. 6d.; each 6d.
   "   **HELDREICHII SUPERBA.** Similar to the preceding but deeper colour   each 6d.
   "   **MONTANUM.** Yellow; a charming plant. Height six inches   each 6d.
   "   **COCCINEUM PLENUM.** Bright scarlet flowers   per doz. 5s.; each 6d.
   "   **MRS. BRADSHAW.** A novelty of sterling merit, with semi-double flowers, fully 2 in. across, freely produced, on long stems, flowering from June to Oct.   each 1s.

GYPSOPHILA PANICULATA. A fine border plant, valuable for cutting   each 6d.
   "   **FL. PL.** A pure white, double-flowered, of the well-known G. paniculata. Valuable for cutting, one of the best recent introductions   each 1s.
   "   **PROSTRATA ROSEA.** A novel and charming variety, producing an abundance of delicate pink flowers on branching stems   each 9d.
   "   **REPENS MONSTROSA.** A fine variety for cutting, flowers pure white, and nearly double the size of the type, each 6s.; ea. 8d.

HELENIUM AUTUMNALE ..   each 6d.
   "   **GRANDICEPHALUM STRIATUM.** Large deep orange flowers, irregularly striped and blotched with crimson ; very erect robust habit   per doz. 5s.; each 6d.
   "   **CUPREUM.** A sterling novelty of recent introduction, flowering from June onwards; deep coppery-crimson flowers, often striped with yellow, splendid for cutting. Height three feet   each 6d.
   "   **PUMILUM.** Beautiful Autumn-blooming plant, eighteen inches high, bearing a profusion of bright yellow flowers.. each 6d.
   "   **MAGNIFICUM.** This forms immense heads of soft yellow flowers, two to three inches across. In flower through Summer until late Autumn   each 9d.
   "   **RIVERTON GEM** (new). Brilliant terracotta red. A continuous bloomer from August to end of October. Three to four feet ..   .. each 1s. 6d.

HELENIUM BOLANDERI. Pale yellow flowers, with brown discs. Height 2½ feet   each 6d.
HELIANTHUS, GOLDEN BOUQUET. Rich golden yellow. Height four feet; very free flowering   ..   .. each 6d.
   "   **LÆTIFLORUS.** Semi-double flowers   per doz. 5s.; each 6d.
   "   **MISS MELLISH.** Much larger flower than Lætiflorus. Height six feet   each 6d.
   "   **RIGIDUS.** One of the best. Rich golden yellow flowers with a black disc   each 6d.
   "   **SOLEIL D'OR.** A fine variety, with deep orange-yellow double flowers   per doz. 5s.; each 6d.
   "   **TOMENTOSUS.** A most distinct and characteristic plant, growing about four feet high, with woolly foliage. The flowers are of a rich golden yellow colour, and three inches across   each 6d.
HELIANTHEMUM (Sun Roses). In beautiful named sorts ..   per doz. 5s.; each 6d.
HELIOPSIS B. LADHAMS. Orange-yellow flowers, medium size, a showy plant, vigorous grower. Height four to five feet ..   ..   .. each 9d.
HELLEBORUS NIGER (Christmas Rose). Fine, pure white, abundant bloomer   per doz. 10s. 6d. & 15s.; each 1s. & 1s. 6d.
HEMEROCALLIS (Day Lily). Handsome for clumps on the border
   "   **AURANTIACA.** Large orange yellow flowers. Height two feet   each 9d.
   "   **MAJOR.** Flowers large, trumpet shape, of a deep orange colour. Height three feet   ..   each 1s.
   "   **FLAVA.** Large umbels of beautiful Lily-like flowers of a bright yellow colour   per doz. 4s. 6d.; each 6d.
   "   **FULVA.** Bronzy orange, shading to crimson   per doz. 4s. 6d.; each 6d.
   "   **KWANSO FL. PL.** Broad foliage and rich bronzy yellow flowers. Height four feet ..   ..   .. each 9d.
   "   **THUNBERGI.** Bright yellow   each 9d.
HEPATICAS. These are amongst the most charming Spring-blooming plants we possess.
   "   **ANGULOSA.** Sky blue; beautiful   per doz. 5s.; each 6d.
   "   **TRILOBA ALBA.** Single white   per doz. 7s. 6d.; each 9d.
   "   **CÆRULEA.** Single blue   per doz. 5s.; each 6d.
   "   **RUBRA.** Single red   per doz. 7s. 6d.; each 9d.
HEUCHERA SANGUINEA GRANDIFLORA. Brilliant scarlet; a gem for cutting   per doz. 5s.; each 6d.
   "   **SPLENDENS.** A bright crimson variety of H. sanguinea. Height two feet, each 1s.
   "   **MACRANTHA.** Loose panicles of white flowers   ..   per doz. 5s.; each 6d.
   "   **EDGE HALL HYBRID.** Large rose-coloured flowers. A very fine variety. Eighteen inches ..   .. each 9d.
   "   **WALKERI.** Large panicles of intense rich crimson coloured flowers   each 1s.
IBERIS SEMPERVIRENS SUPERBA. A fine hardy Candytuft, with pure white flowers; first class for dry rockeries   each 6d.
INCARVILLEA DELAVAYI. Height about 2½ feet with large Allamanda-like flowers of a lovely crimson purple colour   per doz. 5s.; each 6d.
   "   **GRANDIFLORA.** A grand variety of recent introduction, very large, deep rosy-crimson flowers, with pale yellow throat. Very fine and attractive   per doz. 10s. 6d.; each 1s.
INULA GLANDULOSA. A fine hardy plant, growing about two feet high, and bearing large single, Helianthus-like yellow flowers   per doz. 5s.; each 6d.

IRIS GERMANICA.

We have a fine collection of these beautiful flowers, which may be planted any time from September to March.

IRIS GERMANICA ADONIS. Erect petal blue, drooping petals velvety purple-veined white, each 9d.
   "   "   **ALBA.** White. .. each 6d.
   "   "   **AUREA.** Golden-yellow each 6d.
   "   "   **BLUE SKY.** Erect petal blue, drooping petals blue, shading to purple. each 9d.
   "   "   **DARIUS.** Erect petal chrome yellow, drooping petals margined yellow, reticulated white ..   each 9d.
   "   "   **FLAVESCENS.** Erect petal primrose, drooping petals light primrose pencilled brown ..   .. each 9d.
   "   "   **GRACCHUS.** Erect petal lemon, drooping petals pale yellow, reticulated purple, dwarf compact grower. each 6d.
   "   "   **MAORI KING.** Erect petal golden yellow, drooping petals deep velvety crimson ..   ..   each 1s.
   "   "   **MME. CHEREAU.** White edged and feathered, pale blue .. each 6d.
   "   "   **NEGLECTA.** Erect petal blue, drooping petals dark velvety purple, reticulated white ..   each 9d.
   "   "   **NE PLUS ULTRA.** Erect petal chrome yellow, drooping petals pencilled and blotched at base with purplish crimson. each 6d.
   "   "   **PALLIDA DALMATICA (true).** A magnificent variety, producing very large beautiful flowers of a lovely pale lavender blue colour. This is undoubtedly the finest of all the blue flowered varieties, and should be in every collection   per doz. 10s. 6d.; each 1s.
   "   "   **PRINCESS OF WALES.** White, very handsome ..   each 9d.
   "   "   **QUEEN OF MAY.** Erect petal rosy lilac, drooping petals rosy lilac, veined yellow, a very fine and distinct form each 1s.
   "   "   **ROWLANDIANA.** Erect petal white veined and suffused lavender, drooping petals white veined purple   each 1s.
   "   "   **VICTORIA.** Erect petal white, blotched purplish blue, drooping petals purple veined white ..   each 1s.

THALICTRUM AQUILEGIÆFOLIUM.

Hardy Perennial Flowering Plants (continued).

PÆONY CANDIDISSIMA.

IRIS PUMILA. Beautiful dwarf growing varieties from the Crimea, only six or eight inches high, very early flowering. Six choice named sorts   per doz. 5s.; each 9d.
  „ **ATRO CŒRULEA.** Flowers large, with purplish blue .. .. each 9d.
  „ **CŒRULEA.** Flowers large, pale blue, tinged purple .. .. each 9d.
  „ **LUTEA MACULATA.** Pale yellow
       each 9d.
  „ **PURPUREA.** Large purple flowers, very free .. per doz. 7s. 6d.; each 9d.
  „ **FŒTIDISSIMA.** Bright evergreen foliage, large seed pods with bright red seeds
       each 9d.
  „ **OCHROLEUCA MAGNIFICA.** A noble species, with large white and yellow flowers. Three to four feet .. Clumps, each 1s.
  „ **AUREA.** Yellow variety of the preceding .. .. .. each 1s.
  „ **STYLOSA.** A lovely Winter-flowering species, having beautiful light-blue flowers, with yellow blotches, produced in January; as it blooms so early, should be protected or planted in a warm, sheltered spot; near the sea it does well .. each 6d.
  „ **KÆMPFERI.** Large, splendidly coloured flowers of grand effect. A warm, moist situation is the best. These are an important group of hardy Iris, quite distinct from any other, of strong, vigorous growth, stems stout and branching. Choice mixed. 6d. each; per doz. 4s. 6d.
Splendid named sorts, 9s., 12s., and 18s. dos.
LATHYRUS LATIFOLIUS, WHITE PEARL. A superb new variety of the well-known Everlasting Pea. With very large pure white flowers double the size of those of the old variety .. .. each 1s.
  „ **ALBUS (The White Everlasting Pea).** Useful hardy climber. Height 6 feet, June to September .. .. doz. 8s.; each 9d.
LITHOSPERMUM PROSTRATUM. Blue each 9d.
  „ „ **"Heavenly Blue" (new)**
       each 1s. 6d.
LUPINUS ARBOREUS (The Tree Lupin). Yellow. Height five feet .. each 6d.
  „ „ **SNOW QUEEN.** Pure white. Height five feet per doz. 7s. 6d.; each 9d.
  „ „ **POLYPHYLLUS.** Blue .. „ 6d.
  „ „ **ALBUS.** White .. „ 6d.

LUPINUS POLYPHYLLUS ROSEUS. A charming variety of the perennial Lupin, perfectly hardy, flowers of a soft rose-pink colour, which darken with age and are produced in great profusion   per doz. 5s.; each 6d.
  „ **MOERHEIMI.** A grand variety with stately spikes of rose and white flowers, good for cutting, lasting and pleasing   each 1s.
LYCHNIS CHALCEDONICA. Height about three feet. Brilliant scarlet, very showy
       per doz. 5s.; each 6d.
  „ **DIOICA [RUBRA PLENA.** Heads of double, rosy crimson flowers; very pretty
       each 6d.
  „ **VISCARIA SPLENDENS PLENA.** A distinct and splendid variety; large double, brilliant rose-coloured flowers
       per doz. 5s.; each 6d.
MORINA LONGIFOLIA. Rosettes of deep green spiny foliage and stout spikes, three feet high, of rose-coloured flowers each 6d.
MYOSOTIS DISSITIFLORA. Large blue flowers. Height six inches.   per doz. 2s. 6d.
  „ **SEMPERFLORENS.** Perpetual flowering Forget-me-not, sky-blue flowers; requires a damp situation.   per doz. 4s. 6d.
NIEREMBERGIA RIVULARIS (The Cup Flower) Thick carpet of foliage covered during Summer with large creamy-white flowers. Height eight inches per doz. 5s.; each 6d.
ŒNOTHERA ACAULIS VERA. A beautiful dwarf-growing species, with large white flowers .. per doz. 5s.; each 6d.
  „ **MACROCARPA.** A trailing mass of foliage covered with large soft yellow flowers .. .. per doz. 5s.; each 6d.
  „ **FRUTICOSA MAJOR.** Height two feet, with deep golden yellow flowers; a first class hardy plant per doz. 5s.; each 6d.
OREOCOME CANDOLLEI. White flowers, with handsome, graceful foliage. Height five feet .. .. each 9d.
PAMPAS GRASS. Beautiful white plumes
       each 1s. 6d. and 2s. 6d.
PHYSALIS FRANCHETTI (Winter Cherry). A now giant species, growing 1½ to 2 feet high, very showy .. per doz. 5s.; each 6d.
  „ **POLY-MOERHEIMI.** A grand variety with stately spikes of rose and white flowers, fine for cutting, lasting well each 1s.

PÆONIES.

Herbaceous. We have a fine collection of these.
PÆONY. ACANUM. Purple, beautiful each 1s.
  „ **ALBIFLORA SIBIRICA.** Deep pink, very attractive .. .. .. each 1s.
  „ **AMABILIS GRANDIFLORA.** White, guard petals, centre yellow .. each 1s.
  „ **CANAIRE.** White, tinted primrose „ 1s.
  „ **COMTE DE PARIS.** Flesh, yellow centre .. .. .. each 1s.
  „ **DELACHEII.** Purplish crimson
       each 1s. 6d.
  „ **DON JUAN.** Purple, splendid each 9d.
  „ **DR. BRETTONNEAU.** Satiny-rose, with shining pink centre .. .. each 1s.
  „ **EXCELLENT.** Guard petal rose, centre sulphur shaded rose .. .. each 1s.
  „ **FELIX CROUSSE.** Brilliant crimson
       each 1s.
  „ **GENERAL HAVELOCK.** Deep rosy pink, edge slightly shaded .. .. each 1s.
  „ **HALŒUS.** French white, guard petals blush .. .. .. each 1s. 6d.
  „ **JUGURTHA.** Flesh colour „ 1s. 6d.
  „ **LILACEA FIMBRIATA.** Blush rose
       each 1s.
  „ **SUPERBA.** Beautiful lilac, with white centre .. .. each 1s. 6d.
  „ **MILLAIS.** Maroon; splendid each 1s.
  „ **MARIE LEMOINE.** Creamy white
       each 1s.

PÆONY. MRS. BRICE. Rose yellow each 1s.
  „ **NIVALIS.** White, shaded yellow, very sweet .. .. .. each 1s. 6d.
  „ **PLENISSIMA ROSEA SUPERBA.** Rose
       each 1s.
  „ **PRINCE CHARLES.** Pink, beautiful
       each 2s.
  „ **PRINCE PIERRE DE GALITZEN.** Peach blossom, primrose centre, prettily fimbriated .. .. .. each 1s. 6d.
  „ **PRINCESS BEATRICE.** Pink guard petals, yellow and pink petals each 1s. 6d.
  „ **PULCHERRIMA MODESTA.** Rosy flesh
       each 1s.
  „ **SININGIA.** Rose guard petals, shaded deeper and edged white .. each 1s.
  „ **VICTORIA TRICOLOR.** Rose, rose and white centre .. .. each 1s.
     And many other fine sorts.
Choice named sorts, our selection, in beautiful variety doz. 12s., 15s., 18s., 24s., and 30s.
PÆONIES, SINGLE.
  „ **ACHILLES.** Cherry rose each 1s.
  „ **EMILY.** Bright pink „ 1s.
  „ **EUGENIUS.** Lilac .. „ 1s.
  „ **HUMEII.** Tender rose, edged white
       each 1s.
  „ **NYMPH.** Guard petal white, centre yellow .. .. each 1s. 6d.
  „ **OFFICINALIS.** Rosy purple .. each 1s.
PAPAVER NUDICAULE (Iceland Poppies). Most useful and beautiful hardy flowers. Height one foot.
  „ „ Bright pale yellow
       per doz. 4s.; each 6d.
  „ „ **ALBUM.** Pure white
       per doz. 4s.; each 6d.
  „ „ **MINIATUM.** Brilliant orange scarlet
       per doz. 4s.; each 6d.
  „ **ORIENTALE. BLUSH QUEEN.** Blush pink, deep purple blotches .. each 1s.
  „ „ **BRACTEATUM.** Deep blood crimson and black blotch .. each 6d.
  „ „ **MAHONEY.** Very dark crimson, nearly black .. .. each 1s.
  „ „ **MRS. MARSH.** Crimson scarlet, white blotch .. .. each 1s.
  „ „ **MRS. PERRY.** A peculiar shade of orange chrome. Height five feet each 1s.
  „ „ **PRINCE OF ORANGE.** Orange scarlet .. .. .. each 9d.

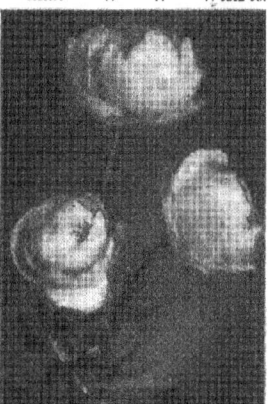

TROLLIUS ORANGE GLOBE.

Hardy Perennial Flowering Plants *(continued)*.

PAPAVER ORIENTALE SALMON QUEEN.
Lovely salmon scarlet .. .. each 9d.
  ,,   ,,   **SILVER QUEEN.** Lovely silvery
white with a very faint blush hue each 9d.

PERENNIAL PHLOXES
Magnificent large-flowered varieties, blooming from July to October. Our collection
includes many of the finest of recent
introduction.

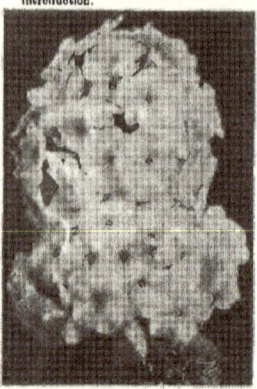

PERENNIAL PHLOX.

PHLOXES. Splendid varieties with names, our
selection .. per doz. 4s. 6d. and 6s.
                 Per 100, 30s. and 40s.
  ,, **ETNA.** Brilliant scarlet, very fine each 1s.
  ,, **FRIEFRAULEIN VON LASSBERG.** Pure
white, very large flowers .. each 1s.
  ,, **GRUPPENKONINGEN.** Lovely pale rose
with carmine eye, very large flowers
                         each 1s. 0d.
  ,, **LE MADHI.** Rich violet blue, very
distinct .. .. .. each 1s.
  ,, **LEONARDO DA VINCI.** White, maroon
centre, splendid .. .. each 1s.
  ,, **MISS PEMBERTON.** Salmon rose, enor-
mous heads of large flowers .. each 1s.
  ,, **TAPIS BLANC.** Pure white, only one foot
high .. .. .. each 1s.
PINKS. All the best named Garden kinds,
including the most beautiful laced sorts.
Our selection, 6 for 2s. 6d.; per doz. 4s.;
                         per 100, 30s.
POLYGONATUM MULTIFLORUM (Solomon's
Seal)   per doz. 4s.; each 6d.
POLEMONIUM CŒRULEUM VARIEGATUM.
A variegated form of Jacob's Ladder; useful
either as a pot or border plant. Height
two feet .. .. .. each 1s.
PYRETHRUMS. These fine plants produce
a great variety of beautiful flowers in many
shades of colour in May and June.
  DOUBLE-FLOWERED. Strong plants in
choice named variety, our selection, in-
cluding the finest sorts per doz. 4s. 6d. & 6s.
  SINGLE-FLOWERED. In brilliant varieties
to name .. .. per doz. 4s. 6d
RUDBECKIA LACINIATA FL. PL. (Golden
Glow). Large double golden yellow flowers
              per doz. 5s.; each 6d
  ,, **LÆVIGATA.** Large yellow flowers, produced late in Autumn Height four to five
feet .. .. .. each 6d.
  ,, **NEWMANII.** Flowers golden yellow with
black centres   per doz. 5s.; each 6d

RUDBECKIA MAXIMA. One of the finest and
most distinct of our Autumn flowering
plants. It grows to the height of about
four feet with large glaucous blue foliage.
The flowers are a deep golden yellow with
black centre. .. .. .. each 1s.
  ,, **PURPUREA.** Height two feet; large
purplish flowers with black centres; very
striking .. .. per doz. 6s.; each 6d.
SCABIOSA CAUCASICA. Large, handsome,
pale lilac-blue flowers per doz. 5s.; each 6d.
  ,,   **ALBA.** A pure white variety
of the beautiful Scabiosa Caucasica each 9d.
SEDUM TELEPHINUM. Pink. Height 1½
feet. .. .. .. each 6d.
SENECIO PULCHER. Purplish crimson with
yellow centre, three feet high
             per doz. 5s.; each 6d.
SIDALCEA. Rosy Gem. This is a distinct and
pleasing plant, producing long, graceful
spikes of bright rosy flowers. Height four
feet .. .. .. each 9d.
SOLIDAGO ALTISSIMA. A fine showy plant
about 4½ feet high, with large panicles
of deep golden yellow flowers each 1s.
  ,, **GOLDEN WINGS.** By far the best of
the Golden Rods, long arching sprays of
bright yellow flowers. A.M., R.H.S. Height
six feet .. .. .. each 1s.
SPIRÆA ARUNCUS. A handsome, stately-
growing border plant, from three to five
feet high, with magnificent plumes of
creamy white flowers .. each 1s. 6d.
  ,,   **KNEIFFI.** The most graceful of
this class; large plumes of white flowers
with elegant finely divided foliage. Very
distinct .. .. each 1s. 6d.
  ,, **ASTILBOIDES.** A beautiful species,
about two feet high, producing dense
plumes of feathery white flowers; grows
in pots or borders per doz. 5s.; each 6d.
  ,, **FILIPENDULA FL. PL.** Corymbs of
double white flowers and pretty foliage
             per doz. 5s.; each 6d.
STOKESIA CYANEA. Lavender-blue flowers,
three inches across. Height two feet
                      each 9d.
**THALICTRUM ADIANTIFOLIUM (The Maiden-
hair Thalictrum).** A beautiful plant rivall-
ing Maiden-hair Fern in delicacy of foliage,
and quite hardy .. doz. 7s. 6d.; each 6d.
  ,, **AQUILEGLÆFOLIUM.** Large plume-like
flowers .. .. .. each 6d.
  ,, **DELAVAYII.** A novelty, with attractive
rose-coloured drooping flowers and pretty
glaucous green foliage. Height two feet
                      each 1s.
TRITOMA CORALLINA. Brilliant scarlet,
dwarf .. .. .. each 9d.
  ,, **GRANDIS.** Scarlet and yellow. Height
four feet .. .. .. each 6d.
  ,, **TUCKII.** Bright red, changing to yellow
                      each 1s.

TRITOMA UVARIA GRANDIFLORA. One of
the grandest of the group; large brilliant
spikes of orange red flowers .. each 6d.
TROLLIUS ASIATICUS. Foliage and stems
dark, flowers bright orange .. each 6d.
  ,, **EUROPÆUS** (Potten's variety). Splendid
variety; flowers nearly double the size of
the old "Europæus" .. .. each 1s.
  ,, **ORANGE GLOBE.** Very large, deep
orange flowers; a strong grower and free
bloomer .. .. .. each 1s.

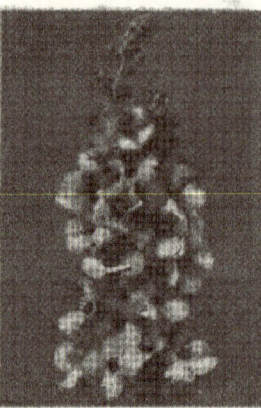

VERBASCUM.

TROPÆOLUM SPECIOSUM. Producing a blaze
of scarlet flowers in late Summer and
Autumn; it grows rapidly, preferring a
light, alluvial soil, and in a somewhat
shaded situation .. .. each 6d.
TUNICA SAXIFRAGA FL. PL. A pretty rock
plant with pink double flowers, a neat little
Alpine, lasting in flower from June till
Autumn .. .. .. each 1s.
VERBASCUM FANNOSUM. Tall spikes of
bright yellow flowers, large woolly leaves.
Height five feet .. .. each 6d.
  ,, **CALEDONIA.** Grand spike of sulphur,
shaded lake flowers. Four feet each 6d.
WALLFLOWERS—Strong, transplanted.
  Blood Red .. per doz. 9d.; per 100 5s.
  Cloth of Gold .. .. 9d.;   5s.
  Vulcan .. .. .. 9d.;   5s.

DANIELS' SPECIAL COLLECTIONS OF HARDY FLOWERING PLANTS.
    We have much pleasure in recommending the following collections, which contain a very choice
selection of the above, specially arranged for brilliant and varied display of colour and a long
continuance of bloom in the open garden.

COLLECTION A.	100 in 50 fine varieties, our selection	..	25s. 0d.
COLLECTION B.	50 in 50 fine varieties, our selection	..	17s. 0d.
COLLECTION C.	50 in 25 fine varieties, our selection	..	15s. 0d.
COLLECTION D.	25 in 25 fine varieties, our selection	..	9s. 6d.

Our own selection, per doz. 4s. 6d., 6s., & 9s. All strong, established plants from single pots, Carriage Free.

PLANTS SUITABLE FOR ROCKWORK.
    We have a splendid collection of dwarf-growing plants suitable for rockeries, including the
finest of the Arabis, Aubretias, Campanulas, Drabas, Herniaria, Phlox frondosa, Saxifrages, Sedums,
Thymus, &c., &c., which we offer from single pots at the following low rates, Carriage Free:—
        Our own selection, per doz. 4s. 6d. and 6s.; per 100, 21s. and 30s.

CARNATIONS—Perpetual, Border, &c.

The Perpetual or Tree Carnations form a beautiful free-flowering class for Winter and early Spring blooming under glass. They are invaluable as cut flowers for Bouquets, Button-holes, &c. Will thrive in any moderately heated greenhouse. The plants we offer are all growing in five-inch pots and are in bud and bloom.

Perpetual Carnations.

Strong plants in 5-inch pots, our own Selection from the following list. Per doz. 15s.
Young plants in 2-inch pots, ready in March, per doz. 6s.

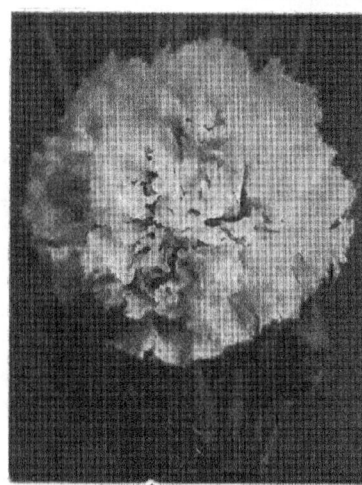

	each s. d.	per doz. s. d.
AFTERGLOW. Rosy cerise, large and shapely flowers	1 6	16 6
AURORA. Buff flaked with pink, very free bloomer	1 6	—
BEACON. Light orange scarlet, very sweet	1 6	16 6
BLACK CHIEF. Deep velvety crimson, sweetly scented	1 6	16 6
BRITANNIA. Crimson scarlet, one of the best reds	1 6	16 6
CAROLA. Very dark crimson, large and sweet	—	—
CRIMSON QUEEN (new). A beautiful sweet scented variety	2 6	—
ENCHANTRESS. Soft pink shade, perfect form	1 6	16 6
FAIR MAID. Lively pink, very free and early	1 6	16 6
FORTUNA. Pale chrome yellow, strong and free	1 6	16 6
HARLOWARDEN. Very rich crimson, and sweetly scented	1 6	16 6
LADY BOUNTIFUL. Glistening white, very good	1 6	16 6
MAY DAY (new). A delightful flesh pink	2 6	—
MRS. H. BURNETT. Salmon pink, rich clove fragrance; easy grower	1 6	16 6
MRS. T. W. LAWSON. The famous cerise pink	1 6	16 6
ROSE PINK ENCHANTRESS. Lovely shade of pink	1 6	16 6
WHITE PERFECTION. A pure white, blooms very early	1 6	16 6
WINSOR. Silvery pink, strong, free and easy grower	1 6	16 6

Malmaison Varieties.

In 3-inch pots, 1s. each, 10s. 6d. doz. ; our Selections, 9s. per doz.
In 5-inch pots, 1s. 6d. each, 18s. doz.

BLUSH WHITE. Very large and full.
HORACE HUTCHINSON. Brilliant glowing scarlet, very fine.
LADY GRIMSTON. A pinkish white marked rose, the flowers a good size.
MARMION. White blotched and suffused rosy red.
MARY MEASURES. Darkest of Crimsons, with spicy fragrance.
NAUTILUS. Most charming flowers of a delicate flesh colour.
NELL GWYNNE. The finest pure white, strong grower, and good size.
ROBERT BURNS. Bright salmon, of a pleasing shade.
SOULT. Deep salmon, very fine.

BORDER CARNATIONS AND PICOTEES.

	each—s. d.
ALICE AYRES. Pure white beautifully striped with carmine, of exquisite form and substance	0 6
ALICE CONEGRAVE. Large, white, broad, smooth edged petals	0 6
ASSELI. Pink self, a very densely built flower, sweetly clove-scented, a strong grower and good bloomer	1 0
BLACK PRINCE. Deep crimson, almost black	0 9
BRODRICK. Yellow ground, beautifully flaked with rosy red	0 9
CASSANDRA. A lovely delicate flesh colour	1 0
CECILIA. Large clear yellow of splendid form	1 0
CINNAMON. Very pleasing shade of crimson and orange	1 0
COSMOS. Pink, suffused with heliotrope	0 6
DERVISH. Primrose yellow, beautifully margined with rosy lilac, quite distinct; flowers handsome in form and large in size	0 9
DOROTHY. Buff-ground, edged and flaked with pink ; very robust and free	0 9
DUCHESS OF FIFE. A delicate rosy pink, with fine flowers of great substance	0 6
EUTERPE. Large flowers of good form and habit, a bright scarlet band on buff base	1 0
FANTASTIC. Rose striped maroon	0 6
FULGURANT (new). A large and very full flower of an intense bright scarlet, robust habit and profuse bloomer	2 6
GERMANIA. Pure yellow ; a beautiful flower	0 9
GLOIRE DE NANCY. Pure white; deliciously scented	0 6
GRAHAM WHITE. Very dark crimson, strongly scented, very good	1 0
HELIOTROPE. Heliotrope, shaded salmon	0 9
HELMSMAN. Pure white; very fine	1 0
ISMALIA. Cinnabar-red, very bright, extra good	0 9
LADY HINDLIP. Brilliant crimson scarlet of perfect form and substance	0 6

	each—s. d.
LORD ROBERTS. Clear yellow, very large flowers, strong grower and very free flowering	1 0
MIDAS. Orange buff, suffused scarlet, large and fine	1 0
MISS AUDREY CAMPBELL. Yellow self ; one of the best	1 0
MISS REEVES. Apricot, shaded crimson	0 9
MRS. CHAS. DANIELS. Deep rosy pink, very sweet scented and of fine form	0 6
MRS. MC. RAE. A very fine dark scarlet	0 9
MRS. NICHOLSON. Deep rose pink ; very fragrant	0 6
MRS. REYNOLDS HOLE. Salmon apricot ; a fine variety	0 9
NONI. Salmon pink	0 9
OLD CRIMSON. The true old clove-scented variety, very dark crimson ; deliciously scented	0 6
PHILOMELA. A very clear salmon pink, flaked bright scarlet	0 6
QUEEN ALEXANDRA. Pale buff, large full flower; a splendid variety	1 0
RUBY CASTLE. Soft salmon pink, beautifully fringed petals	0 6
REBECCA BURNETT. Rosy pink, pleasing colour	0 6
ROSALIE RIEFFEL. A remarkably fine Picotee of extraordinary size, the colour pure white with deep bright bluish margin	0 9
ROY MORRIS. This is without doubt the brightest and largest scarlet border Carnation in commerce, the plants are of robust habit, the grass being broad like that of the Malmaisons; it is a very free bloomer	1 0
STEPHANIE. White, finely edged with crimson purple	0 9
STROMBOLI. A dark velvety crimson, nearly black, the petals are broad, well-shaped, and good substance	1 0
SYLPHIDE. Buff with orange, edged and suffused heliotrope	1 0
TROJAN. Pure white with broad purplish edge	1 0
URIAH PIKE. Deep crimson, strongly clove-scented ; very free	0 6

Choice varieties, our own selection to name, per doz. 6s. and 9s. 25 for 17s. 6d.
Selected Border Carnations unnamed : all good double flowers in fine variety, strong plants, 6 for 2s. 6d. ; per doz. 4s. 6d.

GREENHOUSE AND STOVE PLANTS.

ACACIA DRUMMONDII   — each 2s. 6d.
" ARMATA .. " each 1s. 6d.
ADIANTUM CUNEATUM (Maiden-hair Fern)
each 6d., 1s., and 2s. 6d.
" FARLEYENSE. Very fine variety
each 1s. 6d., 2s. 6d., and 3s. 6d.
ALLAMANDA HENDERSONII. Beautiful stove
plant .. .. each 2s. 6d. and 3s. 6d.
" WILLIAMSII. Very fine variety, flowers
rich yellow, very free each 3s. 6d. and 5s.
ARALIA ELEGANTISSIMA ...   each 5s.
" GRACILLIMA. A pretty variety, with
finely cut leaves ...   each 5s.
" SIEBOLDII ..   each 1s. to 2s. 6d.
" " VARIEGATA. Beautiful plant
each 2s. 6d. and 3s. 6d.
" VEITCHII. Very graceful   each 5s.

ARAUCARIA EXCELSA.

ARAUCARIA EXCELSA. A fine plant for the
conservatory ..   each 2s. 6d. to 5s.
ASPARAGUS PLUMOSUS NANUS
each 1s. 6d. and 2s. 6d.
" SPRENGERI   each 1s. 6d. and 2s. 6d.
" TENUISSIMUS ..   each 1s. 6d.
ASPIDISTRA LURIDA each 2s. 6d. and 3s. 6d.
" " VARIEGATA. A very beautiful and
distinct plant, with handsomely variegated
foliage ...   each 3s. 6d. and 5s.
AZALEA INDICA. We offer a choice collection,
finest varieties, all in good healthy flowering
plants, varying in height from about ten
inches to sixteen inches from the pots.
Our own selection
per doz. 24s. to 50s.; each 3s. 6d. and 5s.
" MOLLIS. A splendid class for the greenhouse, or for forcing. Fine plants, well set
with flower buds
each 2s. and 2s. 6d.; per doz. 18s. to 24s.
BEGONIA, GLOIRE DE LORRAINE. A charming Winter bloomer, bearing a profusion of
bright pink flowers ...   each 1s. 6d.
BEGONIAS, REX VARIETIES. Beautiful
foliaged plants .. each 1s. 6d. and 2s. 0d.
BOUGAINVILLEA GLABRA SANDERIANA.
The splendid new high-coloured variety
each 1s. 6d. and 2s. 6d.
" MAUD CHETTLEBOROUGH. The largest
and brightest flowers each 1s. 6d. to 3s. 6d.
CALADIUMS. The most beautiful varieties
each 2s. 6d. and 3s. 6d.
CAMELLIA JAPONICA. Our collection includes
all the finest of the English and Continental
varieties. Height of plants from pots varies
from about a foot to eighteen inches. Our
own selection — each 2s. 6d.

CANNAS. Crozy's new dwarf varieties
per doz. 6s., 9s. and 12s.
CAREX MARGINATA GRACILIS each 1s. 6d.
CHOISYA TERNATA ..   each 1s. 6d.
CHOROZEMA LOWII   each 2s. 6d.
CLERODENDRON BALFOURII. Useful climber
each 1s. 6d. and 2s. 6d.
" FALLAX. Lovely bright red panicles of
flowers, strong broad dark foliage; very
effective and useful ..   each 1s. 6d.
COBÆA SCANDENS VARIEGATA. Useful
greenhouse climber each 1s. 6d. and 2s. 6d.
COPROSMA BAUERIANA VARIEGATA.
Beautiful greenhouse plant with variegated
foliage   each 1s. 6d. and 2s. 6d.
CROTONS. A fine collection of choice sorts in
nice young plants each 2s. 6d. and 3s. 6d.
CYPERUS ALTERNIFOLIUS ..   each 1s.
DAPHNE INDICA ALBA. Pure white,
deliciously scented variety
each 2s. 6d. and 3s. 6d.
" " RUBRA. Very sweet
each 2s. 6d. and 3s. 6d.
DRACÆNA AUSTRALIS. Fine for furnishing
each 1s. 6d. to 2s. 6d.
" BRUANTII. Excellent for rooms
each 2s. 6d.
" GODSEFFIANA Green foliage spotted
with creamy white; very distinct
each 1s. 6d.
" GRACILIS. Very useful for decorative
purposes .. each 2s. 6d. to 3s. 6d.
" DOUCETTII. A very beautiful variegated
form of D. Australis. Graceful dark leaves
with very distinct white stripe; does well in
a room ..   each 5s. and 10s. 6d.
" TERMINALIS. Well-known and useful
variety   each 2s. 6d. to 3s. 6d.
ECCREMOCARPUS SCABER ..   each 1s.
EUCALYPTUS CITRIODORA. Deliciously
scented   each 1s. and 1s. 6d.
EULALIA GRACILLIMA. One of the most
elegant grasses, splendid pot plant each 1s.
" ZEBRINA. Very handsome   each 1s.
EURYA LATIFOLIA VARIEGATA. Handsome
decorative plant, with golden variegated
foliage   each 2s. 6d., 3s. 6d., and 5s.
FERNS, GREENHOUSE. A fine selection of the
most useful and ornamental
per doz. 6s., 9s., 12s., and 18s.
FICUS ELASTICA (India-rubber Plant)
each 1s. 6d. and 2s. 6d.
" " VARIEGATA. Beautifully varie-
gated with yellow each 2s. 6d., 3s. 6d.,and 5s.
GARDENIA INTERMEDIA. Well-known stove
plants, pure white, deliciously scented,
double flowers   each 2s. 6d. to 3s. 6d.
GENISTA FRAGRANS   each 1s. 6d.
" ANDREANA. The gold and crimson
Broom; a beautiful pot-plant each 1s. 6d.
GLOXINIAS. In beautiful variety
strong plants, per doz. 9s. and 12s.
" SEEDLINGS. Very choice strain, ready
in May ..   per doz. 3s. 6d.
GREVILLEA ROBUSTA   each 1s. and 1s. 6d.
HOYA CARNOSA. A charming stove climbing
plant, producing wax-like flowers
each 1s. 6d. and 2s. 6d.
LAPAGERIA ALBA. Lovely pure-white, wax-
like flowers; very beautiful
each 5s. and 7s. 6d.
" ROSEA SUPERBA. Beautiful climber for
the cool greenhouse
each 2s. 6d., 3s. 6d., and 5s.
MYRTLES (Myrtus). Nice young plants
each 1s. to 1s. 6d.
OLEANDER (Nerium). Well-known Greenhouse Shrub, requiring plenty of moisture
until after flowering. Flowers on well-
ripened wood. Pink and White
each 1s. 6d. and 2s. 6d.

PALMS. A nice assortment of choice plants
suitable for the dinner-table and general
decorative purposes, including :—Areca
sapida, Cocos Weddelliana, Corypha
Australis, Kentia Belmoreana, Kentia
Canterburyana, Kentia Fosteriana, Latania
Borbonica, Phœnix reclinata, etc.
each 2s. 6d., 3s. 6d., to 21s.
PANDANUS VEITCHII VARIEGATUS
each 2s. 6d. and 3s. 6d.
" UTILIS (The Screw Pine). A well-known
variety, very useful ..   each 2s. 6d.
PASSIFLORA PRINCEPS. Lovely stove
climber, with large scarlet flowers
each 2s. 6d. and 3s. 6d.
POINSETTIAS. Very showy greenhouse plant,
with large scarlet flowers or bracts
valuable for Winter decoration
each 1s., 1s. 6d., and 2s. 6d.
PRIMULA OBCONICA GRANDIFLORA. A fine
variety, with handsomely fringed flowers
each 6d. and 1s.
RHODODENDRONS. All the best sorts for
Greenhouses ..   each 3s. 6d. to 5s.
SCHUBERTIA GRANDIFLORA. The best
sweet-scented white flowered plant for
cutting   each 2s. 6d.
SMILAX (Medeola asparagoides). Strong plants
each 1s. and 1s. 6d.
STEPHANOTIS FLORIBUNDA
each 2s. 6d., 3s. 6d., and 5s.
STREPTOCARPUS. White, and hybrids
each 1s. and 1s. 6d.

DRACÆNA BRUANTII.

SWAINSONIA GALEGIFOLIA ALBA. Lovely
clusters of pure white Pea-like flowers;
splendid for pillar or wall in the cool greenhouse, and very useful for cutting
each 1s. to 2s. 6d.
" SPLENDENS. Fine, showy variety, bearing lovely bright carmine flowers
each 1s. 6d. and 2s. 6d.
TACSONIA EXONIENSIS. A fine variety
each 1s. 6d. and 2s. 6d.
" VAN VOLXEMII. Brilliant climber for
the greenhouse   each 1s. 6d. and 2s. 6d.
TECOMA JASMINOIDES. Valuable greenhouse
climber   each 1s. 6d.
GREENHOUSE PLANTS in choice variety, our
selection, per doz. 18s., 24s., 30s., and 40s.

MISCELLANEOUS BEDDING PLANTS.
READY FOR SENDING OUT IN MAY.

BEDDING GERANIUMS.

Autumn-struck good healthy plants from single pots.

This magnificent class of bedding plants is as popular as ever, and may fairly be considered as indispensable for garden decoration. The superb varieties, "King Edward VII," "Scarlet King," and "Paul Crampel," are especially recommended for their splendid effectiveness in the garden.

	per doz.		per 100	
	s.	d.	s.	d.
KING EDWARD VII. (new). Deep crimson, very dwarf ..	4	0	—	
SCARLET KING (new). Brilliant deep scarlet ..	3	6	30	0
PAUL CRAMPEL. Deep scarlet, very striking	3	6	30	0
HENRY JACOBY. Dark crimson, very fine	3	6	30	0
MASTER CHRISTINE. Beautiful clear pink ..	3	6	24	0
MRS. C. LOWESLY. Bright salmon-rose	3	6	24	0
VESUVIUS. Brilliant scarlet	3	0	21	0
QUEEN OF THE BELGIANS. Pure white, beautiful	3	6	24	0
CRYSTAL PALACE GEM. Beautiful ..	3	6	24	0
GOLDEN TRICOLOR. LADY CULLUM	4	0	30	0
MRS. HENRY COX. Splendid; gold crimson foliage ..	4	0	30	0
VERONA. Golden foliage, pink flowers, beautiful variety	4	0	—	
SILVER TRICOLOR. LASS O'GOWRIE. Charming variety	4	6	—	
MRS. JOHN CLUTTON. Very handsome	4	6	—	
SILVER-LEAVED. FLOWER OF SPRING. Very free ..	3	6	24	0
MRS. MAPPIN. White flowers	4	0	30	0
PRINCE SILVERWINGS. Dark flowers	3	6	24	0
BRONZE-LEAVED. BLACK DOUGLAS. Scarlet blooms	4	0	30	0

From Mr. W. SMITH, Hatfield Peverell.

March 9th.
"I am pleased to say I had excellent results from your Flower Seeds last year, especially the Asters. I took First Prize with them at our Show."

MISCELLANEOUS.

All strong young plants from single pots.

	per doz.		per 100	
	s.	d.	s.	d.
BEGONIAS, FIBROUS-ROOTED, SEMPERFLORENS ROSEA. Rose, very pretty, dwarf-growing variety ..	2	6	17	6
VERNON COMPACTA. Bright red flowers, dark foliage ..	2	6	17	6
BEGONIAS, TUBEROUS-ROOTED. From single pots.				
Single-flowered, in beautiful variety ..	4	6	30	0
Double-flowered, selected, mixed ..	6	0	42	0
CANNAS. Fine varieties, mixed, strong plants ..	4	6	30	0
CANTERBURY BELLS. Mixed, strong plants ..	2	6	17	6
CALCEOLARIA, GOLDEN GEM. A fine bedder	3	0	21	0
CENTAUREA CANDIDISSIMA. Silvery white foliage ..	3	0	21	0
DAHLIAS, CACTUS-FLOWERED. Choice named sorts				
4s. 6d. and	6	0	—	
POMPONE. Fine named sorts 3s. 6d. and	4	6	—	
HELIOTROPES. Choice named sorts for bedding ..	3	0	21	0
HOLLYHOCKS. Choice mixed Seedlings ..	3	6	—	
In six choice colours; separate ..	4	6	—	
LOBELIAS, KING OF THE BLUES. Dark blue ..	1	6	10	6
TRIUMPH. Dark blue with white eye ..	2	6	17	6
LOBELIAS, WHITE PERFECTION. Pure white ..	2	6	17	6
MARGUERITES. White, from single pots ..	3	0	21	0
PELARGONIUMS. Ivy-leaved, beautiful varieties, named	4	6	—	
PENTSTEMONS. Beautiful free-flowering plants, throwing up handsome spikes of bloom from July till late Autumn. Height about 18 inches.				
Choice named varieties from our fine collection, 3/6.				
SALVIA, "PRIDE OF ZURICH." Brilliant scarlet ..	4	0	30	0
VERBENAS. In distinct colours from cuttings, mixed ..	3	0	21	0
Brilliant scarlet, pink, white, blue or purple	3	6	24	0

DOUBLE DAISIES.

Well known beautiful and brilliant little plants for edgings of beds or borders, which continue in bloom throughout the months of April and May; the dark crimson and pure white are very handsome.

LARGE CRIMSON, double — — per 100, 16s.; per doz. 2s. 6d.
LARGE WHITE, double — — per 100, 16s.; per doz. 2s. 6d.
LARGE PINK, double — — per 100, 12s.; per doz. 2s. 0d.

MYOSOTIS. (FORGET-ME-NOTS.)

Well-known beautiful flowers, indispensable for Spring gardening.
PALUSTRIS SEMPERFLORENS. Lovely sky blue flowers, very free bloomer .. .. .. per doz. 1s. 6d.
DISSITIFLORA. Beautiful free-flowering variety, bright blue, strong plants .. .. per doz. 2s. 6d.
ROYAL BLUE. Deep blue, long sprays .. .. per doz. 2s. 6d.

OUR GUINEA HAMPER OF CHOICE BEDDING PLANTS.

We annually sell large numbers of these Collections, which contain the very liberal assortment named below. As, however, provision must be made for supplying in accordance with the list given, we shall be glad if our customers will kindly send in their orders as early as convenient.

30 Geraniums, assorted	6 Chrysanthemums
12 Verbenas, assorted	6 Dahlias, named
12 Calceolarias, yellow	6 Fuchsias, named
24 Pyrethrum, Golden Feather	6 Phloxes, choice perennial
18 Lobelias, dark blue	6 Heliotropes
12 Petunias, mixed	4 Pentstemons
12 Pansies or Violas	12 Hardy Flowering Plants

Half the above quantity 11s. 6d.; double quantity 40s.

No Charge for Hampers or Packing. Ready for delivery in May.
Orders executed in same rotation as received.

We do not pay the Carriage of these Collections.

MISCELLANEOUS SPRING-FLOWERING PLANTS.

The above photograph illustrates the beds and lawn adjacent to the Royal Pavilion in the grounds of the Royal Agricultural Society's Show held at Norwich in June last. We were honoured with instructions from the Society to carry out the entire floral decorations both of the interior and exterior of the Royal Pavilion, and received a special Large Silver Medal from the Society as well as an expression of approval from His Majesty King George, conveyed through the Acting President, Sir Ailwyn E. Fellowes, K.C.V.O.

The large bed was designed by us in the shape of an Imperial Crown in honour of the Coronation and of His Majesty's Presidency of the Show. Many thousands of plants were used including 750 pots of Lilium Longiflorum, 150 large plants Scarlet Rhododendrons (Dr. Hogg), 250 Golden Euonymus, 50 White Dorothy Perkins Climbing Roses, 2,000 plants White and Purple Violas, as well as a large quantity of Verbena Stocks, Calceolarias, Golden Privet, etc. Everything used was in full growth and planted in the bed, which retained its beauty for nearly a fortnight, and was much admired by thousands of visitors and admitted on all hands to be one of the features of the Show. We also received the Societies Gold Medal for our Exhibits in the Horticultural Tents.

BEDDING VIOLAS.

BLANCH. Creamy white .. .. per doz. 4s.; each 6d.	**ROYAL SOVEREIGN.** Deep golden yellow, rayless; very fine	
BLUE BELL. Violet, shaded blue; free bloomer per doz. 3s.; each 4d.	per doz. 5s.; each 6d.	
BLUE CLOUD. White, heavily edged .. per doz. 4s.; each 6d.	**SIR ROBERT PEEL.** Primrose yellow .. per doz. 3s.; each 4d.	
CHARM. Soft lilac lavender; rayless .. per doz. 2s. 6d.; each 3d.	**SOUVENIR.** Rich lavender .. .. per doz. 4s.; each 6d.	
JOHN QUARTON. Light mauve; a grand bedder per doz. 5s.; each 6d.	**VIOLETTA.** White, medium size, very compact per doz. 3s.; each 4d.	
LUTEA MAJOR. Rich clear yellow; compact per doz. 3s.; each 4d.	**WM. NEIL.** Pale rose .. .. .. per doz. 3s.; each 4d.	
MRS. SCOTT. Pure white; very compact .. per doz. 3s.; each 4d.	Our own selection, ... per 100, 21s.; per doz. 3s.	

PRIMROSES AND POLYANTHUSES.

A beautiful and indispensable class of brilliant Spring-flowering plants, blooming at the same time as Narcissi and many other bulbs; the single-flowered Hybrid Primrose include the most beautiful shades of crimson, scarlet rose, &c., to pure white.

SINGLE, MIXED HYBRIDS. Very fine and brilliant. Strong seedlings	**POLYANTHUS-PRIMROSE.** Large-flowered yellow and orange shades,
per 100, 17s. 6d.; per doz. 2s. 6d.	very beautiful varieties .. .. per doz. 4s. 6d.
POLYANTHUS, GOLD-LACED. Fine seedlings .. per doz. 3s.	**G. F. WILSON'S SINGLE BLUE.** A very fine selected strain of the most
POLYANTHUS-PRIMROSE. Large-flowered hybrids in splendid mixture	beautiful dark violet blue flowers; splendid per doz. 5s.; each 6d.
per 100, 21s.; per doz. 3s.	**PRIMROSE, MISS MASSEY.** Dark crimson per doz. 4s. 6d.; each 6d.
PRIMROSES.—Double, White, Lilac, Yellow	— — — — per doz. 4s. 6d.; each 6d.

GARDEN PINKS.

	per doz.			per doz
ALBINO. Of the purest snow-white throughout; a very smooth		**MRS. SINKINS.** Large pure white flowers; very fragrant ..	3 0
heavy petal, and fine, full globular form, of extra size	4 0	**OLD DOUBLE WHITE FRINGED.** Very sweet ..	2 6
ASCOT. Soft fleshy pink, with deep carmine centre; erect habit	3 6	**PADDINGTON.** Deep rose, dark centre, edged fringed ..	3 0
EARLY BLUSH. Blush pink, large double fringed flowers	3 0	**SAM BARLOW.** White, with crimson centre; very free bloomer ..	3 6
ERNEST. Lacing rich ruby red; large flowers ..	3 6	**SARAH.** Dark velvety red, laced	3 0
ERNEST LADHAMS. Blush, fine claret centre; extra large	3 0	**SNOWDRIFT** (new). A splendid free-flowering variety. First	
EURYDICE. Rosy red lacing; a very fine variety ..	4 0	rate for cutting. The very large blooms, which resemble those	
HER MAJESTY. One of the finest and best White Garden Pinks	3 0	of Carnations, are white slightly marked with pink ..	3 0

Choice named varieties. Our selection, per dez., 3s.; per 100, 21s.

MISCELLANEOUS SEEDLING & OTHER PLANTS,
FOR BEDDING, &c.

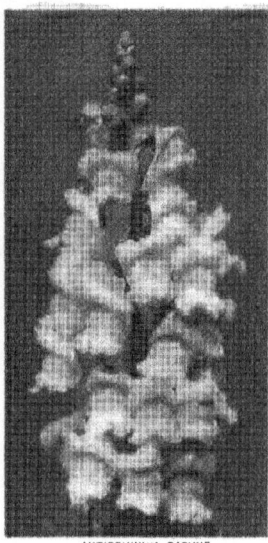

ANTIRRHINUM, DAPHNE.

Well-grown transplanted Seedlings of the following can be supplied during May and June at moderate prices as below—CARRIAGE PAID.

	per doz. s. d.	per 100 s. d.
ASTERS, DANIELS' GIANT OSTRICH PLUME. Mixed ⎫ A fine class for exhibition	0 6	3 6
„ „ „ „ White ⎭	0 6	3 6
„ COMET. Choicest mixed ⎫ Excellent varieties for cut flowers	0 6	3 6
„ Pure white ⎭	0 6	3 6
„ VICTORIA. Choice mixed ⎫ Beautiful varieties for bedding	0 6	3 6
„ Pure white ⎭	0 6	3 6
ANTIRRHINUM, DAPHNE. Rose and white (new) ⎫	1 0	7 0
„ AURORA. Scarlet, white throat .. ⎪ Superb varieties for garden	1 0	6 0
„ NIOBE. Dark crimson, white throat ⎬ decoration.	1 0	6 0
„ BLACK PRINCE. Dark maroon crimson ⎪ Height about 18 inches.	1 0	6 0
„ GOLDEN QUEEN. Pure yellow ⎭	1 0	6 0
„ WHITE QUEEN. Pure white, very fine ..	1 0	6 6
„ TOM THUMB. Scarlet ⎫	1 0	6 0
„ „ „ White ⎪ Dwarf-growing varieties, only about 6 inches	1 0	6 0
„ „ „ Rose ⎬ high.	1 0	6 0
„ „ „ Yellow ⎪ First-class for edgings of beds or borders.	1 0	6 0
„ „ „ Mixed ⎭	1 0	6 0
„ Tall Varieties, choice mixed, very fine, height 2 feet ..	1 0	6 0
CARNATIONS, MARGARET. New large-flowered double, mixed	1 6	10 6
DIANTHUS HEDDEWIGI. Fine mixed, double ..	1 0	6 0
HELIOTROPE. Large-flowered hybrids, choice mixed ..	1 6	10 6
KOCHIA TRICOPHYLLA (Summer Cypress), fine decorative plant ..	1 0	7 0
MIMULUS. Large-flowered hybrids, mixed ..	1 0	7 0
NEMESIA STRUMOSA GRANDIFLORA. Choice mixed ..	1 0	7 6
NICOTIANA AFFINIS. Long white tubular flowers, sweet scented ..	1 0	7 6
„ SANDERÆ hybrids, mixed, very showy ..	1 6	10 6
PANSIES, DANIELS' PRIZE BLOTCHED. Magnificent strain ..	1 6	10 6
„ BLUE KING. Bright blue, good bedder ..	1 0	6 0
PENTSTEMONS. Large-flowered hybrids, choice mixed ..	1 6	10 6
PETUNIAS. Large-flowered, single, very fine strain ..	1 6	10 6
„ Dwarf bedding, rosy carmine ..	1 6	10 6
PHLOX DRUMMONDI. Finest sorts, mixed ..	0 6	3 6
PYRETHRUM, GOLDEN FEATHER. Useful for edging ..	0 6	3 6
STOCKS, DANIELS' LARGE-FLOWERED TEN-WEEK. Choice mixed ..	0 6	3 6
„ „ „ White ...	0 6	3 6
VERBENAS, Large-flowered hybrids, splendid mixed ..	1 6	10 6
ZINNIAS. Large-flowered double, finest mixed ..	1 0	7 6

SEEDLING PLANTS OF CHOICE FLORISTS' FLOWERS, &c.
READY IN JULY AND AUGUST.

	per doz. s. d.	per 100 s. d.		per doz. s. d.	per 100 s. d.
CALCEOLARIAS. Very choice strain ..	1 6	10 6	PRIMULAS, ALBA MAGNIFICA	2 6	—
CARNATIONS. Choicest double; fine ..	1 6	10 6	„ BLUE. Very fine strain	2 6	—
CINERARIAS. From a grand strain ..	1 6	10 6	„ CHOICEST MIXED	1 6	10 6
PRIMULAS, CRIMSON KING	1 6	10 6	„ STELLATA VARIETIES, MIXED..	1 6	10 6

VIOLETS --(SWEET-SCENTED).

The plants we offer are strong, well-rooted, and with good flowering crowns. If planted out in May, when flowering is over, in good soil on a shady border, they will make fine clumps for lifting in Autumn, for blooming under glass.

SINGLE-FLOWERED VARIETIES.

	per doz. s. d.	each. s. d.
ASKANIA (new). The finest winter flowering violet; an improvement on " Princess of Wales," the best of all single varieties ..	9 0	1 0
CYCLOPS. A very fine variety, with tall handsome foliage. The very large flowers are of a rich violet blue, the centres having fine little white petals 3 for 2s. 6d.	—	1 0
CALIFORNIA. Very large beautiful flowers on long stems	4 0	0 6
LA FRANCE. A superb variety. The flowers are of extraordinary size, of a beautiful purplish-blue ..	4 0	0 6
PRINCESS OF WALES. A grand variety, producing very large, beautifully formed, rich violet blueflowers	4 0	0 6
THE CZAR. Blue, large, an almost constant bloomer ..	3 0	0 4

DOUBLE-FLOWERED VARIETIES.

	per doz. s. d.	each. s. d.
COUNT BRAZZA'S WHITE. Large, double, pure white flowers, deliciously scented	4 6	0 6
DE PARMA. Deliciously fragrant flowers of a delicate pale lavender purple, in great profusion ..	4 0	0 6
MADEMOISELLE BERTHA BARRON. A fine vigorous compact grower; flowers of a beautiful indigo blue, deliciously scented	4 0	0 6
MARIE LOUISE. Large double flowers, rich lavender blue	4 0	0 6
MRS. ARTHUR (new). An improved " Marie Louise," the best of all double varieties	7 6	0 9
NEAPOLITAN. Lavender blue, flowers very large and double, profuse bloomer ..	4 0	0 6

CUT FLOWERS. This most important department of our business continues to receive our very careful attention, and the designs we supply may be relied upon as being exceedingly artistic and in the prevailing fashion. To ensure all blooms being freshly gathered, we cultivate large quantities of Flowers especially for this work, and they will consequently travel well, and arrive at their destination in splendid condition.

All designs are most carefully packed in special cases, and our system is such that they will stand a journey of twenty-four hours, if necessary, and arrive quite fresh. It is much the best plan to keep the boxes closed and in a dark cool place until needed, so as to hold the moisture about the flowers, and thus retain their freshness for a longer period.

MEMORIAL WREATHS, CROSSES, ETC.

These are most beautiful and artistic in appearance, being made up of freshly cut flowers. They are composed either of white flowers, or with violets and other coloured blooms introduced according to the wishes of our customers.

We are continually asked to make up special designs and emblems for Masonic and other funerals, and we shall be most happy to be entrusted with instructions for these special occasions.

Each 5/- ; 7/6 ; 10/6 ; 12/6 ; 15/- ; 21,- ; 31/6 ; 42/-, and upwards.

WEDDING AND OTHER BOUQUETS.

All orders for Bouquets are made up with the choicest flowers in season, and the important details of artistic arrangement and blending of colours receive most scrupulous attention ; we are glad to say we invariably give the highest satisfaction.

It is most important that instructions should be given at the time of ordering, as to whether "Shower" or hand bouquets are desired, also the colours of the dresses which the flowers used in the Bridesmaids' Bouquets are to match.

BRIDES', PURE WHITE FLOWERS. Either with or without "Showers." Each 7/6 to 42/-

BRIDESMAIDS', WHITE OR DELICATELY TINTED FLOWERS. Each 5/- ; 7/6 ; 10/6 ; and upwards.

PRESENTATION BOUQUETS FOR BAZAARS, FETES, ETC. Each 7/6 ; 10/6 ; 21/- ; and upwards.

GENTLEMEN'S BUTTONHOLES. White or coloured flowers. Each 6d. and 1s.; per doz. 5s. and 10s.

LADIES' SPRAYS. Beautifully made up to order, any colour. Each 1s. 6d. and 2s. 6d.

LOOSE CUT FLOWERS AND FERN. For Wedding, Altar Vases, and other decorations
in liberal quantity in boxes. Each 2/6 ; 3/6 ; 5/- ; 7/6 ; 10/6 ; 15/- ; 21/- ; 31/6, and 42/-

IMPORTANT.

All orders are despatched promptly on receipt, if required, but customers should, if possible, give at least two days' clear notice before the flowers are required, also full particulars for forwarding. Orders from unknown Correspondents must be accompanied by remittance. We would suggest that orders for Wreaths, &c., should be marked URGENT on the Envelope.

DANIELS' NATURAL PERFUMES.

CARNATION   LAVENDER   SWEET PEA   WALLFLOWER
HELIOTROPE   LILY OF THE VALLEY   PARMA VIOLET   WHITE ROSE

Each bottle is packed in a dainty box, they will travel quite safely by post, and as an acceptable present nothing could be found more suitable. Each kind of scent is offered in three sizes as follows:—

1 oz. Bottle, including box   ..   ..   1s. 6d. each.   Post free 1s. 8d. each.
2 oz.   "   "   "   ::   ..   3s. 6d. "   " " 3s. 9d. "
3 oz.   "   "   "   ..   ..   5s. 0d. "   " " 5s. 3d. "

Plate of Box and Bottle (much reduced).

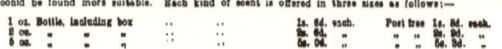

Spring 1912 — ORDER SHEET — *Spring 1912*

Please use this Form when sending an Order to

DANIELS BROS. LIMITED, { Seedsmen by Appointment to H.M. KING GEORGE V., and Nurserymen by Appointment to H M. QUEEN ALEXANDRA } NORWICH.

Name.. Date................... 1912.

Address..

Post-town.................................County.................................

Nearest Railway Station } ....
and distance from same)

AMOUNT ENCLOSED:

	£	s.	d.
Cheque			
Money Order			
Postal Order			
Coin or Stamps			
Total			

CAUTION.—According to Post Office Regulations, Letters containing coin MUST be registered. The Registration Fee is only 2d., and this ensures a safe delivery.

. In filling up this form it is of the greatest importance to write clearly the Name and Address of the sender. **The Railway Station should always be given.**
Attention to this will save trouble, and prevent unnecessary delay.
For Terms of Business, &c., see inside front cover of this Catalogue.

KITCHEN GARDEN SEEDS, POTATOES, &c.

QUANTITY REQUIRED.	NAMES OF ARTICLES.	PRICE.		QUANTITY REQUIRED.	NAMES OF ARTICLES.	PRICE.	
		s.	d.			s.	d.
	Carried forward, £				Carried forward, £		

☞ Spaces for Flower Seeds, &c., &c., provided overleaf.

.	d.	No.	s.	d.	QUANTITY REQUIRED.		s.	d.
						Brought forward, £		
Carr. for. £						*Total, £*		

INDEX.

Flower Seed in Alphabetical Order, see pages 78—107.

	PAGE
Abol Insecticide	57
Almonds	124, 134
Anemone Seed	78
„ Bulbs	113
„ Plants	150
Antirrhinum Seed	78
„ Plants	159
Apples	117, 118
Apricots	121
Aprons, Nail Bags, &c.	59
Aquilegia Seed	79
„ Plants	150
Arabis Seed	78
„ Plants	150
Artichokes	52
Aster Seed	75-77
„ Plants	159
Asparagus Seed and Plants	51
Aubrietia Seed	79
„ Plants	150
Auricula Seed	79
„ Plants	151
Azaleas	137, 150
Beans, Broad	16
„ Dwarf French	18
„ Runners	17
Bedding Plants	159
Beech	134, 140
Beet	19
Begonia Seed	80
„ Plants	110, 157
Birch	134, 140
Blackberries	123
Bone Meals	56
Borecole	22
Bouvardias	157
Box	134
Broccoli	20, 21
Broom	134
Brussels Sprouts	22
Cabbage	24, 25
„ Field	53
Calceolaria Seed	82
„ Plants	157
Campanula Seed	83
„ Plants	149, 151, 157
Canna Seed	82
„ Plants	112, 157
Canterbury Bells Seed	83
„ Plants	157
Capsicum	30
Cardoons	52
Carnation Seed	84
„ Plants	155, 159
Carrot	27
„ Field	53
Cauliflower	28
Celery	23
Centaurea Seed	83
„ Plants	157
Cherries	120
Cherry, Double Blossomed	134
Chicory	30
Chives	52
Chrysanthemum Seed	84
„ Plants	146, 147
Cineraria Seed	85
„ Plants	159

	PAGE
Clay's Fertilizer	56
Clematis	132
Climbing Plants	133
Clovers, Rye Grasses, &c.	53
Coleus Seed	86
Coniferous Plants and Shrubs	138
Corn Salad	30
Couve Tronchuda	25
Cress	30
Crosnes	52
Cucumber	29
Currants	122
Cut Flowers	160
Dahlia Seed	86
„ Plants & Roots	112, 142, 145
Daisy Seed	86
„ Plants	157
Dandelion	52
Delphinium Seed	87
„ Plants	151
Egg Plant	52
Endive	30
Fencing Plants	139
Ferns	156
Figs	134
Filberts	124
Firs	140
Flower Seeds Collections	69
„ Cottagers' Packets	108
„ by Weight	109
„ Novelties	62, 63
Forest Trees	140, 141
Fruit Seeds	52
„ Trees	117-124
„ in Collections	124
Fuchsia Seed	88
„ Plants	149, 151
Fumigators	57
Gaillardia Seed	88
„ Plants	151
Garlic	52
Geranium Seed	101
„ Plants	157
Gladioli	114
Gloves, Gardening	57
Gloxinia Seed	89
„ Plants	156
Godetia	89
Gourd	30
Gooseberries	122
Grafting Materials	59
Grape Vines	124
Grass Mixtures	53
„ Seed for Lawns	54-55
Greenhouse Plants	156
Hardy Climbing Plants	133
„ Perennials	150-154
Heliotrope Seed	90
„ Plants	157, 159
Herbs, Sweet and Pot, Seed	35
„ Plants	51
Holly	135, 139
Hollyhock Seed	90
„ Plants	157
Hyacinthus Candicans	113
Indelible Ink	60
Insecticides, Plant Wash, &c.	57

	PAGE
Iris	152, 153
Kale	22
Kohl Rabi	53
Knives, &c.	58
Labels	60
Larch	140
Laurels	135, 141
Lawn Grass	52
Leek	31
Lettuce	32-33
Lilac	135
Lilies	111
Lily of the Valley	112
Lobelia Seed	92
„ Plants	157
Logan Berry	124
Mangels	53
Manures	56
Marguerites	157
Mats, Garden	60
Medlars	124
Melons	34
Michaelmas Daisies	150
Mignonette	94
Montbretias	112
Mulberry	124
Mushroom Spawn	60
Mustard	30
Myosotis Seed	94
„ Plants	153-157
Myrobella	139
Nasturtium	95
Nectarine	121
Nuts	124
Ornamental Trees & Shrubs	134-136
Onions	36-39
Paeonies	153
Pampas Grass	153
Pansy Seed	97
„ Plants	159
Parsley	35
Parsnip	40
Peaches	121
Pears	119
Peas	8-15
Pelargonium Seed	101
„ Plants	148
Pencils	59
Pentstemon Seed	101
„ Plants	157
Perfumes, Natural	160
Petunia Seed	98
„ Plants	159
Phlox Seed	99
„ Plants	154
Picotee Seed	84
„ Plants	155
Pinks	154, 158
Plums	120
Polyanthus Seed	101
„ Plants	158
Poppy Seed	102
„ Plants, see Papaver	153-154
Potatoes	45-50
„ Onions	52
Potting Mould	56
Primrose Seed	101
„ Plants	158

	PAGE
Primula Seed	100
„ Plants	156, 159
Pumpkin	30
Pyrethrum Seed	102
„ Plants	154, 159
Quince	124
Radish	41
Raffia, Tar Twine, &c.	60
Rakes, Hoes, Spades, &c.	58
Raspberry	123
Rhododendrons	137
Rhubarb Seed	52
„ Plants	51
Roses, H.P. and H.T.	127-129
„ in Collections	127
„ Tea Scented & Noisette	130
„ Climbing, &c.	131
Salsafy	44
Salvia Seed	104
„ Plants	157
Savoy	26
Scissors	58
Sea Kale Seed	52
„ Plants	51
Seedling Plants	159
Shading Materials	59
Shallot Bulbs and Seed	52
Silver Sand	56
Spades, &c.	58
Spinach	40
Stock Seed	70-72
„ Plants	159
Strawberries	123
Stove Plants	156
Swainsonia	156
Swede	53
Sweet Pea	65, 66
Thermometers, Barometers	50
Thorn	136
Tigridias	113
Tomato	42-43
Tools for Gardens	58
Trees for Fencing	139
„ Forests	140-141
„ Underwood	141
Tropaeolum Seed	95
„ Plants	154
Tuberoses	112
Turnip	44
„ Field	53
Vegetable Marrow	43
„ Seed Collections	5-6-7
„ Novelties	2-3
Verbena Seed	106
„ Plants	157, 159
Viola Seed	97
„ Plants	157, 158
Violets	159
Wallflower Seed	106
„ Plants	154
Wall Nails	59
Walnuts	124
Watson's Lawn Sand	56
Wikeham's Weed Eradicator	59
Whitethorn	139
Willows	136, 141
Yews	139

Flower Seed in Alphabetical Order, see pages 78—107.

TO GENTLEMEN REQUIRING GARDENERS, &c.

We keep a register of Gardeners seeking situations, and have almost always on our list the names of some first-class men requiring situations as head or under Gardeners, Farm Bailiffs, &c. We shall be happy to hear from any of our customers requiring such, and will at once put them in communication with men we consider suitable. We are always most careful to recommend only men of excellent character and good experience. We make no charge either to Customer or Gardener.

www.ingramcontent.com/pod-product-compliance
Lightning Source LLC
Chambersburg PA
CBHW020009030726
47500CB00002B/514